Abby

Charlotte Hardy

PIATKUS

For more information on other books published by Piatkus, visit our website at www.piatkus.co.uk

Copyright © 2001 by L. B. Carter

First published in Great Britain in 2001 by
Judy Piatkus (Publishers) Ltd of
5 Windmill Street, London W1P 1HF
email:info@piatkus.co.uk

The moral right of the author has been asserted

A catalogue record for this book is available from the British Library

ISBN 0 7499 0553 0

Set in Times by
Action Publishing Technology Ltd, Gloucester

Printed and bound in Great Britain by
Butler and Tanner Ltd, Frome, Somerset

Part One

Chapter One

Kilnevin, 23 Sept, 187-

Dear Fergus,

Don't mind us writing so soon after our other, but we were wondering whether you got it safe. Everyone here is well, and sends their love as always. But the reason we are writing again is the same as before. That the harvest has been wiped out entirely, so we don't have the twenty pounds we were counting on, and at this moment don't know how we are going to manage through the winter. Sorry to bother you about this, it's not such good news, and you with worries of your own, I dare say. But when we heard you were working with the New York and Erie Railroad, naturally we were pleased for you, all power to you Fergus, and if ever a man deserved luck it was you, fine fellow that you are.

But the problem is we have the rent to find for the second half now at All Saints, and the arrears too, and at this minute don't know where it's to come from, God help us, and half the homes in the townland in a like plight. Rory says the Land League is going to band together to help the poor farmers, but that seems a long hope at this moment. What can the Land League do against a great man like Sir George Pelham, and him a magistrate with the weight of the county behind him? Mr

3

Scott the agent was here on Saturday, yelling and bawling that we'd be out in the *bohreen* if we didn't pay.

So, if you could see your way to letting us have maybe twenty to tide us through the winter, we shall be ever after in your debt, as we are anyway, a kind and careful son and brother to us as you are.

Hoping this finds you as it leaves us,

I remain, your loving sister,

Abby

As she finished reading, there was a moment's silence. Her father lifted his head, stroking the stubble on his chin, and frowning. 'I wonder he never wrote before.'

'Maybe he moved from the other address?'

'But then he'd write wouldn't he, to tell us?'

'Maybe it was lost in the post?'

Abby pushed the hair back from her face, the thick long glossy black hair of which she was so proud, and tried to sound cheerful. 'He is going to write – sure, he's been busy – and him with a job to do – Fergus would never forget his family.'

She screwed down the top of the ink bottle, and carried it to the window sill with the bundle of quills. Outside the rain had stopped, and a fitful sun made a late afternoon appearance. She looked across the small field behind the cottage. Sunlight glistened in raindrops hanging on the long rich grass, and the thorn hedge was still thick and showed no sign yet of changing colour. Somewhere she could hear the blackbird singing. She rested her chin on her hand for a moment, staring out.

'The rain's stopped, anyway. Maybe we could get the hay cut tomorrow if it holds off.' The afternoon sunlight slanted into the room, and she looked down on her father's thinning hair, and his hunched shoulders in his old waist-coat, glowing in the warm light, and felt a rush of affection for him.

'It'll never be dry enough. It should have been cut a

4

month ago.' Da shook his head, and Abby placed her hand on his shoulder.

'Now, come on, I'll make us a cup of tea, and maybe a scone. Fan, put a sod of turf on the fire, there's a darling.'

Fan, her younger sister, who was thirteen, and had been slumped in a chair opposite, roused herself grudgingly, and crossed to the fire, which had burned to a low sultry glow, a small heap of embers in a sea of white ash. Pushing among the consumed turf with a stick, she inserted two large black bricks of dried peat.

Rory still had not spoken. He had been sitting with his hands clasped on the table, his shoulders hunched, staring downwards as he listened to Abby's letter. At last he looked up.

'Abby, why do you say that? The Land League is our only hope! If the tenants can only band together, what can Sir George do? Nothing! Don't you see it?' He leaned across the table towards his father. 'Think, Da, after centuries, after generations and generations in this village, think of the people who have grown up, brought up their children and grown old, people who have died in this village, paying rent to the Pelham family. Think of it. Generations who have gone by and never had the courage to refuse. But now we'll refuse! We will! We'll go together and tell him – no rent until he agrees an abatement!'

Da reached across and ran his hand across the boy's head. 'You're a grand lad, Rory, and I'm proud of ye. I am. But ye see – ye won't remember, but thirty, forty years ago, in the bad times, there were families turned into the *bohreen*, sticks of furniture standing in the rain, and thatch pulled down from the roof. I saw it. Sir George is not maybe such a bad man – not in himself – but there's the others urging him on, and Mr Scott telling him he's got to stand firm.'

'But now it's different, Da! It's not like it was in the old days! Now the people are banding together. Over in Liscarney, over in Bohaun, it's the same. There's no going back now.'

5

Abby watched Rory's face glowing with enthusiasm, his eyes shining, the handsomest boy in the village, in the barony. Where was there such a boy to be found in the four parishes round? Such a boy on the hurling field, such a boy for the wrestling, who else could carry a full grown sheep under either arm, or push a barrow of turf up from the bog and never pause to breathe, and no wonder the girls turned their heads in the village – there wasn't a handsomer boy in it – and yet never impudent or vain, every inch a gentleman, and never a profane word either, not even when he had drink taken – which (she admitted to herself) he did sometimes – why, wasn't he a man like any other now, and him nineteen, and wouldn't he take a drink with his friends? And such a dancer too, whirling the girls in the jig or reel, and how they vied to dance with him, or catch his eye, but he'd laugh at them, and say, 'Easy girls, I can't marry you all!'

Da was shaking his head slowly. 'You don't know,' he said slowly, 'you haven't seen it.'

Abby was seventeen, and since her mother had died two years earlier, had taken command of the house. Sometimes her father called her Little Mother (though she was as tall as he was) and would say, 'I remember when your mother came to this house—' and then he would sigh, and she would slide her arm round his waist, and say, 'I'll take care of you now, Da,' coaxingly, and smile her dark-eyed smile, and give him a quick kiss on the cheek, before turning away. 'But now there's the scones to bake – I'll just do that now, and then we'll all feel better.'

Later Rory went out into the little field behind the cottage, to inspect the grass. But when he came in again he only shook his head gloomily.

'Well, the hay's lost.' They looked at each other round the table. 'That leaves the geese.' Abby was writing. 'The rent of the half year is £16, not counting the arrears . . .' She stared at the figures as Da and Fan watched anxiously. Rory

6

was on the other side of the table. 'We'd have to sell the last two cows to pay it.'

Rory leaned forward and took the sheet of paper. He studied it for a moment. 'If we sell the cows to pay the rent we'll have nothing left. Can't he see that? What does Mr Scott think we're going to live on? Would he rather have his rent even if we have to starve? There's nothing for it, Da—' he turned to his father who was watching him carefully. 'We'll have to refuse the rent! We'll have to. Mr Scott will have to wait till things get better. We'll pay him when we have the money – maybe next year the oats will be better. But this year it can't be done.' Rory shook his head as if to convince himself. 'Or else I'll go to England to seek work—'

'What'll you do?'

He shrugged. 'Go on the buildings maybe. But it sticks in my throat that we should be sitting here counting our money and his honour of the big house can take the last few pounds out of our pockets till we have nothing left and then turn us off our farm. It sticks in my throat! And us having to go north, south, east and west to find work, without even the right to our own land which we have farmed for generations . . .' His voice sank in bitterness.

Abby touched his shoulder gently and he caught her eye. 'Or I can get a job,' she said encouragingly. 'In a hotel maybe—'

'And who's to care for Da? No sister of mine goes out to work. We'll stick together.' He smiled wistfully. 'You're the heart of the family, Abby. Where would we be if you were off working in some hotel? We'll stick together, come what may.'

They set off before dawn.

Rory had gone out to the barn in the dark, with a candle in an old lantern, and rounded up the geese, and with a stick in his hand, had them grouped in the haggard, as Abby emerged with a thick black shawl wrapped warmly

7

round her head and shoulders. She carried a basket filled with eggs, with two great wedges of bread and cheese wrapped in a cloth, on top of them.

Gradually the sky lightened, as they made their way through the lanes, the fields began to be visible on either side, and then the dim outline of the mountains not far away, with the unmistakable conical shape of Croagh Patrick.

Day was breaking as they arrived in Westport, warm now from their walk, though there was an autumn chill in the morning. The little houses stood grey, the early morning smoke rising from their chimneys; the door of The Goat was already open, and a breath of warm air wafted past them, cigar and pipe smoke, and the reek of stale porter.

In the half light cows shambled and shuffled through the muddy streets, bumping each other, twisting up their heads, sniffing the unusual smells of the town and lashing their tails; black long-horned Kerry cattle, red and white short-horn dairy cows, shoving and lowing as they came through the narrow streets. Behind them in their long-tailed coats, hats pulled down over their faces, farmers prodded with their blackthorn sticks, shouted and cursed while at their heels ran wiry black and white dogs. There were sheep too, excited, panicking as dogs kept them together, and pigs. A man, his stick under his arm, had a pig with a string tied to its hind leg and women shawled like Abby carried baskets of eggs, cakes, or hams.

As they came into the square, stalls and standings were being erected; ass carts, propped on barrels, were covered with patchwork quilts stretched on bent rods; while underneath their owners squatted on their hunkers surrounded by their wares – scallions, porringers, remnants of checks, and 'ready-me-daisies'. Breakfast was already on offer: hot pigs' feet with a mouth-watering smell in the cold morning air, whiskey punch in steaming jugs, and black puddings. Shops were opening and young lads were taking down

8

shutters. The square was filling and the air was alive with the sound of bargains being struck, friends hailed, oaths exchanged, prices called, the state of trade discussed.

Rory had the greatest difficulty in keeping the geese together; they had the tendency to run in among the cattle's hooves; now a drover headed his six cows across their path, then three or four sheep came up beside them; on all sides was the confused shouting of boys and men with blackthorn sticks – and here was a man carrying two live chickens by their feet, hanging helplessly, undignified, their wings half open. Now a man was edging through the crowd leading a massive bull, the curly head, and short stubby horns lowered as he held the rope short to the nose-ring. Somewhere a cock crew, but the air was thick with neighing, lowing, braying – and the ground thick too with dung, so that Abby watched carefully as she walked. She and Rory had arrived in good time, and her eggs were quickly sold. 'Three shillings. That's something anyway,' she said.

For a moment they both stared at the coins, as he turned them over in the palm of his hand; stared at the queen's head, worn with handling. Why were such trifles so important? How could such a little thing, this scrap of metal, mean the difference between them living safe and snug in the home they loved, and . . .

Rory looked gloomy, but Abby gave him a quick smile of encouragement. 'I'll just get in a bit of sugar and tea, anyway.'

Leaving him for a moment, with her list in her hand she set off through the fair crowd, pushing between the burly shoulders of two farmers, their hands slapping on a deal, and now a man shouting across her to someone else, and here was a man leading a calf away, the poor thing crying piteously, confused and frightened by the laughing, joking, gesticulating crowd round it.

With her head down, she found herself abruptly in front of a tall horse, a magnificent grey hunter, and couldn't help stopping in admiration. For a moment she forgot her

9

worries as she ran her hand over his neck, then took his mouth and stroked his nose.

'Easy, honey, he's got a temper on him.' A heavy, middle-aged groom turned as he felt the tug on the reins he was holding. He looked her over, and she noticed his companion watching her too.

'Looks like you've got a customer,' the other said with a smile.

Slightly nettled by the sarcasm in his voice, she blushed, and turned to the horse again.

Abby could never pass by a horse. They were the passion in her life. She could not, of course, afford to own a horse but, as long as she could remember, she had begged a ride from anyone in the village who had one, and every inhabitant knew the sight of Abby O'Leary galloping by, and every horse owner was familiar with her entreaties, her flatteries, her blandishments, only for the chance of a ride. Maybe it was her aunt Eileen's hack; or it was Mr Tremayne, and she was offering to clean out his stable, if he would let her ride Firefly; or she was buttering up Sean, Mr O'Hare's man, and enduring a snatched kiss from him too, in the darkness of the stable . . .

'He's a darling,' she murmured, rubbing his neck.

The groom who had been watching her, was now beside her. 'I should think he is. The master paid fifty guineas for him last year at Ballinasloe.' He turned self-importantly to the other man. 'You'll know Mr Thorpe – over by Ballintober? A great judge of horse-flesh.'

The horse sidestepped a moment, and Abby took him by the bridle and soothed him.

'Why is he selling him?' asked the other casually, approaching the horse, and eyeing Abby too as he took hold of the bridle opposite her.

The groom coughed. 'Oh, he needed the space – for his new racer.'

The wealthy stranger was looking intently at Abby. 'Think you could handle him?' he asked casually. She

10

noticed that he had an English accent.

She lit up. But the groom had heard him, and was looking her over too with a cocksure manner. ''Tis grand ye'd look on a horse like that one, to be sure – with two men to hold the reins! Emperor's not a horse for a girl.'

Stung by this she turned without thinking. 'I could handle him.'

'He'd break your neck first,' the other man said dryly. Embarrassed at the way he had been studying her, uncomfortable at the look of money about him – the polished leather gaiters, a well-cut tweed jacket, a stone glinting in his necktie – she turned to the hunter again.

'Oh,' Abby sighed, 'he's a darling,' she ran her hand over the horse's nose again, and he instinctively responded. 'See, he loves me already. You're a lovely boy, a big strong boy, but you'd be gentle with me, wouldn't you, my beauty?'

She sighed but then, remembering her shopping, was about to turn away when the stranger said quietly, 'A guinea says you couldn't stay up.'

Abby turned and found herself, to her surprise, in a crowd of men waiting to hear the outcome of this. She looked again at the man, who was watching her with a steady look. The groom had also become aware of the other men who had turned to hear the conversation, but before he could speak she had decided.

'He's a sweet-natured creature, and wouldn't harm a fly, and I'll prove it. Give me a foot up.'

The groom, though, seemed to be having second thoughts. If the girl came off it might rule out his chances of selling the horse. 'There's no lady's saddle—' he began.

'Never mind for that. Aren't I well used to a man's—'

The groom looked round at the others, but it was too late in any case. The gentleman had given her a foot up and she swung her leg astride the wide back. There was a cheer, and Abby was quite carried away. 'Stand back! – give him his head! I'll just take him down the Mall and back.'

And in a moment she felt the huge thrust of his strong legs, the spirit that was dying to race, and they were away, pushing through the fair, the farmers, the old ladies in their shawls, a young man with a couple of calves, a girl leading six geese which flew to either side hissing angrily, until she came to the head of the wide Mall with its elegant Georgian houses, its rows of trees, and the river between. And here the fair folk were scattered to either side as she gave the horse his head. At the bridge, the heart thumping within her, the blood pounding in her veins, her eyes blazing, she drew up. 'I'll just take you to the quay, oh you're ready for a gallop, my boy –' she leant forward and rubbed the gelding's neck – 'you're dying for a run, aren't you?' she whispered. 'You've been so frustrated, so pent up, standing in the market as the men prod you and poke you, and pull your mouth open, a splendid fellow like you, the indignity of it! And now we're together we'll fly like the wind, and take no notice of any one!'

She gave him his head again, and in an instant was in a flat-out gallop, crouching low against the magnificent beast's neck, holding him lightly by the rein, and standing lightly in the stirrups, so that the animal stretched his head forward, ears laid back. The great smooth shining body rose and fell beneath her; the wind was in her ears, and the thudding of the hooves on the damp earth vibrated all through her. Her hair now flying about her shoulders, where it had broken free from its ribbon, it was a matter of minutes to gallop, past the gates of the marquis's demesne, the mile or so down to the harbour, where the tall grey warehouses stood along the quay. At last, heaving on the reins with all her strength as they came to a halt, she sat back in the saddle and paused to breathe, feeling the salt sea breeze cooling her hot cheeks, her flushed and exalted cheeks. She pushed her unruly hair back from her face as she sat for a moment, gazing out into the bay but seeing nothing, only feeling her heart beating, and placing her hand on her breast for a moment to steady her feelings.

Was there ever anything like it? What could be more glorious, more bold and splendid? In those few seconds she had forgotten everything, Da, Rory, all her worries, the rent, everything swept away by the exhilaration, the thudding of the blood in her, the exultation of the strong animal beneath her. Oh, if she could only go on, riding for ever, just Emperor and her—

As she arrived back at the market, where the groom was waiting in the crowd of farmers, there was a roar of laughter and applause.

'Give her the guinea, master! The guinea! You wagered, and she's fairly beaten you, the *cáilin dhas*!'

The gentleman pulled a gold coin from his waistcoat pocket, and spun it high in the air as she still sat on the horse recovering her breath. She caught it deftly.

'I'd pay it again a hundred fold for the sight,' he called gallantly.

The groom, sensing his opportunity, now approached him again and, glancing round at the others, proclaimed loudly, 'You see what a horse that is, master, as mild as a lamb – would just suit a gentleman like yourself – forty guineas—'

'He certainly is a magnificent animal.' The man strolled forward, one hand in his whipcord breeches pocket, and ran his other across the hind quarters.

He glanced up. 'Almost as magnificent as his rider,' he murmured.

Abby was running her fingers through her hair, arranging it and retying the ribbon. She caught his eye, and read the unmistakable message. She blushed, and for a second was at a loss.

But she had already caught sight of Rory, and the crowd was cheering as she slipped to the ground and crossed to him. 'Oh Rory did you ever see the like, isn't he a beauty?'

As she was moving away with Rory, she glanced back. 'Thank you for the ride, sir!' and caught the eye once more

13

of the man with the guinea, still watching her, then turned quickly back to Rory.

'Oh Rory, will you look at that fellow! And wouldn't I look just grand on him, in a fitted habit, and a tall hat and veil!'

Rory was not laughing. As they turned away, he shook himself free, frowning. 'It's a month to the rent day, Abby, we'll never have the money in a year; we could be put out on the mountainside, and you go making an exhibition of yourself to a crowd of loafers. Have you no shame?'

'Rory – don't be hard on me! I didn't think – and look!'

She was offering him the little gold coin but he ignored it. 'Didn't think is right!'

She took his arm again. 'It was only for a bit of fun – don't you see?'

'I don't see! Even if we weren't about to be put into the road, there's no call for you to be showing yourself off – and riding astride, Abby, no better than—'

'Than? Than what?'

Rory wouldn't look at her. 'You know well enough what I mean.'

'I do not know what you mean!' She pulled herself away and stopped. They had been walking through the market crowd. 'Rory! What do you mean?'

But as he turned to her, he seemed tired and harassed. 'Have you no dignity, Abby?' he said softly. 'What'll the fellows say to me when they hear you were careering through the town like a circus performer?'

She didn't hear him; all the anger had gone out of her as she saw his face. She crossed to him, and slipped her arm through his again. 'You'd know I'd never do anything to hurt you Rory. Shall we be friends? I can't bear to see you like this. And don't be too hard on me. I'm allowed to dream; a girl can dream, can't she? Where's the harm in it?'

He put his arm round her waist. She felt the long sigh through him. A moment later he brightened. 'I sold the

14

geese anyway, that's something. And Abby, there's to be a meeting! The Land League – here – and Mr Parnell is coming to speak. Didn't I tell you! The Land League will save us – and Mr Scott can whistle for his money.'

Chapter Two

She swung the shawl about her shoulders.

'Fan, I'm going over to Aunt Eileen's. I'll try and be back before six. Will you feed the pig before then? And tell Rory I'm going to see Father McMichael. I don't want him to know I'm going over to Aunt's.'

'Why?'

'He thinks I might try to borrow from her.'

'What's wrong with that?'

'That's what I say. But Rory won't accept it, so we have to keep quiet – have you got it?'

'Yes. But I can't feed the pig – I'm going to see Susan Gilhooley anyway.'

'Try and do it, love, Rory and Da are in the field above to get the hay cut while the rain holds off. They won't be in till late, and this is my only chance.'

Fan stood in the room with a scowl on her face, as Abby went out.

It was two miles to Aunt Eileen's, but that was nothing to a strong, long-legged girl who walked with any easy swinging gait, in a rusty red dress, her shawl about her shoulders and head, and long lace-up boots, her hair, thick and abundant, tied in a ribbon and hanging to her waist.

Eileen was her late mother's sister, and a widow. She had married well – married above herself – and since her husband's death was a careful farmer, with the aid of two lads who came in from the village, so that she was able to live in a bit of style. She had a horse and trap, and on Starlight, a little undemanding cob, Abby had learned to ride.

The low cottage was fresh whitewashed, the path from the gate was lined with flowers, and the slab before the front door was scrubbed. The door had recently been repainted dark green and there was a brass knocker on it. Inside, the chairs in the best room had lace covers to their backs, there was a canary in a cage, and when Aunt Eileen set down the tea tray, there was a fine china teapot on it.

'You'll know why I'm here then, Aunt?' Abby said hesitantly, after a few opening remarks.

'The oats are ruined, is it?'

Abby nodded. 'And we've had no word from Fergus, that we were hoping for.'

Aunt Eileen grunted. 'I'm in much the same shape myself,' she said at last. 'We all are. And the price of butter falling has hit me hard. I'd like to help you—'

Abby waited and then hesitantly, 'It would be maybe – ten pounds? To pay the rent, and maybe have a bit over against the winter?'

Aunt Eileen shook her head slowly, pursing her lips. 'I wish I could. You've not sold the cows?'

'Rory would never do that! If we sell the cows we'd starve.'

'You haven't the oats to feed them this winter.'

Abby was uncertain. 'Rory will never do it. He's all for the Land League and to make a stand against our landlord.'

Aunt Eileen raised her eyebrows. 'The Land League? A lot of hot air, and self-important fellows puffing themselves up. Lawyers and schoolmasters making themselves political careers on the backs of the farmers – it's not them to be put out of their farms, for sure—'

'We've got to do something! Oh God, I'd go and seek work in a hotel or something, or maybe as a lady's maid –

17

but who's there to see after my Da? Since mother died, it's only me—'

'And Fan.'

'Fan's too young.'

'She's not too young to do her share of work, the lazy baggage. How's your father taking it?'

Abby looked down. 'He's destroyed, Aunt. It's as if the stuffing went out of him. Ever since mother died. He was never the same after.'

There was a pause as they thought of Abby's dead mother – Eileen's younger sister.

'Your father used to be a fine man, Abby. It's hard to see him now – so down.' She heaved a sigh. 'But it's yourself and Rory will have to find your way. You'll get no help from him.'

As they came out of the cottage, Abby turned. 'I'll just maybe say goodbye to Starlight before I go?'

'Why not?'

In a paddock behind the cottage a chestnut cob grazed peacefully. As she heard Abby's voice, she lifted her head, and ambled slowly across to her. Abby had taken a knob of sugar from the bowl before she left the house, and leaning on the fence, she offered it to the horse. Starlight knew Abby, and was happy to let her run her hand down her nose, and stroke her neck.

'You don't know anything about eviction, do you, old girl?' she murmured. 'Even if Aunt Eileen sold you, you're so gentle and well behaved, she'd be bound to sell you to some kind lady who'd look after you, and you'd take her out on jaunts and go trotting through the *bohreens*—' As she leaned against the fence, rubbing the horse's shiny coat, holding the rope bridle with the other, Abby fell into a dreamy reverie. 'Some fine lady,' she murmured, 'how proud you'd be to carry her, perhaps in a beautiful velvet habit, made to measure, and her hair in a net under her tall hat –' and then – 'we'd look good together, you and I. Us two together, in a point to point? Eh? You'd carry me over

18

anything, old girl, wouldn't you? And wouldn't we just show them!' She chuckled, and gave the horse a playful slap. 'Oh, very likely. Here's me maybe thrown out of our house in a month or less, and bletherin' about point to points, and riding with the gentry!'

The following Saturday she walked with Rory into Westport to the meeting of the Land League. The whole town centre was filled with men, and as night fell, flaming pitch torches were lit, which threw an eerie and uncertain light over the men in their pot hats and capes. Many gripped sticks. As Abby looked about her it occurred to her that she was probably the only woman present. There was a long wait, and the crowd – jostling, talking, and sometimes singing – waited cheerfully, until finally four men climbed onto the platform. Abby had never seen any of them before.

'Mr Parnell is the tall gentleman with the beard,' Rory whispered, as a hush fell over the crowd.

The first speaker, however, was unbearded, a young man, good-looking with a modest, educated manner. He introduced himself as Mr J.J. O'Toole, a lawyer from Castlebar.

Mr O'Toole outlined the problem which they all knew, the wet August and the poor oats harvest. On top of that was the disastrous fall in the price of butter due, he said, to American imports. They were all gathered that night he said to do something about it (cheers), to found the Land League of Mayo, and he was grateful that the leader of the Irish members in the House of Commons, the member for Meath, Mr Charles Stewart Parnell, had come to Westport to speak to them.

Mr Parnell was rather stiff, unsmiling, and had a strangely forbidding, serious expression and when he began Abby was astonished to hear him speak like a English aristocrat.

She turned to Rory and whispered, 'Sure, he's never an Irishman?'

19

'He is, from Wicklow, but the poor fellow went to Cambridge University – they must have rubbed the brogue off him.'

'What's an aristocrat doing speaking for the Irish farmers?'

But she soon found out. Mr Parnell was electric; he had barely opened his mouth, and a dense hush fell on the crowd. There was a force in his voice, a force in his eyes – he held himself rigid, controlled, his voice, though light, was clear and cut through the night air so that everyone there was gripped by it.

'A fair rent is a rent that a tenant can afford to pay according to the times.' It was like a judgement from on high. 'But in bad times the tenant cannot be expected to pay as much as he did in good times. If such rents are insisted upon, what must we do to induce the landlords to see the position? You must show them that you intend to hold a firm grip of your homesteads and lands!'

There was a deafening cheer.

And as they walked home afterwards through the silent lanes hearing sometimes others, their neighbours, all talking excitedly, Rory could not contain his excitement.

'Keep a firm hold of your homesteads and your lands! That's it Abby! With the League behind us – didn't I say it! It's our only chance! We'll organise a meeting in Kilnevin.'

The next night Rory went from cottage to cottage in the village speaking to the villagers, and urging them to come to a meeting in his house.

And three nights later men began appearing, till the kitchen was crowded. Da was on his feet, offering a bottle of spirits, 'to keep out the cold'. Twenty men were packed into the kitchen, their faces distorted by the dim glow of the peat fire and a flickering rush light.

Rory turned intently to Da, and the old man began uncertainly, 'Friends, you all know the condition we're in. The rent is due in a month and we'll never have the money—' Heads were shaking, and there were murmurs of agreement.

'So what we're asking for is your help so that when Mr Scott comes round, and the sheriff and the bailiff, and all of them, you won't stand by and see us thrown out of our home—'

'We'll stand by you, Joseph,' murmured an old bearded fellow, chewing on a pipe, his face lined by years of leading his cattle across the bare mountainside. The younger men kept quiet until the old ones had had their say.

'I don't pretend it'll be easy – whatever Rory says – we know what happened in the bad years. You John Donohue, and you Sean Hickey – you've seen landlords and their agents with the dragoons and peelers—'

Another villager, Donal Cavanagh, cut across. 'No rent! And if any one does pay their rent, why we'll teach 'em what it is to betray their friends.' He finished his drink. 'No rent!'

'And if anyone should be evicted, let no man take his farm,' cried another. 'Let it stand idle so the landlord can get no good by it! Let it rot, and he'll learn he can't go throwing honest men out of their homes and think to get away with it.'

'But the Land League will never have any success unless we all stick together. The landlords stick together and so must we,' Rory couldn't help interjecting.

'Aye, stick together!' Men joined in as the whiskey warmed them.

'And what'll we do with anyone who does pay?'

'Burn 'em out! Ruin 'em! Traitors, they're on the landlords' side!'

'Friends, I hope you're all going to stick by us, because me and my da, and my sisters, we can't afford to pay the rent this half year, and still owe from the last, and if you don't stand by us, we'll be thrown off our farm for sure.'

'We'll stick by you, Rory, aye, stick together boys.'

'Stick together and beat the landlords down!'

21

'Aye, down with all English tyrants who think to grind the face of every honest Irishman in the mud of his own land!'

'We'll show 'em!'

'Mr Donohue, Mr Hickey, Mr Branagh, you'll be there? You'll not let us down when the bailiff comes?'

'We'll stand by you, Rory.'

Abby watched Rory, who was heartened and strengthened by the support which shone in every face round the fire. Rory was on his feet now.

'Because what is Sir George Pelham and his family? What are they all, but a set of vultures that prey on the vitals of the Irish people, that suck our blood and feed on our flesh? Did we ever ask them to come over from England? Did we ever invite them to come over and be landlord? Is the Irish farmer so helpless that he needs a landlord over him? It amazes me that we have stood it all these years, paid our rents year in and year out like sheep, obeyed our lords and masters who are strangers in our land, never invited, and hated by all. I say, No rent!'

Rory sat down and seemed stunned for a moment by the effect of his own words. The others, who had been listening open-mouthed, burst into a cheer. 'That's it Rory! We won't stand for it! We'll stick together. We'll be behind you.'

'We'll send a notice to Mr Scott that we refuse to pay our rent until Sir George Pelham grants a reduction. If everyone writes such a notice whenever their rent is due, there's nothing he can do. I'll write it now, this minute. Abby, do you have a piece of paper?'

The men made way for her as she brought the paper, the ink bottle and the bundle of quills to the table, and set them out.

Rory dictated and she wrote:

Sir,

Mr O'Leary's compliments and begs to inform that he will not be paying his rent due as of 1st Nov, owing to his inability to meet this sum. He respectfully calls on you to make an abatement of the rent so that he will be able to honour this commitment on future occasions. You are no doubt well aware of the circumstances that make it difficult to pay rent at this moment. Mr O'Leary has the full support of the Land League in this matter, and begs to remain, my dear sir,

your obedient servant,
Joseph O'Leary

Abby shook the sheet as the ink gradually dried and then read it back to the meeting.

'I'll see it posted,' she said.

But Da had been crouching in his chair, listening with a worried expression over the table. 'It'll never do, Rory, I know it. Sir George is maybe not such a bad man – but the others would never let him. They'll stick together, and Mr Scott at him too.'

'Da, the whole village is with us! We'll face him down, we'll refuse our rent until he agrees on a reduction. It's happening all over the country. We can't fail.'

Da was shaking his head. 'Rory, I know him. He won't listen, no matter what we say.'

'Da, we're going to make him listen. If we don't pay the rent, if no one in the town land pays their rent, he'll have to listen. He'll have to.'

Da sighed and looked into Rory's face. 'He won't listen, Rory.'

Chapter Three

Abby undid a button of her dress and slid the letter inside and, as the men rose one by one, and took their leave, she stood in the open kitchen doorway bidding them good night, and then strolled out into the *bohreen* to breathe the sweet night air after the smoky atmosphere of the kitchen.

Another very different thought was in her mind.

Threats were not enough. Rory was her own darling brother and she would die for him, but she was old enough, and had heard enough, to know that her father was very likely right. Sir George Pelham would not come alone to claim his property. The newspapers were regularly filled with reports of dragoons, detachments of the Royal Irish Constabulary, and armies of Orangemen imported from the north to do the dirty work. More than threats and defiance was needed.

Before delivering the letter she would try another approach.

'Fan, come in here.'

Abby had taken out her three dresses and laid them on the bed. 'Help me now – I can't decide between the sprigged blue cotton, or this old orangey-goldy one – which I can hardly button, I've got so big round the top.'

She was trying to button the dress over her bosom, which at seventeen was fully developed.

Fan stood in the doorway. 'What in the name of all the saints are you doing?'

Abby crossed quickly and pushed the door to behind Fan. 'Have Rory and Da gone out?'

'Yes.'

'Fan, this sounds daft maybe, but I'm going to see Sir George Pelham.'

'*What?*'

'It's just a chance. Like Da says, he's maybe not such a bad man – if you get to know him. It's Mr Scott always at him to stand fast. Maybe I can persuade Sir George to give us a postponement, or an abatement – anything till Fergus writes.'

Fan watched her with her mouth open. 'You're going to – but the letter—'

'Don't argue now. Just tell me – is it the orangey-goldy, or the blue?'

Fan looked her over. 'Faith, that is a bit tight on you; you look stuffed into it.'

Abby turned round in the dim little room. 'Oh, if only we had a glass big enough! You think it's too small?'

Fan grinned wickedly. 'Depends what you want, Abby. You look as if you're – *bulgin'* out o' that one! But maybe when Sir George catches a sight of you—'

'What do you mean, you minx?'

Fan sniggered. Abby began hurriedly to unbutton the dress, pulling it roughly down over her shift and petticoats, round her ankles, and treading it on to the floor as she snatched up the blue. 'Here – button me up the back.'

'Ooh, you've got your stays on, quite the lady today—'

'I won't have him think we're some sort of lower form of life! We've as good a right to stand in the sun as he has. I'm not going crawling to him. I'm going to borrow Aunt Eileen's dog cart.'

'You're going to arrive in a horse and trap? He'll think we're rich. He's never going to give us an abatement.'

Abby stopped. This was true. She bit her lower lip.

25

'Maybe Rory's right. Maybe I should just send the letter – except I know what his answer will be. But Fan, I know if I once speak to him, if I can once explain to him that there's the four of us, and we're hoping for a letter from America – I'm sure he'll – it's worth the try, anyway.'

The blue dress was now buttoned up the back.

'How do I look?'

Fan put her head on one side. 'Ah now, the other was better for you. 'Tis a stronger colour on you Abby, and the tighter fit too. So to say, it does you more justice.'

It was in the middle of the afternoon that she found herself walking down a gravelled drive through the oaks of Westport Lodge. It had been an hour's trudge from Kilnevin. At the gate she changed from her boots into her lighter shoes, stuffed the boots into a capacious bag and left it with the gatekeeper.

The carriageway curved and she came out of the oaks. To her right a lawn ran down to a lake, still, tranquil, fringed with flags, and with a little wooden jetty where a rowing boat was tied up. Ahead of her was the house – how could she describe it? Tall chimneys all carefully decorated, long mullioned windows in diamond-paned glass, a wing jutting forward here, another squarer part, with a tall gable end, and a turret beyond. Ivy reached up one grey wall, along another flower beds overflowed thick with colour. A mighty cedar sheltered the far side. The house stood still, silent, in the fluctuating afternoon sunshine. She had never seen anything so beautiful, and stopped, suddenly afraid of her own impertinence in trespassing where she had no right to be. Surely some servant must come out and order her roughly away? She must be crazy even to think – to ask the owner of all this – but then another thought intruded, and she stiffened. Yes, it was magnificent – but who had paid for it? Her own family, and the families of her friends and neighbours. She started forward for the door.

She was seized with doubts again. Should she go round

to the kitchen? Or walk boldly up the front steps and knock?

She swallowed, and made up her mind. Maybe she shouldn't have come, but now she was here, she certainly wasn't going to sneak round to any kitchens. She set forward boldly along the gravelled carriageway, and was about to ascend the steps when she noticed the curtain move in a window. Someone had seen her.

Her heart was beating. This *was* madness, and no doubt some servant would give her her marching orders in double quick time. Taking a huge grip on herself she stepped up to the door. At one side hung an iron handle. She gave it a hard pull expecting to hear the clang of a bell. She heard nothing but the faint scrape of the metal. It was as if the wire just disappeared and was lost in the immensity of the house above her.

She waited. Her heart was beating so hard she wasn't sure she would be able to speak a word – but now there were footsteps, a lock was turning, a heavy, rich-sounding lock, and the door opened. A neatly dressed servant with white gloves, and polished shoes, looked at her without expression.

She swallowed. 'I was hoping to speak with Sir George—'

'Sir George is from home, Miss.'

'Ah.' There was a pause as they looked at each other. At least the servant was an Irishman.

'What was your business with him? If you're seeking employment, you should apply at the servant's door for Mr Shaunessy—'

She stiffened. 'Thank you but my business is of a private nature.'

The servant was about to close the door, when a man appeared in a doorway behind him.

'What's the matter, Mick?'

'Nothing at all, sir.'

The servant turned again to where Abby was narrowly framed in the slit of the door and was about to close it when the man spoke again. 'Let her in.'

Mick opened the door, and Abby took a hesitant step into the hall. It was high, spacious, and yet there was an oppressive feel about it. There was too much: too much furniture, a huge oak table and umbrella stand, dark paintings on the walls, a chandelier overhead, suits of armour on either side of an arch, which was swagged in heavy gloomy red, a fretted staircase in dark wood running upwards.

Abby was half conscious of all this, as her eyes fixed themselves on the man opposite her.

He nodded casually towards a door. 'Come in here. You can go, Mick.'

The servant disappeared, and she passed the man into a long drawing room. Again, it was too much to take in at once: enormous sofas in faded gold brocade on either side of a marble fireplace, a circular polished table with a large vase of flowers on it standing before one of the wide latticed windows, looking out over the lawn and the lake. Portraits hanging on the walls. She was taking all this in with one part of her mind, but another was in a whirl. She had met this man before.

She turned and they faced one another.

She coughed. 'I came to see Sir George—'

'The guv'nor's out. But you can talk to me.'

She still hesitated.

'I'm his son,' he explained gently.

'I see.' There was another long silence. Her mind was a blank. 'I didn't know—'

'Why should you? I've been overseas for years.'

'Ah.'

'Anyway, what did you want to speak to the old man about?'

Abby was still searching in her mind to explain this man – and yet she surely should have known Sir George Pelham had sons?

'Lost your tongue?' He smiled slightly. 'You were bolder the other day.'

28

She turned away, embarrassed.

'Yes,' he went on after a moment, in an amused tone, 'the best guinea I ever spent. But I little imagined we would meet again so soon.'

'It's about the rent.' She was writhing her fingers together looking down and speaking in a low quick voice. 'I've come to see your father. It's my family, you see, the rent's due at All Saints, and we're overdue from last May, and we were expecting a letter from America, but it hasn't come and the oats were ruined in August – the rain, and the potatoes nearly all gone, and we just don't have—'

She came to a halt. For a moment they stared at each other.

'I see.' Then, after another pause, he looked round. 'Damme, this is uncivil – would you like a cup of tea?' He crossed to the fireplace and pulled at a bell rope.

'Oh – that is—'

'The family in difficulties, eh? But why have you come? Don't you have a father or mother?'

'My mother is dead sir, and—'

'You're alone in the world?'

'Oh no! There's my brother and sister—'

'I see. And you have to take care of them, eh?'

She was silent.

'Well,' he perched himself on the corner of a table, then got up again immediately. 'Look, why don't you sit – I'm the devil of a host, aren't I? That's the trouble with barrack life – a fellow tends to forget the niceties. It's a long time since I entertained a lady to tea. Sit down – go on.' He motioned her to one of the spacious sofas in front of the fire.

A woman had appeared at the door in the distance.

'Bring us some tea, Mrs Toone,' he called lightly. The woman disappeared. The man threw himself into the sofa opposite her.

'To tell you the truth, this is a treat I hadn't anticipated on a dull afternoon. Time does hang cursedly on one's

29

hands here. I've been moping round the place. Don't know any one much you see, and the guv'nor's out on business all the time. So – all I've got is a pair of sisters for company, and they spend their time trimming gowns and chattering about their beaux.'

She had now got her breathing under control, and was able to relax slightly and take in the man sitting opposite her. He had been abroad, he said. It was obvious – he was tanned, and his face etched. Yet beneath the tan it was as if he were pale too; perhaps he had had diseases, perhaps he had endured hardships in India or Africa which left him slightly gaunt? There were lines about his mouth, there was something slightly bony about his face, he had a spare light frame . . .

The woman reappeared and set a tray between them on a low table.

He looked it over.

'Er, do you want to—'

As he gestured over the silver tray and the fine bone china, Abby was all nerves again. Aunt Eileen had nothing like this. She took yet another grip on herself. She had to get this man on her side. If he could speak for her to his father . . . she took up the teapot.

'To tell you the truth – by the way, what's your name? There's no one here to introduce us. Randolph Pelham.' He held out his hand across the tea tray.

'Abby O'Leary, sir.'

'Pleased to meet you, Abby, and don't call me sir. Yes. Well, to tell the truth, I know nothing of local politics, the estate, and all that. The guv'nor keeps a tight grip on it, and I've been overseas the last six years.'

There was a pause as she poured the tea, and handed him a cup. He sipped at it.

'So you're afraid the guv'nor might throw you out, eh?'

'Oh, I'm sure he wouldn't sir, if only he knew – if only I could explain the situation. We only need a little time; we were expecting a letter from America, you see.'

'Well, Abby, I'll undertake to speak to the old man and explain it myself. Where's your farm?'

'Over by Kilnevin, Mr Pelham.'

'And he knows you, I expect? If I mention your name?'

'The agent, Mr Scott, does know us, yes.'

'Now, Abby, tell me something else. Why did you come today? Couldn't your father or your brother have come?'

Abby set down her cup and stared at the intricate workmanship of the silver tray.

'My father – well, he's not actually so well at this moment, and is in bed; he couldn't ever make it over here. And my brother,' she swallowed, 'my brother is only thirteen years of age, sir.'

'I see.'

A pause. She sipped her tea. It had a peculiar taste, one she did not recognise.

'Tea all right?'

'Oh yes, sir – Mr Pelham, I should say—'

Another pause as he leaned back in the great sofa, engulfed in cushions, but looking at her all the time. 'Well, this is very nice. Very.'

She felt it was time for her to say something. 'Did you say you had been overseas, Mr Pelham?'

'Africa mostly. Devilish hot. Terrible climate, Abby, could kill a man. Nearly did kill me. Malaria. A lot of fellows couldn't take it. They started drinking. And once you start down that route it's only a matter of time ... Still,' he drew a breath, 'it was interesting, I learned a lot. The blacks – we had more than a few skirmishes, I can tell you. I got out with my life hanging by a thread once or twice. You'd look out over the veldt, can't see a thing – bush, scrub, the odd tree, as far as the eye can see. And there are a couple of hundred men, maybe three hundred there – they're all there – only you can't see 'em. They belong to the land you see, they just melt into it.' He paused, thinking. 'But a proud race. Tall men, fine warriors – I came to respect 'em, Abby, in the end. But I've sold

31

out. Had enough of all that, barrack life, dusty parade grounds, black faces everywhere, thought it was time to get back to my own people, time to settle down—'

Abby was much more relaxed now. 'You're looking for a wife, Mr Pelham?' she said unexpectedly.

He was silent for a moment, looking at her carefully. 'I am,' he said at last, holding her gaze. He had known women, it was clear.

She stood up and turned away towards the window, conscious of his eyes following her. She was suddenly possessed by the spirit of playfulness, of impudence. 'You'll find no end of girls here, I dare say.'

'I dare say,' he paused. 'Only, I'm a younger son; I shan't get a penny from the estate. I'm looking to marry money, Abby.'

'Ah now – that takes a bit longer. You'll have to work harder for that, Mr Pelham. And you mustn't be too ambitious – times are hard just now. Fortunes aren't to be found on every tree.'

'You obviously know a great deal about it. My sisters are too green. Perhaps you can advise me? Where shall I start my search?'

'Well now,' Abby pretended to think. 'There's the Misses Markham, at Ballina Lodge, they're said to be worth fifteen thousand apiece. Only Miss Eliza Markham wears green spectacles and reads improving tracts, and Miss Stephanie Markham does good works among the poor and distributes pots of her own preserves. Neither will see thirty again. Then there's Miss Georgina Reilly – she's said to be very fast, and will put her horse at anything – she might do for you, though I believe her fortune is under ten thousand – only there's been a bit of a shadow over her since that incident at Miss Greenslade's coming out ball, when they found her in the arms of Mr Jasper Flynn, that's forty and the father of five children. Or—' she paused, 'Let me see. Oh, of course, I was forgetting Miss Maria Bennett – they say she has four thousand acres, and no parents

32

living. You'll find her rather red in the face, due to a fond-
ness for cherry brandy, the wicked rumour has it – and she
is a *leetle* too much in the company of her gamekeeper Matt
Brady, that is a great strapping fellow, only not too bright
in the head—'

'Stop!' Pelham was rocking with laughter. 'I think I've
heard enough for one afternoon!'

Abby turned towards him again and they looked at one
another; she was elated by her success and, in the silence
that followed and as they stared into one another's eyes, it
was as if they recognised each other.

The door opened at the far end of the drawing room, and
a young woman walked in. She stopped as she saw Abby.
Randolph, who was sunk among the cushions of the sofa,
looked round.

'Randolph?'

Abby stiffened. The girl was elegantly dressed, a dainty
afternoon gown, silk slippers on her feet, her hair carefully, and yet negligently, tied up in a ribbon. Everything
about her spoke understated wealth.

Randolph had turned casually on the sofa cushion. 'What
do you want, Beatie? Can't you see I'm engaged?'

'Evidently.' She came forward and gave Abby a close
inspection. Abby felt inadequate, out of place, all her fears
returned.

'Won't you introduce me?' Beatie said coldly.

Randolph got up lazily. 'It's none of your business, but
as a matter of fact this young lady is here on a private
matter.'

'And do you usually interview tenants in the drawing
room?'

'You were just going weren't you, my dear?' He turned
to her with his lazy smile.

Abby said nothing, and crossed to the door.

He followed to the great front door, and as he opened it,
came out with her on to the step. 'Listen Abby – you can see
what it's like here. What I told you – the sisters spying on

33

me, and no doubt running to tell tales to the guv'nor. Now listen. I'll have a word with him, and let's see, if we could –' he was thinking – 'Suppose we say next Tuesday, eh? And, to save you walking all the way over here again—' He appeared to have an idea. 'You know The Goat in Westport? Let's say we'll meet in The Goat next Tuesday at three – and I'll see if I have any news for you.' He smiled a big smile.

On an impulse, she reached up and kissed him. 'Oh you're a darling! I'll not fail.' She turned, hurried down the steps and away across the gravel.

Chapter Four

All the way home she was on air. Her plan had worked. She had known it would. She was certain – they needed only to talk. Once Sir George knew of her family's circumstances he would understand and give them time – she hurried along.

Only she must be sure not to tell Rory. Suddenly the idea of Rory and Randolph – no, she must be very careful. It would never do. She hurried along. She was already late. They would wonder what had kept her, Rory and Da would be waiting for their dinner.

It was late in the afternoon, the sun had lost a little of its strength, and there was again that faint chill of autumn; she breathed in deeply, yes, autumn was coming, and to be thrown out of their home as winter came down – she had done the right thing. To be thrown out now! It was not to be thought on. She had been right. They had to make every effort possible.

Her thoughts returned to Randolph Pelham: how kind he'd been, not a bit embarrassed to have a farm girl in his drawing room. He was very considerate, she thought, giving her tea – and such beautiful china too, Aunt Eileen had nothing to it. Oh that was a house – to think people could live like that – every day, born to it, brought up in it, knowing no other. That sister – Abby had seen the contempt in her eyes, she hated her. What right had she?

Yet Abby had been intruding in her home. Oh, Randolph was such an interesting man – he'd been everywhere. It was more than she could imagine – to go to Africa! She felt warm inside – they would meet again.

When she got home Fan was waiting. Fortunately, Rory and Da were still out.

'What happened?' Fan's eyes were saucers.

'Where's Rory and Da?'

'Oh – they went over to Castlebar to sell the cows,' Fan took her by the arm, and dragged her into the kitchen.

'Sell the cows? But Rory said—'

'He said there was no point keeping them, the price of butter's so low. But come on, Abby, tell me, what happened? Did you speak with Sir George?'

Abby unwound her shawl and threw it over a chair, and turned to the fire.

'Were you about to let this fire go out, Fan? Do you never think?'

'Abby! Never mind the fire! What happened at the Big House above?'

Abby took a couple of pieces of peat from the creel, squatted in front of the fire, and began to fit them in among the low heap of smouldering ash, pushing and shaking a little with a stick, to nurse the fire back to life.

'Bring in some water, we've got to get supper ready—'

'*Abby!*'

Abby straightened, and dusted her hands together. She looked at Fan, and broke into a grin. 'Only get the water, Fan dear, and I'll tell you everything.'

Fan's eyes filled with glee. She snatched up the bucket and disappeared out of the door to the well up in the field.

There was a bit of cold bacon which Abby set on the table and began to chop into small pieces. There wasn't much of it left, though; this was the last of it. She frowned as she turned and took up two handfuls of potatoes, and set them on the table. There weren't many of them left either.

Fan returned heaving the bucket with two hands.

'Just pour a little in that bowl and wash the spuds. The men'll want their supper on the table when they get in.'

'Abby?' Fan was pleading.

Abby was busy chopping the bacon into small pieces. 'Well now, Fan,' she began, 'Sir George lives in a beautiful big house, you may be sure. I never saw the like before – save only the marquis's of course – a beautiful house with a lawn running down to the lake, and a private boat on his private lake – only imagine—'

'And what did Sir George say?'

'Well—' it came out in a rush, 'I didn't see Sir George but his son was there – his younger son.' Fan was closely following her, watching her face intently, 'I never knew about him – but he's been away for years in the army—'

'An officer!'

'He's left the army now, Fan,' Abby hurried on. 'That's why he's here – he was away in Africa before – and all them sort of places—' she added hurriedly.

'Is he handsome?'

Abby looked into Fan's eyes for a moment, and then grinned slyly. 'He's *very* handsome,' she whispered.

Fan squealed. Abby went on quickly, 'He was the perfect gentleman, Fan. He invited me in to his drawing room, he gave me tea – on bone china and a silver teapot, it was so dainty, and him so kind and asking after the family, and was so good, and said he was going to talk to his father about us, and oh it was the most beautiful house, you can't imagine—' she paused.

'Well!' Fan's eyes glazed. 'You took tea with the landlord's son . . .' she breathed. 'I wonder, is he married?' she looked up wickedly.

'He is not.'

Fan squealed again. 'It's a fairy tale—'

'Fan! It's very likely he'd want to marry me, I'm sure—'

'You never know, Abby! He may be thinking of you at this very moment.' She struck an attitude. '"I don't care what my da thinks. Disinherit me if you will, but I love her, and no other shall be my bride!"'

'He said he wants to get married, Fan—'

'There!'

Abby was more prosaic and returned to her chopping. 'He has to marry money.'

Fan shrugged, and there was a moment's silence.

That night Rory and Da came in from Castlebar. They had sold the cows, and realised seven pounds.

'Butter's down again,' Rory said as they sat round the table. 'Three pounds ten the hundred weight.'

He put the coins on the table. 'That's it for the winter, Abby. Twenty-seven pounds, plus the money from the geese. If we paid the rent and the arrears we'd be left with nothing.'

Abby listened carefully. It was all she could do, not to speak. With any luck she wouldn't have to explain at all. If Randolph were careful, nothing need be said and Rory would never know. She glanced across at Fan, and caught her eye. Fan's glance was full of meaning. Fan was a chatterbox, a silly vain girl, if the truth were known, and Abby was nervous about her. She had told Fan everything. On no account must Fan breathe a word.

'Fan, bring in your da a glass of spirits,' Rory said after a moment.

Fan rose and went out silently.

And as she poured Rory and Da a glass, again there was silence in the little kitchen. Da had not spoken since they had returned, and Abby could see the misery in him, and even more than to Rory she wanted to tell him, that maybe not *everything* was lost, and maybe there might be a ray of hope yet . . .

'Cheer up, Da.' She leaned across and laid her hand on his shoulder.

He sighed but said nothing.

It was not until she was on her way into Westport that

doubts arose. Should she be going into a public bar with a strange man? It seemed an odd sort of place – she had never been into a public house in her life. Girls didn't. People might take her for some kind of fancy woman . . .

The Goat was crowded, men and women too, thank God, and no one took any notice of her.

For a moment she stood on the threshold, as the smoke wafted past her, the acrid pipe and cigar smoke, and the stale smell of porter, the warmth of human bodies; it was stuffy and smoky, but everyone was occupied with their own business and took no notice of her.

She hovered in the doorway, hoping to see Randolph, then turned out into the street again. She could not bring herself to enter alone.

A moment later he came out, and stood close over her, speaking softly. 'Abby, you came, good girl. Come in.'

'Oh Mr Pelham – did you speak to your father?'

'Hey! Not so fast! Come in, and we'll have a drink first. All in good time.'

She followed him in, and a moment later he placed a glass of hot whiskey punch in her hands. She seldom drank it. Whiskey was for men. 'Oh—' She stared down at this strange glass in her hands.

He clinked her glass and raised his own. She took a tiny sip.

'So, you got home safely?'

'Oh, yes, thank you. Er – my father has had to sell the last of the cows—'

'I thought your father was bedridden?'

'Well, he is—' she swallowed, 'but he got someone – a friend – to take them over to Castlebar—'

Around them people passed, pressing them together. Randolph looked round with a slight distaste at this crowd of poor, ragged humanity. Abby sensed this and looked round her too. If any one should recognise her . . .

'You know, it's deuced awkward here – no place to talk—' He was thinking.

She glanced round again, wondering why he had suggested it.

'Tell you what, Abby,' he began again awkwardly, 'I had a word with the landlord before you came – he said there's a room upstairs we can use. Much better than this – peaceful – we can have a nice cosy chat all by ourselves.'

She was confused. Why couldn't they just go out in the street?

He seemed to read her thoughts. 'Tell you the truth, the old man's a bit of a tyrant, likes to think he runs the place – which he does of course – and my sister was a bit shirty after you'd gone, the silly goose. So it might be just as well if we keep this secret – just a secret between you and me—' he smiled.

Abby didn't know what to think.

'Look, it's number nine – just up the stairs – out there—' He pointed. 'Up the stairs, turn right, and it's in front of you. Number nine. You go up now – it's open – and I'll come up in a moment. Just finish this.'

Without thinking she set the drink on the bar, and looked round. Just outside the bar door she saw the stairs. Uncertainly she made her way up, and found number nine. She opened the door and went in.

It was a bedroom and almost filled by a double bed.

She bit her lip. It didn't seem possible. She was more confused than ever. What was she doing here? Why hadn't they met in the street or in the marquis's park – down by the harbour – anywhere? She was tense, waiting, leaning against the wall, huddling her shawl round her.

The door opened silently, and Randolph slipped in. He smiled, as he closed the door. For a moment they watched each other.

'Well,' he said, 'this is nice.'

'Mr Pelham,' she began hurriedly, 'I don't have long. Can you please tell me, did you speak with your father?'

'Hey, not so fast, everything in good time. Let's make

40

ourselves comfortable. I brought your drink up, by the way – you hadn't finished it.'

He set the glasses down (he had replenished his own) on the bedside table.

'You know Abby, I've been thinking of you since we spoke. Couldn't get you out of my mind. I've never met a girl like you. And do you know, the more I thought about it, the more I thought how alike we are. We are kindred spirits.'

He looked hard at her. She was still standing with her back to the wall, her hands behind her. He held his hands out to her, and at last hesitantly she offered her own. Gently he drew her away from the wall towards him. Her heart was thudding. What was going on? One thing, obviously. She wished she were outside, but said nothing, waiting.

'You were more forthcoming last time,' he went on, 'I couldn't stop you. Do you know, Abby you made me laugh so hard – I couldn't remember the last time I'd enjoyed anything so much. I just wanted it to go on. And when you kissed me—'

He was holding her hands. With difficulty she pulled away from him. He could see her distress and confusion.

'Mr Pelham, I beg you—'

'I haven't forgotten the first kiss you gave me, Abby—'

'That was nothing!'

'Nothing? You mean it?'

'Oh, well, no, not nothing – but I was just so grateful to you for thinking of me and my family, and saying you would speak to your father about us – have you spoken to him?'

He seemed upset, and pulled away from her. 'Well dash it all. I thought you cared for me. I mean to say, if a girl kisses a fellow, it usually means something, unless she's just some common flirt—'

'No! It wasn't like that, sir!'

'For God's sake, don't call me sir! My name is Randolph.'

41

'Oh I'm sorry, sir – Randolph. I never meant to lead you on, it was just that you were so kind and I – well, I just did it without thinking.'

He paused, and was more subdued. 'You led me on?'

'I like you, sir of course—'

'Well, then, if you like me, can't you show it?'

'But Randolph, sir, how can we – I mean – you a gentleman and me a poor girl with nothing—'

'Damn it, Abby this is a poor show – you lead a fellow on, and now you blow cool. What a way to behave! I'm not asking for very much. I've thought of nothing but you for the last week, can't get you out of my thoughts.' He took both her hands again, now speaking softer and lower. 'Abby, I've never met a girl like you. Won't you at least let your hair down for me? You have the loveliest hair I ever saw.'

Standing away slightly she loosened the ribbon and shook her hair free, spreading it over her shoulders and back. He reached his own hands and ran his fingers through the heavy black tresses. He seemed mesmerised.

'The loveliest hair . . .'

There was something hypnotic about that motion, something deeply sensuous and she couldn't help responding to the motion of his hands. The lulling effect calmed her as he took her shoulders gently and sat her on the bed beside him.

He spoke softly, still running his fingers through her hair. 'You can't send me away unsatisfied now? At least give me a kiss?'

The trouble was that, beneath all her confusion and uncertainty, she did actually find him extremely attractive. She had never met anyone remotely like him before. He was completely different from any man she had ever met, quite unlike the village boys.

His hands still round her head, his fingers in her hair, he gently bent his face over her, and as they kissed, she was powerless to stop him. And then, in spite of herself she was carried away, and they were kissing passionately. She had

42

lost all sense of her bearings. In this strange situation, with a man whom she scarcely knew, the sense of danger, that someone might have seen her as she came in – everything served to confuse and disorient her. As they kissed Randolph lowered her on to the bed, and they kissed again.

'I say, can't you take off this thing—' This was her shawl which was still draped round her shoulders. They were kissing again, and now he was over her, his knee between her legs, forcing them apart, his hands running up and down her body, urgent, pressing, down her back, across her bottom, and then up her thighs and across her belly and breasts. She was being taken over, invaded and, willing and afraid, a part of her wanted it.

She pushed him away suddenly, her head swimming, and tried to raise herself on one elbow.

'What is it?'

'Oh wait, you'll have to let me think—'

'Think? What is there to think about?'

'I don't – this isn't right—'

'Abby! Don't let me down now! Can't you see I'm dying for you? You're beautiful. I've never met a girl like you. You're beautiful. For God's sake, don't go all bashful now!'

She was afraid, the blood racing in her, her brain confused. 'I never meant to lead you on at all. Mr Pelham, you'll have to let me think! This is all wrong—'

'For God's sake, stop worrying. I'll speak to the guv'nor – it'll be all right, I tell you. Trust me.'

'You promise?'

'I promise!'

He leapt off the bed and drew the curtains, so that the room was thrown into a dim gloom, and returned to the bed, stripping off his collar and tie.

'Come on – take those boots off—'

'You won't—'

'Trust me! Stop worrying. We'll just—'

He had begun to unbutton the top of her dress.

43

Through her all her blood seemed on fire, her mind confused – she no longer knew what to think – and could only cling on to one thought: at least they would be safe now. That was the main thing. He had said so – but oh, he was so pressing, so urgent, so—

Half an hour later she walked quickly down the stairs, through the little entrance way and out into the street, still feeling shaky and weak, her hair awry, hoping she wasn't blushing, pulling the shawl over her head, hurrying down the street.

It was undoubtedly wrong and if she were to confess it to Father McMichael, the Lord only knew what might be the penance. But she had done it at least for the family. For Rory and Da and Fan. She told herself over and over . . .

Chapter Five

I have fallen.

She was trudging through the lanes, wet after the recent
rains, unconscious of the puddles, the muddy ruts, slipping,
unconscious, unseeing . . .

But Randolph will save us, I know he will. And that will
make it right. But how can I confess to Father McMichael?
How could I tell him I have lain with the landlord's son?
And himself strong for the Land League, and was at the
meeting last week. I can never tell him. I can never tell
anyone, not even Fan. If I told Rory he'd kill me, I know
he would; then he'd kill Randolph. Oh Randolph, why did
you have to do it? Suppose a baby were to come? I'd be
dead. Dead. He would never marry me; he told me he
wanted to marry money. Him, a fine gentleman to marry a
poor girl with never a penny to her fortune? Oh Blessed
Virgin Mary, what have I done?

People passed her in the road; she didn't notice them,
walking hunched forward, staring at the muddy track in
front of her.

I'm done for. I can only pray he'll speak to his father and
we'll get a bit of time till the letter comes from America.
What a fool I am! And yet, he wasn't rough was he? She
tried to clear her thoughts and remember. He wasn't rough,
he used me gently, and him so handsome, such a man of the
world, he would never harm me, would he? Yet he has

harmed me, so. If a baby were to come—

And how can I ever be married now, me no maid, when Father McMichael told us that chastity is a jewel, and there's no race on earth to compare with the Irish for the purity of their womenfolk, and here's me— She stumbled on, pulling the shawl over her head more snugly as she felt a waft of rain borne on the wind, and the clouds gathering and massing over the mountains.

Let it rain. Rain on me, let me be cold and wet, I deserve it, oh Holy Mother of God, how am I to show my face ever in the village again? Surely they'll know? Won't it show like a mark on my forehead – the sign of a whore? Abby O'Leary, the whore that lay with his honour of the Big House? Oh Jesus Mary and Joseph, was there ever such a miserable girl as I?

The rain coming on stronger now, cut like a whip across her face, and she bent into the force of it. But still after all, he said he would talk to his father, and if only we can keep the house, all is not lost, it was worth it in the end, and Rory would thank me if he knew. Oh Holy Jesus, I hope he never does know.

Does he love me? Shall we meet again? It was the right thing to do. Wasn't it? And he will come to see me when he can. Yes, he will. He has to go to London for a spell, then he will find a way to come to me. And he gave me his medal as a token. But will he want me now that he's – now that we have – done it? Oh sure, him such a good man, gentle too, it cannot be that he would desert me now? And he did say he would come to see me when he could. Oh, but he must never come to the cottage. He said he had to go to London – on important business no doubt. I wonder what he will do? But then he could never marry me—

So her thoughts went round and round, always coming back to the same place.

When she arrived home, the others were sitting by the fire,

46

and looking up sometimes at the steady downpour and the dim grey of the afternoon.

'Where've you been?'

'Oh,' she said casually, 'down in the village.'

'There's tea in the pot, Abby,' Fan said, 'take off them clothes. You're soaked through.'

Abby went through into the little bedroom she shared with Fan, and unwound her shawl, and sitting on the edge of the bed, unlaced her boots, crusted with mud.

Fan came in and closed the door behind her. Her eyes were alive with interest.

'How did it go?' she whispered.

Abby looked up and shook her head wearily, and glanced to the door. 'Not now,' she whispered.

Fan sat beside her on the side of the bed, her face alight. 'But you did see him?'

Abby nodded, and pointed silently to the door. 'I'll tell you tonight. Not a word now.'

But what could she tell her? When they were in bed that night – they shared a bed – what could Abby say? Not even to her sister, who pestered her and would give her no rest till she had heard all.

'I think he's a good man, Fan, I do,' she whispered, 'and he promised he'll speak with his father—'

'He said that last week.'

'I know ... I think there was ... anyway, he hadn't had a chance yet, but he said he would – faithfully. Oh Fan—'

She clasped the girl to her, and couldn't help her tears. 'I'm sure it'll be all right—'

Fan was alarmed. 'But what happened? Abby – what's the matter? Why are you crying?'

For a moment Abby wept helplessly. Fan was frightened. 'Surely – you didn't do anything you shouldn't?'

Abby shook her head silently.

'Well, then, what is it – you're never in love with him?'

'Why ever should I be such a fool? Don't talk daft.'

47

Abby pulled away and sniffed, wiping her eyes on the edge of the coarse linen sheets.

'Well, what is it then?'

Abby heaved a sigh that shattered her whole frame. 'I can't say.'

Every day she watched out for any sign of a letter from the landlord's agent, Mr Scott, or from Fergus in America.

When All Saints passed, the atmosphere in the cottage became tense. They sat round the table again, and Rory counted the money.

'Not even enough for the rent, and even it was, we'd have nothing for ourselves.' He moved the little piles of coins about the table for a moment aimlessly. 'There's been no reply to the letter. Not that I expected any.'

Abby could feel Fan's eyes on her, but ignored her.

'Ah well, I suppose no news is good news,' she said at last. 'Maybe he's thought better of it, and means to leave us alone?'

'Leave us alone?' Rory looked incredulous. 'Sir George Pelham leave us alone? He'd skin us for the last penny of his money.'

One morning the following week, one damp grey autumn morning, after Da and Rory had gone out, there was a rap at the door and, as Abby opened it, a stout middle-aged man in a thick overcoat confronted her, his tall hat jammed low on his brows. Behind him a constable in his green uniform and pointed helmet sat on a horse, holding the bridle of another. A rifle rested across his saddlebow.

'Mr Joseph O'Leary?'

'My father is in the field beyond.' She pointed. 'What do you want?'

'No matter. Where did you say?'

Abby pointed.

'Will you show me?'

She went into her room to pull on her boots, and led

them up the *bohreen* a little way and then into a field where Rory and Da were digging the last of the turnips.

The two men followed her, the policeman still on his horse. The constable halted at the gate of the field as Abby led the man across the muddy turnip patch. He seemed used to it, and was quite expressionless.

'Mr Joseph O'Leary?'

Da and Rory had stopped work and had been watching them.

'That's me.'

The man pulled a sheaf of paper from his inside pocket and thrust it into Da's hand. 'This is an order from the magistrates' court in Castlebar, to pay all outstanding arrears of rent, or quit this farm as of the third of next month.'

Abby who was standing a few yards away almost rocked on her feet.

But before Da could take it, Rory had seized and thrust it back against the man's chest. 'Take your order! We'll accept no order! We recognise no such order, and will not give up our farm, and we call upon Sir George Pelham to grant an abatement!'

Abby watched with frozen concentration.

The man was clearly well used to this. He was expressionless and the document fell to the mud. 'I have discharged my office,' he said woodenly. 'The order has been served.'

He turned back across the field. Abby watched him bewildered; what was this order? What did it mean? Surely the landlord didn't mean to go ahead after all?

The policeman on his horse had lifted his rifle as he saw Rory coming after the process server. The man did not slacken his heavy tread, but said half casually over his shoulder, 'I am an officer of the court. I advise you not to lay a hand on me.'

'Tell Sir George we'll not give up the farm!'

The man swung himself heavily on to his horse. 'Tell him yourself. I'm only here to carry out the law.'

He turned his horse's head, and the policeman turned with him, and they made their way out into the *bohreen*.

Rory turned back to his father, who was still standing in the middle of the field, with the muddy document at his feet. Rory snatched it up, so angry he could scarcely speak.

'He can take his order—'

Abby came to him, and took it out of his hand. 'Let me see.'

Concentrating as hard as she could she read through the legal jargon. Why had she trusted Randolph Pelham? She was mad. Completely and utterly mad. Of course he had never had any intention of helping them. The dirty sheets of the order hung in her hand as she looked into Rory's face.

'Oh Rory—'

He had turned to her, she opened her arms, and they clung to one another.

That night Rory went through the village, telling what had happened, and calling on everyone to be present when the bailiff came and to resist his attempt to repossess the farm.

Fan was frightened. 'But what'll we do, Rory, if the bailiff comes? Where will we go? Maybe we could pay a little off the arrears?'

'We'll pay not a penny. Every man in this townland will be with us. The landlord would need to bring a regiment of dragoons to get us out of this.'

Rory spent the day constructing a stout wooden frame intended to fit into the doorway. Short of a cannon shot that door would be impossible to break down. The response in the village had been strong; Father McMichael was with them, and with his encouragement, the villagers were committed.

Early on the morning of the third, mild, grey, overcast, the door was open at an early hour, as Rory worked to complete his wooden frame. The villagers began to appear in twos and threes, and Da was among them with a bottle of

50

spirits against the morning damp. They had come armed with sticks, pitchforks, and other agricultural implements. As they stood about in the *bohreen*, they talked to give each other encouragement.

Aunt Eileen was there too.

The door being open on this morning gave their house a curious air, as if it were no longer a private home, but a stage on which was about to be enacted a public act. Tonight they would have a home – or not . . .

It was an hour and a half's walk from Castlebar. But the bailiff would come early, wouldn't he?

Then they heard him. Heard a tramp of men, and the jingle of bridles. Everyone turned in the crowded lane, tense, waiting. At the turn of the *bohreen* a man appeared on horseback, and then another, and two more, officers, one in red, one in green. Then came the military. How many? Fifty? A hundred? As they came up the narrow lane, they seemed to go on appearing at the corner, as if there was no end to them. But now there were more, only in green now – these were peelers, constables of the Royal Irish Constabulary with carbines over their shoulders. The sound of marching was loud, the horses, too, and then – oh God, there were more still, labourers now, men with sticks and crowbars . . .

The officers drew up before the cottage, and a sergeant rapped out an order. The troops came to a disciplined halt and there was silence for a moment. Abby, Fan and the men were standing before the door.

Mr Scott on his horse pulled out a sheet of paper. 'Joseph O'Leary. In the name of Sir George Pelham, I call upon you for the payment of rent owed as of 1 November last, together with arrears dating back to 1 May. In the sum of thirty-two pounds. Do you have it?'

Before Da could say anything, Rory stepped forward. 'No we do not! In the name of Mr O'Leary, I refuse this sum, and call upon Sir George Pelham to grant an abatement of the rent. And I further wish it to be known that we

51

have the support of the Land League in this matter, and will resist any attempt to deprive us of our home.' He looked about at the crowd. 'Won't we, lads?'

The crowd gave a rousing cheer.

The agent looked at the officer, and the officer looked at the leader of the labourers who had now come up with him. He nodded, and turned to his men. 'Turn 'em out.'

As the men moved forward, a sergeant barked another order, and the red-coats turned, snapped into a well-rehearsed military manoeuvre, and in a second presented their bayonets to the faces of the crowd about them. The people as they crowded forward found eighteen inches of bright steel in their faces.

In the very act of setting his wooden frame into the doorway Rory felt himself seized by two heavy men, thrown two yards away, the frame pulled out in an instant, and hurled to one side.

The crowd were shouting, screeching, anything they could think of, sods of turf came flying through the air, raining down on the soldiers and police. It made not the slightest difference. This was something they had practised; something they were prepared for, used to. These were men who had been in Africa, in India, who had marched through blazing deserts, and over mountain passes. They were professionals. A few villagers were as nothing.

Abby and Fan were together watching with horror, unable to see what they could do.

Pieces of furniture were being carried – or thrown – out of the house, chairs, on their sides, carelessly thrown through the door, the sideboard, an old picture of Daniel O'Connell falling and breaking its glass . . .

Da, who up to now had said nothing, as he saw his home being demolished before his eyes, at last found his voice. And before Abby could stop him, breaking free from her grasp he launched himself at the agent's leg, as he sat on his horse, and seemed inflated with more than human strength.

52

'You scoundrel!' He was hoarse, red in the face, incoherent. 'You blackguard! It's *my home*!'

For a moment it seemed he would have pulled Mr Scott to the ground, but in the same second, as the troopers jostled about them, one of them turned and, with one blow of the butt of his carbine, felled him to the ground.

Rory threw himself on the trooper's back and pulled him over. As they rolled in the mud, two, and three others fell on him, and struggle though he might, Rory disappeared beneath four soldiers. One of them was beating Rory about the head as the others held him, and Abby screamed, and threw herself upon them so that, one of them struggling to his feet, pulled her and flung her away. Fan crouched against the wall, her head in her hands, screaming.

'Take that man into custody.'

'You villains!' Rory was on his knees, his hands bound behind his back, his shirt torn, his face, his clothes crusted with mud. 'Will you watch the old man! Look to the old man – you've killed him!'

Da was lying still, flat on his face, almost beneath their feet. Abby and Aunt Eileen knelt by him, and with difficulty turned him on his back. He was unconscious. Fan screamed.

'Oh God, they've killed Da!'

A man was now on a ladder pitchforking straw to the ground, and there were holes appearing in the roof. Everywhere about them now lay their furniture, the sideboard, beds – grotesque in the lane – a cabinet, pots and pans, all their household spread out to view.

As Abby knelt over her father, spread-eagled unconscious in the dirt, the officers conferred, then one of them turned to the troops.

The sergeant barked, and the troops formed themselves into line. The agent, buttoned up, his tall hat jammed over his brows, turned in his saddle to the villagers, still struggling and shouting behind the fence of steel. Despite his bluster he seemed less sure of himself.

'I remind you that there is such a thing as the right of property. The law upholds that right. This house and farm are the property of Sir George Pelham. And I should like to see the man bold enough to defy the law.'

As he turned his horse's head, a sergeant glanced at Rory. 'Bring him away.'

Rory, his hands bound behind his back, was roughly urged down the *bohreen* amid the soldiers. He looked back desperately. 'Abby! Take care of Da!'

Chapter Six

As the troops disappeared down the lane, the villagers crowded round Abby and Fan who were kneeling over their father lying on his back, his face muddy, unconscious.

Abby wiped her hand across his face to clear off some of the mud. 'Send for a doctor, someone!'

Aunt Eileen knelt beside her and examined Da. She looked up. 'Tell Dr Fagan to come over to my house. We must get him inside, Abby. Seamus Mallon, will you bring your ass cart, and we'll get Joseph to my house.' She looked up. 'Thank God it's not raining anyway.'

'Poor Da! Will he be all right Aunt Eileen, think you? Will he ever wake up?'

Aunt Eileen glanced at her, shaking her head. 'I pray to God—'

Father McMichael was with them. 'Abby, you're a sensible girl. Listen. Your aunt will take care of your father. I'll get a couple of neighbours to collect your furniture. We'll store it in my barn for the moment. Paddy Byrne and you, Mrs Reilly, you'll lend a hand now?'

Once Father McMichael had organised them, the confusion and chaos was a little reduced, and villagers began to carry individual items down the lane to the presbytery. Father McMichael lived in a house far too big for one man, with only a housekeeper for company.

'Thank you, Father.'

A few minutes later, Seamus Mallon appeared at the bend in the lane leading his ass cart. Together Father McMichael and he lifted the unconscious body of Da on it.

'Fan – you go with Aunt Eileen and look after Da. I'll stay here and help with the things.'

As the cart set off, bumping and jolting down the lane, Abby turned to where the villagers were all helping to carry the family utensils into the village.

She must not think. Don't think. Just get on with what had to be done. There was nothing else for it. Because if she once stopped to think what had happened—

All morning they tramped up and down the *bohreen*, until everything had been got in. Abby stood in the barn with the priest and looked at her family things – what had once been her home, stacked up, in any order, what did it look like? A few simple things? A few bits of cheap furniture? The bed she and Fan had slept in every day of their lives? A chair? A table? A pile of kitchen utensils? She would not think.

'Thank you, Father. I don't know how we'll ever repay you, that's sure. But thank you.'

'What will you do now Abby?'

She shook her head. 'Rory gone to prison, Da struck down—' She looked down. 'My aunt will take us in for a day or two – after that—'

She was silent. The priest laid his hand on her shoulder. 'Go and see after your father, Abby. I'll go into Castlebar and find about Rory.'

'Oh thank you, Father.' Impulsively she kissed his hand, and turned quickly away.

She was about to turn back up towards their cottage, but stopped herself. No. She would never go that way again. That way was barred to her. She tightened inside herself, and struck out through the field towards her aunt's house.

When she arrived, she found the doctor had come and gone.

56

Da was on a bed in her aunt's spare room. He had recovered consciousness, though he was very weak, and could neither move nor speak. He barely recognised Abby as she knelt beside him and took his hand between her own. She had been holding herself in check all day, the events crowding in upon her so thick and furious, but now, suddenly, with the immediate pressure off her, the sight of her father on the bed was too much for her.

'Oh Da—' And she knelt, the tears running down her cheeks, holding his hand, unable to speak, the two of them looking into each other's eyes.

Only at length, very slowly she rose, wiping her eyes on her apron, and tucked her father in more comfortably, fussing about the bed a moment, and then at last returned to the kitchen. Her aunt was sitting with Fan, waiting for her.

The older woman was grave. 'Your father received a terrible blow in his back,' she said. 'The doctor is not sure at this moment whether he'll ever walk again. Whatever happens it'll be a long time before he will be able to get out of bed.'

Fan was sitting at the table with them, confused and frightened.

'It's a blessing you are to us, Aunt,' Abby heaved a long sigh. 'I'll never be able to thank you. But I promise we won't be a burden to you, will we Fan?'

Fan shook her head vigorously.

'We won't!' Abby went on quickly. 'Whatever happens you won't regret this. We'll work and—' she hunted for words – 'anyway, do everything in our power to repay your kindness. And I promise faithfully, we won't be any kind of a burden—'

The aunt laid her hand on Abby's. 'You've not to worry,' she said kindly. 'You'll remain here as long as need be. Have you heard about Rory?'

'Father McMichael said he would go into Castlebar to ask about him. I'll go over to the presbytery tonight to see him.'

'Now,' Aunt Eileen became practical. 'You and Fan can sleep in the loft above.' She pointed to the half loft that effectively roofed in the little room where Da lay. A ladder reached it. 'We'll get in a handful of straw for a mattress, and you'll be snug up there – 'tis warm behind the chimney.'

Before Abby could return to the presbytery however, there was a knock on the door towards dusk.

Rory, dusty, his face still dirty, his clothes covered in mud and looking like a scarecrow, stumbled into the cottage. He was exhausted, and stood staring round at them as they waited in trepidation.

'Where's Da?' he whispered hoarsely.

'In here,' Abby said quickly, and opened the door into the little room behind the fireplace. Like an automaton, Rory crossed the room and entered. They were behind him. Da lay still barely conscious.

'The doctor came. He said he didn't know how long he would have to lie here – he thought maybe the back was broken – he can scarcely speak.'

Leaning over his father Rory was able to exchange a couple of words with him in the gloom of the darkened room. Then he turned and came back into the kitchen.

They helped him to a chair, and he sat heavily. Abby sat by him. 'They let you go?'

He sat for a moment, his head on one hand, and nodded slightly. The two sisters watched, helpless.

'Rory darling,' Abby looked round to her aunt. 'Aunt, Rory must be famished—'

Eileen turned to the hearth where the remains of the stew hung in an iron pot over the fire. She placed a bowl in front of the boy.

Abby sat beside him, and spoke gently. 'Rory darling, here's something to eat. Have your supper, and then tell us what happened.'

At last Rory lifted his head. She had never seen him so

grim. He looked grey, heavy. 'God rot them all to hell,' he muttered at last.

'But – what happened?'

Slowly Rory took up the spoon and began to taste the stew, staring down at the table. The three women sat round the table watching him. 'My curse on George Pelham, on him and his family to all eternity,' he said still looking down, and in that same low monotonous voice. 'The Land League! What help was it? Abby, we have been used worse than cattle. Da maybe crippled for life, thrown off our own land, what is there to live for? Let's hang ourselves and be done with it.'

They watched silently. At last he glanced up at them. 'They threw me out. Just kept me in the cell for a few hours then threw me out.'

Abby's spirits lifted. 'So – no charges?'

He grunted in a tired, cynical laugh. 'I wasn't important enough,' and lapsed into silence, spooning up his stew, his elbow on the table, his head lowered, not looking at the others, and saying nothing.

At length, Fan plucked up courage, and whispered, 'What'll we do now, Rory?'

Rory did not reply. Abby was frightened. She had never seen him like this. The silence in the kitchen hung over them in the dim lantern's light, like a pall. It was as if someone had died.

Rory slept on a mattress of straw on the kitchen floor. Above, in the loft, Fan huddled against Abby beneath the coarse blanket. 'It'll be all right, won't it Abby? Aunt Eileen won't throw us out?'

Abby whispered a few comforting words. 'Rory will know what to do.'

'But Abby,' Fan was near to tears, 'Rory was so down. I've never seen him like it.'

'Hush now. We can talk about it in the morning.'

*

In the dawn of a December day, a misty morning, they struggled up. Abby had slept fitfully. She still had not absorbed what had happened. In a strange way, she kept expecting to wake up and find it had all been a dream. Everything she had built her hopes on, still so recent, was fresh in her mind. She still would not accept that Randolph Pelham had betrayed them. There must be another explanation.

Rory was recovered. He washed his face in a bowl on the kitchen table, ran a comb through his hair, and shook out his coat at the doorway. While Eileen and Fan prepared a bit of breakfast, a bowl of stir-about, he and Abby sat at the table. She waited for Rory to speak, constantly watching him anxiously, till he should be ready. He noticed this, and turning suddenly smiled, his old self, reached his hand and covered hers.

'Don't worry Abby. I've thought it out. There's nothing for me here. No chance of a job in Mayo, or anywhere in Connacht. So – I'm off to Dublin, or maybe England. There's always work if you look hard enough. I'll find something – then I'll send you word, and you and Fan can come and join me –' he frowned – 'though that depends on Da – whether he'll recover or not. Look, we have to have money. Aunt Eileen's been kindness itself but we cannot be here eating her food—'

'Hush boy!'

'No. Aunt Eileen, I will not be a debtor to you! And I don't know where we'd be this minute if it weren't for you. I'm going to Dublin today, and I'll write the moment I've found a job and then, depending on how Da is, we can arrange something, and then we'll all be together again.'

Abby threw her arms round his neck. 'Oh, I knew you'd know what to do. Rory my darling!'

'Now Fan, my little sister,' he looked across at her, Abby's arm still round his neck, 'you're to help Abby and your aunt. Be good and take care of Da, and do all you can.' He pulled some coins from his pocket. 'There's twenty pounds and a bit here.' He stared at it, 'Aunt Eileen, I'll keep a couple of pounds just to get me to Dublin and then to keep me a few days till I find work. You understand – I'd give you every penny for we owe everything to you. But I promise I'll pay you back in full.'

Eileen, who was standing at the fire, shook her head. 'Don't say any more, Rory. The girls and Joseph will be safe here till you can write, never fear.'

Soon after, Rory, who took few things – a spare shirt rolled up in his pocket – set off to Westport for the train. Abby walked with him. On the way they said little, each full of their own thoughts, and as they stood on the platform as the train prepared to depart, the steam gently hissing behind her, standing close on the busy platform as passengers came past, and doors slammed, still unable to speak then, with a little sigh, taking each other in their arms, and hugging, hugging, as if they might never meet again. She took his head, and kissed him on his cheek, hard, long, and he could feel the wetness of her cheek.

'God watch over you, Rory my darling, darling boy; I'll pray for you every night.'

As the train pulled out, gently gathering speed, she could scarcely make it out for the blur of her tears.

She was walking back through the town, still in a kind of frozen hibernation, still waiting for something in her to reawaken, waiting for her customary energy and strength to return.

She found herself passing The Goat, and glancing up at it, a shock passed through her; the scene was visible to her clearly again, and now at last there was the fierce heat of anger in her, a vivid redness in her sight.

Rory was right – they had been used. She had been used – worse than a whore. If she had been a whore at least it would have been an honest transaction, and she would have been paid. But to be fooled, to be made use of for an idle hour's pleasure and fobbed off with worthless promises –

61

she turned along the street and out of the town.

She walked fast. Anger was in her now. Anger against Randolph Pelham, against his family, against the peelers, the dragoons, all of them, that had conspired to throw her family out of its home. Oh, one day there would be such a reckoning! That an honest family might not be left alone to go about its business, to raise its children, to plant its crops, to harvest, to tend its herds, but they must be harried and bullied by such a set of blood-suckers . . .

When she arrived at her aunt's, she found Da had recovered his strength a little, though his face appeared sunken, and he looked old, ill.

Abby knelt by him, and took his hand. It was cold. 'Da?' she whispered. 'How are you now? Are you feeling better?'

He could scarcely croak. 'Abby . . . your aunt—'

'Yes?'

'Your aunt has been very good . . . but I can't—'

'Hush, don't try to speak.' Abby adjusted the coverings, afraid to look her father in the face for a moment. He seemed so ill, she thought, He's going to die.

She turned to her aunt. 'Aunt Eileen, did he manage to eat anything?'

Eileen bent over her where she was still kneeling by the side of the bed. 'He was able to take a little breakfast.'

Da, who was listening, nodded, and whispered, 'It was good.'

Abby stood up again, her hands writhing together. She turned. 'Aunt, we must talk. What to do—'

'Don't fret yourself, my dear. Sure, you'll stay here as long as need be.'

Having tucked her father in comfortably, she returned with her aunt to the kitchen.

Later they were at the table.

'Aunt, we cannot just live off you like this. It isn't fair. Fan's too young yet, and you must have someone to help to

62

look after Da. But I've been thinking. Maybe, I can get a job.'

They swung round on her.

'I can! Listen. Once, in Westport, there was this groom with a hunter he was selling, a giant of a horse, and I begged him to let me ride him. Well, he was a big creature all right – but not too big for me. I galloped him from one end of Westport to the other, and the people cheered!' She hesitated as she remembered Randolph and his guinea but then went on. 'He said he worked for Mr Thorpe.' She turned to her aunt. 'That would be Mr Thorpe over by Ballintober?'

The aunt nodded, and Abby looked at her inquiringly. 'And would he be, do you think, a suitable employer?'

Eileen shrugged. 'I don't know much about him. I dare say he would. But why do you think he would give you a job?'

'I don't. But I could try. Don't you think?' she added hesitantly.

Eileen was thoughtful. 'And do you think Rory would want you to go off and get employment? To go away to live?'

'What do you mean?'

'I wonder now – would he be happy to think of you living in some strange house, with all them grooms and stable boys all day long? Rory was always careful for you both, for your good name.'

Abby was silent. What was her good name worth? A sudden vision of Randolph in The Goat boasting of the girl he fooled and tricked into bed so easily. She bit her lip. 'Aunt, I'll take my chance with Mr Thorpe.'

Chapter Seven

Ballintober House was a substantial grey cube on three floors, with little windows peeping from the roof above a low parapet. Before it was a wide carriage sweep of raked gravel, and beyond that the smooth rolling grass of the demesne, dotted with oaks. It seemed to be Abby's fate to find herself walking up drives to gentlemen's residences. The stables must be at the back, she imagined. She could see through trees that there were outhouses and other offices to the rear and side.

The rain had held off, thank goodness, and it was a crisp clear winter day, good for walking the seven miles. But she had a sinking feeling in her stomach, and cursed herself for not bringing anything to eat. She stopped for a moment to get her bearings. There could be no going to the front door this time. What a fool she had been, standing on the front doorstep! And much good it had done her.

The stables were spacious and well tended, clean and neat, but it was midday, and there seemed to be no one about. She could hear horses in their stalls, stamping sometimes, the chink of a chain, a snort or snuffle and, crossing to one half door that stood open, she peered in. In the gloom a chestnut mare turned in her straw and glanced at her.

'Hullo my beauty,' Abby said softly. 'Are you happy here? Do they treat you well? Hm?'

The horse watched her for a moment and then turned again to the manger and pulled a mouthful of hay.

I could do with something myself, Abby thought, and turned again to the yard, its black crinkled tiles neat and scrubbed down, and looked up at the back of the house. All was silent. A face appeared at a window, and a moment later a woman appeared at a door.

'Oh excuse me, ma'am, but could I speak to the head groom?'

'He's having his dinner.'

'Would you tell him there's someone waiting to speak with him, in the yard, then, please?'

The door closed.

It seemed for ever she waited, half an hour, an hour, she had no idea, and all the time she got hungrier and hungrier.

At last the door opened, and a stocky man in breeches and gaiters, wiping his mouth, came over. She started towards him.

He stuffed his handkerchief into his pocket, stopped and looked her over. She was better able to take him in this time. He was a middle-aged man, unshaven, his collarless shirt open at the neck, and a greasy neckerchief tied in it; heavy, self-important, but with a certain obstinate, stupid expression.

'Oh sir, you'll maybe not remember but once in Westport I rode a big hunter you were selling, and I was hoping – wondering – whether there might be the chance, you know, of a job?' She swallowed. 'I have a letter here of recommendation from our priest.'

His face crinkled into a slight smile. He took a deep breath of satisfaction and pulled at the lobe of his ear as he continued to inspect her – for all the world as if she were a horse. He glanced at the letter and as he continued to stare at it, she went on,

'It's for Mr Thorpe – if you could show it to him—'

He continued to inspect her in his leisurely way. 'To be sure, honey. Now I remember you. That day in Westport

65

on Emperor. That was a day to remember. I never saw a colleen the like of ye—' he laughed.

She had already taken a dislike to this man, felt uncomfortable, and wondered whether this had been a good idea. But she had to get a place. He viewed her with a proprietorial air.

'And what could ye do, think ye?'

'Oh anything you want, sir, cleaning the stables, exercising the horses and tending to them, treating cuts and bruises, applying embrocations and liniments, poultices and pills. I've lived with horses all my life, sir.'

He stroked his chin now, the other hand in his pocket, still thinking.

'Would you show the letter to Mr Thorpe, please?'

'Oh I will, to be sure.'

'Er, do you think, like, you could show it to him now, sir? You see I've walked over from Kilnevin, sir, and should like if possible to know . . . today . . . if possible—'

He grinned at her and winked. 'I'll see if the master is in. Wait here.'

She was being led through the kitchens. Servants paused in their work to look at her and there was a smell of food that made her dizzy. Along a narrow dim corridor, up stone steps, they passed through a door, and now were in the family's part of the house. The ceilings were higher, and the windows large; there were carpets and they were going up a wide staircase, across a spacious landing through beautiful polished doors, and she found herself in an airy drawing room, with long windows looking across the park. Two women, an elder and a younger, mother and daughter perhaps, sat on a sofa. Even as she was taking everything in she was thinking, there's enough turf on that fire to keep us warm for a week.

A solid-looking man in breeches and gaiters, substantial, with greying hair, slightly receding, and a plump rubicund face, got up from a desk.

66

'Beggin' your pardon Mr Thorpe, but this girl might do for stable work—'

Abby was conscious of the grovelling of the groom, so different from the tone he had taken with her in the stable below. She held out her letter, curtsying as she did so. 'If you please, I have a letter of recommendation from our priest, Father McMichael—'

He looked at her with a mild smile as he took it. 'What's your name, girl?'

'If you please sir, Abby O'Leary.'

He broke open the seal, and glanced across the contents. 'I don't understand – is Father McMichael a horseman himself?'

'Oh no sir! Only you see, he's known me since I was little and—'

'I selected her, sir,' the groom interrupted in his ingratiating manner. 'I've seen her mounted, she has a good seat, sir, and could be a useful girl about the stables. And I'd keep a good eye on her, never fear.' He shook his head with a cute smile.

The lady on the sofa called across, 'Are you a papist, girl?'

'Yes, ma'am.'

She clucked in disapproval and, heaving a disagreeable sigh, went on, 'Henry, how many grooms have we in the stables?'

He turned mildly to her, and then back to the groom, 'How many, O'Farrell?'

'Three sir, including myself.'

'And how many horses, Henry?'

'Twelve, my dear—'

'But I take particular care of the racers, my lady,' the groom interrupted.

'And do we really need another groom – and a girl at that?'

'Well—' Henry hesitated, then turned to O'Farrell.

'Oh, 'twould be a most admirable addition to your staff,

sir,' the groom was at his most affable and confidential. 'I think most convenient and fitting – and maybe to show off the yearlings? When you're selling a horse, sir – there's nothing like a pretty colleen mounted on her to show her to advantage. The horse will sell herself—'

'Yes sir!' Abby burst in, 'like that time in Westport.'

She felt an intense pain in her foot, as the groom went on unhurriedly, 'And since Josiah left us in the spring, we've felt the loss sorely.'

'What was that – about Westport?'

The groom took her by the elbow and gripped her hard. 'I saw the colleen on a horse in Westport, sir, owned by another gentleman, and the interest sir, why that horse was sold in minutes.'

There was now also a severe pain in her arm where the groom gripped it. She looked up at him in confusion.

'And you really think?' The master was looking her up and down.

'I do, sir.' O'Farrell was the soul of confidence and assurance. He released her arm.

But at last the swimming feeling, of which she had gradually become aware, was stealing over her, more and more urgent, and Abby rocked slightly on her feet. She was becoming lighter and lighter, and felt she might float away at any moment. Her body was quite hollow; she was empty, weightless and without strength. She wondered whether she might hold on the groom to steady herself, and then quite suddenly, blackness swept over her.

There was a terrible roaring in her ears, and she was in the midst of a violent dream of brilliant flashes of light and colour, strange rushing sensations, flickerings and incomprehensible noises.

She opened her eyes. Faces were staring down at her, a crowd of faces, and in a moment she recognised Mr Thorpe and the groom and the girl. Behind them was an elderly woman. This lady, who was dressed in a sober gown of black, with her grey hair drawn tightly back from her face, now pushed through the men and knelt by her. Abby realised that she was lying on a chaise longue.

'It's all right, my dear,' the lady said in a kindly voice, 'you fainted, that's all.'

Abby made an attempt to get up, but fell back immediately as an intense pain shot up through her neck into her head. She closed her eyes and groaned.

'Perhaps a tot of brandy, Mrs O'Connor?'

The lady was studying Abby carefully. 'You're as white as a sheet, my girl. When did you last eat?'

Abby felt terribly embarrassed. 'This morning, ma'am.'

The old lady stood up. 'What she needs is food, not brandy. Thady O'Farrell, you kept the girl waiting in the yard near on an hour while you were filling that fat belly of yours.'

She was in the kitchen, seated at a large scrubbed table. Two servant girls were sitting opposite her drinking tea as they watched her eating from a bowl of stew. Nothing had ever tasted so heavenly.

'Oh, I can't thank you—'

'So what persuaded you to walk seven miles from Kilnevin and never a crust for your dinner?' The housekeeper stood over her.

'I didn't know it was so far. I thought it was only about four miles or so – and never thought to bring anything to eat.'

'Hmm. Well do you think you're going to be strong enough to ride today – after your fainting fit?'

Abby started from her chair. 'Oh yes, ma'am.'

'Very well, I'll tell Mr Thorpe.'

Abby tried to smile a very small smile to the two girls watching her. She felt utterly mortified. How would she ever live it down? To faint in the master's drawing room and make such a spectacle of herself! She had ruined her chances. And did she really have the strength to ride now? She still felt quivery and weak. And why had she fainted

69

anyway? She never fainted, not even after a seven- or eight-mile walk – which she had done many times, to Castlebar and back, and thought nothing of it. But the stew, and the fresh air as she came out into the yard again steadied her, and she gained a little confidence.

Another, younger groom was holding two horses. 'Ye can have the two year old, miss – 'tis a nice gentle horse, fit for a colleen.' He winked at her.

'Thank you,' she said in a weak voice. The horse was fitted with a side saddle.

'Thady says ye rode Emperor like a man?' he grinned. 'Only don't mention it to the master.'

But now Mr Thorpe appeared at the corner of the yard, pulling on his gloves, and grasping a riding crop. He looked her over. 'It's put some colour in your cheeks, anyway. Are you fit for a ride?'

'Oh, yes sir!'

The groom gave her a foot up, and in a moment she was in the saddle, her left foot in the stirrup, her right leg hooked round the pommel of the lady's saddle. She rearranged her skirt about her as demurely as she could. 'Here, miss,' the groom handed her a cane.

'We'll just take a turn through the park, Miss O'Leary.' And he led the way through the gate of the stable yard, round across past the front of the house, and beneath the old oaks that dotted the green.

For a while they walked the horses side by side.

'And where did you learn to ride, Abby?'

'You see, sir, I've been on and off a horse's back ever since I can remember. I guess I was just born to it. Sometimes I rode my aunt's cob, sometimes I helped a farmer in the village and he would let me ride. Mr O'Mahoney – he's a bachelor man with only an old lady to cook for him, and has three horses, and rides out to hounds too – he would show me, and let me ride his mares. And he knew about treating them too when they were unwell, and taught me ever such a lot. I told Mr O'Farrell—'

'Tell me.'

'Oh, sir, all kinds of treatments for the ailments of horses, such as colic, and gravel, and making up embrocations and liniments—'

'Father!' There was a call from far behind them. She turned and saw a young girl galloping towards them. As she drew up, Abby recognised the girl she had seen in the drawing room.

'I'm just taking this young lady for a ride, Marianne. This is my daughter, Abby.'

The girl, who Abby thought was probably fifteen or sixteen, smiled sweetly, and Abby liked her at once. 'Have you recovered from your faint?'

Abby shrugged and smiled back at her.

She followed Mrs O'Connor up the narrow clattering steps into the attic. Off a short corridor a door gave into a room with a sloping ceiling and a window low in the wall immediately behind a stone balustrade, through which she glimpsed the park. Two beds stood at right angles, covered with coarse blankets. The bare boards had no covering. In a corner stood a wash stand, with a bowl and jug on it.

'That's your bed. The other belongs to Teresa, a parlourmaid. You bring the hot water up from the kitchen for you both, Abby, at six. At six-thirty you have a bit of breakfast in the kitchen, and at seven you're to report to Mr O'Farrell for your duties.'

'Thank you, Mrs O'Connor.' Abby gazed round the little room.

Mrs O'Connor was turning to the door as Abby deposited her bag on the bed then stopped. 'Abby, a word of advice. Mr Thorpe is a kind master and you'll find none better in the county. Deserve well of him. Do you understand me?'

'Oh I understand, Mrs O'Connor. I'll never be able to repay him as long as I live. We've been thrown off our farm, Mrs O'Connor, and we were that desperate I don't know what we might have done. Mr Thorpe taking me in

71

has been the gift of heaven itself and I shall bless his name as long as there is breath in my body. And I shall send back all my wages to my aunt. She's taking care of my sister and da, who's been in bed sick ever since a dragoon struck him down, the cowardly blackguard!'

The older woman chuckled to hear Abby's vehemence. 'There now, and you're very welcome to Ballintober House,' she was about to go out, but turned again. 'One other thing. You watch out for them grooms in the stable below – they're a wild set, Abby. Take good care now – especially of Thady O'Farrell himself.'

Teresa, with whom she was to share her room, was a mild, round-faced girl a year younger than herself.

'I'm so glad to have you here, Abby. It was lonely on my own.'

That night as she and Teresa were in bed, the girl gave her some of the background to the house she was in.

'Oh Mr Thorpe, he's your only man for the horse-flesh – doesn't he spend scores and hundreds of pounds on horses – him and Thady for ever at Ballinasloe fair – and thinking to enter a runner for the Longford Stakes next year. Every morning they're out exercising the racehorses. And Mr Thorpe is a most liberal man – the easy-spoken gentleman entirely, Abby, you'll find no better master in the whole of Connacht. And thinks only of the horses – and his daughter the same. Only Mrs Thorpe cannot abide 'em – never goes near the stables and for ever complaining about the smell, poor woman; railing against her husband tramping through the house in his muddy old riding clothes, and stinking the house out, and saying he's ruining the family and spending his daughter's inheritance, and the girl will have nothing at all when she comes into her property bar only a mess of nags.'

Abby couldn't help giggling at Teresa's description.

Chapter Eight

It was raining the following morning when she got to the stables.

These were set round three sides of a yard behind the house, and over each door the horse's name had been painted in neat flowing letters in gold. Above the centre block was a small lantern with a weathercock over it. It was obvious to Abby as she peered into the stalls, that Mr Thorpe maintained his horses in style: twelve in all, four of them farm horses, six hunters and, his pride and joy, two racers. Gazing round the yard in the dim early morning, and the light rain, she could still scarcely believe her luck that she found herself actually working here. It was the job above any in the world she could have wished for.

There was still no one about, and Abby was not sure what to do, but finally, pulling a piece of old sacking over her head, after she had been looking into the stalls for a while, she decided, 'Well, there is one thing I'm certainly going to have to do, so I might as well start.'

Accordingly, after looking into a barn where she found a large fork, she set to and began the salubrious job of mucking out. After half an hour of this and as she was well warmed up, a young man, the same she had seen the day she first called, came across the yard from the kitchen door, and found her in a stall busy with her fork.

'Well! If that isn't grand! Abby, you're a jewel! Are you alone?'

'I am.'

'Have you fed them?'

'I don't know where to find the oats.'

'True for you. Mr O'Farrell has the key and he's still at his breakfast. I'll get it.' He disappeared and shortly after reappeared with a sack of oats and began feeding the horses as Abby continued shovelling and forking the manure into the yard.

'You're a good strong girl for the job, anyway,' the groom called.

'You're Sam, aren't you?' she stopped a moment.

'Indeed I am.'

They stood in the doorway looking out across the yard.

'We all heard about your ride on Emperor, Abby. You caused quite a sensation. But why do you think Thady was selling him?'

She shook her head.

'Mr Thorpe bought Emperor on Thady's say-so. Only, when they got him home they found he was too much for Mr Thorpe altogether. And that put Thady on the spot. You can imagine Thady wouldn't want Mr Thorpe to know you'd been able to sit a horse he couldn't handle himself? See, Mr Thorpe trusts Thady O'Farrell in everything. But between you and me, Thady has never the eye for the horses.' He shook his head. 'Emperor was an expensive mistake for Mr Thorpe. It's lucky for Thady Mr Thorpe is the easy-going gentleman he is.'

'Has Thady caused him any other expensive mistakes?'

'A few.'

Sam had the key to the tack room, and showed her how to light the fire.

'Tomorrow morning, Abby, you light the fire first thing.'

She nodded as she gazed round in wonder at the racks of harnesses, saddles, bridles, bits, curry combs, brushes,

74

pots of saddle soap – every kind of horse equipment, and everything neatly in its place. Some of the saddles looked expensive, too, and she couldn't help running her hand over one side saddle, beautifully made with inserts of tapestry work – a floral pattern in green and red.

'Miss Marianne's,' Sam commented, 'made to her own design in London.' He crouched again to stoke the fire which by now was going merrily. Abby came over to warm her hands. 'She's the apple of his eye, Abby, as ye've probably seen by now, and a proper little minx she is too. But ye don't have to worry. She's Mr O'Farrell's particular responsibility. He takes care of that; nothing's too much trouble for her little ladyship.' He grinned.

'What's funny?'

He thought for a moment. 'Oh, you'll find out.'

Much later, after she and Sam had fed the horses, and finished tidying the yard, Mr O'Farrell finally put in an appearance. He made a tour of inspection, criticised her preparation of bran mash, gave her several jobs to do, including rubbing down one of the mares for Miss Marianne who would be riding out later that morning, and disappeared again.

After he had gone, Sam reappeared, and gave her a wink. 'Back to the kitchen for another cup of tea,' he chuckled.

'I could do with one myself, Sam,' she said. It was three hours of a cold damp morning since she had risen.

'True for you, Abby, you deserve it. We'll have a cup ourselves in the tack room. I'll call Willy.'

Willy was an older man, who had appeared earlier, grunted a few words, and then led off one of the farm horses.

Abby found Moonbeam, a sweet-natured, docile four-year-old, and spent an hour rubbing her down, till her chestnut coat shone.

While she was back in the tack room, feeding the fire, a

slim figure appeared in the doorway. 'Where's O'Farrell?'

Abby leapt to her feet. 'Oh Miss Marianne!' she was flustered.

'He's supposed to have Moonbeam saddled,' the girl said brusquely.

Abby swallowed. 'Er – if you'd just wait in here out of the cold, Miss, I'll have her saddled for you in an instant.' She looked round at the massed ranks of saddles on the wall. 'Which—'

The girl stamped her foot. 'Why isn't O'Farrell here to do it?'

'He's busy miss – er – the master sent him out with one of the racers, but if you'll just wait, I can fetch him!'

Marianne grimaced and twisted on her ankle in the doorway. 'Just like Papa,' she muttered. 'That saddle.' She pointed with her riding switch, and Abby took it out to Moonbeam's stall. The rain had stopped by this time, and the sun was making a fitful appearance.

Abby had had an opportunity by this time to take in the young girl a little more. Marianne was pretty, slender and shorter than Abby, with blonde hair taken up beneath her hat, and a tight-waisted jacket over her riding skirt. Smart little black boots gleamed at her hem as she walked. She was certainly very attractive – and knew it, Abby thought, as she pulled hard at the girth strap, buckling it with practised fingers.

There was a mounting block in the yard, and Abby held the mare's head, as Marianne seated herself. She looked round again.

'Well! If he isn't here, he isn't here. I'm jolly well going on my own! Let go of her head.' Marianne turned Moonbeam's head, and put her into a trot, across the cobbles, and out through the stable gate.

As Abby turned back to the tack room, she saw Mr O'Farrell appear at the kitchen door, just in time to see Marianne disappear through the gate. He hurried across to Abby in alarm. 'Where's she gone?'

'Out for a ride, Mr O'Farrell, I think,' Abby said uncertainly.

'Jesus! She's not allowed to ride alone. I'm supposed to be going with her. Why didn't ye call me?'

'I said you were out with one of the racers for the master, Mr O'Farrell – I could hardly tell her you were in the kitchen drinking tea. It was the first thing I could think of.'

He rushed past her into the tack room and a moment later reappeared with a racing saddle, hurried across to the stall of one of the racers, and two minutes later was galloping through the gates.

Later in the tack room again, where they spent every spare minute, it being the warmest place in the stables, Abby narrated this little drama. Sam shook his head and clicked his tongue.

'Did I do wrong, Sam?' she asked anxiously.

'Oh no,' he grinned mischievously. 'I'd say ye saved Thady's bacon! And it makes a change seeing Thady O'Farrell having to shift himself for once.'

Later she was in Moonbeam's stall putting down fresh straw when Mr O'Farrell reappeared with the mare. She turned nervously, still uncertain whether she had offended him, but he seemed in an affable mood.

'Smart thinking, this morning, Abby,' he said amiably.

'Thank ye, Mr O'Farrell.'

'You've a head on your shoulders. I saw that the first time I laid eyes on ye.'

'Thank ye.'

'And if ye work hard and attend to your duties, you'll do well here. Yes,' he continued as he turned past her towards the door, 'I'll see to it that Mr Thorpe gets a good report of ye.'

He smiled and patted her bottom. She couldn't be certain, but it seemed to her that the hand lingered there just a fraction longer than it should have, and she was left feeling confused, grateful that she had not offended him, but also wondering at the unmistakable suggestion the gesture carried.

A few days later she was summoned upstairs. Mrs O'Connor was waiting for her and led her into a bedroom. Abby gazed round at the beautiful room with its large four-poster bed. On the bed were laid out several riding habits.

'These are the mistress's. But one might do for you. Try that one—'

Abby hurriedly unbuttoned her red dress, and the old lady helped her into the heavy black habit, with its breeches and complicated over-skirt.

'Hmm, you're big, but you could just about squeeze into it.'

'What is this for, Mrs O'Connor?'

'The master wants you to ride with Miss Marianne this afternoon.'

She now caught sight of herself in a long wardrobe mirror. Her heart gave a little leap. This was something! A lady! She turned and tried to catch a glimpse of herself from the side. There was no doubt, it was very satisfying. Her hair was a mess though. She must try to run up to her room to do it before they went out . . .

'Pleased with yourself?' the old lady said sarcastically.

'Oh Mrs O'Connor, it's grand. I never thought, you know – to see myself in a real lady's habit—'

'Don't be getting ideas above your station, my girl.'

'But Mrs O'Connor, why did the master want me to accompany Miss Marianne? Surely Mr O'Farrell—'

'Ask him yourself.'

As they set off that afternoon together, Abby soon found why she had been selected.

'I asked for you,' said Marianne.

'You did? Why?'

'I cannot abide that odious Thady O'Farrell. Father thinks he is such a perfect expert on horses, but I think he's a humbug and a fraud, Abby. And so do Sam and Willy. And I liked you as soon as we met, and thought how perfect it would be to have you to accompany me instead of him.'

'Thank you, Miss Marianne. Very much.' She had noticed Thady's expression as they left the yard. He had not been pleased.

'You have a good seat on Moonbeam,' Marianne went on, glancing over to her, 'you look quite elegant.'

'Hush, you mustn't say such things, Miss Marianne!'

'Do you like me in this costume?' the girl prattled on, she was in bottle-green velvet, and a smart little hat with a feather. It was a habit Abby would have died for, but before she could answer, Marianne pointed with her pearl-handled riding cane. 'Look, you see the monument – there on the hilltop? I'll race you!'

She set the spur into her horse's side and sprang away and Abby started after her. She had no intention of racing the girl, however. Her job was to take care of Marianne – not to beat her in a race. She had landed on her feet in Ballintober with a vengeance; within a few days of arriving she was galloping through this beautiful park dressed in a lady's habit, on a very well-behaved mare ... she would take good care to let Miss Marianne win the race.

Later she was leading the mare into the stall, when she found Mr O'Farrell behind her.

'Well now, are ye glad in your new place, Miss Abby?'

'Very well, Mr O'Farrell, I'm obliged to you.'

'And you're grateful to me, I dare say, for getting it, aren't you?'

She was silent as she unstrapped the saddle from the mare's back, and set it on the partition of the stall. She took up a cloth and began to rub the horse's back.

Thady leant in the doorway watching her. 'The habit becomes ye.' She said nothing. After another moment he repeated thoughtfully, 'Yes, I got ye the place, Abby.'

She said nothing.

79

'Just a word from me, was all it took. Me and Mr Thorpe – we're like that.' He held up his hand and crossed his fingers. 'He trusts me, you see. Just a word, that's all it takes.' He had strolled round into the stall now, and leant against the partition, a few inches from her, so that she was trapped between the bulk of Moonbeam, and him. She had stopped rubbing by now, and had turned. Her heart was beating painfully. He looked carefully down into her face. 'There's girls would do anything for your place, Abby,' he said quietly, 'anything.'

She bit her lip and with an effort turned again to the horse. The conversation seemed to be going in only one direction. She swallowed.

'Of course I'm very grateful, Mr O'Farrell,' she said in a low voice, and then, with an effort, 'but I hope I can keep the place on my own merits.'

'Merits?' He looked her up and down in his conceited fashion. 'Och, ye've merits right enough, Abby. Big merits, bit round merits, as any man will tell ye.'

Every time Abby brought a horse into a stall, to unsaddle her, or feed her or give her a rub down, things which she was doing most of the time, Thady now seemed to appear. He would lean on the partition, and make comments and chat. She was acutely aware what was going through his mind. It had started when he patted her bottom. Then there was a time when she was seated on a mare, and he had affected to find fault with her stirrup, and was fussing with it, but as she quickly found out, only because it gave him the opportunity to run his hand up her leg.

She found these attentions difficult. The fact was, however, there was nothing she could do about it if she wanted to keep her job, and Thady O'Farrell knew it.

'You've a good job here, Abby,' the odious groom remarked one afternoon, it seemed for the hundredth time. He had returned from a trip into Westport, and she had caught the whiff of whiskey on his breath.

80

'True,' said she.

'And you can send money back to your aunt, can't you?'

'True again, Mr Thady.'

'And you wouldn't want to lose the place, now, would you?'

She remained silent.

'Miss Marianne sets great store by you, Abby – you're well in with her.'

'That's for her to say,' she said guardedly. It was all too obvious where this was leading.

'You see Abby, I think you're a grand girl. And I foresee a bright future – very bright. With a little managing,' he added modestly.

'By you?' Astonished, she turned to face him.

'That's right.'

This was going too far, and before she could think she came out with, 'When I need you to manage me, Thady O'Farrell, I'll let you know.'

'Oh I think you will, Miss O'Leary.'

'We'll see, but I rather think not.' She turned back to the horse.

'And I rather think so. You see, Miss Abby, my fine upstanding piece of Irish womanhood, your fame has been getting round.'

'What are you talking about?' She had lost her temper, and had had enough of his endless insinuations. He ignored her tone.

'And I don't mean that day you rode Emperor for his lordship's guinea in Westport,' he went on smugly. ''Twas another kind of ride he gave you, wasn't it, in The Goat?'

Try as she might, she felt gripped in a frozen embrace. Her throat tight, her jaw seemed locked, the skin crawling on her face.

He leant forward and looked carefully into her face. 'Forgotten? Up in room nine?'

She was dumb.

'Oh don't worry,' he went on casually, 'I wouldn't think

of telling Mr Thorpe. Only, don't you think I deserve a little thanks – for keeping your secret?'

He took a step forward as he spoke and looking into her eyes, reached his hand and casually ran it down her front, pressing over her breasts and down to her thigh. Shaken into action now, she stepped back and glanced round.

A window had broken that morning when a gelding had unexpectedly kicked against the wall, and there were still pieces of glass lying where she had not yet had time to clear them up.

Abby snatched up a villainous shard, a dagger of glass and turned quickly on him, thrusting it towards his neck.

'If you don't swear here and now never to breathe a word of it, so help you God, I vow I'll cut your throat.'

He staggered slightly back against the wall, his eyes frozen on to the glinting sliver of glass beneath his nose. 'Abby – don't be a fool—'

'It's not me that'll be the fool,' she hissed, 'if you can't keep your gob shut – swear now! Swear!'

'Abby!' He was beseeching her.

'Swear!'

At last, his eyes bulging, the sweat on his forehead, he gasped, 'I swear!'

'So help you God!'

'So help me God!' he gasped.

She held his look for a second, then slowly lowered her hand. 'And the better for you. Mind you keep your word.'

She threw down the glass and noticed for the first time her hand was bleeding. She drew a handkerchief from her pocket, and wiped it. 'I'd better clear up that broken glass. Someone might get hurt,' she muttered. Thady, who was still pressed against the wall was watching her. 'Abby—' he wheedled.

'Excuse me for being so rough with you, Mr O'Farrell.' She went towards the door.

'Abby,' he called. 'Wait!' She turned, feeling low, drained.

'Call me Thady, won't you?' He came to her. 'Ye don't think I'd ever have spoke a word, do ye?'

'I don't know.' Her eyes downcast, she felt very tired.

'But Abby girl, what I wanted to tell ye was – did ye ever think of maybe going to London?'

'London?'

'Aye. I was there many a time with the master. A girl with your talents – why there'd a grand opening for ye there, to be sure.'

She watched him morosely. 'Is this why you wanted to *manage* me?' she said sarcastically.

'I could find ye a job there Abby would pay ye better than ever ye'll make with Mr Thorpe. We'd be a team, Abby.'

'What makes you think I'd want to team up with *you*?'

'Why not?'

'Why not? Well, for the first thing, Mr O'Farrell, I have a good place here, which I have no intention of leaving thank you, and in the second place, if you were the last man on earth, I wouldn't team up with *you*!'

As she was about to leave the stable she turned again. 'How did you know?' she asked in a low voice.

'How did ye think to keep it a secret?'

As she lay in bed that night she realised she could never trust Thady O'Farrell. She had humiliated him with the shard of glass; he would never forgive her that. Another time, if he chose to exploit his advantage, she would be helpless. She had frightened him and he would resent it; he would want to be even, that was certain.

As if such a thing could be kept secret! In Ireland? In Westport? She was the talk of a crowd of grooms and ostlers. She might have frightened Thady – but how long must it be before the word got out – a chance remark, a jest thrown across a stable yard? How long before the word got back to Kilnevin?

She stared up in the darkness. Her hand was bandaged.

She had told Mrs O'Connor she had cut it cleaning up the broken glass. Teresa was already asleep, and Abby could hear her regular breathing. Lucky Teresa – how easy her life seemed . . .

And what a fool Abby had been ever to trust a man like Randolph Pelham! Curse Randolph Pelham! And curse Thady O'Farrell! She would never be free.

And why not after all? For what was she now? A whore, no better. She was spoiled. Suppose some man asked her to marry him? Could she ever tell him what had happened? And if she didn't wouldn't she be for ever in fear Thady might?

Her only consolation was Marianne. Over the last few weeks they had become firm friends – at least as firm as any friendship can be between mistress and servant. But Marianne was an only child and lonely in the big house, and to have a companion of about her own age – Abby was nearly two years the elder – had meant a great deal to her. Often Marianne would seek Abby out in the stable yard, and they would stand together in the tack room door looking out at a wet winter afternoon, talking. Abby wondered whether Marianne had a sweetheart, but it seemed that though the family had numerous acquaintances in the neighbourhood, there was no one quite her own age. She was well used to flattering remarks from older men – and this had given her a superficial gloss of assurance – but of girls her own age with whom she might be really intimate there were none. Abby became that friend.

Marianne knew clearly that as an only child and an heiress she would be sought after. She knew well enough why the men crowded round to be introduced; this, although it did not lessen the pleasure she took in their attention, did nevertheless force her to be on her guard, to keep at bay any that ventured too close. But it also made her lonely. It was difficult to know what to think; better to be safe than sorry. It was therefore all the more comforting to know that Abby could have nothing to gain by her friendship and must therefore be sincere. Abby could be trusted. She was also physically larger than Marianne, and this gave the younger girl an instinctive faith in her.

It was lucky for Abby too. Having Marianne on her side might one day be useful – if and when Thady chose to make mischief against her.

Chapter Nine

'Oh Abby, do hurry up! There's Sir Thomas, and I want him to see me in my new habit!' Marianne peeped through the gates of the stable yard.

'Give me a moment, Miss; the girth wants taking up a notch.'

Abby threw up the saddle flap and pulled hard at the girth strap. 'Ye'll need to get a snug grip on this lady, Miss Marianne. She's lively this morning.'

'This lady' was Columbine, a sixteen-hands, nine-year-old hunter. A chestnut mare, she was a new acquisition, bought on Mr O'Farrell's recommendation. Cannonball, her favourite hitherto, had cast a shoe and was temporarily lame on the off fore.

'Yes! Only hurry! Ooh look – there's Mr Wentworth; he said he'd come! And Jack Counihan – see Abby, over there! Jack is the very devil of a horseman – he'll go at anything. And look at his horse – did you ever see such a brute! Oh hurry, he's looking this way now! Do you think he'll like me in this? It does become me, doesn't it?'

Abby had got the strap adjusted to her satisfaction as the mare took a sudden side-step and whinnied. Abby pulled at her reins.

'Oh Jesus, she's as frisky as a kitten. Take it easy, you'll have your chance in a minute, ye shameless creature.'

Abby had been in the stable preparing Miss Marianne's

new mare since six, brushing and brushing till her coat shone with a deep chestnut gloss, and plaiting her mane. There might be twelve horses in her father's stable, but if Cannonball was lame none of the others quite suited Marianne's fastidious taste and nothing would do but she must have a new hunter for the occasion. Thady O'Farrell had been deputed for the task; however, as Abby had already found out, the mare was a contrary, highly strung minx with a will of her own. Abby had already had to give her a hard slap with the end of the reins to bring her to order.

'Keep a strong grip on her, Miss Marianne, and let her know who's mistress, or she'll run clear away with you.'

'Oh, never mind for that! If I can't handle a horse now, it'd be a fine thing. Now, tell me, is my hat straight? Oh, if only there were a glass handy!'

She was turning back into the yard when, high on a big grey, and resplendent in his scarlet coat, a man appeared at the gate. He touched his hat with his crop.

'Miss Marianne.'

'Teddy Cavanagh! Abby quick, help me up.'

Abby brought Columbine to the mounting block and as Marianne seated herself, arranged the folds of the habit round her. Marianne smiled with undisguised glee, and Abby had to confess she did look extremely pretty in her russet-red costume, tailored beautifully to her girlish figure, and her tall hat and veil.

Abby gave the mare's head a gentle tug and fed her a handful of barley sugar. Then muttering to her as she stroked her neck, 'Mind, behave yourself now – or Mr Thorpe'll have me scalp,' she passed the reins up to her mistress.

At the front of the house the gravel sweep was already crowded; hounds were arriving now, the air filled with their voices, riders excitedly greeted one another, scarlet coats, green coats, ladies fastidious in tight black costumes, their hats tipped forward over hair scrupulously drawn back into nets, shiny black boots glimpsed in the stirrup; horses

87

whinnying and pawing the ground, restless with anticipation. They knew as well as their masters what was afoot.

Servants appeared with trays of punch, sausage rolls and fruit cake, and passed through the crowd. It was a bright clear morning, the fields beyond still half shrouded with mist, the oaks half emerging from it, and a heavenly scent in the air.

As Abby stood surveying the scene, Thady appeared beside her, looking up.

''Twill clear in an hour.' His attention was distracted. 'I see Miss Marianne's on Columbine.'

'She's too much for her, Mr O'Farrell. I warned Miss Marianne, but she told me to boil me head.'

'Too much? I chose that horse meself. She'll carry her all day, and never tire.'

'Well, I'm riding Moonbeam. If there's any trouble she can change with me,' Abby said dryly, and turned back to the stable.

'We're getting quite the lady this morning, ain't we?'

Abby didn't slow down. ''Tis an old habit of her ladyship's, Mr O'Farrell,' she called over her shoulder, 'which Miss Marianne insisted I wear.'

'Oh indeed. I understand well enough.'

She turned at the touch of sarcasm. 'And what pray is there to understand?'

'That ye've become bosom friends with the little mistress, worming your way into her graces.'

'If you'd rather ride with Miss Marianne, Mr O'Farrell, I suggest you speak to her father. 'Twas by no wish of mine.'

She turned sharply away to the stable to saddle up Moonbeam; since their confrontation in the stable she had found herself being notably freer with Thady O'Farrell. Glancing back, she saw Marianne in a crowd of men, laughing, smiling, primping herself, as they crowded round, eager to talk to her.

Abby was about to turn into the stable yard when she

realised with a shock that among these red-coats on their well-fed, well-groomed horses, was one well-fed and well-groomed man she recognised.

Taking up her skirts, she hurried through the yard and into Moonbeam's stall, stopped in the half darkness, and rested one hand on the partition, staring at Moonbeam, but seeing nothing for a moment. What was he doing here? And what was she to do? He was bound to see her, bound to recognise her. How could she get out of it so late? She ran her hand over her face. And Thady O'Farrell in the secret too.

She hurried through to the tack room and took Moonbeam's saddle from its peg. The fact was, she couldn't get out of it now. Trying to distract herself, she concentrated on saddling Moonbeam. The mare knew it was a hunt today too, whinnying and fretting with excitement. You lucky thing, she thought, you're looking forward to a gallop, aren't you? You're not worrying about any Randolph Pelham with his fine promises, and his, Oh Abby, can't you see I'm dying for you, you can't leave me like this, don't be so cruel – oh God! He could do that to me, and we thrown off our farm, and Rory gone to God knows where, and when I'll see him again, who can tell? And him there now, laughing and flirting with the girls.

She hurried on, slipping the bridle over Moonbeam's head as the thoughts rushed through her head. Standing in the stable door she drew a deep breath, and then without thinking pulled the piece of chiffon from her bowler hat, and re-arranged it round her face and hat as a veil. With luck she could keep out of his way, too, and none the wiser.

Sam was leading two horses out. He stopped as he saw her on the mounting block. 'Abby is that you? Quite the lady today!'

'Don't laugh, Sam, I beg you. There's a reason for it.' She mounted the mare, hooked her legs round the two pommels of the side saddle, smoothed down the folds of the habit, and headed Moonbeam out to where the hunt was ready to move off.

Marianne caught sight of her. 'Abby! What on earth are you wearing a veil for? Take it off at once. You look ridiculous!'

'I'm sorry, Miss Marianne, it's just that I have a terrible sore throat,' she rasped hoarsely, 'and I can hardly speak as it is.'

'What are you talking about? You were speaking perfectly well just now.'

'I know, Miss Marianne. It just came on me. I beg you don't be hard on me. 'Tis only the once.'

Fortunately Randolph Pelham was well away, and in a crowd of a hundred or more riders there was a good chance she would escape him. She caught a glimpse of him once, and felt an unexpected nagging tightness in her insides.

'Well, come along! The hunt's moving off. We're going to draw coverts on Bantry Hill. The Huntsman said – oh Dr Hickey, are you here?'

Her attention had been distracted by a heavy-set middle-aged gentleman who had cantered up beside her, and Abby fell behind as the hunt now funnelled into a farm track, a long line of horsemen and women. The Huntsman was somewhere ahead with the hounds, and Randolph Pelham, who was obviously a 'thruster', was up beside him. She jogged along behind Marianne who was prattling to her companion, giggling and flirting, and tapping him every so often to emphasise her point.

Abby relaxed. Perhaps all would be well. And after all, here she was riding to hounds. There were worse fates for a girl! She cheered up. She was wearing a lady's habit and veil, and on a very well behaved mare about to enjoy a thundering gallop. Things could be much worse; all she had to do was to keep out of Randolph Pelham's way and keep an eye on that mare of Miss Marianne's – which anyway seemed to be quite well behaved for the moment.

After half an hour of this jog trot they came into a field,

crossed it into another, towards some distant clumps of trees scattered along the base of the mountain slope. The hunt fanned out following the hounds who loped along, clustered around the Huntsman with his long whip. As they came to the woods she could see Mr Thorpe and the Master talking while the rest of the hunt scattered about the field. It looked as if they were going to send the hounds in through the woods in the hopes of flushing a fox out. Several older members of the hunt were on 'point' at strategic positions round the covert, to catch the fox breaking cover.

She saw Randolph again, far off talking to another man. He laughed and the other man laughed. Abby again felt a peculiar tightness in her chest. Curse him. Pelham pulled a flask from his pocket and offered it to the man, talking quickly, gesturing, touching the man on the arm. The man laughed again. She saw it all. Perhaps Mr Pelham was telling him about the farm girl he had one afternoon, it had been easy enough old fellow, spin her a few lies, it scarcely matters what, you're never going to see her again, anything will do. She'll believe whatever you say – it's easy – and if she's ruined it's her own fault after all, the little fool should be more careful for her honour ...

Oh God, he was coming towards them. But it was Marianne he was aiming for.

'Miss Marianne! You don't remember me?' He touched his hat with his riding crop.

'I don't believe—'

'Randolph Pelham?'

'Mr Pelham!' She gave a little squeal. 'I haven't seen you for years! Do you remember me?'

'I certainly do.' He pulled his horse alongside her, leaning in confidentially with an impudent smile. 'You were an impossible little madam in short petticoats when I saw you last, with a snub nose, and a frown that froze the blood—'

'Shame on you!' she burst out laughing. 'Why haven't you come to see me before, you naughty man?'

91

'No fault of mine, Miss Marianne, I assure you. Only got back from Africa a few weeks ago. Then a chum of mine invited me for a bit of shooting in Scotland. We were in the regiment together, and I couldn't turn him down.'

'You are *not* forgiven! You should have come to pay your respects the moment you landed.'

So much for that important business in London, Abby thought. She studied his back. Oh she knew that back, the set of those shoulders only too well, she knew the caressing tone in his voice as he set out to charm a woman. Abby hunched in her saddle and jogged along behind them as they flirted. The girl's vanity knew no bounds, and no doubt she was drinking in his lies; as if a man of his experience would be interested in a sixteen-year-old. At one moment he glanced back, and her heart nearly stopped, but fortunately he noticed nothing, and returned to his chatting.

The Huntsman sounded a note on his horn and their attention was distracted. There was a general movement now towards the end of the spinney where the hounds, who had been nosing through, now began to emerge. Then, quite suddenly the fox broke cover and was streaking away across the field. The air was thick with 'holla-ing', the horn was squealing 'Gone away!', the hounds were ahead of them and the horses had started forward instinctively. They were off.

The Huntsman cannoned past Abby. 'Go on Traveller, good old Warrior, Gaylass, Daffodil – good girl, first out of the covert as ever!'

Pelham had already gone as Abby clapped Moonbeam into a gallop beside Marianne.

She glanced across but Marianne seemed quite comfortable. They flashed a grin to one another. This was it – this was the freemasonry, the camaraderie of the chase – now, for these few minutes, Abby could be the equal of anyone. Still, cautious, she held her pace to Marianne's.

Marianne put her mare at a banked hedge and cleared it with no difficulty and a moment later Abby sailed over after her. They were in the midst of the chase, riders scattered over the field. Someone behind them had come off – they could hear shouts – but they neither even turned their heads. The field spread out, and with clear ground ahead of them, the mares lengthened their stride.

But now Columbine, caught up in the excitement of the chase, the racing horses all about her, stretched her neck and streaked away as if her life depended on it.

She's too much for Marianne, I knew it, Abby thought immediately and kicked Moonbeam harder to come up with her mistress. As she drew level with Marianne and glanced across she saw instantly that the girl had lost control of her mare. The horse was far too strong for her and Marianne, terrified, was leaning back hard in her saddle and heaving on the reins. But she was a slender girl and her strength was just not sufficient to hold the horse in check; worse, Abby saw a five-foot bank coming up ahead.

'If the mare goes for that Marianne will break her neck.' She pulled Moonbeam closer and as the two horses galloped side by side, she could see the undisguised terror on the girl's face. Leaning down now, on her off side, Abby took a strong grip on Columbine's bridle near the mouth, and checking Moonbeam at the same time pulled the other horse's head down and round as hard as she was able, leaning back in the saddle till she ached and her thighs strained against the twin pommels as she had never strained before. The mare appeared possessed, her eyes staring, her ears flat back, and at first would not moderate her speed, and the bank was coming up quickly. There was a distinct danger of the horses becoming confused with each other, or bringing each other down. That was a risk she would have to take. Abby leaned back, pulling and straining on Columbine's bridle, pulling her away from the bank, so that at last they slewed round and gradually slowed, and at last, her heart pounding, Abby pulled them to a halt. Dragging for breath, she turned to Marianne.

The girl was frozen in her saddle, her eyes staring; Abby

93

knew instinctively that she had to get Marianne on to another horse and back into the gallop immediately, or she might never mount a horse again.

She slithered to the ground. 'Come down with you miss, and take Moonbeam –' she was authoritative, matter of fact – 'she'll be no trouble.'

She took Marianne's hand and without speaking more, helped her to the ground.

As Marianne touched the ground she turned to Abby, as if coming out of a trance, clasping her arms, staring into her eyes. Abby could feel her trembling. 'Oh Abby—'

But Abby wouldn't give her time to think. 'Come along with ye, miss, or we'll be too late for the kill. Up with you now.'

She was holding Columbine's bridle loosely, as she brought Moonbeam round, and offered Marianne a foot up. Marianne still seemed paralysed, unable to focus. 'Come on miss!' Abby was sharp. 'Up with you!' And as Marianne was at last shaken into action, helped her up into her saddle, arranged her habit about her, and passed the reins up to her.

'Go on now, miss – go for it – they'll be wondering where we've got to.'

Marianne was now coming out of her trance. 'What? Oh Abby, I couldn't—'

Abby could see her still trembling. 'Go on now, go for the bank. You've got dear old Moonbeam under you now and you'll be safe. Off with you now!' She gave the mare a slap, and before Marianne was conscious of it, a whole childhood of training came instinctively into play, and she was once more in charge. She cantered away from the bank, turned and had taken it in a moment.

Abby was left with the recalcitrant and seemingly unrepentant Columbine; they stared at each other. 'You would, would you?' she muttered. 'I'd like to see you try that trick on *me*!' She gave the mare a stiff cut across the rump with her riding cane. '*Now* will ye do as you're told!'

She grasped the pommels and with some difficulty pulled herself up on to the saddle, wrapping her legs round the pommels and finding her stirrup. 'Come on, you contrary creature, let's see you take the bank after all.'

She cantered away from the bank, then turned Columbine's head towards it and sailed over. 'That's more like it. You're well behaved right enough when you've a mind to it, aren't you?'

The hunt was well ahead of her, spread out now across the mountainside, and Abby set herself to catch up, climbing through a patch of slippery, treacherous rocky scree, then on to the bare mountain above, seeing other riders scattered here and there, then through a patch of dead ferns hanging wet, brown and sodden. She heard the horn ahead of her and climbed towards the ridge of a spur of the mountain.

However, as she was just coming over the brow, and could see down the other side she unexpectedly found Randolph Pelham nearby. For a moment she thought he hadn't noticed her, but he changed direction and before she could escape he was beside her.

'I say, wasn't that you I saw just now? You saved that silly girl's bacon. By Jove, that was quite something. The mare had gone mad. I didn't think anyone could have controlled her.'

Abby stared straight ahead and couldn't think of a reply to this. Until she unexpectedly heard herself speaking as if – as if someone else were speaking through her.

'You are very kind,' she said demurely in a low voice still not looking at him, and speaking to her own astonishment in an imitation of Miss Marianne's clipped diction. 'She was in difficulty. I helped her. That is all.'

'All?' he echoed incredulously. 'I should jolly well say so. There aren't many men could have done what you did, let alone women.'

He pulled his horse's head over. 'I don't believe we've been introduced. Randolph Pelham—'

95

'Oh excuse me—' She had caught sight of Marianne in the fold of the mountain below them struggling up through the ferns towards the further ridge, and set Columbine's head down into the narrow glen before he could continue.

What possessed her to put on an English accent? She had never done such a thing in her life, and only the panic of his presence could have caused it. Yet it had come quite spontaneously; it was very puzzling.

But she would not think about him – just get back to Miss Marianne. The hounds had lost the scent among the wet ferns and were nosing up and down the steep sides of the gully. As Abby picked her way carefully over a little stream hidden beneath the ferns, the Huntsman gave a shrill blast again, the hounds had picked up the scent, and riders were struggling up the farther side towards the open mountainside higher up. Abby followed Marianne; she felt confident there would be no more trouble now that the girl was on Moonbeam.

They came out again on to the open mountainside and the riders were well spread out on the rocky open slope. She saw Sam not far away leading Mr Thorpe's spare horse, Mayflower.

'I see you've changed horses with Miss Marianne,' he said as he came over. 'I thought ye might. How are ye handling her?'

'I told her to behave herself.'

Sam laughed.

Shortly after Mr Thorpe came up to Abby. 'Isn't that Miss Marianne's new hunter, Abby?'

'Yes sir,' she hastily pulled the chiffon from her face. 'Er – she decided she would be more comfortable on Moonbeam, after all.' She gave a desperate smile.

The hunt was setting off for the next covert, and once again Abby was tagging behind Miss Marianne. The girl appeared to have completely forgotten her little adventure and was chattering gaily between two men. Flasks had made their appearance, and port and whiskey were being

96

offered. Quite how it happened she didn't notice but a little later she found herself behind Pelham who was in a conversation with a man of about his own age whom she did not recognise. They were exchanging a flask, and Pelham had lit a cigar. Abby who had no wish to be in his presence again would have moved away if she hadn't heard him say, 'You a friend of Marianne Thorpe's?'

'A neighbour.'

'They say she's the apple of her father's eye,' Pelham went on as they jogged together. Abby pulled up behind them as near as she dared. 'Empty-headed little thing, if the truth be told.' He drew on his cigar. 'Look here Tommy, don't mind me questioning you like this. I've been away you see. Old Thorpe – he must be worth a shilling or two?'

'I should say so.'

'And she's still an only child? No others born recently? No little brother?'

'She is an only child.'

'Hmm.' He offered his flask again. They each took a pull at the whiskey, and drew on their cigars. There was silence for a minute.

Then Tommy came to life. 'Anyway, why are you so interested? Isn't she rather young yet?'

'Young? Not at all. They're never too young. The younger a girl marries, the better.'

'Really?'

'Fewer faults for her husband to correct, you see. Oh sorry, you married?'

'Not so far.'

'It's a battlefield, whatever people say,' Pelham went on thoughtfully, looking about the field. 'One side or the other has to be top dog – and if the man intends to rule, the younger the wife the better.'

'And you would like to rule Marianne Thorpe, is that it?'

'Wouldn't mind at that. I'm a younger son, remember; with a younger son's luck, more's the pity.'

His friend shrugged his shoulders. 'Well, good hunting,'

he said cynically, and set off across the field. Abby hurriedly started Columbine into a trot, and crossed through the crowd in search of Sam. Better not to think of Mr Pelham for the moment . . .

It was later in the afternoon. They had drawn other coverts, had one short run before the fox had gone to earth, drawn another without any luck, and now were turning for home. Pelham fortunately had not come near her again, was nowhere to be seen, and she had been able to relax. It had been a narrow escape, but now she could turn her attention to her mistress. After the excitement of the chase everyone was more relaxed and content to walk the horses, chatting peacefully. Mr Thorpe was with Marianne, Abby behind them with Sam and the spare mount.

They crossed down the bare mountainside, through a field, made their way through a patch of woodland, where the afternoon shadows were beginning to lengthen between the trees, and had just come into a dark, narrow lane, where the trees hung low over them on both sides. It happened in an instant. Marianne had pushed a long trailing branch aside as she passed, and casually letting it go, it had swung back with whip-like force across Columbine's eyes.

With a maddened scream, the mare reared vertically, striking at the air, and Abby was thrown. The ground came up and struck her so hard she thought her back must be broken; falling in the cumbersome folds of her habit she couldn't control it and felt the jarring thud right through her. For a moment she was stunned, not unconscious but shaken and breathless, and lay amid the whirl of horses' legs, men and shouts. Mr Thorpe threw himself to the ground and took Columbine's bridle, attempting to soothe her. Sam knelt by Abby.

'Abby, how do you feel? Are there any bones broken? We'll send for Dr Hickey—'

She attempted to lift herself on one elbow. 'I think I'm all right—' then fell back.

She stared dazedly at the trees above her, and in a moment Dr Hickey was leaning over her. 'Take it easy, Abby. Are you in pain?'

She looked up at him. 'I don't think so, doctor.' She lifted herself again and remained on one elbow for a moment. 'No, it's fine. There's nothing the matter.'

Dr Hickey helped her to her feet. Sam was beside him. ''Tis all right, doctor. I'll watch her. Abby, we'll put ye on Mayflower. Mr Thorpe's calming Columbine.'

Marianne had dismounted too and had been watching anxiously. 'It's that horrible horse!' she exclaimed. Still feeling shaky Abby waited as Sam changed the saddles, but then, just as he was helping her up on to Mayflower, a searing red-hot pain shot through her guts, and she slipped down.

'What is it?'

'I don't know – oh!' Again, the jagging pain. She doubled over, clinging to the stirrup.

'Abby, what is it?' The others had gone on ahead now, and she was alone with Sam and Marianne.

For a moment she was speechless but then the pain subsided. She gradually straightened; she felt weak and shivery.

'Are ye well now?'

She drew a breath. 'I think so. Give me a hand up, please.'

But once again as she was arranging herself in the saddle the pain shot through her and she was barely able to cling on to the pommel. Sam watched her with concern.

She doubled forward trying to get her breath back. 'Oh by Jesus, Sam, I've done something, oh!' Another spasm wrenched her gut.

'We'll get ye home as quick as we can.' He mounted Columbine and took Mayflower's bridle. 'Just hang on as best ye can, Abby.'

It was an eternity, mile after mile – she had no idea how far – and the pain would come and go. Sometimes it ceased altogether for a space; she straightened and thought it over. 'I must have strained my insides,' she smiled once briefly to Marianne who was beside her, 'but it's mended now.' And then ten or fifteen minutes later the pain shot through her once more; she would rock and cling on to the saddle pommel.

They were in the stable yard in the dusk, and two men were helping her down, Mrs O'Connor was crossing from the kitchen door, she was being helped in – she couldn't walk very well – they were going upstairs and she was being helped out of her clothes. Marianne had wanted to come up too, but Mrs O'Connor gently advised her to remain below. 'The doctor's coming.'

By the time Abby was being helped into bed, the pain was greater than ever and had become continuous.

Dr Hickey clattered up the uncarpeted stairs, sent the other women out, pulled back the covers of the bed, and drew up her nightdress. His examination was brief. He called down the stairs, 'Bring some hot water and fresh bedding.'

She arched in pain, there was a last thrusting through her, then suddenly it was over. She lay back, her body slippery with sweat, and could feel wetness in the bed between her legs.

As she opened her eyes, Dr Hickey was looking down at her seriously. He studied her in silence for a moment then said, 'Do you realise what has happened, girl?'

'No sir.'

He ran a hand over his forehead, made a small clicking noise, and shook his head wearily. 'You have had a miscarriage.'

Chapter Ten

'Mrs O'Connor, I don't want any of the other servants in here.'

'Very well, Dr Hickey.'

'Now give me a hand to clear up this mess.'

Abby lay inert as they worked round her, washing her, lifting her as they changed the bedding, settling her back. Mrs O'Connor gathered up the blood-stained sheets and went out. Dr Hickey put his instruments back into his black bag.

'You are a strong girl and will get over it with no physical effects. As for the moral effects . . .' He paused. 'I will of course have to inform your mistress.'

She was left alone, and staring at the ceiling, felt only very tired and curiously empty. The candle flickered on the table beside her. Sometimes she would hear from far, far away a door close, or footsteps in a corridor. The house must be preparing for bed. What time was it? Oh, what did it matter? For her there was no time. Only the silence, the flickering of the flame. Why had she not foreseen this? Was there ever a more stupid, ignorant girl not to have known what might happen?

She stared at the ceiling, empty, her thoughts locked, focused in this moment. After the tension and pain, her body was utterly relaxed, as if she were floating above the bed, suspended in time and place. She drifted into sleep.

101

She was being shaken awake. Mrs O'Connor was bending over her. 'I've brought you something to eat.'

Abby pulled herself up and Mrs O'Connor set a bowl of stew before her. 'Put yourself outside o' that.'

The old lady, expressionless, watched as Abby ate. After a while she said, 'You'll be well enough to get up in a couple of days, Abby. You're to say nothing of this to the other servants, do you understand?'

Something strange: Teresa had not come up to bed. In fact, Abby now saw Mrs O'Connor take some dresses of hers from a nail behind the door as she went out.

She was awake again. It was morning now, and sunny outside the widow, out there in the real world, a million miles from where she lay in this room.

Only Mrs O'Connor came and went. The old lady betrayed no feelings, brought her meals, took away the empty bowl. In the afternoon she said, 'You'll be well enough to rise tomorrow morning. Mrs Thorpe will wish to speak to you.' She shook her head slowly before turning away.

The following morning, though she still felt weak, Abby pulled herself from her bed and dressed herself. She still did not know how she felt or what she should feel; in a way she did not know who she was any more. Mrs O'Connor told her the mistress would see her at eleven. When she went down she was to speak to no one; in particular she must on no account speak to Miss Marianne.

She was escorted by Mrs O'Connor to Mrs Thorpe's parlour. The lady herself, in a dress of dark blue silk, her hair done neatly beneath a lace cap, turned from where she had been writing at an escritoire.

She surveyed Abby in silence, folding her lips together into a compressed line. 'Dr Hickey has informed me of what has happened. I must say I am most astonished and dismayed. I had had good reports of you and thought you might have grown in time to be a useful and trusted servant. That of course cannot be – any further association with my

102

daughter is out of the question. I do not wish to hear explanations or excuses . . .' She turned to her desk where a ledger lay open and briefly consulted it. 'Your wages will be made up till the end of the month but you will leave this afternoon.'

She took a metal box from a drawer, opened it and took out some coins, counted them and laid them on the edge of the desk. Silently Abby took them. Try as she might she could not help the tears starting.

'Mrs Thorpe, I won't say anything, I promise, only I'm just very sorry that this has happened. I wouldn't have wanted to cause you distress because you have been a good mistress and I have been very happy here.' She paused to wipe her eyes, 'and especially looking after Miss Marianne—'

Mrs Thorpe's head jerked round. 'How dare you mention my daughter's name? I shudder to think she has been in your company these last weeks. I only pray no damage has been done.'

'Damage? I wouldn't hurt her, Mrs Thorpe. I loved her and was so happy taking care of her.'

'Be silent.' She glanced up at Mrs O'Connor who stood behind Abby and who now touched the girl on the shoulder and whispered to her. Abby dropped a curtsy to Mrs Thorpe and turned away.

But once outside the door she could no longer hold back her tears, and standing in the corridor with Mrs O'Connor she sobbed uncontrollably. 'She trusted me, Mrs O'Connor; I had special care of Miss Marianne, and I betrayed her. I did . . .'

At last the old lady took her in her arms. 'You're young yet to have got yourself into such a scrape. I shall miss you, girl. You should have had a mother to advise you.'

Back up in her room she put her few things into a bag and after a plate of bacon and potatoes went down to the stables. Sam was to drive her to the crossroads. After that she would have to walk.

103

Sam was looking sad as they climbed on to the trap. ''Twas Mr Thorpe said I might drive ye part of the way, Abby. I'm not supposed to talk with ye, but he didn't like to think of ye walking all that way to Kilnevin alone. He's a heart of gold – 'tis only the oul' bitch never liked ye and thought you was makin' sheep's eyes at the master—'

'No! No really, Sam, 'twas not that way at all.'

'What? Well, was it – not Mr O'Farrell makin' bad blood because ye was preferred above him to care for Miss Marianne?'

She shook her head. 'I can't tell you Sam. And don't say any more. I'm that miserable I could drown myself.'

They were just driving out of the stable gates when Marianne darted from behind the gatepost. 'Abby! Wait!' she hissed. Sam pulled up the trap.

'Miss Marianne! I'm not supposed to talk to you—'

'Abby, I couldn't believe it when Willie told me you were leaving. What on earth has happened?'

'I'm that sorry, Miss Marianne, but I can't tell you. I wouldn't have left for anything, but there's no helping it. It must be, that's all I can say – and you shouldn't even be talking to me.'

Marianne could see the tears in her eyes and impulsively reached her hand up for Abby's. Abby grasped it fervently in both hers and couldn't speak for a moment.

'But Abby what did you do? You must have done something – I don't understand.'

Abby shook her head blindly and wiped away her tears. 'I can't tell you. 'Tis impossible. Oh, Miss Marianne—' She turned quickly to Sam. 'Wait just one second.'

Clambering down, she took Marianne by the arm and led her a couple of paces away.

'Miss Marianne,' she whispered. 'Before I go there is just one thing I must tell you.' She paused, biting her lip, and clutching Marianne's arm as she looked carefully into her eyes. 'Did you meet a Mr Pelham at the hunt? A Mr Randolph Pelham?'

Marianne was flustered. 'Yes,' she said uncertainly, 'why?'

'I can't explain why, but – just be careful of him, won't you? You're a sweet, good girl. I wouldn't want you to come to any harm.'

She said this with such a concentration, such a curious authority, that Marianne was visibly disconcerted. She started away.

'Well, really!'

'Miss Marianne, forgive me, I wouldn't see ye hurt for the world! And now I must go – and you must go too. You shouldn't be seen talking to me. Sam, drive on.' She was clambering back on to the trap beside Sam and pulling her shawl round her. She looked back once.

'Remember!' At the stable gate Marianne stood in her flowery print gown, her golden hair, a picture of beauty and innocence. 'Remember!' Abby called again, and as Sam whipped up the horse and rounded the bend in the lane she broke into helpless sobs, and covered her face as she wept.

After a while Sam asked gently, 'What'll you do now, Abby?'

She shook her head and neither spoke again until they reached the crossroads. Sam did not stop, and she looked across at him. 'What are you doing?'

'I'm not leavin' you here to walk.'

'Sam, but Mr Thorpe—'

'It's a disgrace, so it is for you to be gettin' the cold shoulder, and 'tis only that old Mrs Thorpe is at the bottom of it. I know her, Abby!' He shook his head. 'So I'll drop you at Kilnevin, 'twill be no trouble and if Mr O'Farrell says anything, I'll tell him . . .'

But what he would tell Mr O'Farrell, Sam never said.

She heaved her bag on to the table as Aunt Eileen turned and looked up from the fire.

'Abby!' She rose, 'this is a surprise! But how—'

105

'I'll explain all, Aunt, only give me a moment.' Eileen had crossed the room quickly and they took one another in their arms. But already Abby's eyes were on her father, huddled in a rocking chair by the fire.

'Da—'

He had half risen from the rocking chair as she knelt by him and threw her arms round his neck. 'Oh, how I've missed you all!'

'And is the job going well?'

'Oh, Aunt,' she turned, looking up. 'Aunt, how can I tell you?'

That night they sat round the table, Fan, Da, Aunt Eileen and Abby. Gloom hung in the air above them.

'Mrs Thorpe never even gave you a character?' Fan searched her face, her voice rising. 'However can you get another place? They'll ask you where was your last place? And when you say Mr Thorpe's over at Ballintober, they'll say did he give you a character when you left, and when you say no, that's the end of it. Abby, since Rory went, we were depending on you. It's too bad of you, so it is!'

Abby's head was bowed, her hands clasped together on the table. Eileen laid her hand on Fan's arm. The girl was angry, her little face contorted. She pulled her arm away brusquely, and continued, still on that upwardly rising note, that querulous, panicking note, 'Well, what'll you do now?'

'I don't know,' Abby whispered.

'We've still heard nothing from Rory. You've got to do something, Abby!'

Abby nodded slightly, still saying nothing. Then, at last, in a low, hesitating voice, she whispered, 'I could maybe find work in a bar in Westport or Castlebar.'

'In a bar?' her aunt interrupted. 'Pulling pints for all kinds of rough working men? Do you not think of your immortal soul, girl? You could fall into all kinds of temptation—'

106

'Aunt, please don't shout at me,' Abby ran her hand across her eyes, shaking her head again, 'you don't know—'

'Well, you've got to get something, Abby!' Fan cut in. 'We can't stay here for ever.'

'Fan, be quiet! Abby's upset.'

After a moment, Abby said still very quietly, 'I'd go to Rory only we don't know where he is.'

That night when da was asleep and Fan had climbed into the loft, Aunt Eileen squatted by Abby as she banked down the fire for the night, and whispered, 'Abby dear, won't you tell me what's wrong?' Abby only shook her head. 'I can never talk about it, Aunt, so please don't ask me.' She turned back, absent-mindedly heaping up the ash over the dying embers, to keep the fire in for the night, and went on, on a different note, 'I only wonder what became of Rory now? It's strange he hasn't written.'

Eileen, who had seen she was going to get nothing more from Abby, now rose, stretching her back. It was late. 'I expect he wanted to get well settled before writing.' She turned away to the table, and was taking up some dishes to stack on the dresser. 'If he was still moving about in search of work it'd be difficult to write, wouldn't it?'

Abby rose too, and then, as if she had just thought of it, opened her bag, still on a chair where she'd dumped it, took out her purse and opened it.

'Aunt, here's twenty-five shillings,' she said quietly, 'I hope it'll keep us, till I can find something.'

But as she climbed into bed in the loft beside Fan, and was trying to settle herself to sleep, Fan, behind her, with her arm round Abby's waist, started again in a low whisper,

'You've got to get another job or something, Abby. I can't stand it here any longer. Da's useless, and Aunt Eileen's always on at me, do this, do that, I'm sick of it. Every day she finds something to complain of. She won't

107

let me alone two minutes. And being here away from the village I never get to see anybody. I haven't seen Susan Gilhooley since we were evicted. I've got nobody to talk to, I'm going mad with it. You've got to do something.'

Abby said nothing. She shook herself free from Fan's arm, staring alone into the empty darkness.

In the morning, she only wanted some menial chore, any occupation for her hands that would keep her from thinking. She and Fan went out to milk Eileen's eight cows, then there was a clamp of turnips to open. The turnips were cold, but she didn't care. She went out too without a shawl, in the cold winter morning, indifferent, careless, and Eileen had to call her in again.

'You'll do us no good if you're laid up with a chill, girl. Wrap up well,' and Abby, without smiling, without saying anything, meekly allowed her aunt to place the shawl round her shoulders, and turned out of the house again. She didn't want to be inside, didn't want to have to face others, didn't want to face anything, only wanted to work, any dull, repetitive chore, no matter how dirty.

'Urgh! Abby how could you! Da always does that.' Fan stood, her arms crossed, as Abby was forking out the turnips. 'You'll ruin your hands.'

Then she was feeding Starlight. Alone with the mare, Abby felt soothed. 'Dear old girl,' she murmured, rubbing the horse's nose, as Starlight burrowed her face into the fresh hay Abby had piled into the manger, 'you're still here, thank God. You don't reproach me.'

She made up her mind, and that afternoon set off to walk into Castlebar; it was nearly ten at night before she reappeared. She stood in the doorway, her shawl still round her head.

'Where in God's name have you been?' Eileen looked up sharply. She and Fan were at the table, folding petticoats. Abby still hesitated.

'And close the door, girl, we'll all catch pneumonia.'

Abby stepped forward, closing the door behind her. She stared at the two women.

'Abby, what's got into you?' said Fan, 'why are you looking like that?'

'Abby, where have you been?' Eileen asked again. 'We were worried—'

She faltered. Without saying anything, Abby had let the shawl fall round her shoulders. The two women at the table let out a gasp.

Abby turned slowly once. Her hair was cut close to her head, hacked awkwardly with unwieldy shears.

'What . . . Abby . . . your *hair*—'

Still like a sleep-walker, Abby reached into her pocket, took out some coins and laid them on the table in front of her aunt. 'Five shillings, Aunt. It'll help a while,' but there was a catch in her voice, and try as she might, a tear ran down her cheek.

'But Abby – your lovely *hair*, you've never cut it off!' Fan was clutching her fists to her face, contorted.

Abby couldn't speak, her arms hanging at her sides, clasping the ends of her shawl, as the tears ran freer, her face crumpling at last. Eileen took her in her arms, as Abby wept. Fan was watching, horrified, appalled, and kept repeating, 'But your lovely hair, Abby – how *could* you?'

'What good's it ever done me?' Her voice was muffled in her aunt's shoulder.

As the winter wore away, Abby was in a sort of hibernation, any job she could do for Eileen, any journey, any task, however menial, she took it without a murmur. Early in the morning, she was clearing the cowshed, setting off before dawn for market with a basket of eggs, or some butter, digging out turnips from the clamp, her hands raw and cold. She didn't think, didn't wonder where Rory might be. Didn't think of the future at all. Just wanted to do some mindless job, the muddier and harder the better.

She would stand in the market place, tall, yet curiously

stooping, her shawl muffling her head, and half covering her face, looking down when farmers addressed her, speaking low, briefly, a few staccato words, avoiding a man's gaze, silent when a man made a pleasantry, cracked a joke, or tried to engage her attention. It was as if she were an idiot girl, a half-wit, stupid, sullen, unseeing, not listening, only waiting to get her money, and then hurrying back out of the town, hurrying through the lanes, keeping her head down, avoiding other travellers, refusing offers of a lift, only wanting to get home.

And then, in the evening sitting at the fire, when the day's tasks were done, gazing into the embers, and sometimes breaking her silence with, 'I wonder whatever became of Rory now?'

Chapter Eleven

Then one day, the following April, Rory reappeared. He came walking up the *bohreen*, a little bag over his shoulder, looking ragged, poor, dusty; his boots well worn, and down at heel. He was brown, leaner, and seemed older – more a man.

She had been in the field behind the cottage, when her aunt called her, and as she came down and saw him she uttered no words, but only flew to his neck, hugging and hugging him as if she wanted to make up for a hundred years of absence, and he had slowly to pull her off him, laughing at her vehemence.

'Steady, steady,' he murmured. 'Let me look at you.' He stepped back, looking at her and seeing the scarf round her head which he seemed to think nothing of at first.

But already Fan and Eileen were crowding round, and Fan had her arms round his waist, and between the three of them they were pulling Rory into the cottage.

'Rory darlin' you must be parched with your travels – come and have a cup of tea – Fan make up the fire, there's a darlin', oh God, Rory, you can't imagine how good it is to see you after all this time – and us havin' no word from you, and never knowin' whether you were alive or dead, or in England or America – or in Timbuctoo—' she felt the tears smart in her eyes, running her arm round his neck again, and making him sit in the best chair. Already Da had got up from his chair beside the fire, and was shaking his hand.

'Da, 'tis grand to see you – and Aunt Eileen – you've been a friend to us, and sure, will I ever be able to thank you for everything?'

Tea was made, and at last as they sat round the table, and the first rush of excitement receded a little, they began to look more clearly at each other and take each other in, and then it was that Rory noticed her hair. 'Abby? Your hair . . . what—'

She ran her hand quickly over it – the scarf which had covered it, had fallen down in the excitement of their greeting. Her hair had grown back a little way since she had had it cut, but was still very short, and looked most odd about her head.

She smiled. 'Oh, you see we didn't want to be a burden on aunt and I had the silly notion I'd sell me hair! What do you think of that?' She laughed, but not very convincingly.

Rory was silent a moment or two. She rushed on, 'But Rory, how have you been doing? Did you find work? Won't you tell us?'

Da interrupted, 'Let the boy drink his tea first, girls! How far have you come today, son?'

'Dublin, Da. Came over on the steamer last night.'

'From England?'

He nodded, then drew a sigh. 'From Liverpool.'

They waited. He was silent a while drinking his tea, and thinking. She could see more clearly now that he was changed, matured, old for his years, perhaps not so close as he had once been. At last he began.

'It's not been easy Da, and girls, that's why I never wrote. I was hoping to get established in a good place, then maybe write, and one or both of ye could have come to join me. But,' he sighed, 'I got the odd job here and there, you know. In Manchester mostly, on the buildings, a couple of months here, a couple of months there – but never anything permanent, and everywhere there were "No Irish here"

112

signs up as if we were all lepers or something. Oh, it's a busy place all right with factories and mills belchin' out smoke night and day. You'd think you were in Hell itself, seeing all the chimneys and furnaces by night. Those are filthy cities – Jesus! – narrow winding streets, the slops running in the middle of the street, and a whole family in a room sometimes, with the wet running down the walls; and charging half your wages for the privilege – or maybe a man's paid only in tickets at the Tommy shop. That's, like, the factory shop – you have to spend your wages in the owner's shop. And bringing home little enough out of it at the week's end.' Weary, he unconsciously rubbed his eyes. 'Still, aunt, I made a bit, saved up you know and never touched a drop the whole time I was there, though others did. There's a grog shop every five doors in Manchester, and men drinking away their week's money on Friday night. But, well, I made a little bit, Aunt—'

He dragged a small purse from his pocket and placed it on the table. ''Tis a few pounds is all there's in it – but it's yours anyway.'

They stared down at this small purse – all the fruit of Rory's labours. No one liked to touch it.

''Tis a good son and brother you are to us, Rory,' Da said at last.

'What'll you do now, Rory?' asked Fan.

'What can I do? I'll have to go back. There's nothing here, is there? Maybe in the summer I can get work in the fields – there's often the need at harvest.'

'Would it be an idea for me to come over with you?' Abby asked.

Rory smiled at her and took her hand. 'How would you like to work in the mill? Up every day start at six, work, work, work till eight at night – six and a half days a week – how would like it, d'ye think?'

'I wouldn't mind, if we were together. And it'd be a job, wouldn't it?'

Rory thought. And then looked across at Eileen and Da.

113

'Maybe it'd be for the best, Da. There's work enough in Manchester for a girl. We could lodge together, and I could watch over you.'

'And in a few years, if we got well placed, Fan could come over.'

'To work in a factory?' Fan looked horrified. 'Oh Abby, you never mean it?'

Rory was stern. 'Fan, my little sister – how can we go on living off Aunt Eileen's charity? How can you be so selfish? If we have to work for our living there's no shame in it. Besides the pay's good. You'll make more in a factory in Manchester than going into service on a farm in Ireland. What would you rather do?'

That evening there was a celebration. Rory was home again and the bottle was brought out, Da lit his pipe, toasts were drunk, and everyone was more cheerful. Everything was not lost after all. There might be a future yet for them, if only they could once get established somewhere – even in Manchester.

Once or twice Rory glanced at Abby's hair. She felt the embarrassment, and later when they had a moment together, he murmured, 'Abby, I know times are bad, but promise me you'll never cut your hair again?'

She had to force a smile.

'Rory!'

He stood in the doorway, his shirt torn, marks of dried blood on his face, his hair in disarray.

It was late on a Saturday afternoon, Rory had been in town all day, and they had been expecting him home for the last two hours. He lurched into the room, staring across at Abby.

'Rory!' she screamed. 'What happened? You look terrible! Dear boy come in, sit down and let me clean you up. What *have* you been doing?'

He leaned an elbow on the table as he sat and ran a hand over his face.

Abby was still fussing round him. 'Aunt get water, let Rory bathe his face.' But Rory looked up at her, interrupting her.

'The question is – what have *you* been doing?'

She was still fussing about him, getting out a cloth to wipe his face. 'And you've torn your shirt—'

Fan was watching Abby, though she had taken in the point of the question.

'I said,' Rory repeated slowly, 'the question is – what have you been doing?'

He brushed her aside, as she was about to begin wiping his face. She started back. 'What?'

'*Abby!*' He started to his feet abruptly, dashing the chair back behind him, so that it fell. She was about to go to pick it up, but he took her arm in a strong grip. '*I said* – what have you been doing?'

They were face to face, her arm caught in a painful grip. 'I don't understand?'

'You don't?' he jerked her towards him. 'There's men in Westport do, though!'

There was a paralysing silence as they stared at one another. She was speechless.

'I don't—'

Rory glanced round and seemed to notice the others for the first time. Another paralysing silence.

Abby stared at Rory, Fan stared at Abby. Da was looking up fearfully.

Rory, still holding her in a powerful grip, turned and opened the door, dragging her outside. He led her round to the side of the cowshed, and confronted her again. It was late in the afternoon, getting on to dusk, chill, clear. 'Why do you think there's blood on my face?' he said softly, in a controlled voice, looking hard into her eyes. 'What does a man do, Abby – what does he normally do – when someone tells him his sister's a whore?'

'Who?' she gasped.

'*Who?* What does it matter who? He was shoutin' it in

115

me face: I was ready to fight 'em all and would have done—'

'It's a lie,' she gasped at last.

'I knew it was! Abby, I knew you were pure, but why did he say it? It couldn't have been clearer. But why?'

'Why?' She looked away.

'*Why*? Why did he say it? Only tell me!'

'There's nothing to tell, Rory, darlin'.'

'But if there's nothing to tell – Abby, something's happened. What is it?' He was becoming ever calmer – but more determined, and now reached to her and took her by the shoulders. 'Tell me. Tell me everything.'

She couldn't help tears starting, fighting to hold them back, but feeling them forcing themselves through. She wiped her eyes fiercely with the back of her hand.

''Twas on account of the rent.'

'Yes?'

'That letter you wrote, Rory darlin' – I knew it would never work, like Da said, so I had an idea—'

'What idea?'

'I thought I would go and speak with Sir George Pelham and beg him to give us an abatement till Fergus wrote or till we could find the money—'

'Well, what did he say, though I can guess?'

She sniffed and wiped her nose with her wrist. She swallowed and went on.

'I didn't see Sir George,' she stumbled on.

'No?'

She swallowed again. ''Twas his son.'

'Ha! That's right—'

And now it came out quicker. 'It was at his house. I asked him to speak to his father – because Sir George was from home – and he said he would – and he said to meet him in The Goat and he would tell me what his father said. So I went to The Goat – I didn't want to go in The Goat, Rory. I would never go in such a place! Only that he told me to go there, and you see I wanted to hear whether he had spoken with his

116

father – and then, well, he met me there – and it was so crowded and noisy and he said wouldn't it be a good idea if we were to go – well, you see, to go upstairs – because it was quieter and out of the way, and he would tell me everything—'

'And you went?'

'I didn't know what to do! All the time I was waiting for him to tell me what his father said, but he wouldn't. He kept putting it off, and leading me on, so –' she shook her head – 'Rory, I didn't know what I was doin', so I went upstairs with him—'

'Go on!'

'And,' she shook her head, staring down, the tears running down her cheeks, 'he said he would speak to his father. He kept promising, but all the time he was tellin' me he was in love with me and wouldn't let me go, kissing me and telling me how much he loved me. What could I do?'

She broke down completely, sobbing into her hands.

'You mean?'

Still with her face in her hands, she nodded. Rory stared at her, then slowly turned away. 'Randolph Pelham,' he breathed.

He turned away, walking a few yards with his hands hanging limp at his sides, staring down, and muttered again, 'Randolph Pelham. My God—'

At last she looked up to where he was a few yards from her. The light was fading, and it would be dark soon. 'Rory?' she whispered.

Rory turned and leaned against the wall of the cowshed, his elbows above his head, his face against his arms. At last, he turned very slowly, like a man sleep-walking.

'I'll kill him.' It was a breath, a whisper.

'No!'

'No?' He was close in her face, quiet but intense. 'You have the name of a whore in the town Abby! You were *seen*! Don't you understand? How can we ever—'

He realised something, and suddenly stepped back. His

117

tone was quite changed. 'And that was why you cut your hair off, wasn't it? Your shame!' His anger was growing all the time. 'I will kill that man. I swear, I swear – before God and all the saints I will never rest, I will go after that man. I will go after that man, and I will kill him with these hands. That he could do this – when you came to him thinking only to save your family – and he could – oh *God*!'

She was terrified; she had never seen Rory like it. But still fighting her fear she approached him – it was nearly dark now – and tentatively reached a hand. 'Rory,' it was barely a whisper, 'think of aunt, think of Da.'

He stopped and seemed to consider. Then at last by a great effort he appeared to master himself. He glanced round at the cottage, a light gleaming in the one window on this side. He turned to her again. 'They'll be wonderin'. Come on. Let's get in. Ye've never spoken of this?'

She shook her head.

'We'll be calm now, Abby. Wipe your eyes. Be calm now. It'll be all right. Come on, little sister.' As he put his arm round her shoulders, he suddenly drew a shuddering breath. 'Don't worry. Everything will be all right. Only say nothing.'

'I won't.'

Supper that night was eaten in near silence. No one dared to ask what had been said outside the cottage. Rory seemed to have regained complete control of himself, and spoke normally, quietly. Ordinary, everyday things were discussed, plans were rehearsed – when Rory should return to England – the summer hay season would soon be starting; and that Abby should go with him.

The next day they went to mass. Then in the afternoon were out in the fields again, mending a fence; milking the cows.

Fan gave strange looks to Abby but said nothing. Da and Eileen were subdued – neither said anything, but were both obviously thinking very hard. In all, a strange oppressive atmosphere hung over the house.

118

On the following morning Rory announced in a casual way that he had a bit of business in town and would walk in. No one questioned him or inquired further as to what this bit of business might be. Abby stood in the doorway watching him go, and then on impulse, ran after him, and caught up with him in the *bohreen*, clutching his arm.

'Rory,' she began, 'you won't do anything – dangerous, will you?'

He smiled, said nothing, only kissed her forehead. 'I'll not be late. Have tea ready for me,' he called over his shoulder.

Chapter Twelve

Rory did not come home that night.

As afternoon wore on and dusk was falling, Abby became more nervous. She had been filled with foreboding all day. It was obvious that Rory was concealing something from her: she understood that, after their nerve-shredding interview by the cowshed, he was not simply going to forget this matter. Something was going to happen, and very probably something violent. But there was nothing she could do; she could no more stop Rory in his intention than she could stop a landslide. She waited all day in trepidation, and as dusk fell it grew worse.

Night fell, and still there was no sign of Rory. After their supper, as they sat about the fire in the light of a rush candle, she stood, went to the door with her shawl, and was about to go out, until her aunt who had been watching her all day for exactly this, quickly stopped her.

'There's nothing you can do tonight,' she said quietly but firmly, and Abby allowed herself to be led docilely back to the fire. Fan watched her but said nothing, and they all looked at one another; they all thought, but no one spoke.

She did not sleep that night and the following morning as soon as she had swallowed something she set off into town. There was no need to explain, nothing was said. Everyone understood.

All the way into town her whole body was filled with a fearful premonition. She could not be still. It was as if snakes were writhing in her veins. She kept drawing long shattering breaths, trying to inflate herself, or to breathe the tension out of her body, feeling light-headed from lack of sleep, dizzy and unreal. About her other people went about their business; she stood aside as a herd of cows were driven down the *bohreen*, a farmer passed her in a pony and trap, then a group of farm girls. Clutching her shawl she kept on her way, her eyes on the road in front, not hearing, not seeing, not thinking, only possessed by this dread. Something had happened; she must know; must know where Rory was, what he was doing; know he was safe.

The town was busy; it was Tuesday morning; shops were open. Why did everything have such a normal face? Why? And why could everyone else have a normal life with no difficulties, and only they, only she and her family, only she and Rory in such a strait?

'Abby O'Leary!'

Abby swung round. It was a girl from the village – Susan Gilhooley, Fan's friend.

'I'm surprised ye'd show your face in Westport, after yesterday.'

'Yesterday?'

'The whole town's talkin' of it, sure.'

'Talking? What?'

Susan came to her. 'Ye've not heard?'

'Heard? Heard what?'

'Why, that your brother near murdered a man yesterday outside the Imperial Hotel.'

Abby stood frozen for a moment.

'The Imperial Hotel?' She turned and ran away down the street, and didn't slow down till she came to the Mall, and stood beneath the stately façade of the largest and most important hotel in the town.

There was no sign of trouble. Men were going in and out, a maidservant was shaking a rug from a window, a

121

stablehand led a horse past her. She stopped, panting from her run, staring up at the windows, and wondering.

At this moment a servant came to the door and looked round. She darted forward. 'Oh, excuse me sir! I'm so sorry to trouble you – but yesterday – there was a fight I heard—'

He gave her a serious look, and put his hands in his pockets in a casual way. 'Who are you?'

'I'm his sister. But what happened?'

'It was your brother, was it? Well, a fine brother ye have to be sure. The blackguard came roaring up to Mr Pelham as he was mounting his horse; he was drunk, calling him names and threatening to commit murder. Mr Pelham tried to ignore him, told him to be off, but he wouldn't go away, shouting all kinds of foul abuse, not fit for the ears of ladies. Still, Mr Pelham tries to ignore him, tells him he'll call the police if he doesn't take himself off. And we were about to send him on his way with a good kick, when he rushed at Mr Pelham just as he was mounting his horse. He would have pulled him to the ground, he was a madman. In the end we managed to beat him off, and Mr Pelham rode away. Then he went off shouting and swearing like a tinker and making terrible threats.' He looked Abby up and down. 'So you're his sister? What kind of a family are you at all? That live without the bounds of civilised society entirely? Be off with ye!'

Abby stepped back, drawing her shawl instinctively about her head, and at last turned away, scarcely seeing where she was going as she ran those terrible words through her mind. And where was he now? She turned away through the streets, wandering like a mad woman herself, unable to concentrate, looking about her into shop windows, into the doors of public houses, everywhere, going into the church, always hoping and hoping to find him, and having no idea where he could be, near to tears, trying – forcing herself to think of anything she could that might help, and only feeling a terrible weight of help-

122

lessness, that somewhere out there was Rory and he might be in great danger, he might do some rash thing, and she must find him and stop him.

It was dark by the time she reached the cottage. She was deathly weak – she had eaten nothing since breakfast – but the light in the window was comforting.

She prayed that Rory was home too but, as she pushed open the door, it was obvious instantly that he wasn't. The others were all sitting round the table, and the second she saw them they turned their faces to her. She seemed to read everything on their faces before a word was uttered.

'Oh Abby!' Fan cried.

She stood in the doorway, the door still open behind her.

'It's Rory – he's taken for murder!'

At that, the last little strength drained from her body, and she staggered.

'Abby darlin', we'll just get ye into a chair,' and she was helped up, and seated in a chair by the fire, feeling utterly without strength. Eileen gave her a cup of water.

'I'll make ye a cup of tea,' Da was saying, and Fan watched with fearful eyes.

As she drank the water she looked about at the others. 'Murder?'

'This afternoon Mr Bourne came in and said Rory was taken for murder, and is lodged in Castlebar Gaol.'

'Who did he say was murdered?'

'He didn't know. Only that a murder had been committed and Rory was in Castlebar Gaol waiting to go before a grand jury.'

Abby stood. 'We must go—'

But she tottered again, and Eileen took her firmly by the shoulders and made her sit again. 'You're not going anywhere tonight, my girl! You'll not have eaten, I'll be bound.'

She was so weak, she could not even think. Everything had happened exactly as she had feared. She was in a

123

nightmare and entirely unable to influence it, paralysed, watching like a hapless bystander.

She sat like a waxwork doll in the chair. Eileen meanwhile was fussing over the fire, and soon after set a plate before her. 'Eat that,' she said impassively, placing it on the table. 'In the morning we'll go and see Rory and find out. It may only be a rumour. There's nothing we can do tonight anyway.'

Another sleepless night it seemed at first, but at last merciful nature took over, and in the early hours she fell into a deep sleep, and though she had a headache as she woke, and felt strange and ethereal, she could acknowledge to herself that she was a little stronger, and after an early breakfast she and Fan walked into Castlebar and found themselves outside the county gaol.

At first sight this appeared to be a medieval castle, grey rough-hewn stone, with crenellations, and turrets, narrow barred windows and a heavy studded door. At one side there was a iron bell pull, which she rang in the faint hope that someone might answer.

But at length there were sounds, and to their surprise, a smaller door in the larger one opened, and a man in a pointed helmet appeared.

'If you please sir, could we speak with Rory O'Leary – he's our brother—'

'He's in court now.' It was a constable in the bottlegreen uniform of the Royal Irish Constabulary. 'Come in.'

He let them pass through into a stone-vaulted chamber.

'In court?'

'The magistrate's hearing his committal proceeding. If ye wait here ye can see him after.'

'Thank you, sir.'

They found themselves in a cold, unappetising room, smelling of stale tobacco smoke, and sat on a bench along a bare wall. On the wall opposite hung a framed sheet of regulations, some laws or orders which made no sense to her at all, and when she began to try to read it her mind wandered immediately.

But after twenty minutes there were voices, doors were opening, and moments later Rory appeared. He was looking terrible: ill, tired, dishevelled, his shirt torn, a terrible weal across his forehead, and a black eye.

'Rory!'

She was restrained.

'Ye can talk with him in his cell, miss.'

As Rory was led before them she saw he was manacled, and the irons made a clanking sound as she and Fan followed into a short stone corridor, and a cell door was opened.

The door was so low, that they actually had to stoop to enter, and the cell was small, a low bed on one side, and a tiny window high in the wall, with such thick bars scarce any light entered so that the room was in gloom.

'Knock on the door when ye want to come out,' the constable said in an offhand voice, as he closed the door behind the three of them; they heard the sound of a key in a monstrous lock.

'Rory!' They flung their arms round each other, all three of them. 'Oh Rory.' They sat on the side of the filthy little bed, Rory with his arms round the girls' shoulders.

'Rory, we brought you some spare shirts, and a pie, and a bottle of spirits; if there's anything you want, darlin', we can bring it, we'll come every day. Oh my darling, that's a terrible bruise on your forehead, whatever—'

'Oh Rory, tell us what happened,' Fan whispered.

'I'm to stand trial for attempted murder,' he said expressionlessly.

'Attempted?'

Rory drew a breath. 'The gun jammed,' he said in a low voice.

'But they said, outside the Imperial Hotel—'

He drew a long sigh. 'I'll tell you everything. I went to his house, but they said he was in town, at the Imperial

125

Hotel. So I went back into town, and waited outside, and at last in the afternoon out he comes with a gang of his friends, and servants. There were a lot of men there. That was good, I wanted plenty of witnesses. I went up to him. Randolph Pelham, says I, you're a coward and villain, says I, my name is Rory O'Leary and I call on you to fight. He pretended not to know me, and tried to ignore me. You know full well who I am! I shouted at him, don't turn your back on me. He was about to get on his horse, Abby. Turn and fight, says I, you know why I'm here. I've never seen you in my life, says he – be off – as if I was some kind of a tinker, Abby. Are ye a man or a coward, I shouted. Will you fight! No says he, I wouldn't soil my hands on such vermin – or something like that. And he goes to mount the mare again, and this time I was so angry Abby, I took hold of his leg, and at that he cut at me with his crop. I tell you, I was blind with rage – and blinded too, I could scarcely see, with the cut across my face. I'm staggering about blind with pain, and he rides off with his friends, then the grooms and servants of the hotel they're all round me – be off with ye, tinker, and they take hold of me, and thrust me away. I wandered about the town, it was as if heaven itself had cursed me. So I went to a pub I know in town, and there's a fellow I know – have ye got a shooter ye can let me have—'

'Oh Rory!'

'Come back in two hours says he, and that evening – it's dark by now – back I come, and he's got a pistol for me. Have you used one of these before, says he? Show me, I said, it ought to be pretty easy, and he gave it me. So out I went to Westport Lodge. It was night now. I couldn't rest Abby, I hung about in the woods all night. I didn't want to let him get away. I couldn't sleep – well, maybe a couple of hours – it got cold, I was frozen through, stiff, but at last the dawn came, yesterday, it seems years ago – the dawn comes, and I'm ready, waiting in the trees, and at long last he comes out of the house. There's a couple of servants,

126

there – and his father and a woman. I didn't care – I didn't care about anything, Abby. I walked across the grass – they could see me coming but I never faltered. I walked right up to them; they had turned as they saw me, but I never faltered. I was two yards from him. Randolph Pelham says I, you're a coward and villain, and I pointed the gun at him and pulled the trigger.'

He paused. The girls waited breathless.

Rory was staring at the ground. 'The gun wouldn't fire. I don't know why. Maybe it was damp for having been out all night. Of course they were all over me, holding me down, about ten men on top of me.'

There was a long pause.

'And now you're to stand trial?'

He nodded. 'At Castlebar Assizes.' He shivered.

'You've caught a fever from being out all night.' Abby pulled her shawl off, wiped his face, and examined the long weal across his forehead. 'Have you had a doctor to your cut?'

He grunted.

'Oh Rory, this is a terrible thing altogether! You must keep warm and rest. I'll get the doctor to come to you. When's the trial?'

'A month or so. But think, Abby!' He turned to her as she was arranging the shawl about his shoulders. 'To stand trial and him still walking about! I wouldn't mind swinging for his murder; but to stand trial and him still alive! Where's the justice?'

'Do you have a lawyer?'

'Yes. That's a good thing, anyway. Mr O'Toole. You'll maybe not remember him but he's strong for the Land League, and is always on the side of the farmer against the landlords.'

'Mr O'Toole. Where's his office?'

Rory did not know. 'Here in Castlebar maybe.'

'Well, never mind for that, darlin'. We'll come to see you everyday till the trial, won't we, Fan? And once your

127

lawyer tells the judge about, you know, Mr Pelham and me—'

'He won't.'

'Pardon?'

'You won't be mentioned.'

'Rory?'

'Do you think I want my sister's name dragged through the courts for the world to laugh at? I'd rather swing!'

Fan screamed, and Abby cried, 'Don't say such a thing! But darlin', you must tell the judge – you were only doing it to save your sister's honour—'

'Randolph Pelham knows well enough. 'Tis his shame – the coward – if he wasn't man enough to face me. But your name will never be spoken in that court.'

'Rory that's madness. If only you once tell them why you attacked him they'll let you off, sure.'

Rory would not be moved, and soon after they rose to leave. As they were looking round the cell one last time, she glanced at the bottle of spirits she had brought.

'They'll only confiscate this, Rory darlin'. I've a better idea.'

And as they were leaving, she approached the desk sergeant. 'My brother's maybe sickening for a fever, sir; I'm going for a doctor for him now. And sir,' she lowered her voice, 'you're a kind gentleman, I know, and you'll take care of him, won't you?'

She gave him a long look, full of feeling, as she unveiled the bottle from her shawl, and passed it to him carefully behind his desk.

The sergeant got her message. He gave her a wink. 'Don't worry, miss, we'll take care of him. He's a good lad.'

Chapter Thirteen

'Abby!' Fan stopped her the moment they were in the street. 'What did he mean?'

Abby tried to hurry on, but Fan held her arm, determined. 'Tell me! Was it about when you went to see Mr Pelham?'

Abby shook herself free. 'I'll explain, only we must get a doctor to Rory first. He looked so ill. And that cut on his face.'

'But what happened, Abby?' Fan was insistent. 'Tell me! What did you mean about your honour? Did you – I mean – you didn't—'

'Not now, Fan!' Abby hurried on in front of her. 'We'll find a doctor, and then we must go and see Mr O'Toole.' The desk sergeant in the barracks had given her his address.

The following morning they were in Castlebar early. 'He might have to go out, to court over something, we'd best be there early,' she had said to Fan. They had walked all the way back to Aunt Eileen's the previous afternoon, described what had happened, and this morning walked back to Castlebar. By now Abby was in a state above tiredness, in a kind of exaltation, in which her self had been annihilated; as if she were all spirit. Whatever was needed would be done. She would have time enough to rest

129

afterwards. But she was also uncomfortably conscious of Fan all the time beside her, watching her, waiting for an explanation.

She vaguely remembered Mr O'Toole from the meeting she had gone to with Rory. But they had been far back in the crowd – he had been one of a number of men on the platform – she didn't remember much about him.

Outside the door was an inscribed brass plate: 'J.J. O'Toole, Bachelor of Laws, late of King's Inn, Dublin'. It looked impressive.

They explained who they were to a clerk, and waited twenty minutes while Mr O'Toole spoke with another client.

At last the door opened, and they caught the end of a conversation as a heavy, middle-aged man came out still speaking. Immediately behind him was a young man, quick, light on his feet, and he had scarcely bidden farewell to the other before he turned to the two girls, had crossed to them stretching out his hands, was apologising for keeping them waiting and taking them by the hands was ushering them into his office and helping them to chairs, and introducing himself. 'And you are his sisters, Miss Abigail – Abby – and Miss Frances – Fan? This is a very trying time for you both. I sympathise with you most sincerely. Well, young ladies, as you know, we were in court yesterday for the committal proceedings, and I have had another long talk with your brother, and I think things may not be as black as they seem at the moment.'

He was talking all the time as he settled them, with a sort of quiet sure confidence, and at last worked his way round his desk and sat himself behind a heap of documents. As he was speaking she was obscurely conscious of her surroundings.

His office was a light room with a large window on to the street, and was about as cluttered with documents and books as an office could well be. His desk was covered with papers and rolls of parchment, there were rows of black

130

books on shelves numbered on the spines in faded gold Roman numerals, and elsewhere bundles of rolled parchment were stacked.

Mr O'Toole took her by surprise. She didn't know what to expect, but had supposed vaguely that attorneys were elderly gentlemen with spectacles and bony, pointed fingers. Mr O'Toole was young, spruce, energetic, and good-looking. He was also neatly dressed, his hair beautifully brushed, not a hair out of place, his hands clean, his fingernails clipped – she took all this in as he talked to them, the two sisters sitting anxiously forward on their chairs.

'The point is that this was not an isolated, nor spontaneous attack. Your brother had suffered a vicious blow from Mr Pelham's riding crop.' He became serious, looking at them both, 'I shall be taking a deposition from the surgeon who attended him. Mr O'Leary had a legitimate grievance and we shall plead provocation.'

Unable to help herself any longer Abby burst out, 'Mr O'Toole, it is my fault he did what he did! My brother would never speak of it. He'd die first! But he did it to protect my good name! My good name!' she repeated, confused, 'and—' she paused again, looking down. 'Sir, the reason why my brother attacked Mr Pelham was on account of me.' She swallowed.

There was silence as the lawyer waited, and after a moment she collected herself and went on quietly, 'It's on account that we were evicted from our farm, sir, for being behind with the rent. I went to our landlord, Sir George Pelham hoping to obtain an abatement or postponement of the arrears. But instead I met his son, and he promised me that he would speak with his father – and then—'

Mr O'Toole, who had been listening with his eyes down, looked up at her.

She swallowed. 'It's not very easy to explain—'

'You had been evicted from your farm?'

'Yes sir.'

'So your brother had a grudge against your landlord?'

131

'Yes sir.'

'That could be important. Your family have suffered hardship through the Pelham family.'

'Yes sir, but that isn't—'

He leant forward, cutting through her words. 'What you say may be of very great importance, Miss O'Leary. We could build a strong case on your eviction. Your brother – and your whole family had suffered grievous provocation. The Land League will also be strongly behind us. I shall speak to counsel about this case next week, and take advice about it.'

His certainty was so strong that she felt inhibited especially after what Rory had said in the cell. So she said nothing, except a very small, 'Yes sir.'

Fan said, 'So, you think you can get him off, sir?'

He thought a moment. 'That will be difficult. There were so many witnesses. I shall aim to mitigate his sentence. We shall plead not guilty in any case, and use the opportunity to advance your brother's cause in as strong terms as possible. The trial comes on in May and I have got Eoghan MacCarthy to lead for us. He's one of the best briefs in Ireland and a nationalist. We've been lucky.'

Outside in the street with Fan again, she could not contain her enthusiasm: 'Oh, he's such a gentleman, Fan! So handsome, so kind, and everything about him so neat, his hair, his brown eyes—'

Fan gave her a comical look. 'Yerrah! Ye're never fallin' in love with him, Abby?'

As they walked home, Abby was thinking. There was something about Mr O'Toole – that modest manner and quiet air of certainty – you just knew you could trust him. And so handsome too – she wondered whether he were married and – oh, but that was a silly thing, as if it were any business of hers. She could scarcely imagine what sort of a life Mr O'Toole must lead, a lawyer and a gentleman, so smartly dressed, his coat beautifully brushed, his boots gleaming – he must have a man to do for him, at the very least. And that he should want to take up the case of a poor farmer; you just knew you could trust him. She instinctively clasped her hands together. 'Fan, Rory couldn't have a better man for a lawyer. Thanks be to God.'

The trial day came at last, after a worrying time of tending Rory through ten days of fever in his cell, during which he lost weight, and looked haggard, gaunt, almost fanatical. Every day the conversation reverted to Randolph Pelham; Rory was obsessed. But he did make a gradual recovery.

They got to the court house early – but they still weren't early enough. Already a crowd was waiting at the door, and Abby was terrified for a moment they wouldn't get in. But they gradually insinuated themselves forwards, until they were right at the very door itself. 'We'll be the first in, Fan – mind now, that no one gets in front of us.'

The talk didn't give them much to be cheerful about, though.

'He'll swing for it!' said one. Abby turned indignantly. 'Hold your tongue!'

Abby and Fan looked at each other. 'Oh I wish they'd open up, and get on with it. Fan, whatever you do, don't let anyone get in front of us.'

The crowd grew steadily larger, noisier and more vociferous, jostling.

'We'll burn the court house down if he don't get off!' shouted someone, and Abby's heart lifted again as this was greeted by a cheer.

But eventually there were noises from within, the drawing of heavy iron bars, and the doors were opening. The crowd pressed against them, and they were swept helplessly forward, pushed, buffeted, and up the steps.

'Keep together!'

In the push, in the confusion, in the noise and muddle, they struggled to hold hands; Abby lost her basket with their bit of bread and cheese – until later, when they had found their way into the public gallery and managed to squeeze together on to a bench, and it was somehow passed over people's heads, and back into her lap.

As they settled themselves they were able to look round the court room. It was a dingy place, with windows high up, giving a gloomy light. Already the barristers were assembled below them in wig and gown. Abby could see Mr O'Toole in a back row, leaning forward in earnest conversation with one of the barristers, a plump, jovial-looking man, who laid his hand on Mr O'Toole's shoulder and said something with a laugh. That must be Mr MacCarthy, and if he was laughing, surely everything must be all right. She looked along the line of the other barristers, but none of them meant anything to her. They had piles of documents and books and papers scattered all over the desk in front of them, and talked to one another in low tones. Elsewhere there was a beadle in a dark blue cape, and opposite the jury were arranging themselves.

With a shock she now saw the prisoner being led into the dock. Fan gripped Abby's arm as they looked down at Rory. He in his turn looked round the court room, rather out of curiosity as it seemed, and they waved, and Fan called out his name, so that he saw them, and smiled. How pale he looked, tired and thin.

'All be upstanding—'

The judge now came in a red gown and long wig, and took his place, and after a moment's consultation with a clerk below him in the well of the court, the clerk read out the indictment: that on the fifteenth day of April Rory O'Leary did with malice aforethought attempt to murder and kill Randolph Pelham.

The words sounded so chilling, confronting her with the brute public fact. And that her own dear Rory should be exposed like this in public humiliation and shame. And looking so weak and thin after his fever; she could scarcely control herself.

In the meantime the prosecuting counsel was outlining the events leading up to the attempted murder. She knew all this, except that she was astonished to hear him turn every moment of the story somehow inside out: to make Rory sound one minute like a lunatic, the next like a vagabond, the next like a scurrilous and shabby criminal. She wanted to shout out, 'Don't say such things about my brother!' His speech made her deeply uncomfortable, as if she and her family were dirty, and unfit to mix with ordinary, normal people.

The defence counsel now rose. Mr MacCarthy, round, affable, spoke with an easy rolling delivery, and a bass voice which filled the room effortlessly. His client was a man sorely provoked, he told the jury. A farmer, known and respected in the village and surrounding villages, a friendly, generous man, a man of honour, upright with no stain on his character, who had nevertheless been driven to the end of his tether. Due to the bad harvest, which had caused hardship to many farmers – when he and his family, his two sisters and elderly father, when all were in a state of most acute distress – he had been driven from his home by the greed of an unscrupulous landlord. His pleas for a stay of execution had been scornfully ignored, and he and his family had been driven out at the point of a bayonet to starve on the public highway. No wonder he was angry. No wonder he was provoked! Mr MacCarthy then went on to outline the events outside the Imperial from Rory's point of view. His honourable challenge to Randolph Pelham. Mr Pelham's scornful and cowardly rejection of it. No wonder the prisoner O'Leary had been driven to do what he did – anyone who called himself a man would have done the same.

Randolph was called to give evidence. It gave Abby a jolt seeing him again, but she disciplined herself as well as she could to listen, concentrating on his face. Fan was acutely conscious of her sister, glancing as often to Abby's face as to Randolph's.

Randolph had an unaffected manner, was perfectly composed, modest and reasonable, and Abby realised that

135

anyone not knowing the circumstances and watching him today would take him for a pleasant and normal sort of man, civilised, well-to-do, a gentleman. He described the attack as coming completely out of nowhere by a man he had never seen in his life, a ragged hooligan. And after all, it was his father not Mr Pelham himself who had caused the eviction. He himself had taken no part in it. As the questioning progressed, Abby realised that any outsider strolling into the court room, or any juryman, would conclude that the accused O'Leary must be half crazy, a violent, uncontrolled scoundrel, primitive and backward, and that prison was the best place for him.

At the end of the day, she and Fan waited for Mr O'Toole and, as he came out with Mr MacCarthy, she hastened to thank them for what they had done so far.

'We're doing our best girls,' MacCarthy boomed in his genial tone.

Abby took Mr O'Toole's arm. 'Don't mind me sir, if I seem so anxious. I've been watching all day, and there's something – you must tell the jury about me and Mr Pelham. My brother will never get off otherwise. How can they understand why my brother attacked Mr Pelham, if I'm not to be mentioned? It's madness! You must let me give evidence – it's Rory's only hope. You must do it.' There were tears in her eyes.

'Come to my office.'

Abby glanced at Fan, and the three walked off to the office. The clerks were packing up for the night, and the office was soon left empty.

Abby turned to Fan. 'Fan dear, will you wait here?'

'What? Can't I—'

'Please, darling. There's something I have to tell Mr O'Toole.'

They went into his office. Once alone together he invited her to sit, and brought a chair close to her so that they sat almost knee to knee. 'There's plenty of time,' he said gently.

136

Again slowly and haltingly she outlined the story of herself and Randolph Pelham in The Goat.

He was thoughtful for a long time. 'And your brother won't allow you to speak?'

'He was always careful for me, sir – and protected me, like a good brother. He would die rather than any harm should come to me. And when he found out about – what I've said – he was so angry he wouldn't rest until he had punished Mr Pelham. But he is an honourable man. That was why he challenged him. He wanted to give him a fair chance. But I can see that everyone believes Mr Pelham is a gentleman and honourable, and that Rory is just a blackguard and a scoundrel – and that's all wrong! It's exactly the other way about. You must tell the jury – tell Mr MacCarthy, sir. You must! Or my brother will go to gaol for years and years—'

O'Toole reached for her hands, and held them for a while willing her to be calm. His face was filled with sympathy in the golden light of the early summer evening, and she felt a tremendous comfort flowing from him all through her body, sitting still as he held her hands. 'Calm yourself,' he murmured at last, 'we are doing all we humanly can to save your brother.'

'You don't blame me, sir?'

'It is not for me to blame you,' he said gently, looking closely into her eyes. 'You were thinking of your family.'

'Thank you.' She was still looking up into his face, as they sat, face to face as he held her hands and she felt this warm comforting feeling stealing through her. At last he said, 'I will speak of this to counsel and your brother tomorrow before the court sits, and tell them everything you have told me. However,' he looked down, and drew a breath, 'I must tell you, Miss O'Leary, that I am under instruction from Mr O'Leary. It will be his decision. May I say too, that I entirely understand his desire to preserve his sister's good name, and I respect him the more for it.'

She pulled her hands away from his, wringing them

together, staring down and muttering, 'As if I had any good name left. Every man in the town must know why he attacked Mr Pelham. Can't ye tell the judge, Mr O'Toole! Ye must. I couldn't bear it if Rory was to go to gaol because of me – when it was all my fault in the first place.'

Yet when they took their seats the following morning, and the trial continued, there was no mention of her.

Counsel made their closing speeches, the judge gave his summing up. He mentioned the many witnesses who had heard the accused O'Leary threaten to kill Mr Pelham; they heard of the accused's unprovoked attack on Mr Pelham outside the Imperial Hotel; witnesses had described the scene at Westport Lodge when the accused had pointed the pistol in Mr Pelham's face. Whether or not the accused had been evicted from his farm for non-payment of rent was irrelevant to the case. The only question the jury had to decide was – what was the intention in the accused's mind at the moment when he pointed the pistol? Was it merely to frighten Mr Pelham? Or had the accused actually intended to fire the pistol? If so they must find him guilty of attempted murder.

The jury retired. They needed nineteen minutes to decide their verdict, which was unanimous.

They found the accused Rory O'Leary guilty of attempted murder. This caused little reaction in the court, but – and this did take everyone by surprise – they added a recommendation for leniency.

The judge heard them, and asked the convicted man whether he had anything to say? He had not.

The judge then sentenced him to fifteen years' penal servitude.

Abby felt dizzy, and the two sisters clutched one another staring down at Rory. Fan was weeping against Abby's bosom, and this somehow strengthened Abby so that she herself did not break down. Rory looked up at them, and Abby looked down as Rory was led out of the court room.

'We'll go and see him before they take him away,' she murmured. And then, 'Thank God they made the plea for clemency.'

As they stood outside the court room waiting for Mr O'Toole, one of the jurymen passed her and recognising him, she stopped him to thank him on behalf of her brother.

'You're his sister?' He looked down at her contemptuously. 'So you're the one, eh? We heard of ye. That ye had whored with Randolph Pelham, every one of us knew it, and we thought the more of your brother that he never brought ye before the court to buy himself off by your shame.' He gave a contemptuous shake of his head and passed on.

Her face burning, Abby turned away. Fan had heard it too. 'Whored with Mr Pelham? Abby, is that true? Is that why Rory went after him?'

Abby nodded still looking down.

'So Rory's to go to prison for your shame?' Fan went on.

'I wanted him to say it! I asked Mr O'Toole last night to tell Rory to say it was my fault. But he wouldn't.' And now at last she covered her face with her hands and burst into tears.

'Abby, how *could* you!' Fan was beside herself. 'We'll never be able to live here now! What are we going to do? Rory's gone to prison – and you've the name of a whore! Did ye never think? Oh Jesus, Abby!'

'Don't you think I don't know? Don't you think I haven't lain awake this many and many a night and thought it over? I did it for the best, Fan, I thought to save us! And now—'

'And now you've the name of a whore and Rory's in prison,' Fan repeated coldly, 'and what's to become of us, there's no knowing.'

She turned and walked away.

Abby sat facing Mr O'Toole in his office. Morning sunlight streaked through the dusty atmosphere, over the papers crowding the desk where he sat.

139

O'Toole looked tired, slumped in his chair. She had seen that the second she entered the office. Even so, he was neatly dressed, his tie perfectly knotted, his coat brushed. Beyond him she glimpsed the square, people going past the window, morning business, real life.

'And – will he have to serve his whole sentence, sir?' she asked tentatively.

He looked down, examined his fingernails briefly. 'It depends. On his behaviour.' O'Toole looked up at her sympathetically. 'It can be reduced under certain circumstances. For good behaviour, perhaps after eight or ten years.'

She rested her head on her hand on the edge of his desk, until, after a pause, looking up again wearily, 'And do you know which prison he's going to?'

'Portland.'

'Is that in Australia?'

O'Toole smiled slightly. 'England.' The smile disappeared again. 'I'll be honest with you, Miss O'Leary. It won't be easy. English prisons are not pleasant places. And Irish prisoners are not popular with the other inmates.'

Abby took a hold on herself, straightening her back. 'He will be able to have visitors?'

He nodded again. 'After the first six weeks.'

'Can you give me the address?'

He leant forward, scribbled across a piece of rough paper, and pushed it across the desk. She took it, stared a moment at it, then folded it carefully, and stowed it in a pocket.

Then after another moment she stood up, composing herself and looking down at him at his desk, very serious. 'I will never be able to thank you for what you have done.'

He raised a hand, deprecatingly, but she went on, deadly earnest, 'I will not forget this, Mr O'Toole. You have helped my brother, and you have been very kind to me. If there is ever – *ever* – anything I can do for you –' she hunted for the words – for in truth, what likelihood was

140

there that she would ever be able to be of assistance to a man like him? 'Ever,' she repeated, and went on in a whisper, 'I want you to remember that.' Slightly confused, she turned rapidly and hurried out of his door, into the corridor and into the street.

She was crossing the square when she caught sight of a heavy round-shouldered man leading a horse. Even from the back she recognised him at once.

She walked quickly across to him.

'You said you'd take me to London,' she said in an expressionless voice, looking him in the eyes and crossing her arms.

He stopped, taken by surprise, and said nothing for a moment. A sly smile spread across his mouth as he looked her over.

'You could have a big success there, Abby.' He looked carefully into her eyes, with the impudent smile on his fat lips, and went on thoughtfully, 'with the right management . . .'

Abby turned to the horse he was leading, rubbed her nose and ran her hand over the mare's side. 'When do you want to go?' she said without looking at him.

He ignored the abrupt note in her voice, and after a moment went on thoughtfully, 'And if you were prepared to show your gratitude in the appropriate manner . . .' He watched her shrewdly.

'Whatever you want,' she said at last in a low, heavy tone. Then, as he approached her and was about to put his hand on her arm, she stepped back.

'After.'

'Is that a promise?' he said softly, his eyes shining, his lips wet and slightly parted.

'It is.'

Part Two

Chapter Fourteen

She was awake again, as her brain cleared gradually and her eyes focused. A pain nagged in her neck and shoulder where her head had been leaning uncomfortably, and at last, exhausted and unable to help herself, had fallen against the man's shoulder beside her. Pulling herself slowly and with difficulty upright again, she tried to stretch herself despite being pressed between these two men.

The train gave a distant whistle and through the window she saw lights flicker past and then darkness again. She shivered and attempted to rearrange the shawl round her shoulders, but one end was securely fastened beneath the fat man beside her.

In the fitful light of the one oil lamp swinging from the ceiling she looked across at Thady. He was asleep. Earlier, when they had boarded the train at Liverpool, Thady had been lively; loud and assertive. Travelling to London was apparently nothing to him; he told complete strangers he had often been there. Abby had watched in silence as he unwrapped a loaf and some slices of ham from a newspaper and, talking loudly in his offhand manner, absent-mindedly passed a bit of it across to her. The man beside him, compelled to listen, had glanced across at her as he did so, but Thady hadn't noticed, as he pulled a whiskey bottle from his pocket and took a mouthful.

She studied him now, his head propped across the bulkhead, his mouth open; studied the blotched and mottled cheeks, the thinning hair, turning grey and disarranged untidily across his heavily lined forehead; studied the stubble chin, noticed the hairs growing from his nostrils, the dirty open neck of his shirt, and the neckerchief, its knot twisted round to the left.

She tried to think back over the succession of events that had brought her to this moment. Yet think as hard as she might, she was unable to see how it could have been any other way. She had to come.

Had it been only the previous morning that she had said goodbye to her aunt and Da and Fan? It seemed already in another lifetime. Eileen had been implacable. What she was doing was wrong, it was a sin, and she would never be able to return to the village. Abby had tried to explain that it was not like that (or not like that yet, she inwardly corrected herself). It didn't matter what Eileen said, Rory was in England and Abby had to be near him. Eileen shook her head, while Fan watched with a stony glum stare. Finally, after stumbling out a few unconvincing words that it wasn't at all what they thought and that she would send money the first day she got any, she told them she would just go down to the presbytery to look at their furniture, still in Father McMichael's barn, to remind herself of home, and in the hope that they would all one day be together again in one of their own.

It was while these thoughts were running through her mind that she noticed something in her pocket, and drawing it out found it was a medal which Randolph had given her. She examined it. 'Doesn't mean a thing,' he had said in his offhand way. 'One chap gets one, or another – the high-ups haven't the foggiest idea what really happens. Have it if you like.' In her childish enthusiasm, in her simplicity, she had been pleased with the trinket, this talisman of faraway places, of bold and splendid deeds. She stared at it now, turning it over, frowning as she made out the words 'Ashanti Campaign' and the queen's head. It was because of him that she was sitting here now. And, turning the medal over, a coldness settled round her heart. One day, Randolph Pelham, one day ... she didn't know how ... but one day ...

Thady stirred, smacked his lips, adjusted his weight, and went back to sleep. Her attention was drawn across to him. Looking at him now, it seemed incredible she had ever been in awe of him; incredible he could ever have been made head groom. Sam knew a thousand times more about horses than he. So did she, if she thought about it. Yet Thady had a certain brazen, immovable impudence that enabled him to carry off what another man, though more gifted, lacked the confidence to achieve.

Thady had been momentarily abashed when she confronted him with it. 'So, Mr Thorpe's given you your marching orders, I hear?'

He looked at her in an offhand, sideways look. 'Who's been talking to you?'

'Who do you think? Sam, of course. I saw him in Westport.'

Thady snorted. ''Tis little he knows of the matter.' But he bridled as he saw the smile curling on her lip. 'What's funny?'

'It looks like Columbine was one horse too many for Mr Thorpe,' she said mockingly. 'I only hope he didn't lose too much when he sold her.'

Thady scowled. ''Twas a fine mare that only needed handling.'

'A pity Miss Marianne couldn't handle her. I pity for you, I mean, Mr O'Farrell, since she cost you your job.'

Now Thady shifted again, wiped the back of his hand across his mouth, yawned and opened his eyes. Looking across at her, his concentration gradually focused. He grinned, then winked. 'Soon be there.'

She said nothing, only glancing out into the blackness. Somewhere a distant light moved slowly past.

Dawn at last began gradually to filter through the dirty

147

window and the passengers round her were waking, first one, stretching and gaping, then another, and then from somewhere behind her a baby began to cry and a woman could be heard soothing it. Hearing that baby, Abby suddenly asked herself: suppose she hadn't been thrown by Columbine? Suppose that was herself with Randolph's baby in her arms? Staring away out of the window, still in a dull, half-awake state, she could see herself so clearly with a baby, could feel its weight, twisting and stretching in her arms, its eyes staring about it, reaching and clutching with its tiny fingers at her shawl. That would have been good, wouldn't it? That would have been a fine surprise for Aunt Eileen and Father McMichael. The man beside her shifted and she moved to make way for him, braced herself and put away those unprofitable thoughts.

The day had broken as the train pulled in to the station and came to a stop. All around her people reached up for packages, bags and parcels and she reached for her small bundle too.

'Where are we going?' she asked as they made their way along the platform in the crowd.

He gave a knowing shake of the head. 'You'll see.'

She said no more but kept pace by his side until they were outside the station and on a street corner. The crowds from the train were dispersing and already the streets were busy, a heavy haywain lumbering past, a covered wagon, a smart cab clipping along. She was at first distracted by these sights, but turning back she saw Thady talking to a man. She caught the words 'Hyde Park Corner', and the man was saying something and pointing along the road. As he went on his way she said, 'I thought you knew the way?'

'I was just refreshing my memory.'

She shrugged. 'Is that what you call it?'

They set off now, her bundle over her shoulder, and from time to time Thady took a turn to the left or the right. London was very crowded and very big. It seemed to go on and on, as they trudged down one street and then another, till she was faint with hunger, and only when she asked whether they couldn't have some breakfast did he eventually stop in a narrow street where a café opened at the corner. It was crowded with working men in woollen caps, their trousers rolled up to reveal heavy boots, smoking little pipes and drinking tea and spirits. The air was thick with smoke and steam. Thady managed to find them space at the end of a bench at a narrow marble-topped table. Around her men were busy with piled-up plates of bacon and sausages, and she felt quite dizzy, until at last the proprietor leaned across to them, giving the marble a professional wipe with a teacloth as he asked what they wanted. Thady had no sooner opened his mouth when the man straightened, said very loudly, 'No Irish here!' and jerked his thumb at the door. Everybody looked round at them and there was silence, for a second Abby sat frozen, staring up at the man. Thady blustered, 'My money's as good as any man's!' but the man said nothing, only pointed.

She felt grotesquely out of place, aware of the shawl over her head, her face glowing with embarrassment and anger. Without a word, and without looking at Thady, she pushed through the tables and was out of the door. A moment later he followed her, turning to shout, but there were laughs and whistles, and she heard, 'Beggars! Get along with you!'

Her heart beat violently and she stared away down the street till, Thady striding past, she followed him. They stumped down the pavement in silence, as she tried to control her breathing, to still the beating of her heart. In her anger it was clear to her: she was in a foreign country, something which had stupidly never occurred to her before, a country which would never welcome her. In her hurry, the shawl had fallen round her shoulders. She hated it; it made her look like a foreigner, someone to be elbowed aside, to be turned out, overlooked. She reached her hand to touch her hair, still short like a boy's. What a sight she must look; she bent her head, clenching her jaws.

Later they turned into another café, even poorer than the

149

first and to her relief the proprietor was himself an Irishman. Her anger was gradually dissipating.

'Thank God, I thought I was going mad,' she told him. 'We were turned out of the last one.'

'Well, you'll not be turned out of here,' he announced in a Kerry accent. 'What can I get you?'

By mid-morning she had lost all idea how far they had come. She couldn't believe a city could be so big. Thady had to ask the way again and again.

'The great man that knows London like the back of his hand,' she said wearily, as they set off once again.

But after she had given up hope of ever reaching their destination – whatever it was – and she was already beginning to wonder where they were going to spend the night, she glimpsed trees in the distance, and Thady exclaimed, 'Ah!' and soon they found themselves staring through iron railings at a huge public park. Near them, along a sanded trail, men rode on horseback. Nursemaids pushed perambulators, elegantly dressed men and women sauntered. The trees were in fresh leaf and in the distance water glinted in the sunlight. It was very orderly, polite, and well behaved. It was a glimpse of paradise.

'Hyde Park,' said Thady triumphantly.

'It must be very expensive to go in,' she murmured as she looked about her.

'Expensive, you cuckoo! Of course it's not expensive. Anyone can go in.'

'But how much does it cost?'

'It doesn't cost anything. Don't be so ignorant.'

'You mean – we could go in if we wanted?' She was still studying the beautifully dressed ladies and gentlemen parading by, as her hands grasped the railings. Then, slowly pulling herself away at last, she turned and saw herself and Thady, two grotesque scarecrows from a faraway country, out of place, ridiculous.

'And this is where I'm supposed to have a great future?' she asked.

'Trust me. I know where I am now. Come on.'

She followed him along beside the railings for some time, constantly looking through as some handsome cavalry officer would gallop by, or now a lady in a splendid black habit flash past too, and then further ahead, she saw them draw up, and sit talking. She was weary and beginning to get hungry again.

Thady now crossed the road – he never looked back for her, simply expected her to follow – and into a narrow street leading behind a high and imposing white palace-like terrace of what must surely be aristocratic residences. The street led them into a square; they passed across that, and then unexpectedly, he turned into a very narrow cobbled way, under an arch, and they found themselves behind the tall houses on the square in a narrow street of stables smelling of horses, and where several were to be seen, grooms leading them in or out, and one busy combing a large grey. For a moment it reminded her of Mr Thorpe's stables.

'Wait here.'

Thady approached the man busy with the comb, they were in conversation for a moment, then the man pointed up at a window. Thady nodded and crossed to a small door beside an open stable door, and disappeared inside.

She waited. Time passed. The man who had glanced at her, resumed his combing. As she waited she was able to take in her surroundings better. She also felt a distinct relief. She should have known this was what Thady had in mind. A job with horses; it was obvious. There was plenty for her to do here, the pressure lifted, and her heart felt lighter. She would have no trouble fitting in; here she could be the equal of anyone. Why had she had such apprehensions? She had been braced for the worst, and in fact, she could not have come to a better place.

Thady was gone a long time. Minutes passed. The man finished his combing, and he led the grey into the stable, giving Abby another look. There was silence, and for a while the place was deserted.

Now there was a clatter of hooves as two young men came by her under the arch, there were shouts, and another groom ran out to take the bridles as the riders swung themselves to the ground and one of them tossed a coin to the man who caught it in mid air. 'Next Tuesday!' he shouted as they turned towards the arch again, and one of them glanced at her, giving her a minute's appraisal.

She felt slightly uncomfortable at his frank stare, but then they had gone. Now it seemed everyone was staring at her. But even as she wished Thady would hurry up, he reappeared, followed by a stout, middle-aged man in riding clothes, top boots, and a red coat. He had, like Thady himself, a heavy self-important manner, and a large moustache. He stopped as he saw Abby, and Thady turned back to him, was saying something, as the man looked her over. She could have been a horse herself, she thought. Maybe they'd like to see her teeth?

'Abby, this is Colonel Wilkes. I've been telling him about you.'

They stood before her.

'O'Farrell tells me you're a crackin' good horsewoman. Is that so?' His breath smelled of beer, and he heaved audibly as he breathed.

'I'll ride any horse you show me,' she said quietly.

He raised an eyebrow, and looked her over for another second. 'We'll soon find out,' he said dryly, and turned to call over his shoulder. 'Jenkins! Saddle up The Baron for a lady.'

A head appeared at a stable door. 'Did you say a lady, Colonel?'

'What's the matter – you deaf?'

'Right away, Colonel.'

The colonel turned towards the stable door, and she and Thady followed him. Inside they found the groom fitting a side saddle to one of the biggest horses she had ever seen – an elegant 'park hack' – and a stallion.

The groom led him out past her to a mounting block nearby.

'And saddle up Frisky for me.'

'For you – but who's to ride The Baron?' The groom looked round at them in surprise.

The colonel gestured at Abby. 'She is – so she says.'

Chapter Fifteen

Abby said nothing, but ascended the mounting block as the groom held the stallion by the bridle. The groom was looking up at her uncertainly. She ignored his look, seated herself, hooked her legs round the twin pommels of the side saddle, and arranged her skirt as best she could.

'You can let go,' she said dryly, determined to show no expression. She had come all the way from Kilnevin for this, and if she didn't get it right, she might be going all the way back. The groom still seemed uncertain, but eventually handed her up the reins. Immediately, the stallion took a pace to the side, as if to try her out in a preliminary trial of wills. Jenkins had disappeared into another stable. Thady and the colonel were watching her.

'Give me a cane.'

The colonel handed up the one he had been holding. Even so, even as she tried to preserve a cool exterior, she was acutely conscious that this was by far the largest horse she had ever sat, and a stallion, which she had rarely ridden.

The Baron, without any warning, now started turning on himself in a circle, as if to make a fool of her. She leant forward to speak to him. 'Hush now, darling boy, take it easy, and we'll get along fine,' she murmured in the stallion's ear, at the same time taking a gentle grip on the reins. Trying to seem calm, she leaned forward again, still

154

whispering in the horse's ear, and gently straightening his head. For the moment The Baron decided to give up this game.

Jenkins led out another horse, and Colonel Wilkes mounted her. He glanced across at Abby. 'Ready?'

She nodded, and he led the way over the cobbles, beneath the arch. She was acutely conscious, as she walked him across the square, of the height of this horse, his huge strength, the massive haunches lifting and falling behind her, the strength coiled in them. The Baron lifted his head and snorted. A moment later he gave himself a shake. Abby understood him now. This was a thoroughbred who was eating too much and not getting enough exercise. Once she got him into the park, it would take all her strength to hold him in check.

'This horse needs a good run,' she said in a matter-of-fact tone. 'He's fat and out of condition.' The colonel was watching her closely. 'Once we're in the park I'm going to give him his head. After he's worked off some steam, he'll be in a better mood.'

The colonel looked worried. 'Eh? Don't go wearing him out.'

They crossed the main thoroughfare, and through the gates into the park where she found herself on the sandy trail she had been looking at earlier. It was deserted, stretching away beneath the trees. She glanced back at the colonel. 'Here goes.' She leaned forward, hissing 'ss-ss' into The Baron's ear, and loosed his head. The Baron needed no second invitation and launched into a flat-out gallop. She was taken by surprise even so by his impetuosity, caught off balance, and anchoring herself round her pommels instinctively, had to take a moment to right herself. The Baron was stretched full out, his ears laid back, going for his life, and in a few seconds, though she scarcely noticed, they had come down to the lake and were galloping along where the sandy path extended beside it. Two men, who had been walking their horses in conversation, looked round in astonishment as

155

she flashed past, and she was half conscious of them – but not looking very hard – because she was filled with a glorious exulting, that she was in her rightful place, and the colonel could follow as best he might on his tame little mare. As for wearing him out, The Baron wasn't to be worn out so easily.

They had reached the end of the lake and he showed no sign of drawing breath, so they dashed on till the houses were drawing closer. They had almost reached the farther side of the park, and she could see traffic and a large archway, and here she turned him, scarcely pausing in his stride, and set him back along the sandy track beside the lake, which she was better able to appreciate now. The Baron seemed comfortable with her, and in a few more minutes she saw the colonel.

She drew up beside him. The heart was hammering within her, her cheeks were burning, she was in an ecstasy of pleasure. In a few brief minutes, it was as if everything had come right again for her, she was doing something she knew how to do, and she could be on equal terms with anyone.

'You've blown him!' The colonel was distressed. 'I told you not to gallop him.'

'Blown him!' She laughed. 'It'll take a sight more than that to blow this brute. He'd run all afternoon and never be blown. He was dying to gallop. It's a sin to keep him cooped up in a stable.'

'Hmph!' The colonel grunted as he turned his mare. 'You've got a point there. I can't get anyone to take him out.'

When they got back to the stables, Thady was waiting. She slipped down from The Baron's back, taking the reins.

'Which is his stall? I'll give him a rub now.'

'Eh? Jenkins can do that. Jenkins!'

The groom appeared a moment later and took The Baron's reins. Already Thady had approached Colonel Wilkes, and was in quick urgent conversation with him.

156

Abby turned between these two and the horse, uncertain what to do next.

'Is there anything you want me to do?' she called.

'No, wait there a moment.' The colonel turned back to Thady. Somewhat nettled to be ignored after the excitement of her gallop, Abby turned to where Jenkins was unsaddling The Baron.

'You managed to stay on, then?' The groom winked.

She crossed her arms and said nothing, waiting for Thady to finish. She had been so excited to find herself in a stable, and to have had such a ride on this magnificent animal. Obviously Thady had got her this job, but she was annoyed to be left out of the negotiations. Thady treated her as if he owned her.

At last, after what seemed an age, the two men turned back to her. She waited in silence, as Thady explained. 'It's all taken care of, Abby. The colonel's got a job for you.'

She could scarcely resist jumping in the air. 'I'll start now.'

'No, you've to be fitted first.'

'Fitted?'

'For your costume.'

The colonel explained. 'We'll get you kitted out in something striking. Then you take the nags out in the park. If anybody asks who you are, you just refer 'em to me.'

'Your job is to bring in the customers,' Thady explained.

She looked between them. 'And I have to wear a special uniform?'

'In a manner of speaking.' The colonel nodded. 'I'll send you round a woman I know tomorrow. In the meantime your friend here can make himself useful round the stables.'

Thady turned at this; it was unexpected, and a shade of annoyance crossed his face.

She scarcely noticed. Already her mind was filled with the spectacle of herself in a beautifully tailored habit riding The Baron, and drawing admiring glances. They would ask

157

who she was; she would disdainfully direct them to Colonel Wilkes' stables. It was a dream come true.

Soon afterwards they went out to the Bathurst, a public house on the corner which the colonel had pointed out, and were shown to a room upstairs. It contained two beds.

Suddenly overcome with tiredness, she stood in the doorway. 'Where do I sleep?'

Thady pushed her into the room. 'Don't worry. We'll sort something out later. This is all they've got tonight.'

She looked round the room. Fortunately for her there was a screen. Then, suddenly the stresses and strains of the journey were too much for her; Thady left her, she threw herself across one of the beds, and was asleep immediately.

She was being shaken awake. Thady was standing over her. One candle stood on the mantelpiece. 'We'll go down and get a bite to eat.'

Later, she brought a can of hot water up from the kitchen to wash herself. There was a girl down there, Rosie, but she was rushed off her feet as it was, and Abby thought it simpler to bring the water up herself than to wait. She arranged the screen, and changed into her nightgown. Thady was waiting, sitting on the edge of one of the beds. He was watching her intently. There was an awkward silence as she pulled back the covers of the other one, and climbed into it.

'Abby—'

'What?'

'You remember? Your promise?'

'I told you. I said – after.' He made a move towards her, but she repeated quickly, 'After.'

He made another ingratiating gesture. 'Aren't you going to thank me – for getting you the job? Aren't you going to thank your old Thady?'

She slipped down into the bed. After a while, she muttered, 'I'm tired. I'm going to sleep now.'

*

The following morning she was taken by the colonel to a house in a back street nearby where a dressmaker, Mrs Cadogan, took her measurements. She seemed a real expert, because she made Abby strip down to her shift, and took a lot of trouble to get the most exact measurements she could.

Over the next few days the colonel kept both her and Thady busy in the stables. Then she was sent to be fitted for her new habit. She knew the way now but the colonel insisted on coming too. 'I'm paying enough for this,' he explained. He waited in the front parlour as Abby went into the fitting room at the back. There on a dummy hung an ensemble in fiery red velvet. It was of a semi-military cut, with tassels and frogging across the front, and a stand-up collar with gold lace ornament. Rather unmilitaristically, however, it was short at the ankle, and had a vent at the front as far as the knee. Altogether it was the oddest costume she had ever seen, quite unlike the elegant ensemble Miss Marianne had worn.

Abby undid her dress and as it slid to the ground, Mrs Cadogan in a matter-of-fact tone said, 'That too,' gesturing at her chemise.

Abby didn't understand and stood staring at her for a moment.

'Get it off, love,' the woman repeated.

'But—'

'The colonel wants it made to measure.'

'I don't understand.'

'It's simple enough.' The woman was fiddling with the red ensemble, easing it off the dummy.

For a moment Abby stood clutching the chemise about her, staring at the woman. The woman did not look round again. So, not quite knowing what she was doing, Abby pulled her chemise over her head, naked now to the waist, in drawers, her stockings and boots.

'Now –' the woman, a mouthful of pins, turned and was holding a pair of red trousers, and held them so Abby could

159

step into them. She buttoned them up, tight, figure hugging. Then Mrs Cadogan eased the costume off the dummy and Abby and she worked, fitting it round her, as Abby slipped her arms into the sleeves. 'Turn round.' The woman began doing up the hooks and eyes, as Abby watched herself in the looking glass.

'Now I understand.' She surveyed herself as the woman adjusted the costume at the back, taking in every last inch of material till it was skin tight, without a wrinkle. '"Fitted" is the word. Any tighter and I shan't be able to breathe.'

'How does it look?' They heard the colonel calling.

The woman threw open the door, 'See for yourself.'

He appeared in the doorway and looked her over. Abby, feeling like a dummy herself, turned slowly round. 'It doesn't leave much to the imagination, does it?'

'That's the idea.' He looked round the room. 'What about the hat?'

Mrs Cadogan turned and picked up a little military-style cap from a chair. 'Try that.'

Abby adjusted it as best she could, tucking up the ruins of her hair beneath it.

The colonel looked her up and down. 'We'll get you a pair of boots.'

'All right, that's enough. I'll have it ready tomorrow.' The woman shut the door in his face.

As Abby dressed herself again and the woman hung the costume on the dummy, and was fiddling with it, putting in pins, and making a small adjustment with a pair of dress-maker's scissors, Abby was filled with rather mixed feelings. She had imagined herself in something like one of Miss Marianne's habits, elegant, refined. But this scarlet outfit was like something out of a circus. What on earth were people to think of her riding in the park in an en-semble like that? She was very thoughtful as they walked back to the stable. The colonel, however, was ebullient. 'That woman knows what she's about.' He breathed in with

160

satisfaction. 'I couldn't have designed it better myself. My God, what an effect you're going to make! Every man in London is going to be beating a path to the stables. It'll be the making of us. A stroke of genius, even if I say so myself!'

A day later a small girl appeared at the public house early with a brown paper parcel, and Abby carried it up to the room. Thady was still in bed, dishevelled from sleep and looking out blearily as she came in clutching the parcel. But he sat up quick enough when he realised what she was carrying. 'Let's see it!'

She left the parcel on the bed and went down to the kitchen. 'Rosie, will ye just spare me two minutes to help me into this outfit they've sent? I can't ask that Thady . . .'

The kitchen maid wiped her hands, and followed her back upstairs. Thady was still in bed sitting up in anticipation. But Abby arranged the screen and, huddling behind it, Rosie helped her into the ensemble, doing up the innumerable hooks and eyes down the back. Rosie was impressed. 'Cor! Don't you look something! Like a princess!'

Princess! thought Abby. A tart in a circus, more like.

But the effect on Thady was even stronger. His eyes stood out as he devoured this apparition, and Abby felt even more embarrassed. It was going to be like this all round the park.

'Thanks, Rosie,' she said as the girl hurried downstairs. She took up the little cap. 'Well, better get to work, I suppose.'

161

Chapter Sixteen

She stopped in the doorway, thinking.

'There isn't even a lookin' glass. How does me hat seem?'

Thady still in bed, was still mesmerised. 'Ye look like a queen,' he breathed.

'You'd better get out of that, there's work to be done. The colonel'll be after you.'

'But Abby,' he wheedled, 'aren't ye grateful to your old Thady for gettin' ye the job?'

'You're doing all right out of it, aren't you? I haven't seen any money yet.'

He was more confident at this, leaning back on the pillow and shaking his head. 'Ah, don't worry about the money, 'tis all taken care of.'

'Does that mean I get any wages?'

'The colonel and me have come to an arrangement,' Thady smiled knowingly.

There was a moment as she surveyed his unlovely form in the crumpled bed, then she pulled herself together. 'I'm off – to work.'

At the stable Jenkins and the other grooms gathered to admire her and, as Jenkins led out The Baron she felt very self-conscious, arrayed in this brilliant striking outfit among the scruffy unkempt grooms and the piles of manure.

'Don't get any mud on your boots.'

Abby had as usual provided herself with a paper bag of broken sugar lumps, and fed a handful to her horse as she greeted him, rubbing his nose, talking to him softly. By now he knew her; she had brushed him down many times, stayed with him in his stall talking to him, stroking him, making friends with him.

As she rode across the square and into the park, she felt every eye must be upon her. 'They'll all be thinking, who's she? Is the circus come to town?' she thought. But then she drew a deep breath and took a grip on herself. She was here to do a job; this was work. She was being paid – at any rate, Thady was being paid for them both. She'd better just get on with it.

She set The Baron into a gallop, down through the park to the lake. It was a glorious day in June, the summer leaf was out, thick and fresh, and there was a lightness in the air. Seeing the morning sunlight glinting on the water, and to be riding such a splendid and strong horse – her heart rose. Only thinking back a few weeks it was astonishing how her luck had changed. She had fallen on her feet again; and she must make the most of it. She cheered up. She would enjoy her ride, and if she were accosted by anyone, well, she could just do the colonel's bidding. That was the agreement.

There were other riders in the park, scattered here and there, and two children on ponies who turned to watch her as she galloped past. But then, as she had completed a circuit of the lake, and was walking The Baron, wondering how long the colonel expected her to stay out, she noticed two men on horseback who had been watching her, and who now started towards her. What was she supposed to do? Wait for them? Something in her revolted at this, colonel or no, and without thinking she gave The Baron a touch of the spur, and he was off again in an instant. But as she was galloping away, she couldn't resist turning and sure enough they had set off in pursuit of her. A smile came

163

quite spontaneously to her lips, and she gave the stallion another touch of the spur, loosening the rein as he lengthened his stride. 'They'll never catch me,' she was certain. Neither was on a horse to match hers – a couple of hired nags, no doubt broken-winded long ago. And after ten minutes, by which time she was almost at the other end of the park, she drew up, turned and saw them, far away behind her.

And as she saw them still struggling to catch up with her, she couldn't help giggling aloud, as she realised this could be great fun. What a mystery she would be! No one would know who she was – she would become the talk of London – the mysterious woman on that huge stallion. Tongues would wag! All the handsome rich young men would be dying to find out her identity – but none should. That was for sure. She would remain anonymous, the mysterious rider in red. Who was she? The town would be on fire to know! Articles would appear about her in the press. Songs would be sung in the music hall. Sums of money would be offered for her identity – perhaps offers of marriage? Crowned heads of vague far-off European countries would vie for her hand but they should never know her identity – she would disappear – and . . .

She sobered up as she began to cool in her saddle. The men had turned away in any case. This was not what Colonel Wilkes was paying Thady for. She wasn't supposed to be running away from them: her job was to entice them to his stable. She frowned and turned The Baron's head. But even as she did so, she almost ran into two men – two other men – who had come up. They both raised their hats before she had a chance to think.

'Good morning!'

And she had to reply, 'Good morning.'

They were both young, good-looking, and well off too by the look of them. They were smiling. She smiled. It was difficult not to.

'Well, this is a treat,' said one of them. 'I don't think I

ever saw a horse go like that. Did you, Darke? What a vision!' He was blonde, pale complexioned, and rather heavy in the body. His accent was English and aristocratic. He turned to her again, in a free and easy way. 'Tell us, young lady – what's the secret? You must be made of iron.'

'Don't be such an oaf. What a thing to say,' the other one intervened. 'As if she were made of anything so vulgar. What are little girls made of? Sugar and spice and all things nice. Isn't that so?' he appealed to Abby.

The first one – the heavy one – looked serious. 'Well now, only the young lady can answer that.' He brought his horse up beside her. 'Strictly in confidence, of course, which is it to be – iron – or all things nice?' He raised his eyebrows.

'Oh – all things nice, of course,' she smiled again, quite helpless with such concentrated attention on both sides.

'By Jove, an Irish girl! What a coincidence, eh?' Mr Darke, who she noticed had dark eyes too, turned to his companion.

'Rather.' The two of them were now on either side of her, and they began walking their horses back towards the lake.

She looked between them. 'What coincidence?'

'My friend there,' Mr Darke pointed across with his crop. 'From the old emerald sod, too.'

She looked back. 'Really?' He certainly didn't sound like it.

'Limerick.'

'An Irishman! Just like meself!' She turned to him in astonishment.

He too appeared delighted, and held out his hand. 'O'Shea. But call me Willie.'

She too held out her hand, but by some sudden instinct withheld her name. 'Delighted, I'm sure.' In that moment, too, she remembered her job. There was a momentary pause. Clearly they had expected her to tell them her name. She smiled at each in turn as she realised this.

'Isn't it a grand day for a ride?' she said cheerfully. 'Come on, gentlemen, you see the teahouse?' She pointed with her cane. 'I'll race you!' She clapped her spur to The Baron's side and shot away from them. In an instant, they were off too, and she could feel them on either side, close behind. She turned, grinning to one of them.

'Come on! Give her the spur!' Urging the stallion faster, she drew away from them, and by the time she reached the teahouse by the lakeside, they were urging their labouring mounts on with difficulty.

'Livery stable nags, gentlemen,' she called. 'They'll never do. Next time come round to Colonel Wilkes' in Bayswater. The best in town! Cheerio!' And she set her horse off again across the park and left them sitting. She turned once to wave, and saw them watching her on their exhausted horses.

'Ten shillings.' He counted the money in his hand. 'That's pocket money,' he added, 'and you're to get yourself some nice clothes too. We'll get that woman to run somethin' up for ye.' A candle burned on the mantelpiece in the summer evening. The window was open and they could hear children calling to each other in the street. Thady and she were sitting on their beds facing each other.

'You mean – all this – is for me? Just for me?' She stared down at the coins.

'All for you. The colonel's very pleased with ye, Abby. You're a hit.'

Ten days had gone by since her first day in the park. By now she was at home in her scarlet ensemble. Dozens of men had accosted her, and she had found some repartee to satisfy them all. She had seen them turning up at the stables later. The colonel was very pleased.

'Now Abby—' Thady jingled the coins in his hand as she stared down at them. 'You remember your promise?' he looked up into her face. 'Ye've done well. And this is only the beginning. But it's time to reward old Thady. You

166

wouldn't be here today, only for him ... don't forget old Thady ...'

She looked him square in the eyes, then stood abruptly, and held out her hand. As he placed the coins into it, she put them into her pocket, then began undoing the hooks and eyes down the back of her dress with quick practised fingers. The dress fell about her ankles. She swept the chemise over her shoulders, pushed down her drawers, trod them to the floor, threw back the bedclothes, and lay down.

'Only mind, there's to be no baby.'

Thady, his hands shaking, was wrenching at the flap of his trousers. 'Ye mean it?'

'I said it, didn't I? Do what you want.'

'Oh Abby, oh God, dear Jesus, you're a queen, a goddess—'

In a moment Thady, still dressed, had flung himself on to her. She turned away her face; she had said nothing about kissing. As he squirmed on top of her, hurriedly finding his way into her, she stared at the bright square of the open window. And as he thrust himself in, she concentrated on listening to the sound of the children calling to each other. They were playing some pavement game, chanting in a sing-song repetitive rhythm she had never heard before, then for some reason breaking into laughter. It was the wonderful sound of innocence, a simple game, that seemingly went round and round in a never-ending loop, starting in on itself, never wearying.

He was soon done, falling beside her with a small gasp. She turned on her side with her back to him, and concentrated on the children singing in the street. After a while she was aware of Thady getting off the bed, and then she heard him, in a small voice:

'Abby?'

She did not reply.

'Will we go for a drink downstairs?'

She said nothing, did not move.

'Abby?'

167

Nothing.

'I'll – I'll see ye in a while, then?'

A moment later she heard the door close. She still lay, her mind empty, listening to the sound of the children. After a very long time, when it was completely dark, she turned on her back, staring at the ceiling. She shivered slightly, and pulled the covers over her. She must write to Rory. She must find out when she would be able to go down to visit him. That was the main thing. And she must write to Aunt Eileen to let her know everything was all right.

'What do you think?'

An extraordinary vision had walked into the bar of the Bathurst. She put down her glass in frank astonishment and for a moment was speechless. Thady was transformed. A black velvet smoking jacket, fawn trousers, shiny patent leather boots, a quilted waistcoat with a gold chain across it, a curly-brimmed bowler hat, a silver-topped walking stick.

'What—'

'Aren't ye going to say anything?'

'I don't understand, Thady, I mean, how – they must have cost—'

'Never worry about that! Things are looking up.' He waved at the barman. 'A large whiskey – hot and strong. This is how it's going to be from now on. Abby, we're going to live in style. We're on the way up!'

'But Thady, they must have cost—'

'Leave old Thady to worry about the money. Me and Colonel Wilkes, we've got it all arranged.'

He brought his glass to where she was finishing the remains of a plate of beef and potatoes. 'And you're not to be forgotten. The colonel—' he coughed. 'I thought, Abby, you're to have more new clothes too. We're going round to Mrs Cadogan's this afternoon to talk about clothes for you. We're going to live in style from now on.'

Abby was in fact already wearing the new dress Mrs Cadogan had made for her; it was a huge improvement on her old red dress, and tailored to her figure. Abby had not had the first notion of fashions and when Mrs Cadogan had made the dress, had had to take her ideas entirely on trust. Still, in the few weeks she had been riding in the park she had learned fast. Every afternoon from five to seven the whole of society crammed into the park, particularly along the south side – 'Rotten Row' – and watching them, she realised what in a way she already understood, that the red outfit the colonel had put her into was grotesquely inappropriate and quite unlike what real ladies wore. As she watched, from a distance, she saw that the understated grace and distinction of real ladies was wholly separate from the garish and vulgar display she was making. How could men ever take her seriously dressed like this? When she had tackled the colonel over it, however, he waved her aside. 'I'm not paying you to be a lady. Your job is to get the men in here.' She bit her lip and was silent.

'And Abby, we're getting out of here!'

She sat up.

'I know ye weren't so happy living over a public house – ye see, old Thady is only thinking of ye – so I've had a word – I've been puttin' out a few feelers here and there and I think I've found us something – very snug and just the thing!'

'You mean—'

'Exactly! A house of our own and not so far off, just down the road, near Marble Arch.' He reached into his pocket and produced a key.

'Thady!' She snatched it from him. 'You've done it already! A house! When can we go?'

'Now!'

'Now!' She squealed, pushing away the plate and snatching up her hat, she crammed it on her head. 'Oh let's go! I can't wait!'

Not so far away they found a quiet square, trees now in

169

thick leaf on a sunny afternoon, and four or five doors along Thady turned up a few steps to a front door. The key fitted, and they were inside, looking first into a comfortable, though not large, parlour crowded with plush arm chairs and a sofa, pictures on the wall, and a gas lamp hanging from the centre rose on the ceiling. A carpet, a little faded and worn by the fireplace, where a brass fender and a coal shuttle stood, empty now in summer. Wondering at this, and silent as she took it all in, Abby looked into the snug little dining room behind it which in turn looked out into a neglected garden. Here, too, everything was in readiness, a dining table for eight, a side table loaded with a tray of wine glasses. Another door gave into the kitchen and scullery at the back.

'I've engaged a woman to do for us.'

'Thady, it's paradise, I've never seen anything so beautiful but Thady – who's to pay for all this? I mean it must be ever so expensive.'

'Never you worry about that. Have a look upstairs.'

The front bedroom was almost filled by a wide double bed. Her heart sank; of course she should have known: this was the catch. She leaned against the wall staring at this great bed with its brass posts, as the realisation sank in. But at the very same time a resolution hardened in her. Never in a million years would she share a double bed with Thady O'Farrell.

Thady was behind her. 'That's your room, Abby,' he said cheerfully. 'Mine is at the back.'

She turned and encountered his beaming face. 'Will it suit do you think?'

'Suit? It's wonderful! But I still don't understand—'

'I told you – don't worry! When are ye going to understand? It's all taken care of. And we're to have a house-warming party.'

As they were walking back to the stables she noticed the name on the wall: Connaught Square. 'Thady, it's an omen! We've come home!'

170

Chapter Seventeen

She surveyed herself in the looking glass, picking uncertainly at the rows of little silk bows which hung in a series of descending cascades across the apron front of the gown.

'Don't you think they're . . .' It was difficult to find the words. What exactly was it? All she could think was, Miss Marianne wouldn't have had them. She would have had – well, something simpler. Abby frowned, and caught Thady's eye over her shoulder. He was enthusiastic, insistent.

'They're the fashion. That's the style this season. D'ye want to look like some simpleton from up the country?'

She drew another breath. The dressmaker, Mrs Cadogan, over her other shoulder, was watching in silence. Abby stretched, drew herself to her full height, and tried to believe in the gown. It was in satin, old gold, and certainly suited her colouring. It had the fashionable bustle, which involved her upholstering herself with a wire contraption strapped beneath it. It was meant to be a lady's dress, and yet there was something, she couldn't put her finger on it, only it all seemed so – well, overdone – there were too many flounces, it was cut too low across the bust, she thought, 'If I sneeze, I'll pop right out of it!' – it was cut rather short at the ankle to reveal layers of frilly petticoats – and there were too many bows. She felt horribly torn. In a way, all her life she had longed to see herself in a gown like this. And yet now that she was here, there was something about it – oh, she couldn't say exactly what it was ...

And as to what it cost ... as always, whenever she raised the subject, Thady was breezy. 'Leave it to Thady!'

And now there was to be the house-warming party. When she had asked, 'But who are we going to invite?' Thady had exclaimed, 'Abby darling, they'll be climbing over each other to get in!' And when, in her innocence, she blundered on, 'Who will?' He laughed, 'I suppose ye've not noticed, then, the gentlemen in the park so eager to make your acquaintance? Ye've a wide circle of admirers, Abby. The cream of society all begging to make the acquaintance of the girl in the red dress.'

She brightened at this. Of course, they must have begged an invitation from Thady. She was flattered.

So, on the night, she was ready at ten in her golden gown. The cook had been busy all day baking – various bits and pieces she didn't recognise, which now stood on the sideboard in the dining room. Thady was ready in a hired evening dress, and had managed to shave for once, and comb his thinning hair. He had already had a few whiskies; in fact, during the evening as they were setting out ashtrays, and a box of cigars on the mantelpiece, she had had to tell him to leave the whiskey bottle alone. 'You're the host,' she hissed. 'They do the drinking – not you!' as she wrenched the bottle out of his hand.

And now, at ten, she drew a breath, glanced again in a hand glass to check her hair, which a woman had come in to put up for her, the ruins now disguised by a chignon. So long as it doesn't work loose, she thought, surveying herself, with her bare neck, and her low-cut bosom, and decided that well, perhaps after all, she didn't look too bad ...

Then they were pouring up the steps and hammering at the door, and ten-year-old Sarah, the cook's daughter, was opening it as young men, old men, some very withered ones too, were crowding up to her, all eager to shake her hand – one man even bent to kiss it. It was all very flattering, she was smiling her welcome, Thady was behind her with a bottle in each hand, and it took some time before she began to see that quite a few of them were drunk. In fact, it was only when one man, pretending to bend to kiss her hand, actually planted a wet kiss on her left breast, and giggled as his friend pulled him off. She managed to laugh it off, but felt a stiffening inside.

Thady was affability personified – the cigar box now in his hand, offering one to all comers, whiskey and champagne were pouring into glasses, the talk was uproarious. It occurred to her gradually that for some reason none of the men had brought their wives, and wondered whether she was destined to be the only woman at this party, when as the door knocker crashed again, yet another high-spirited young man staggered in with his arms round the neck of two young women, whom, in somewhat incoherent fashion, he introduced. 'Martha! The Belle of the Burlington!' He swept his arm round, 'And, damme—' he stared at the other girl for a moment, till she leaned forward and whispered in his ear, at which he burst into a shrill laugh, 'Of course! Charley! Girls, allow me t'introduce – the gamest girl ever to sit a horse, the toast of the turf!' He freed his arm from Martha's neck, and reached across to clasp Abby, 'The prettiest—' and planted a kiss on her lips before she could see it coming.

Someone had opened the piano – hired for the night – and was beating out the tune of 'Champagne Charlie', and, as she circulated, she couldn't help thinking everyone seemed to be having a good time, and that was what parties were for, and – but now another man had stopped her, and insisted on refilling her glass, and then another man was beside him, and they were all asking her questions, and then another man, a rather forceful one, for some reason had a bank note in his hand which he had rolled tightly into a long spill and, as he leaned forward, he deftly tucked it down the front of her dress and, at the same time, she felt

173

his arm round her waist as he kissed her long and hard on the lips. The other men were cheering, though she heard one protesting, 'I say, Morton – unfair advantage, don't you know!' The man, whose breath smelt of whiskey, gave her a self-satisfied smirk and turning to him said something like, 'And cheap at the price, I'd say', and other men now began reaching bank notes from their pockets.

She pulled herself away, muddled and flustered, trying to smile but uncertain how to react, when the front door was savagely beaten yet again and, using this as an excuse, she pushed her way into the hallway in time to see two men she recognised – Mr O'Shea and his friend Mr Darke. She felt relief; these were real gentlemen at least.

O'Shea looked about him and was effusive. 'I say, splendid little place you've got! O'Farrell told me about it but, well, this is very nice. Now, what about a drink, eh?'

Behind him, Mr Darke gave her his dark-eyed smile, and as O'Shea was pushing into the crowded parlour, took her hand casually. 'Looks like a lively party?'

'You could say that,' she gave him a rueful grin, turning to the parlour door, and Darke, in a fatherly and comforting way, slipped his arm through hers.

As they came into the room Thady was greeting O'Shea. ''Tis grand to see ye, sir,' he said, cringing in a servile caricature of an Irish servant. 'What'll ye take – whiskey, champagne?'

She turned to Mr Darke. 'Can I offer you anything, sir?'

'What are you having?'

'Oh, I'm trying to drink as little as possible. Got to look after the guests. But you must take something.'

'Well, perhaps – a little whiskey.'

O'Shea turned to her. 'I say, Abby, are you the only girl here?'

'Oh no, there are some others, they must be next door.'

'Or upstairs?'

'Pardon?'

O'Shea burst into uproarious laughter. 'Hear that,

174

Darke? Or upstairs? Eh what?'

She turned in mystification to Mr Darke. He still held her by the arm, and gave her a small squeeze. 'Only his little joke,' he said impassively.

Now another drunken guest heaved before her, his hair dishevelled, his bow-tie twisted to one side. He was holding up a long stick-like thing which she recognised in an instant as another bank note closely rolled. 'I say, my turn, you know! Fair's fair!' He thrust it drunkenly into the front of her dress, and lurched against her. She would never have avoided his kiss if Mr Darke, his arm still through hers, had not turned her and interposed himself very neatly between them. He plucked the note from her bosom, and handed it back half over his shoulder. 'I'd hang on to it, you might need it for a cab,' he said, and before the man could reply, helped her through the crowd into the hall.

She turned to him in astonishment, uncertain what to say. He wasn't smiling, but looked at her thoughtfully. 'Got to draw the line somewhere, don't you think?' he said at last raising an eyebrow.

'Thank you.' She recovered her breath. 'I was just beginning to feel taken for granted . . .'

He was looking at her carefully, and after a moment went on, 'How long have you been over here?'

'Oh,' she tried to think, 'weeks. Let me see, we're into July now, aren't we? That must make it, oh, I don't know, so much has happened, er—' she giggled, 'five weeks? Six? I've lost track.'

He frowned. 'Lost track?' He looked round and up the stairs, from where, as if in answer to O'Shea's joke, they heard voices, a shout, and a shrill peal of woman's laughter. 'Is this your house?'

She sobered a little. 'Of course, why?'

He shrugged. 'Oh, nothing,' but glanced up again, and she felt suddenly rather embarrassed as she too took in the sounds from above.

'You're living here with O'Farrell?' he went on.

175

'In a manner of speaking.' She was awkward. 'We're not – you know – only he brought me here, and got me the job with Colonel Wilkes. So we're—' she lapsed into silence, uncertain how to finish.

Darke nodded, seeming not to notice her confusion. 'You've done well.'

'D'you think so?' she asked eagerly.

He looked round again. 'It's a nice house. And here you are, in a new gown—'

'Oh, do you like it?' Again, she wanted his approval.

He studied it carefully. 'Do you really want to know?'

She was taut. Mr Darke seemed to know so much, to understand her too easily. She waited, and then, 'Tell me.'

He considered a moment, his head on one side as he surveyed her. 'Did your friend O'Farrell design it?'

'Well, he did speak to Mrs Cadogan, that's the dress-maker, about it, yes.'

'Hmm.'

'Why, I mean – can you tell?'

'Oh you can tell, all right.'

'I don't understand.'

'To tell you the truth, Abby,' he went on in his even way, 'it doesn't entirely do you justice. You could do better for yourself.'

'In what way?' she said uncertainly.

'Well,' he surveyed the gown again. 'These bows, for instance. I'd have those off. Spoils the line of the gown – muddies the silhouette—' he took her gently by the shoulders and turned her sideways, studying her outline. 'Simplicity is the heart of elegance.'

He looked into her eyes. But she tried to break his spell; there was just a bit too much of Mr Darke; he was too assured, he knew too much . . .

The door opened and Thady reached for her arm, pulled her across to him, and whispered urgently. 'Come and talk to Captain O'Shea.'

She turned helplessly one last glance to Mr Darke, as

Thady pulled her bodily into the parlour.

'I was just telling O'Farrell about the first time I saw you in the park ...' Captain O'Shea was loud and full of himself. 'By Jove, thought I to myself, there goes a vision. Diana herself, I thought. And nothing would do but I must make her acquaintance. I'd made up my mind, the O'Sheas are all alike in this, O'Farrell –' he breathed on Thady briefly, '– once we make up our minds, don't you know, we're not to be stopped. So up I go to her, bold as you like – "What are little girls made of?" I asked her, "Sugar and spice and all things nice!" Eh what? Pretty apt, what? Look at her, like something off a cake, eh? Makes you want to eat her all up! And in a gown fit for a queen. That's what I shall call her – the Queen of the Row. By Jove, she puts the others fairly in the shade.' He reached for her hand, and held up her arm, as he inspected her. 'A queen!' He brought her hand to his mouth and gave it a lingering kiss.

Dawn had broken as she and Thady sat together amid the ruins of the party. Thady still had a whiskey glass in his hand. Abby, slumped in a chair, stared glumly into the back garden where the birds were singing.

'We have done well,' he said complacently taking a mouthful of whiskey and smacking his lips. 'I couldn't have asked for more.'

She looked up at him wearily. 'Thady, could you please get those people out of my bed? I'm tired to death.'

Thady rounded on her, scandalised. 'That is Lord Morton! Would ye have me turn a belted earl out of his bed, Abby? Think of it! The aristocracy asleep beneath our very roof! The honour of it! And think – only think, where's it going to lead? When word gets round? And it will get round – the O'Farrells entertaining aristocracy! Oh Jesus, but we're only made for life! I can see it now! The society column!' He put on a mincing English accent. 'Mr O'Farrell entertained a select party to supper on Saturday night, assisted by his comely companion Miss O'Leary, the

177

Irish belle and fair equestrienne who has been delighting society by her dashing exploits this season ...'

Abby rested her head on one hand. 'I want to go to bed ...'

'Abby darlin', can't ye see? Ye've been a smashin' success! There's no stoppin' us now. This is only the beginning.'

She shifted her position slightly, and felt something in the front of her dress. Reaching in, she plucked out the rolled up bank note and, carefully unrolling it, she found it was for twenty pounds. As she stared at it, Thady reached over and took it out of her hands.

'That'll go towards the cost of the party,' he waved it before putting it into his breast pocket. Then patting it, he looked at her again. 'It'll not be the last.'

Lord Morton was still sound asleep when Mrs Dodds arrived at eight to clean up. Abby stole into her bedroom where the 'belted earl' lay tangled up with the girl called Martha, extracted an old dress from the wardrobe, changed, and went downstairs again to start the task of clearing up after the party. All morning they worked, sweeping up the broken glass in the fireplace; shaking cigar ash out of the rugs as she stood on the doorstep on that quiet Sunday morning, washing up wine glasses, which had to be returned to the public house on the corner, and the breakages paid for, she thought, as she shovelled broken glass into the dustbin. And, as she was on her knees trying to scrape the remains of a terrine off the carpet then, as she wiped the dining-room table and saw the cigar burns on the edge, she wondered what the landlord would make of it. Thady had gone to bed.

Later that morning when there was still no sign of the earl, and she seemed for the moment to have got past her tiredness, she walked round to the stables and took The Baron out for a canter to clear her head. Alone at last, breathing the clean morning air, seeing families walking in the park after church, and children sailing boats on the Serpentine, ordinary people doing ordinary civilised things, she felt soothed after the rackety night before.

Thady, however, had got the bit between his teeth, and was not to be stopped.

'That was only the first step,' he said to her when he rose in the afternoon.

'The first step to what?'

'Into society!'

'*Society?*' she echoed. 'A groom from the County Mayo going into society? Thady, I know you were drunk last night, but you're not drunk now.'

'I know what I'm doing! Trust me. From now on, we're going to move in select circles.'

She shook her head.

'Abby! Listen to me, I know what I'm talking about. Now next week we're to have a few gentlemen to dinner – influential gentlemen, that Captain O'Shea – he's an MP – and others,' he added.

'*Him?*' She wrinkled her nose.

'He's very influential.'

She had managed to get most of the stains out of the dress, and surveyed it now as it hung on the front of her wardrobe. Looking at it, at the rows of little bows across the front, she remembered Mr Darke. Why didn't Thady invite him to dinner instead of that oaf O'Shea? Mr Darke was – she stopped and thought of him carefully. He was the only man who understood about the bows. The others had been more interested in looking down the front of her dress. She remembered the way he had slipped his arm through hers in that comforting and fatherly way.

Chapter Eighteen

'Captain O'Shea, sir! Come in, come in!' Thady was at the
door, doing his Irish servant act again. She could hear him
as she stood in the parlour, checking herself in the looking
glass over the fireplace. She had got most of the marks out
of the dress and was just hoping he wouldn't notice the
worst one, which was low down on her right side. She
would try to sit turned away on that side.

She pulled at the bust of the dress, and turned her head
to check her earrings. These were Thady's idea too. It
had been a painful fifteen minutes, but she had had
them done. The earrings had been chosen by Thady. They
were glass, but he said, 'In candlelight you can't tell the
difference.' She believed him, and thought they looked
pretty.

She had put a sort of tiara-like comb in her hair – also
glass, but Thady said – oh it didn't matter, it caught the
light as she turned her head, and she liked the effect. She
smiled at herself, and stretched the dress down over her
stays, turning to inspect the sideview.

'Come in, sir, come in.' Thady rubbing his hands,
ushered their first guest into the room. She turned and tried
to behave as she believed a gracious London hostess might,
advancing towards him, her hand outstretched.

'You're very welcome, Captain.'

He was all smiles. 'Oh, call me Willie, please.'

'Let me offer you something to drink. Thady, what can we offer Willie?'

Thady scurried across to a small table where some bottles waited.

'Whiskey for me.'

'Whiskey it is, sir,' Thady grovelled.

'Have you had a hard day, Willie – in the House?' She tried to sound relaxed, as she offered him a chair.

'Oh – the House isn't sitting. No, I'm just hanging around till the end of the season, then I'm off for a bit of shooting. Bit of a dead time now – fag end of the season. Most folk have gone already.'

'Really? And where do you hunt?'

'Hunt? You mean shoot?'

'Hunt, shoot,' she waved her hand vaguely.

Thady crossed and pressed a large whiskey into Willie's hand.

Twenty minutes passed, and no other guests appeared, then little Sarah poked her head through the door and said, 'Cook says dinner's ready, Miss,' and Thady gave her a glance, and she turned to their only guest and said, 'Perhaps you'd like to wash your hands before dinner, Willie?'

While he was out of the room, she turned to Thady. 'Hadn't we better wait for the others?'

'Ah,' he looked shifty. 'Actually, Abby darlin', I meant to tell ye – there aren't any others.'

'What?'

'But listen, he's very important, an MP, so be nice to him, ye understand? He can be very useful – and make us all kinds of contacts.'

'Useful?'

'Ye don't want to go on working for old Wilkes for the rest of your life, do ye?'

She was mystified.

'London is ours for the asking.' Thady was excited. 'Why do I have to keep tellin' ye? Can't ye see it? With

181

your looks and my brains, we're a partnership – like I always said. So be nice to Captain O'Shea, there's a darlin'.'

Fortunately Willie was happy to do all the talking, to her. Thady acted more in the way of a butler, hurrying in and out of the room to see where the girl had got to with the Brussels sprouts or the gravy, and having whispered altercations in the hall just outside the door, which she – and Willie – could hear clear enough.

After dinner they moved back into the parlour, and Abby poured Willie a glass of port; he had had quite a lot of wine already. Thady reached for the cigar box. It was empty.

'Where are the cigars?' He struck his forehead. 'Bless me soul! If I didn't only forget the cigars! Captain O'Shea, sir, will ye ever forgive me? Abby, girl, whyever didn't ye remind me about the cigars?'

'I thought you—'

'Captain darlin', I hang me head in shame.' He looked round for a moment. 'But all is not lost! Abby, d'ye think that tobacconist on the corner—'

They both watched him. 'Just ye wait there the pair of ye and Abby, why don't ye entertain the captain while I run down the road for the cigars?'

He gave her a huge wink, as Willie looked round unsteadily. 'Yes, you run along, O'Farrell, we can entertain each other.'

She handed him another glass of port, and he settled himself on to the sofa. She watched him as he tossed back the port and set the glass unsteadily on a side table.

'Damme, this is convibial – bonvicial – con – a lot of fun, don't you know. Don't know when I've had such an evening, very gracious hostess, charmer, beautiful girl, figure of an angel,' he hiccuped, 'sugar and spice, look just a fairy on a cake, makes a fellow want to eat you all up—'

He looked at her for a long moment as if he might do just that.

'I say Abby—'

'What is it?'

'You're an awful long way off, why are you so far away? Come here and sit beside Willie. Let's be con – friendly, I mean.'

'I'm quite comfy here, Willie, thank ye.'

'That's no good,' he stood up unexpectedly, reached for her hand and dragged her suddenly on to the sofa beside him. 'That's better. That's more friendly. Friendly.'

She wondered how long Thady was going to be. Willie put his arm round her waist, and sat staring into the fire. She thought he might be falling asleep.

'This is nice,' he said dreamily after a while.

She didn't like to push his arm away, and was silent for a moment, not wanting to hurt his feelings. 'Yes,' she said faintly in the end.

'Yes, very nice,' he went on in that dreamy tone. 'It's nice for you too, isn't it?'

She glanced round wondering again where Thady had got to. 'Yes,' she repeated after a while, uncertain what to do.

Then she was conscious of his hand – the one round her waist – pulling her towards himself, then creeping up under her arm towards her breast, then more confidently, reaching more fully over it. His other hand now reached across her waist and up over her bosom too.

'My God, you're—' he turned towards her, his face pink and his breath suffused with wine. He ran his free hand up over her bosom to her head, pulled her towards him and kissed her, loosely, a wet sloppy kiss which slurred round to her ear as she turned her head away in disgust.

'Willie—'

He twisted himself half on top of her, seemingly unaware of her reaction, pressing her into the corner of the sofa where it was impossible to move, his knee between her legs.

'By God, you're lovely, you're the most beautiful—' He was kissing her neck then, slipping down and burying his

183

face in her bosom, he covered her breasts with kisses. He was heavy, and it took a moment to recover from the shock, and then another to heave him away, so that he fell across the edge of the sofa and on to the floor.

He pulled himself unsteadily into a sitting position staring up at her in surprise. 'I say, what's the game?'

She was sitting up, her heart hammering, and straightening the bust of her gown. 'Game?' she said angrily. 'There isn't a game, so far as I know.'

He pulled himself up by the end of the sofa into a kneeling position, dishevelled, his tie half undone. 'Well, this won't do. Dash it. You're leading me up the garden path. I won't have it, I tell you.'

He reached for her hand, but she shook him free, stood up and retreated a pace, looking down at him, where he knelt awkwardly by the sofa. 'Get off! Who do you think you are?'

'Damme, this is no way to carry on.' He stared up at her drunkenly. 'You make all kinds of promises—'

'What promises?'

'He said you'd do anything I wanted.'

'Who did?'

'Don't you know? Your pal Thady—'

'Thady said that?'

'This is a sell! You mean you don't know?'

'I don't know anything! Are you telling me that Thady O'Farrell promised you—'

'He told me that you were in love with me and wanted – you know – to do it with me. Dash it, I paid him enough.'

'*Paid him?*' She was white with anger, shaking.

There was a long silence as they both stared at each other. Willie seemed to be sobering up. At last she said, quietly, 'I think ye'd better wait here and ask for your money back.' She turned to the door.

'I say, where are you going?'

'I'm not sure.' She ran up the stairs two at a time into her room. She could feel herself shaking as she wrenched

184

the wardrobe door open, tore down the three dresses and the coat and threw them on the bed, ducked down to pull her boots out from beneath it, threw them together and wrapped them in her red riding outfit.

She was out on the landing and heard Willie's plaintive voice at the bottom of the stairs, 'What are you doing?'

She ignored him but, on an inspiration, turned into Thady's room, threw her bundle on the bed and quickly ran her hands through the pockets of the coat hanging behind the door. She found a twenty pound note, recognised it as the one which had been rolled up, stuffed it into her pocket, snatched up her bundle, and ran quickly down stairs. Willie was still standing in the doorway.

'I say—'

She stopped at the front door and turned to him, but then, with a shake of her head, dashed down the steps and along the street. She didn't want to think. She mustn't think. How could she have failed to understand? She must have been blind and stupid, it was so obvious. Oh God she was such a fool, the tears smarted in her eyes now, a mixture of anger, humiliation, hurt pride. She hurried on. Only don't let him come after her, that was all, though she didn't know what she would do if he did. She hurried on, through the streets, dark now on the summer evening, and within ten minutes found herself at the door of the Bathurst. She pushed her way in through the late Saturday night crowd, to the bar.

'Oh, Mr Winchester, I'm sorry to trouble you, but could I have my room back?'

She lay on the bed in the darkness looking at the window, uncurtained, a lighter square in the darkness, trying to straighten out her thoughts.

Anyway, it wasn't as if he was doing anything so very strange, was it? Looking back over her weeks in London, it seemed obvious. Everything had been leading up to it. Everyone must have known. Every one but her, that is. She was only the innocent one, the dim, stupid one, the idiot of the family, who couldn't see what was staring everyone else in the face. 'Ye could have a great career there, Abby. I foresee a great future for us.' Oh, of course, a great future – 'with the right management'. How could she have been so stupid? She turned over.

She turned over again. And what now? She had completely lost sight of why she had come to England. Rory. Before she did anything else she must go to see him. Poor boy, how he must have been thinking of her, alone in a cold cell. She had a bit of money, she would go and see her brother. After that she could try to think things out more clearly.

She heard a knocking at the door below the window. The Bathurst was closed by now, shut up for the night, everyone in bed. The knocking repeated. She tensed, waiting, then she heard Thady's voice.

'Abby?'

She lay silent, rigid.

'Abby!' Louder, more insistent.

Another pause.

'*Abby!* Answer me! I know ye're there!'

With a sudden bound she was off the bed, and threw up the window. She could hardly make him out in the dim light below her.

'What do you want?'

'Ye've robbed me! Come home this instant or I'll call the peelers! Ye're a thief – I'll have ye arrested and indicted.'

'I'm not coming home,' she said decisively, and added, 'it was my money, and you'll never go for the peelers, Thady O'Farrell.'

'I will!'

Another window was thrown up and a woman's voice shouted. 'Stop that row!'

'I'll go for the peelers this moment if you don't come straightaway home with me this instant.'

'If you fetch the peelers I'll tell 'em you was pimping.'

'*Pimping?*' Thady sounded outraged. 'What a thing for a young girl to say! And ye misunderstand, Abby darlin'—'

186

'Will you shut that row!'

It was time to finish this. She looked down again at the dim shape of Thady. 'All right. Wait there a moment,' and turned into the room. On the wash stand stood a large jug of cold water. She carried it carefully to the window. 'Thady?' she called quietly.

He caught her tone, and replied in a conciliatory mood. 'I'm here, me darlin'.'

'Thady, I've got somethin' for you. Are you ready?'

'I'm ready, me darlin'.'

'Now, stand still then.' Aiming as carefully as she could, she emptied the jug over him. It was a perfect shot. Thady leaped, screaming as the water cascaded over his head, hopping about and shaking himself. She closed the window but waited, listening intently, tensely, clutching herself.

Silence. After a long while, she went cautiously to the window, and without opening it tried to see whether he was still there. She waited. He seemed to have gone away. She returned to the bed, and lay down, fully dressed, uncertain what to do, wondering whether he had gone for the police. And then came the reaction. After a few minutes she began to shake, and before she could help herself the tears came, she couldn't help it, and her whole body shook as she wept out her tension, all the events of the nights, the shock of Willie's attempt on her, the rushing out of the house, the row with Thady, like some stage washerwoman in the street. And what was she to do now?

Before long, mercifully, as her weeping slowed and at last exhausted itself, a huge relaxation stole over her and, in spite of everything, she fell fast asleep, still dressed and lying on top of the bed.

She woke the following morning, cold and stiff, and feeling dirty, her face sticky and unwashed. But she brought a can of hot water up from the kitchen, stripped herself naked and washed herself all over, and afterwards felt better.

She was half way through her breakfast, eaten in the bar

where early morning workmen were refreshing themselves with tea and hot spirits and bacon when, inevitably, Thady appeared again. He looked terrible – the stubble chin and bleary eyes. Abby did not take her eyes off her plate, stolidly cutting up her bacon and eggs, taking bites of bread and butter, and sipping her tea as he sat beside her on the bench pleading with her.

'I brought ye over. I found ye the job. You can't desert me, Abby.'

'You brought me under false pretences.' She munched on. 'Oh, don't even talk to me! I can't bear to think of it. You used me! All this time – my God, all this time, you were foolin' me. Thinking only how you could make me your whore—'

'Abby honey,' he was wheedling, 'Look, we'll say nothing of the twenty pounds, ye've earned it. We'll forget that if only you'll come back.'

'It was my money. And I'm not coming back.'

'I understand it was a shock for ye. I understand. Maybe I should have ... but then ye see, I thought ye'd understand when I told ye of the opportunities.' His voice sank to a whisper, as he leaned in on her. 'Only think of it! My God there's a fortune to be made out there. Can't ye see it? We had it all, Abby! Right there in our hands. Ye could be rich! Ye could have your own carriage. Servants and all. That Captain O'Shea – that Lord Morton! Didn't he only tuck a twenty pound note down your frock – just for a kiss – think of it! My God, the possibilities!' he was hissing in her ear.

'I'm not coming back,' she said stolidly. 'I didn't come all the way to London to be a whore,' she said in a suppressed whisper.

'Well, what did ye come for?' He was angry for a moment.

She ate in silence. He changed his tone, wheedling again. 'Abby, honey, ye won't desert me? You can't desert old Thady?'

She finished her breakfast and stood up.

'Where are ye going?'

'Where do you think? To work.'

All the way to the stables Thady followed her, attempting half heartedly to repeat his arguments. She said nothing.

In the stables she found Colonel Wilkes. 'Colonel Wilkes, do you still want me to go on working for you?'

'Eh?' he was taken by surprise. 'Of course I do. What are you talking about?'

'From now on you'll have to pay me – direct.'

Chapter Nineteen

'Colonel Wilkes, where is Portland?'

'Portland? You mean Portman. Portman Square. Just off Oxford Street.'

He went up the stairs, and she watched his back.

Did she? She was confused. Was it in London? Surely not? She approached Jenkins after the colonel had gone. He was rubbing down a mare.

'Jenkins. Do you know where Portland is?'

'You mean Portland Bill? Down in Dorset.'

She was even more puzzled. Mr O'Toole had said nothing about a Bill.

'Portland Bill,' Jenkins went on, 'down by Weymouth. You know – big stone quarries, naval station.'

'Ah.'

'Why do you want to know?'

''Tis this cousin of mine – he works there.'

'Works there? There ain't nothing there – only the navy and the quarries – and the prison.'

'Ah.'

Jenkins laughed as he came out from behind the mare. 'What – is he doin' time?'

'Oh no,' she hesitated, 'only, he has a job down there, and I wanted to visit him. I haven't seen him—'

He straightened up, and looked at her shrewdly. 'Cousin, eh?' He winked. 'Sweetheart more like?' He grinned.

She turned away, as Jenkins laughed, but after a moment turned back. 'How would I get there?'

'Train, of course.'

All through her journey down to Portland, the hours sitting in the train, she gazed out at the passing landscape; she had never realised until this day how beautiful the English countryside was in summer – softer than Ireland, and somehow more tamed.

Things weren't so bad. Of course he was in prison, but still, in such beautiful countryside, she had never seen anything so beautiful, and by the seaside too, such a relief after the pavements and chimney pots of London. Her spirits lifted; she would be seeing Rory, and perhaps, who knew but his sentence might be shortened for good behaviour? Of course, he would be a model prisoner – they would be bound to let him out before too long, and even if it were eight years – that would make him twenty-seven – not too old – no age at all really, there was still time enough ... she breathed deeply, her eyes drinking in the vista, and so glad she had come.

The train came into Weymouth, and as it waited, she could smell the sea air, and hear the seagulls over the roof tops. Then it was moving off again, round a bay where she could see navy ships, iron-clads at anchor, flags fluttering at their mastheads.

But now the scenery changed; she saw coming up ahead a great hill, a forbidding rocky mass, and guessed that this must be Portland Bill.

Here she got out of the train, straightening her hat, taking her basket, and set forth up the narrow street of a little village, Fortuneswell. A good omen, she thought, 'Fortune's well', and quickened her step, glad to walk after the hours in the railway carriage, glad to breathe the salt air after the acrid train smoke smarting in her eyes. The village street ran steeply up; she passed the church, the village petered out, and she found her way steeper still, till she was pulling and dragging for breath. Her new boots, bought for the occasion, were tight on her feet.

When she came out on the summit, she could see stretching away on the other side a vast panorama to the west, the sea and a mighty curve of the beach fading into the incredible distance.

All round her were the stone quarries, a bleak and dismal prospect, a tangle of jagged and gaping holes in the earth, stone and dust, glaring in the midday sun. She was hot by now and her boots pinched, as she set down her basket and looked about her to get her bearings.

And as she did so she beheld, across the desert landscape of the quarries, a long bleak stone building, a high fortress, forbidding, unfriendly and, bare in the summer day, with a few small red-brick houses in a row nearby; the most depressing, despairing place, devoid of all human warmth, quite unresponsive to the season and the setting, as if to say, It may be summer and the sea may be glittering and friendly, but we are not here to welcome you. We are here to punish you, amid these harsh stones.

She was admitted through that same little-door-within-a-door she had known in Castlebar, and officers with key rings on chains from their belts, scanned her expressionlessly. She was led across a courtyard towards a stone building with long rows of tiny windows high up, and through a small door, opened from the key ring at the warder's belt. Her heart sank and sank, and she had to take a real grip on herself, clutch herself, strengthen and brace herself, and remind herself that Rory would perhaps be changed. He had been several months in prison now, and . . .

She was in a stone corridor. To her right, separated by stone buttresses, were a series of small openings in the wall, each heavily barred. The warder pointed to the first of these, and she waited.

Then Rory appeared at the aperture. She started forward. But oh, what a shock! Rory, her Rory, in that hideous uniform, that grey-striped, coarse-woollen ill-fitting uniform. And his head was shaved almost bald. How ugly it made him, and his face, grey, pasty, unhealthy as if he never saw the sun – oh Rory! She clutched the thick bars, pressing forward to see him better in the poor light, trying to still herself, forcing her voice down, and spoke quietly.

'Rory darlin' it's good to see you, and you're lookin' so ... oh my darlin', are they treatin' you well?'

Rory was staring at her, taking her in, as if wondering how she came to be there.

'I have a job now darlin',' she hurried on, 'in a stables in London, exercising the horses, and gettin' wages and all.'

Rory was still staring at her, still silent. She slowed to a stop.

'Rory? Will you say hullo?'

'What do you want?' His voice sounded strange, as if rusty with lack of use.

'What?' she swallowed. 'To see you, of course.'

'Why?'

She searched his face. Cold, inexpressive, he continued to stare at her.

'Rory,' she pressed on, 'I know what you're thinking but I did speak to Mr O'Toole and told him everything. I wanted you to tell the judge about me – there was no need to cover up for me—'

He was still staring at her, but now looked down and, to her horror, she saw he was weeping, not looking up, but unconsciously reaching and wiping the back of his hand savagely across his face.

'Oh Rory – don't!'

'I'm sorry, it's seeing ye after so long, Abby.' He wiped his eyes fiercely, and went on in a low monotone, 'it'd drive ye mad, Abby, six weeks I was in solitary, all day, all night, with never a fellow to talk to, you can't imagine. They take us out to the quarries, and we're all day there breaking stones, with never a kind word, and if ye do utter a word, they punish ye. I hate it. I look up, I try to pray,

193

but I think God has turned his face away from me, to put me in here for fifteen years. I can't even imagine it. I'd top meself only for the thought that it'd grieve ye. The days going by, I feel as if I've been here for ever and not even one year has gone by, and I've got fifteen to do. Every day the same, every one the same, and the screws picking on me because I'm Irish. It's always, "Get on, bloody Fenian." God, I hate it, Abby, I hate it! I'd go mad if it wasn't for your letter, and the thought of seeing ye . . .'

There were tears in her eyes too, though she tried to stop herself. She so wanted to comfort him, but he was behind the bars, and she could only touch his fingers, touch him, when she would have given all she possessed to clasp him in her arms and soothe him. 'Don't cry, Rory darlin', I'll come and see you regular. Don't pine and grieve, because I'll always be near you. And even though we're parted, you'll always be in my thoughts – and I'll come as often as I can. Oh Rory –' she wiped her eyes '– don't cry, I can't bear it.'

At last she tore herself away, wiping her tears, scarcely able to see as the warder opened the door and then, turning for one last moment, called, 'I'll come again soon, Rory darling, and I'll write,' and then she was led across the yard, weeping helplessly, and at last much later, in the train, utterly, utterly drained, staring out of the window, seeing nothing, weak, hopeless, and eventually falling asleep.

When she awoke it was evening, and the train was still chugging through the countryside. Sitting up she collected her thoughts and decided, weeping was no use. She must be stronger. What use was it to Rory? It must only have made him sadder still. She must be his strength from now on. It was her job to help. She would be his sanity, his normality. She would write every week.

A month went by, and business was slack in the stables.

'Everyone's gone down into the country,' the colonel told her.

194

She went out every day exercising the horses, and Thady was occupied in the stable. She tried to speak to him as little as possible, but one day he stopped her. She waited for him to get to the point.

'The colonel's on me back, Abby.'

'What?'

'How do you think I paid for the house? And the food and drink? I was dependin' on ye, Abby. He's threatenin' to sue.'

'What do you expect me to do?'

He looked at her longingly. 'We had it made, Abby,' he wheedled. 'Ye could have been riding in your carriage and pair—'

'Don't start again! I didn't ask you to go borrowin' money. 'Tis your own greed brought it on your head. Now get out of my way, I've got work to do.'

But as she mounted her horse – a young mare the colonel had bought recently – she looked back. Thady was bending over his fork, shovelling manure. There was something ridiculous, something pathetic about him. Annoyed with him – and with herself for some reason – she urged her mare under the arch, and out into the square.

Why should she feel responsible for *him*? She urged the mare into a stiff trot. The animal had picked up some bad habits under another owner, and her job was to straighten her out.

The cheek of it. Thady had brought *her* to London – not the other way about. He had deliberately misled her about Willie O'Shea. She drew a long breath; he was no responsibility of hers – let him sink or swim – in any case, she had no money so she couldn't help. Yet, and she still couldn't fathom the reason, she was concerned. The sight of that back, bent over the pitchfork . . . she kicked the mare into a gallop, to push Thady out of her thoughts.

All the rest of the month she worked away in the stables or the park.

And then one fresh morning in early September, she was

195

in the park, still busy training her difficult mare. It was one of those beautiful clear mornings of early autumn, the light falling long across the grass still wet with dew, and glowing through the leaves now turning to gold. The park was almost deserted, and swans sat motionless on the lake.

The mare was still playing up on her, and she was concentrating on getting her to behave, so that she didn't notice the man cantering across the park towards her, didn't even see him till he came up to her and spoke.

'Good morning.'

She looked up. 'Mr Darke!' She gathered herself and smiled spontaneously. 'This is a pleasant surprise. I haven't seen you since—'

He pulled his horse up beside her. 'I've been out of town the last few weeks. What about you?'

'Oh, I've been busy you know.' She patted the horse's neck.

'And how is Mr Thady?'

'Oh,' she hesitated. 'Well, there was a rearrangement of, well, I mean, we had a – but things are all right now.' She finished off quickly.

He didn't reply to this, and for a few moments they walked their horses in silence, as she tried to work out what he was thinking.

'A rearrangement?' he said at last in a light tone, 'with your friend Thady?'

She swallowed. 'Yes,' she said faintly, looking away.

'I hope it wasn't too painful.'

She drew a breath and turned back to Mr Darke, who she found studying her carefully.

'Not for me,' she said decidedly.

'Hmm. But for him – perhaps more so?'

She grinned. 'You could say that.'

'A misunderstanding?'

She nodded.

He was silent again, still studying her. 'I had an idea,' he said at last softly.

'Did you?'

'Mm.'

'In what way?' she asked uncertainly.

'Oh, it was obvious you weren't suited.'

'Obvious? That obvious?'

'Obvious to anyone who cared to look. He spoke to me you know, about you. I mean, when he invited me to your "party".'

'Did he? What did he say?'

'Can't you guess?'

'Oh,' she paused. 'Now you mention it, I suppose I can.'

'Then when I came that night, and saw you again, I realised it wasn't going to last long.'

She felt a huge relief as he said all this, and a warmth, as she bathed in his attention, in his interest in her. They walked a little further in silence.

'You know Abby –' he said at last. She turned quickly, ready. 'You know, it would be nice to go out one evening together. The two of us.' She was studying him, his face, all over him, taking him in. He could read her answer easily. 'The only thing is, I can't get out early in the evening, not till ten. Would that be a problem?'

'No, of course not.'

'Would any evening suit you specially?'

She shook her head vaguely. 'Any,' she said faintly.

He gave it a moment's thought. 'Well then, say – Friday? At ten? We'll get a bit of supper. Anywhere special you like to go?' She shook her head helplessly. 'I expect I can think of something. Let's see – where shall I pick you up?'

'Oh, I'm staying at the Bathurst at the moment, the corner of Sussex Square, Bayswater.'

'Good. I look forward to it.'

For the rest of the week she was in a huge dither, on tenter-hooks, filled with uncertainties. Mr Darke was a gentleman, so neat and precise, so quietly spoken, so beautifully dressed. What on earth could he want with her? The smell of the stables on her, and her awful dress?

The night before, she hung the dress up on a hanger and studied it. It was the best she had. But it wasn't good enough for him. How could he even bear to be seen with her in a dress like that – so tarty and vulgar; she could just see it through his eyes. She sat on the end of her bed, staring at the dress. If only – if only she had some money to buy a real gown, something to do him justice!

Well, there was one thing she could do. She picked up the pair of scissors she had borrowed, and took them to the dress. At least there would be no bows.

When she had finished she studied the gown again. It was a bit better. And then, it was cut very close to her figure – Thady had seen to that. That was one thing – the man wasn't born that didn't like to see a woman in a close-fitting gown. Anyway, it was the best she had. And it would be at night . . .

At night. For the first time she wondered what Mr Darke had in mind. He had mentioned supper. But what about after supper? That was what it was all about, usually. Supper was just the prelude, wasn't it? She studied the dress, and then with a gesture of impatience shrugged away her thoughts. Events would just have to take their course; she would know what to do when the time came.

She was waiting outside the pub at ten, a shawl wrapped round her shoulders. That evening she had stripped herself naked and scrubbed and scrubbed at herself. Especially her hands, under her fingernails. Yet still she wasn't sure whether she had got rid of the smell of horses. All her underwear was fresh, she had washed her hair, and dried it in front of the fire, and then as best she could, crammed it beneath a hat. She had cleaned her boots. Everything she could think of. She had tried on Thady's glass tiara, but rejected it. Thady might not notice the difference, but Mr Darke would.

There was just a touch of chill in the air. People were elbowing their way in and out of the door, as she stood on the pavement, and one or two men addressed her. She moved away.

Perhaps she should have waited inside? But, then, she didn't like to think of someone so nice and genteel as Mr Darke having to make his way in through that crowd, all that laughter and smoke, the shouts, the singing of working men and their wives. It wasn't his sort of place.

She stood on the pavement's edge and ignored the remarks.

A carriage drew up, sharp on the hour, and she saw his head, in the gloom at the window. 'Abby?'

In a moment she was inside beside him. He rapped on the ceiling with the silver knob of his cane, and they moved off.

Chapter Twenty

When she found herself outside the Bathurst again, it was half past one in the morning. Nick Darke got out, and helped her down.

He held her hands, thinking for a moment, looking down at her in the light of the lamp post on the corner. 'I'm not quite sure what I'll be doing for the next few days. But you're in the park every day, aren't you?'

'Pretty well.'

'I'll be able to find you there, then?'

She nodded and then. 'Oh Nick—'

He was climbing back into the carriage, but turned to say, 'Sleep well!'

'Nick, thank you!'

He leant out of the window. 'Thank *you*.'

As she came into her room, in total darkness, she threw herself on her bed and simply allowed herself to luxuriate in her happiness. It was the most beautiful evening she had ever spent. Everything had just been so perfect: the restaurant – she had never been in anything so elegant. Not too big, and the tables quite crowded together, so that there was a cosy and intimate feeling; then the walls were covered with portraits – opera singers and actors he told her; famous men and women of the boards. What boards, she had asked? He laughed. The boards? Don't you know that?

The theatre, of course. We're in the midst of the theatre district. She had no idea. Her ideas of London were extremely sketchy.

When they first came into the light, and she took off her shawl, she had been tense with nerves, suddenly aware of the other women about her, all beautifully dressed, aware of her hair crammed up beneath her hat, aware of this awful gold dress.

He looked down at it, 'You've got rid of the bows I see.' He smiled into her eyes and winked as if they were in a subtle conspiracy together – a conspiracy against bows. A waiter helped her to a chair, and a heavy leather tome was placed in her hands. As she opened it, flicking over pages, uncertain where to begin, Nick looked over his. 'Shall I order?' he had asked. She nodded. Obviously, since she didn't understand a single thing on it. It could have been written in French for all it meant to her. In fact, when she said that, he replied, Well it *is* all written in French, and they laughed again.

'Fancy soup, or whitebait? They do a very good *consommé* here.' She stared at him, and then he said thoughtfully, 'I see there's a lot I'm going to have to teach you, Abby.'

She was silent for a moment.

'Would you like that?' he went on leaning over the table.

She nodded, caught by his eyes.

'I don't like to presume, Abby, but you know, for a young woman, you learn very quickly.'

She brightened. 'Thank ye, sir.'

'Don't call me sir.'

She giggled. 'Oh sorry, Mr Darke, then.'

'Nick.'

She sat up straight, smiled broadly, and held out her hand. 'How de do, Nick.' And he laughed.

And then afterwards, in the carriage, he never laid a finger on her. She was ready – in fact she would have welcomed it. She would have had no problem with Nick in

201

her arms; he could kiss her any time he liked, as often as he liked. But he didn't. He was very careful, considerate, helped her in and out of the carriage as if she were a real lady, and then on the pavement shook hands with her, and wished her sweet dreams.

She wriggled on the bed. He was just the most perfect man she had ever met. But then doubts started. Why didn't he kiss her? Perhaps he didn't find her attractive? Perhaps he could smell the horses on her? He hadn't made any assignation. He hadn't told her where he lived. In fact, as she thought back over the evening, he hadn't told her anything about himself at all. All the conversation had been about her. Of course she had been very happy answering his questions, she was very happy to do *anything* he wanted; she prattled away, especially after she had had a couple of glasses of white wine. She was more than happy to learn from him. He would point out little things, which fork to use, what to do with the napkin, silly things but she hadn't had the first idea, and would have been more nervous if the wine hadn't relaxed her. Nick chose the wine, Nick chose everything.

'Do you think your colonel would give you a couple of hours off this afternoon?'

She was uncertain. 'I could ask. Actually, he usually takes a nap after lunch. He's never around much between two and four.'

'I'll call at two.'

And now they were clip-clopping through the suburbs, a quiet leafy street, where large single houses stood back from the road, discreetly hidden by trees and thick high laurels. She gazed about her. This was a part of London she had never seen before. She had no idea where they were, or why they were here, but she had a shrewd idea.

Nick was taking her home; and that meant only one thing. She smiled at him, answering some question, she didn't remember what, as she ran the possibilities through her mind. Why else were they here?

And at that moment the carriage pulled into a driveway, she could hear the sound of the wheels changing as they crunched over gravel and came to a halt. She threw open the door and jumped down before he came round to her side, and looked up at this beautiful villa. It was on three floors, though the lowest was partly submerged, and she glimpsed down through iron bars into the kitchens. A few wide steps led up to a broad door painted a glossy black. The blinds in the windows were down.

He went up the steps beside her, found a key and after a few attempts managed to open the door. There was something strange about this, and it crossed her mind that perhaps he was a stranger here too.

The house was cold as they went in, and seemed deserted. A spacious hall with black and white chequer marble floor, from which an elegant staircase curved up and round to a landing. To the left, broad double doors opened into a room, carpeted and furnished. He went ahead of her, crossed it, and opened the shutters at the window. This window gave out on to a garden behind the house, and as she inspected that, he crossed to the other end of the room and opened the shutters there too. She was now able to look about the room, furnished in light colours, pale rose and fawn. A large mirror over a marble fireplace, wide comfortable chairs, a long sofa facing the fire, a writing desk in the corner. She was still gazing round at this as he crossed the hall again and threw open another pair of double doors.

'The dining room.'

Her jaw really did drop now as she looked in at the long polished table, and quickly counted fourteen chairs round it. Fourteen to dinner!

Still saying nothing, he led her up stairs, opening the doors of bedrooms, and she gazed in, but more and more puzzled. Obviously this wasn't his own home. Unless he had more than one? But where were his servants? He must have them – he had his own carriage standing outside the door.

Sooner or later he was going to explain all this.

When they got downstairs again he motioned her to a chair. 'Sorry I can't offer you any refreshment. Servants aren't in.' She waited. 'This isn't my own home – as you guessed, though I do own the house. I usually let it, but the lease fell in, and I've got it back and – well, I had a thought.'

He sat opposite her, and leaned forward his elbows on his knees, his hands clasped. 'Abby, there is something I've got to tell you first – before I say anything else.' She could feel herself tensing. She clasped her hands together, in unconscious imitation of him, and concentrated on his face. 'Perhaps you're wondering why I haven't taken you to my own home. The fact is, I'm married. Before you say anything, let me finish. My wife doesn't know I'm here. You see, she's an invalid. We've been married six years, but only a few weeks after we married she was struck by illness – difficult to describe – a sort of wasting disease. She picked it up in north Africa on our honeymoon; nobody understands it, but it's just sapping her strength. She's confined to a couch for the moment – at least we can still get her up every day; she can be dressed, and sit in the drawing room. But she gets very tired, sometimes sleeps all day. Occasionally I take her to the park in the afternoon. I'll have to get back soon, as a matter of fact.' He paused. 'I'll be perfectly frank with you Abby. We married for love. And I do still love her, nothing would induce me to abandon her. But, I wonder whether you can understand? Not so easy to describe, you know – I'm a man and – well, seeing you on your horse that day, I had an idea about us – from the very moment that I saw you. Strange isn't it?'

She was silent, taking this in, but as he paused, she couldn't help murmuring, 'Not so strange, Nick.'

He looked up. 'What do you mean?'

'I had an idea about you too – the first time I saw you.'

204

'Did you?'

She nodded.

'Can you guess what I'm going to ask you?'

'I think so.'

'Are you sure? I mean, can you guess why I've brought you here?'

'To talk – in private?'

'More than that. I want you to come and live here. I'll pay you of course, pay all your bills, get you some servants. You'll live in comfort – in style – and then we can meet, and be together, do things, you know—'

He paused again. Her eyes had dropped, as she tried to take in what he was saying. Live here? In this house? All of it? Before she could confront this, however, there was one other thing she had to be sure of.

'Do I take it, Nick,' she was looking down, awkward, 'that your wife can't – be a wife to you?' She looked up at last into his eyes.

He nodded. There was a long silence, then she said, 'Where do you live?'

'Mount Street, Mayfair.'

Another long pause. She didn't know what to think. Part of her wanted to accept at once. Another part was unsure – it was such a leap – all this house. What did she know about houses and servants? She lived in a room over a public house. And why had he picked her when there must be thousands of women – English women too – who were better educated than her, and knew about all these things.

He saw her hesitate. 'Perhaps I've taken you by surprise. Do you want to think about it for a day or two?'

At last she swallowed and said huskily. 'Perhaps I should, Nick. It's just so much—' she gazed round again at the drawing room, glancing out into the autumn garden, the leaves beginning to fall on the grass.

'Are you afraid you wouldn't be able to handle it?'

'I don't know.'

'Something tells me you could.'

205

She looked up. 'Really?'

'As I said, you're a fast learner.'

He grinned, and she relaxed. 'Just give me a day or two, Nick.'

It was the wife she was thinking of. She had to know about the wife. And all unknown to Nick, as he dropped her off at the stables, she ran into the Bathurst, hurriedly changed, dashed back into the stables, saddled up the new mare and within fifteen minutes, was galloping through the park towards Mayfair.

Jenkins had given her an idea where Mount Street was.

'Just up a way from the Achilles statue – a bit below Grosvenor House.'

She was now familiar with these landmarks. Standing among the trees a little way off she waited. The august frontages of aristocratic residences faced across Park Lane towards her blinking sleepily in the low western light of the autumn sun. It was a quiet afternoon, almost no one about; Park Lane was empty.

She waited. Mount Street was one of the narrow streets running into Mayfair from the park. Perhaps Nick would take his wife out in his carriage. In fact she now realised there would be no way of telling which was his – black carriages were all much alike – and began to think she was wasting her time. But then to her astonishment, she saw him, pushing an invalid carriage, across Park Lane, through the gates and into the park. She retreated behind the trees, watching carefully.

It was Nick, just like anyone else, pushing a long invalid carriage, in which a woman was carefully wrapped, though it was a mild September afternoon, a travelling rug round her legs, a thick fur collar to her coat, her hands in a muff. The invalid looked up and said something; Nick stopped the carriage, went and tucked the rug more comfortably round her feet; he fussed with her collar for a moment, adjusting it, then resumed his journey. They went quite slowly, and

Abby began judiciously to follow them, as they made their way down to the Long Water. They seemed to be continuously in conversation; she could see the invalid turning her head from time to time, obviously speaking to Nick, and he would lean forward too. They reached the lake; he settled his wife facing the water, and brought a chair to sit by her.

Very soon a number of ducks and geese began to gather. Nick handed her a paper bag, and from her seat in the carriage she threw bits of bread at the birds and they eagerly gathered round to snap them up. Nick got up and waved away one or two bolder ones who came too close.

Abby saw it all. Nick was devoted to his wife. Her heart beat painfully as she took this in. 'He loves her,' was the thought that went through and through her mind, and at last Abby turned her horse away, walking her as she turned over the events of the afternoon.

All evening and that night in bed she was filled with these thoughts. Nick was devoted to his wife, the invalid. What a hero he was! And what a fortunate woman his wife was.

But where did that leave Abby? She wished in a way she hadn't seen what she had seen. She wished she didn't know Nick had a wife. It would have been better if he hadn't told her. But then, she asked herself whether this were true. Nick had been noble, he had been a true gentleman; he hadn't tried to seduce her, he hadn't lied to her. Everything he had done had been upright and honourable.

And he wasn't asking her to usurp his wife's place, was he? That was the point. Abby wouldn't be taking away anything that rightfully belonged to her. It was coming clearer now. His wife couldn't be a wife. And Nick was a man – a fine man, who had a man's needs. She paused and at last confronted her decision, 'And that means – in so many words – he would like *me* to act the part of a wife to him.' She paused again. The fact was, there was nowhere she would rather be than in bed with Nick Darke. '. . . And he did say he would provide for me, and . . . I'll do it! So what if we're not married? It's not like whoring. I'll be faithful to Nick.'

She sat up, alert with her decision. 'I'll do it!' she repeated. 'And I'll be able to do something for Fan and Da.'

It came to her in a flash, sitting up in bed, as the possibilities flashed into her mind. If he gives me money—

That settled it. She wanted to leap out of bed and run to Nick there and then. But she lay back on her pillow, her heart beating, as vision upon vision presented themselves to her. If she had money, she could send Fan to school, to be educated. And Da could have his own home, she could pay the rent and they wouldn't have to depend on Aunt Eileen any more . . .

Chapter Twenty-one

That morning they met in the park. He saw by the smile on her lips, as they were approaching each other, saw before she spoke, what her answer was.

'I'll get some servants for you, Abby, and get in some fresh linen, have the place cleaned and dusted, and get something done about the garden ... that'll take a few days. Let's say a week. Next Thursday you can move in. Can you give notice to your colonel?'

She nodded, almost too excited to speak.

'Eh? Give notice? You can't give notice! I need you. I've invested in you. What about that dress? That cost me seven guineas. That's real gold lace round the collar, you know.'

'I'm leaving.'

'I know what this is. You've found some young buck to set you up, haven't you? I might have known. It always happens. Well, listen my girl, you've got an obligation here.'

'I'll work till Wednesday.'

'You'll work till you've paid off that dress.'

She swung on him. 'I've paid off that dress over and over! Don't pretend different. You know the business I've brought in here. You've done well enough out of me, Colonel Wilkes. And you can have your dress back!'

Thady was watching anxiously, and hurried after her as

she strode out of the stable in the direction of the Bathurst.

'But Abby,' he caught her sleeve, 'what about me?'

She turned on him, too. After her row with the colonel, she was in no mood to conciliate. 'What about you?'

'You're not leaving old Thady?'

He was pathetic. For a moment she was at a loss for words.

Thady wheedled. 'I brought ye here! Surely you won't desert old Thady?'

Clenching her jaws, she stared at him for a moment, taking him in, the rounded shoulders, the grovelling, the hands rubbing together. 'You knew what you were about,' she said quietly but firmly. 'You thought to make me your whore. I'll never forgive you for it. You'll have to sink or swim on your own.' She turned away, but called back over her shoulder, 'The colonel will keep you on, I expect.'

He called after her, 'So you're going off to be someone else's whore, is that it?'

She ignored this, striding away.

The following Thursday she was ready with her few possessions rolled up in an old dress, standing at the corner of Sussex Square. She had told no one when she was leaving, but even so, Thady had been watching her carefully, and managed to be near by, hovering at the corner. She tried to ignore him, but felt very self-conscious, as the shiny black carriage drew up. The door opened from the inside and, as she stepped in, Nick was waiting.

'Say goodbye to the stables, Abby. You've not brought that red outfit, I hope.'

She shook her head, expectant, suddenly uncertain. Nick had still not laid a finger on her. She wanted to kiss him, but felt inhibited. She had never met a man before who seemed to hold aloof like this; it was strange because it meant he kept all the power. She could do nothing but wait.

As they rolled through the London streets, he was expansive. 'I think you'll be pleased. I've got you in a few servants – a cook, a parlour maid, a girl to clean. They should be able to take care of you. Of course, if you need anything you only have to ask. You can have anything you want.'

At this her resistance broke and unable to help herself she threw herself across him and kissed him on the lips. He smiled knowingly.

'Plenty of time,' he murmured.

The driveway had been swept, the gravel freshly raked. As they stepped out of the carriage, Nick turned to the driver.

'By the way Abby, this is Blake. You'll see him again.'

The man on the box touched his hat. 'Ma'am.'

'In the meantime I've engaged with the livery stables round the corner. Whenever you need a carriage, send a girl round to let them know. Now,' he rapped on the door, and a moment later a maid in a black dress with a clean starched pinafore and a white cap opened the door and dropped a curtsy.

'Sir, and ma'am.'

As they came into the hall she found two other women also in black and white uniforms lined up to greet them. The women also dropped a curtsy.

'Abby, this is Mrs Casey your cook. She's Irish like you.'

'Oh that's grand!' Abby shook her hand readily.

Nick introduced the other girls. 'Jane and Mary. Now, whenever you need to plan your meals, you may summon Mrs Casey and give her your orders.'

A fire had been lit in the drawing room, and the place cleaned and freshened. Obviously the curtains had been washed, the surfaces dusted.

Nick turned as she took everything in.

'Tea I think, first.' The servants all disappeared to their quarters and she was left alone by the fire with Nick.

First? That was interesting.

During tea, as they sat on either side of a low table

where a dainty tea service was set out, his eyes explored her, contemplatively and slightly amusingly, but always with a complete certainty that he was in charge, and had everything arranged to his satisfaction.

So that when he rose without a word, and took her hand to lead her upstairs she had no hesitation. And as he carefully undid the hooks and eyes down the back of her bodice and first pulled the dress away from her shoulder, brushing his lips across her skin, a shudder ran right through her. She turned and they kissed passionately.

'Gently does it. This is going to last a long time . . .'

Later he said thoughtfully, 'Hester.'

This meant nothing, but he repeated, 'Hester,' as if trying out the sound. She turned towards him, lazily, relaxed, pulling a sheet over her. He was staring at the ceiling. 'Yes,' he murmured, 'You're not an Abby. You're a Hester. Let's see. You shall be Hester Moncrieffe. It suits you much better. And something else – you are never to call anyone "sir" again. When my friends come, Hester, and you do the honours at dinner, which you will do with perfect skill and composure, you will give them your hand to kiss, and they will, one and all, feel grateful that you have stooped to notice them at all. Tomorrow we shall start on your elocution, though you have a good ear. You are going to master the English tongue – and learn a bit of French too. It adds tone to one's conversation.' He turned on one elbow, running his hand over her breasts and down over her belly. 'And there is much else to learn. We're going to do *everything* . . .'

Later still, he got out of bed.

'I must be getting back,' he murmured, glancing at the pretty eighteenth-century French clock on the mantelpiece. She watched him dressing. Although it was the first time she had ever watched a man getting dressed (apart from Thady, she tried not to remind herself), there was nothing strange about it. It was nice; it was pleasant, intimate. Her eyes dwelt lovingly on his body.

As he fitted the collar to his shirt, he turned to her. 'I'll call for you at ten tomorrow, and we'll go shopping. Would you like that?'

She nodded.

'Whenever you need anything, just pull the cord—' he indicated the tassel hanging near the bedhead. 'Goodbye my dear. See you in the morning,' he kissed her and was gone.

Distantly she heard the front door close, and stretched herself out in the bed. It was so comfortable, the sheets smelled so clean and fresh – and were so rumpled, she thought, surveying the ruins after their love-making. She felt deliciously relaxed and happy. Nick had been more than she could have hoped for.

He had been a most tender lover; of course he must have had other women, she told herself, yet there was something in his manner almost hesitant, gentle; he was as shy as she was, it seemed, so that they explored one another for the first time, wonderingly, tenderly, gratefully. And the bedroom: it was paradise, she thought, as she opened her eyes and looked about her; the pretty pastel colours, the pale blue and pink paper on the wall, the gold-rimmed mirror, the pretty chairs, the wardrobe, the thick rug before the bed. She twisted over, and could just catch the faint smell of Nick among the rumpled sheets. Why had she been singled out for such stupendous good fortune?

Then she was restless. She must inspect her new domain. And she must order some supper. Making love makes you hungry, she thought, grinning to herself, and it was past six as she saw from the clock on the mantelpiece. She sat up in bed, and surveyed her clothes scattered about the floor. Poor shabby clothes. And seeing them she was filled with doubts: they were her real self – not this fairy-tale house. She, the real Abby O'Leary, the stable girl. She looked about the room and chewed her lip. But she could trust Nick, couldn't she?

213

She remembered the tassel by the bed, and gave it a pull. Well, she would just have to put on her old clothes. One more day, then she would enter her new life.

The girl knocked gently at the door, and Abby pulled the sheet round her. She gave the girl an embarrassed grin, and asked for hot water. Their love-making had been noisy at times. Had the staff been listening in, she wondered? Was that a sly grin the girl gave her, as she went out? And what was her name – Jane or Mary?

Abby washed herself and with a small grimace pulled on her old dress. She was definitely hungry. She took herself down to the drawing room, still amazed to find herself here, staring round at the pictures on the wall, and absent-mindedly pulled the bell by the fireplace. The room was rather chilly.

A girl appeared – the other one – or rather one of the other ones.

'I'd like something to eat . . .'

'Shall I send cook, m'm?'

Abby nodded. And soon after the short round figure of Mrs Casey waddled into the room. Abby recognised her; she was Irish, and not easy to forget.

'Will ye have somet'in' to eat, ma'am?'

Abby gave her a huge grin, a sort of relaxation and recognition, and then paused, 'What is there?'

'Mr Darke ordered your supper, ma'am. Shall I serve it now?'

'Yes please! And – could I have some more coal on the fire in here?'

'I'll send the maid.'

Twenty minutes later she was seated at the dining table which normally held fourteen persons, slightly intimidated by the paintings on the wall, the candelabrum on the table, and the silver cutlery ranged out on the snowy tablecloth. A small decanter of red wine also stood before her. She poured a glass, and the wine sharpened her appetite.

214

Eventually a girl brought in a bowl of turtle soup, thick, glutinous, green, delicious.

'There's a sole and cutlet to follow, ma'am, and the syllabub.'

By the time she had waded through this banquet, and finished the wine, she sat back in her chair of state, all inhibitions flown. A dish of fruit sat on the cloth before her. She picked a grape at random, and sat, slightly stupified by the wine, still stunned by this transformation.

Nick had done all this for *her*. She was still trying to take it all in. How was she ever going to recompense him for it? Could she love him enough to make up for it all? Nick was going to want a lady for his companion. He was rich, he lived in elegance; could she ever measure up to his needs? Would he get tired of her? Would she wake up one morning and find herself in the gutter – like someone out of a fairy tale – to find it had all been a dream?

If only Nick could have been here. It was wonderful to eat and wonderful to be here – but being alone somehow diminished it.

Still he would come tomorrow. She rose slightly unsteadily and wandered back through the rooms, still trying to take it all in.

'Now, we've a busy day ahead, Hester. We'll get you a few things this morning to be going on with, then we'll take you to a very good dress-maker I know, and she can make you some really nice things. Winter's coming on, and you're going to need warm clothes.'

'Yes Nick.'

'And we're going to make a start on your elocution.'

'Pardon?'

'Your speech.'

'Oh yes. I want to speak like a real English lady. So you won't know the difference.'

'By the time we've finished, *you* won't know the

215

difference. Later we'll go for a ride. And once you have your new habit—'

'Oh Nick—' she jumped – 'shall I have a real lady's habit, in black?'

'We'll have you fitted for it this morning.'

She squealed with joy and kissed him spontaneously.

'I want you to have your own mare too. We'll go to Tattersalls.'

'Oh Nick . . .' she breathed, 'that'd be heaven . . .'

He was silent for a moment. 'In a way, you know, Hester, I'm not doing you any favours, whatever you might think. It's been six years since my wife was taken ill, and all this time, I've not been able to do any of these things – the things a man wants to do for a woman. And now – being able to do them for you . . . I'm very selfish really.'

She was sobered by this, and took his hand. 'You won't be sorry,' she whispered, kissing his cheek. He placed his other hand over hers, and they were quiet for a while, as the carriage rolled through the traffic into town.

These were shops she had looked into once or twice in the past; sanctums where august ladies and gentlemen came and went, stepping in and out of carriages, people she had watched as if they were creatures from another world. Nick knew his way about them, though; he seemed perfectly at ease, and the shopkeepers, who had seemed to her so dignified, so forbidding, jumped about with alacrity when Nick gave his orders.

Nick inspected things, turning over coats, mantles, fur-lined cloaks, woollen dresses, winter skirts. 'These are things we can have ready in a couple of days, Hester. The others will take a little longer.'

Then they were in a haberdasher's. Nick seemed perfectly cool as he inspected the underwear. 'We want something nice for you.' He was turning over chemises, drawers, nightgowns, stockings. 'Yes, we want nice things . . .' he murmured, and parcel after parcel was made up.

216

'We'll take a few things today at least. Then you won't have to wear that old dress any more.'

'Thank ye, Nick.'

'Thank *you*,' he said without expression.

'Thank *you*,' she repeated, and from then on, as he spoke she would repeat his words, repeat his accent, his intonation. 'Hyde *Pahk*,' she giggled. 'Riding in Rotten Row,' she enunciated, exaggerating the consonants, rolling the Rs. 'Repeat after me . . .' she had a good ear. She remembered the time, which now seemed in a former life, when she had done an imitation of Miss Marianne's clipped diction, to put off Randolph Pelham.

She was sitting at her escritoire – the pronunciation of that took a little work – chewing the top of her pen. She was wearing a soft blouse in ivory silk, closed at the collar by a cameo brooch, and a long skirt of fine black wool, silk stockings, and pretty Persian slippers. Nick had chosen perfectly for her colouring, and height, and she had been extremely pleased as she had surveyed herself in her glass.

But it had taken her some time to settle how she was going to explain her new situation. She began to write.

Rory darling I do hope you're well, and maybe just a bit more cheerful. You were so miserable when I saw you, my darling, and so was I. I could scarcely bear to think of you in that horrible place. But do try to look up. Things won't always be this bad – one day you'll be free again, and we'll be together just as we used to be in the old days. I look forward to that, and think of it every day. We shall be free again and together.

I have a great piece of news. I have a new job working for a very kind gentleman, looking after his horses just as I used to for Mr Thorpe. It's a lovely job, I don't have too much to do – he has three horses, two for the carriage, one for riding. The other servants are very friendly, and we all get on together very well.

And I am earning a bit of money too, so if there is anything I can do for you, anything you would like me to bring you, please tell me. I plan to go over to Ireland soon to see how Fan and Da are, and I will write and tell you everything.

If you can write Rory darling, address your letter to me at 16 Acacia Road, St John's Wood, London NW.

Your loving sister,

Abby.

The horse was a grey, sixteen hands, a four-year-old mare.

'Oh, she's lovely, Nick! I shall care for her myself.'

'Blake can go out with you when I'm not here.'

Blake, who was standing behind him, came forward and gave her a foot up into the saddle. She was wearing her new black riding habit, and took a moment to arrange the folds of the skirt about her. A gleaming new boot found its way into the stirrup. This was what a lady *should* wear.

As she was being fitted for this ensemble by the dressmaker, she remembered the red outfit Colonel Wilkes had had made for her.

'Make it fit good and tight, Madame Brocquet,' she'd told the dressmaker. She wanted to please Nick so badly, and she hadn't been disappointed. The first time she appeared in it, coming downstairs as he waited in the hall, she had seen his eyes as he caught sight of her. That moment, that quickened interest, that half step forward . . . it gave her a fierce pleasure. It was power, a power – she quickly told herself – of giving pleasure to the man she loved.

Chapter Twenty-two

Loved?

Oh yes, she loved him. When did she first know it – consciously? Was it as he made love to her? Bringing her to her climax so surely, so skilfully, so fully, so that she clung to him, gasping out her soul to him, reaching up to cover his neck, his face, his chest with her kisses? Or when they had been in the carriage and he told her he was only pleasing himself, because he was grateful to her for being there for him? Or as she sat alone in the window looking out into the October garden thinking about him?

Or this morning, as he presented her with this magnificent mare, a most delicate shade of dove grey, flawless, and such a gentle nature, a horse who responded to her immediately, whom she had got to know within half an hour of their meeting as she fed her a handful of barley sugar, stroked her nose, talked to her soothingly?

'Oh Nick, she's beautiful; oh, I do love you.' It had come out quite without thinking. Nick had said nothing, his arm round her shoulder.

As she rode out into the park that afternoon – after Nick had gone – herself and Blake riding so decorously together, though anyone could see that Blake was her servant, and she the mistress – she felt that this was the true moment in which she arrived, in which she felt her transformed status. Now she really *was* a lady.

After the first few weeks of her new life, she drew a deep breath, and turned her thoughts to her family. Something had to be done about Fan. The girl was now fourteen, and if she, Abby, had had the chance to be educated and made a lady – well, Fan deserved as much.

This was the other compelling reason, she reminded herself, for being here: through Nick she was able to help her family. Just so long as none of them took it into their heads to come and pay her a visit, she thought; it would be safest if she went over herself.

'Oh Mrs Moncrieffe?'

Abby – or Hester, as she was getting used to being called – turned from where she had been staring out into the unkempt garden.

Mrs Casey was waiting at the drawing room door; by her side stood a youth of sixteen or thereabouts, a big lad, with a well-pleased expression and a thatch of sandy hair.

'Might I have a word?'

'Come in, Mrs Casey.'

'It's me son Mick. I was thinkin' – now ye have your mare and such a fine mare as all the world can see – whether ye wouldn't be needin' a boy to care for her?'

'I'm really quite happy to look after Dewdrop myself, Mrs Casey,' she said uncertainly.

'Oh but a lady like yourself, such a fine lady as ye be, Mrs Moncrieffe, should be havin' a boy to tend the mare. Ye can't be down in the stables doin' all them dirty jobs – it'll ruin your hands entirely, and spoil your beautiful clothes, and make ye all smelly.'

Would it? She had never thought of her hands before, had never thought of her smell, and as for her clothes . . . But then Nick, perhaps, if she were to be introduced to his friends . . .?

She came over to them. 'Have you worked with horses before?'

'Oh Mrs Moncrieffe,' his mother went on, as the boy grinned, 'he thinks of nothin' else. Wasn't he only brought

220

up wid horses? He dreams of 'em at night, Mrs Moncrieffe.'

'Very well. Come with me, Mick. You can return to the kitchen, Mrs Casey.'

She led the way down to the stables, where Dewdrop was in her stall.

'Now Mick you can give her a rub. There's a comb – and there's a cloth on the peg.'

Mick began to rub the mare down, and as he did so she watched him.

'Where have you worked?'

'I was in Mr Roper's stables, Mrs Moncrieffe for two years, and at the Midland Railway depot before that.'

'Why did you leave?'

He laughed gaily. 'Oh 'twas nothing' at all, missis – just a difference of opinion! I'll give Dewdrop a good rub never you fear. Just leave her to me! Go on now – a fine lady like you has all kinds of business to attend to. Just leave Dewdrop to me.'

Uncertainly she turned away.

She had been waiting twenty minutes for a jug of hot water. This was ridiculous. She pulled a dressing gown about her – it was chilly in the early October morning – and went down to the kitchen. No one was there, except one girl – Jane – who was on her knees in front of the range, and appeared to be raking out the ashes. It was twenty past seven.

As Abby came into the kitchen, the girl turned her head, gawping up at her mistress. 'I rang for some hot water.'

'It's all right Mrs Moncrieffe,' the girl said airily. 'As soon as I get the range going I'll be up with it.'

'As soon as – but why isn't it lit already?'

'Oh sorry miss – only Mary's brother's home and we all went round to meet him.'

'Mary's brother?'

'He's a sailor, miss,' Jane went on with her raking. A

221

newspaper was spread out before the range and she was scraping the ashes on to it. 'And don't get home that often, so we had to go.'

'I see.'

'And then, it went on longer than we expected. You know what it's like. Don't worry miss, I'll bring the water up as soon as I can.'

'Oh, well, thank you—' Abby returned upstairs, rather puzzled.

But after a few minutes she could not wait any longer. More to the point, Dewdrop couldn't wait, hot water or no. Irritated, she hurried on her clothes and went down to the stables.

Mick looking unwashed, unshaven, was carrying in some hay to Dewdrop.

She surveyed him in silence. 'At least you're here. Didn't you go to the party?'

'Oh sure I went, missis. 'Twas a grand night, to be sure.'

'Are you going to muck her out?'

'All in good time, missis!' Mick said cheerfully, 'give her something to eat first, anyway!'

Mick seemed to be in charge here, and she returned to her room. The hot water still had not arrived.

She went back downstairs to the dining room, and rang the bell. 'Bring me some breakfast,' she said as Jane came in.

'Very good, miss.'

The clock in the hall chimed eight o'clock. She couldn't make out what was going on. But she drew a long breath. After all, if Mary's brother was home from the sea, it was not unreasonable – heavens – they were human beings like any one else! Who was she to spoil the fun? Abby was confused.

But she did like to be in the stable by seven to check that the horses were comfortable. It was ingrained in her. She might have a hundred servants, but she would still be in the stables by seven. And she must have her hot water at half past six. She must.

Fifteen minutes went by, and Jane reappeared with her breakfast. As the girl lifted the cover from the plate, it seemed as if the bacon and eggs had simply been thrown on to it.

'Did Mrs Casey go to the party too?' Abby asked sarcastically.

'Well, you did say you were in a hurry, miss,' Jane said irritably. 'Cook was only doing her best. Shall I bring in the coffee now?'

'If you wouldn't mind.' Abby tried to control her temper.

Later that morning, she had been giving instructions to Jane, and was turning up the stairs. Was it her imagination? She paused on the stair, and looked back as the maid disappeared through the door connecting with the downstairs. Her words were still echoing in Abby's ears.

'Eau yayers, Mrs Moncrieffe. Thet'll bay neau trahble, Mrs Moncrieffe.'

Abby stood thinking, and slowly descended the stairs again and crossed into the drawing room. Was that girl being funny?

She couldn't be sure, but she could have sworn the girl was making fun at her attempts at an English accent. Abby had thought at first she had a good ear for an accent. But as she worked at it, she saw it would be a harder job than she thought.

She bit her lip, wandering among the acres of furniture, the vast carpet. If only Nick were here! She could only see him a few hours a day; she had understood that from the beginning; but it left her hours and hours and hours alone. It was almost more than she could bear. All she had for company were the servants, and it seemed as if they were ganging up on her. Especially that Jane – Abby had the feeling she was the ringleader, and egged the others on.

Mary was a docile little thing. But she didn't want to complain to him. She was sure of this. Nick would expect her to order her servants herself. But how could she? She had never had a servant in her life. She had *been* a servant.

She took a turn about the room. They seemed to do just as they liked. They had never said anything to her last night about going to a party. Shouldn't they have asked permission? She was bewildered. And when she went into kitchen at twenty past seven, Jane hadn't been the slightest abashed, or apologetic about being so late. In Mr Thorpe's house the kitchen fire was alight at six heating water. Maybe it was being in London. Maybe they did things differently here.

Still he did come, and while they were together she forgot all her worries, and was just happy to be with him.

One afternoon they were in bed together; she lay with her head on his chest, his arm round her, happy, relaxed, at peace together, and out of nowhere she said, 'Tell me about your family, Nick.'

After a moment he began. 'The family comes from Bolton in Lancashire originally. I'm not supposed to tell you this, Hester as a matter of fact; the family likes to forget it. But great-grandfather Josiah Darke founded the family fortunes: cotton. Darke's threads and yarns. Take a look in your work basket some time – if you have one. You'll find the name on the cotton reels. We still have relatives up there, though we try to forget 'em. The family don't like to be reminded where the money came from. My mother especially.'

'Your mother?'

'Oh I haven't mentioned her, have I? That is one lady you aren't going to be introduced to, Hester.'

She giggled, snuggling against him.

'My mother is a great one for the family. The name of Darke must be upheld at all costs. No one is exempt, my brothers, my sisters, my cousins and uncles and aunts.

224

Everyone is bound to uphold the family honour.'

'Where are they?'

'Where do they live? Well, my mother lives in town – got a house near me as a matter of fact, calls in pretty regularly to see Caroline.'

'Is that – your wife?'

'Mm.'

There was a silence. 'What about your brothers?'

'Well, one is in the army, and the eldest is in Lancashire, minding the business.'

'Do you have anything to do with the business?'

'Oh yes. I go up once a month. Less than I used to, what with Caroline. But my family don't like to refer to it. It's a sort of sordid secret, where the money comes from.'

'What about your sisters?'

'I've two. 'Tilda is seventeen and coming out next year.'

'Coming out?'

'Presented at court – you know – a debutante, all the balls and parties, the great marriage market. My other sister Lily is married and has two children. Her husband's away a lot – Hong Kong, the Far East, import and export. Tea, wool, and all that. So she has a lot of time on her hands – well, as much as you can have with two small children. She comes round to sit with Caroline too.'

Abby was thoughtful. 'Is she there now?' she said at last.

'My mother is.'

'So when you're with me – one of them is keeping your wife company?'

He laughed, and turned over to look at her. 'Why are you interested?'

'Of course, I'm interested!' she burst out. 'I want to be able to picture you when you're not here. I want to know all about you – and your family.'

He ran his hand over her hair. After a moment, he whispered close to her head as he kissed her, 'You're very good to me.'

She was astonished. 'No! It's you who are good to me!' She rolled over on to her back, as he propped himself above her. 'You, you, Nick, you've done everything for me.'

And she so wanted to be what Nick wanted her to be. She worked on it every day. After her elocution lesson, she would practise at home.

'How do you do? I am Mrs Hester Moncrieffe. How d'ye do – do you do – I am Mrs Hester Moncrieffe.' She paused, staring at herself in the wardrobe mirror. 'Isn't it warm today? Do you find it so? I am sure I do. Do. Do.' She pouted into the glass, struggling for that long 'oo' sound. '"There is much ado about the new revue *Moonlight in Peru*, due in June at Boosey's Jubilee Rooms".' She paused again, took a deep breath, then holding the parasol in one hand, the other on her hip, she posed once again in the glass. 'My husband? I am afraid poor Moncrieffe was taken in India. The cholera, you know. It was a terrible blow, most affecting. I am sure I don't know how I survived. Still, one does one's best, doesn't one? One bears up, you know.'

She threw down the parasol and sat on the end of the bed her chin on her hands. This was ridiculous. How could anyone ever take her for an English lady? She was sitting staring glumly into own eyes when she heard a very slight rustle outside the door and a sound of suppressed giggles, then the noise of feet on the stairs. She sat up straight, furious, mortified. It didn't matter how well she did. The servants would always know, would always be on the look out for the telltale sign that gave her away.

She was eating breakfast when Mary brought in the morning mail. 'There is one strange one here, Mrs Moncrieffe . . .' the maid said.

Abby bit her lip as she saw the postmark: HM Prison Portland.

Dear Abby,

I got your letter. Many thanks. At last I am permitted to write letters, thanks to Her Britannic Majesty's gracious clemency. It was grand to see you, and I was grateful that you made the journey all the way from London. A long way to be sure.

I get a lot of time to think sitting in here, as you can imagine. And I count the days – what am I saying, since I don't know how many days there are going to be – still I count them, take it how you will. I have a lot to think about, a lot on my mind. And most of all, Mr Randolph Pelham is on my mind. It's the one thing I always keep my sights on. Oh Mr Randolph Pelham, there's going to be such a reckoning! I wonder where he is now? Does he know I am thinking of him, I wonder? Is there some telepathic message warning him? Or has he forgotten all about me? Perhaps he has? Perhaps he has no idea that I am thinking about him, plotting and planning for the day when I get out of here; plotting and planning the day of reckoning. It's like a fire in my guts, Abby, knowing that one day I will even the score with that scoundrel, and call it quits. It doesn't matter if it's in twenty years or fifty years – if I have to wait all my life, but I'll even with him for putting me here. It keeps me sane, you know that?

I am glad you have such a good job, and hope that Mr Moncrieffe is a kind and generous employer. It is a good sister you are to me, to have come over here to the land of the Saxon, to put up with all their airs and graces, their snobbery and callousness, just to be near me. I thank you for it from the bottom of my heart, and bless you in my prayers every night.

God bless you my dear sister,

Rory

She held the thin grey sheet of paper to her lips, shutting her eyes tight as she felt the tears start in them. Oh God,

Rory my dearest brother, to be so far away and shut up in that foul and horrible place, surrounded by rocks and stones, and no blade of grass to be seen.

And as she held the letter like that an anger rose in her against Pelham. She had tried to forget him all the time she had been in England, but reading Rory's letter brought him back. Oh yes, Rory had good reason for revenge. And so had she! Yet what could *she* do? Go back to Ireland, and plunge a knife into him? She could almost have done that, as she sat there, reading and rereading Rory's letter. That her brother should be in that inhuman place, wearing his young life out . . .

Chapter Twenty-three

Abby stopped just outside the stable door. Someone was inside: there was a giggle, a sigh, then silence, with only the slight sound of clothes rustling.

'Oh Mick,' in a long drawn sigh. More rustling, then, 'Oh – no!' in a hoarse whisper, then a moment later in an agitated whisper, 'No Mick, no!'

There was a low chuckle from him.

Abby, immaculate in her tight-fitting riding habit, the pretty little top hat tilted forward on her head, her riding cane in a gloved hand, stood frozen as she listened. How much further was this going to go? She took a breath and strode into the stable. Mick was pressing Mary against a stable partition, one hand on her waist, the other leaning against the partition.

He turned easily as if he had been expecting Abby. 'Mrs Moncrieffe! I've got Dewdrop all ready for ye. She's in spanking form! I'll bring her out to ye directly. Mary, tell me mother thanks for the pudden.'

Mary, red-faced, embarrassed, bobbed a curtsy to Abby and hurriedly squeezed past her as she stood in the stable doorway. Abby watched Mary go in silence. She turned back into the stable and they walked to Dewdrop's stall. How was she supposed to react to this? Wasn't it their private life? They were only human weren't they – and if Mick was flirting with Mary, why shouldn't he? Yet she was painfully reminded of the advances she had had to endure from Thady O'Farrell all that time ago at Mr Thorpe's . . .

She bit her lip, and bent down to examine Dewdrop's off-fore hoof. 'I told you to saddle Mountain Ash. You were going to take Dewdrop to the smith this morning.'

'I'm goin' this very minute, Mrs Moncrieffe. There was a bit of urgent business this morning, and I never had a chance till only this minute.'

She turned to him, severe. 'I told you yesterday afternoon. This shoe is definitely loose. And what urgent business?'

'It is that.' Mick shook his head wisely as he examined the shoe as if for the first time, though he had had a good look at it with her the previous afternoon. 'That is a very loose shoe, and I'll be round to the smith's this minute.'

'What urgent business?' Mick had straightened, was already untying her loose headband and beginning to back Dewdrop from her stall. Abby stepped aside. 'What business?'

'Oh 'twas nothing at all, Mrs Moncrieffe. Just a little thing that come up, and Mother asked me wouldn't I run to the grocer for something – 'twas nothing.'

Abby tried to contain her anger. It was a fine, clear, sharp morning and she had been looking forward to a ride. 'Before you take Dewdrop, put a saddle on Mountain Ash.'

'Very good Mrs Moncrieffe, 'twill be the work of a minute.' Mick was irrepressible, and a moment later led out the little bay mare.

As she rode Mountain Ash into the park, the scene went through and through her mind. What was she to do? Could she sack a servant? Nick paid their wages; still, the boy had been given the job on her initiative – because Mrs Casey had asked her as a favour, and she didn't like to say no.

She had taken him on – how could she sack him? She was intensely irritated – and with herself. She tried to reason it out. Mick was a charmer, as all the maids knew –

230

a happy-go-lucky young lad. Surely she couldn't be too hard on him? You're only young once ... But then, thinking it through again, it came to her – it was the horses which were suffering. Never mind herself, she was letting down the horses. It was their welfare which was suffering through her ignorance. It was still less than two months since she had come to Acacia Road. She didn't know what to do; how could she? And she didn't like to mention it to Nick.

He came that afternoon. They seldom went out together; he would call almost every afternoon, and they would spend their time together in bed. He was very grateful, and often told her so.

'You can't imagine what it's been like for me, Hester. Before we met I had dreamed and dreamed of something like this. That I could be with a beautiful woman and that we could do everything together with no barriers between us, no inhibitions ...'

There certainly were no inhibitions. She only wanted to please him, and if he hinted he wanted to try something out, something different, she was ready. Sometimes too, she was ahead of him. She discovered in herself a wicked shamelessness in bed which took her by surprise, and might have made her blush, but only made her giggle.

'Let's try it this way, dear ...' she would smile knowingly.

'I've got six years to catch up on,' he told her more than once. Perhaps this was why they never went out together.

But this afternoon, as he came into the house, took her in his arms, and was already running his hand over her bottom, kissing her passionately on the side of the neck, and moving her in the direction of the stairs, she told herself despondently, 'That's all he wants.'

Still in a raw mood after the morning's events, she allowed a rare bitter note to creep into her voice. 'I'm going to Ireland,' she said abruptly.

231

'Ireland? Why?'

'It's my sister, Fan. Now that you have given me all this money I want to help her. Do you mind?'

'Mind?' He had heard the defensive note in her voice and reacted to it. 'Why should I? I suppose you'll want to bring them all over next.'

'What?'

'Isn't that what you Irish do? Bring over all your eight brothers and sisters and your aunts and uncles. I expect I'll come round one afternoon and find the house overrun with them.'

'I haven't got eight brothers and sisters,' she started up on one elbow. 'Is that really what you think of me?'

He was looking away.

'Have I ever asked you for money?' she went on.

He was silent, and had rolled over away from her. 'Well, have I? Nick?' She climbed out of bed, and came round to stand naked, confronting him. 'Nick! Have I ever asked you for money? I've *never* asked for a penny! You give it to me and I'm truly grateful, and I do everything I can to be nice for you and do everything you want—' She stopped as she felt tears smarting in her eyes. 'How could you *say* that?'

He was watching her almost as if he had never seen her before.

'I must be mad,' he whispered at last, and reached his hand towards her. She did not respond, the marks of tears on her cheeks.

'Hester – forgive me,' he was still staring at her. 'I'm such a fool. It's just that you hear stories from other fellows and for one stupid moment I thought you were like the others. Please darling, for God's sake you'll kill me if you don't say you forgive me.' He took her hand and drew her back to the bed. 'Of course you must go and see your sister. Go to Ireland if you want of course – I don't care if you bring your uncles and aunts and—'

'Nick, I'm not going to bring anybody – I only thought,

since you've helped me and been so good to me, I should help her too. That's all.'

Two days later she was on her way to Ireland. The scene was still raw in her mind; there was something there which she could not properly understand. It was as if Nick did not want to know about her background, her family, her childhood; he never asked her about it. He had deliberately given her a different name, he was training her to be an English lady, the clothes he had bought her, her speech lessons; it was as if he wanted her to begin her life from this moment on, and to have no past.

It was little more than six months since she had left Kilnevin yet as she arrived she found she was seeing it already with a stranger's eyes: the muddy track into the village; the low cottages with their mouldy thatch, the piles of dung in the roadway, the pig going in and out of a cottage. She saw the tall church steeple as if for the first time and, as she wound her way up to her aunt's farm, she felt as if she were seeing that too for the first time.

She had prepared the family for this visit in a letter; primed them well with news of Mr Moncrieffe, and his generosity. Her costume had been chosen with care. She had to look smarter than when she went away – yet not too smart. She was still conscious of the atmosphere between them when she had left in May.

Still, Eileen was civil enough at first, and Abby was glad to see her father. He pulled himself out of the old chair as she came in, and she flew across the room to take him in her arms.

'We had your letter,' he remarked a little awkwardly as she held him.

Eileen made a cup of tea, and they sat round the table. Abby was not at all sure how to break her news, but fortunately they had a piece of news for her.

'We had a letter from Fergus, in Chicago.' Aunt Eileen

233

brought it out, and passed it over. Abby read it eagerly.

'He's got married!'

'Pity he didn't write before,' Fan grunted watching her, her elbows on the table, 'and we might still be on our farm.'

'He had his reasons, I'm sure.'

She was saving her important news for a good moment. Before that moment could arise, however, Abby went out to see Starlight. Fan followed her, and they leant on the fence together as Abby stroked the horse's nose.

'Well, I am very pleased for you,' Fan started immediately. 'To land such a good place and have such a kind master. Some people have all the luck, is all I can say.' She rested her chin on her hand, with the familiar scowl on her little face. 'Life goes on here just the same, I am so bored and frustrated I could scream.' She drew a sigh. 'Aunt Eileen drives me to distraction. Go and fetch the water, peel the spuds, clean the pail, take the geese to market, always orders, who does she think she is, my mother? She is not my mother, Abby, and she has no right to order me about – she does it only because you're not here. Da is no good, he just sits in the chimney corner muttering to himself, and staring at the fire, and never offers to do any of the work.'

'Poor Da. It's awkward for him, living with Aunt Eileen.'

'I was surprised to hear you went to see Rory,' Fan began again. 'Frankly, I shall be happy if I never hear his name again. How could you bear to go into a *prison*?' Abby shrugged but said nothing. 'I know I should die if it was me,' Fan went on. 'I can scarcely bear to go into the village, someone is bound to ask about him. I cannot abide their pitying glances, the evil hypocrites. I know they're laughing behind my back, the shame of it!' She turned and clutched Abby's arm. 'Abby, can I come and live with you? Please say yes! Please, please, Abby, I cannot abide it here a day longer, please say I can.'

234

'I was going to tell you—'

'What?'

'Well, wait a little. I have some news Fan – and I want to tell you all together.'

Fan's eyes lit up. 'What news? Is it good news? About Mr Moncrieffe?'

Abby nodded. 'Only wait, Fan dear, and I'll tell you all.'

After supper they were all seated round the table in the light of the paraffin lantern.

'There's a bit of news I've been saving up for you,' she began hesitantly. 'You see, as I mentioned in my letter, my employer Mr Moncrieffe is very kind and I want for nothing, everything supplied. He has three horses and I have the responsibility of caring for them. He is a very elderly gentleman, and goes out in his carriage and pair; the other is for riding. Only he never goes riding any more – he's quite frail – so I take Dewdrop out myself. Now,' Abby was getting into her stride, more confident. 'Mr Moncrieffe often asks after my family, he's for ever round the stables chattin', and so kindly, I have told him all our woes (excepting only about Rory you may be sure) how we were thrown off our farm, and reduced to such straits. So,' she drew a breath, 'last week he summons me to his sitting room – and me in all my dirty old clothes. Abby, says he, I have been thinking of what you told me and I wish to help you, says he. Help me sir, says I, how is that? You say you have a younger sister and would like to send her to school. I believe I may be able to help, says he. Oh sir! I cried—' Abby was in full flow now – 'Yes, says he, I am willing to pay her school fees. Do you go tell your aunt and ask her how much the fees may be and then we'll see about it, says he. Oh sir, I cried, and took his hand to kiss it. That's all right, says he, drawing his hand away – it was the smell of the horses, I'll be bound – but then the rich English people are so nice and fastidious in their habits, Aunt, he would not want a smelly groom clasping him, to be sure.'

235

'Go to school?' Fan breathed in awe.

'So, dearest Aunt Eileen,' Abby went on, 'you must make some inquiries and look out a nice school for Fan. I should be so proud that she could have an education, which she deserves if ever a girl did.' She reached a hand to Fan.

They had been watching her in awe and there was a moment's silence as they digested this news.

'Go to school! Abby you're a darlin'!' She threw her arms round Abby's neck. 'Aunt, I'm to go to school!' She turned to Eileen. 'What school do you think?'

Eileen was frowning as she tried to take in this news. 'We'll ask Father McMichael,' she said after a moment.

Chapter Twenty-four

A week later she was home again in Acacia Road, alone, thinking over the trip. On the whole she was pleased with the way things had gone. Eileen had changed her attitude once she saw Abby was able to do something for her sister. The heavy expression with which Abby had been seen off in May was changed now that Abby had a bit of money to dispense.

She drew a breath, rousing herself. In the meantime there were things to be done. And the first thing was the horses. Before even changing, before washing her face, she took up a paraffin lamp, threw a riding coat over her shoulders and went out to the stables. It was dark but she could hear the horses inside. Setting the lamp on the ground she undid the stable door, and went inside. It was chilly, and damp. She held up the lamp. The horses were all there as usual. Still it was strangely cold; she set the lamp on a window sill, and went into the first stall to check on Dewdrop. She seemed well, but when Abby went into the next, she saw immediately that Mountain Ash had a chill, and a moment later heard her hoarse breathing. The horse shuddered, and coughed.

Abby was thoroughly alarmed, and looked round thinking. Where was Mick, first of all, and second, why was it so cold in here? As she stood beside Mountain Ash she noticed something else. At first she thought she was standing on fresh straw, but in a second she realised that this had merely been tossed down over the old, and that the horse was actually standing in inches of sodden, cold, stinking, straw.

She went through into the tack room next door and knelt at the range. No need even to open it. It was stone cold.

She walked quickly back in to the kitchen, which gave across the courtyard directly on to the stables. Mrs Casey was preparing dinner with a maid helping her.

'Where's Mick?'

'Oh Mrs Moncrieffe! 'Tis grand to see ye!'

'Where's Mick?'

'Ah now, Mick, ye see—'

'Is he here?'

''Twas a very urgent business took him, Mrs Moncrieffe, but he will be back directly—'

'Did he know Mountain Ash has a severe chest cold? The fire in the tack room is out, the mare hasn't even a blanket over her, and she hasn't been mucked out properly.'

Mrs Casey raised her hands. 'Not even a blanket! Oh the poor creature. Jane, run out directly, and put a blanket over the poor thing!'

And the girl would have done it, but Abby had turned to the door. 'I'll get the blanket, and I want to speak to Mick the instant he comes in. Jane, bring some firewood and kindling. I want the fire lit in the tack room this instant.'

The girl hurried after her as she strode back to the stables.

The first thing was to put a warm dry blanket on Mountain Ash. Then, as Jane knelt before the little iron door of the range raking out ashes, stuffing in newspaper, firewood, and getting a fire started, Abby was already mucking out the stall and spreading fresh straw. Once this was done she returned to the tack room, ladled some bran and oats into a bucket, crossed back to the kitchen, and was adding hot water from the kettle.

'Oh Mrs Moncrieffe! Ye mustn't soil your hands with

238

that! Sure, I can do it!' Mrs Casey would have taken the bucket out of her hands if Abby had let her.

'I'm doing it,' Abby said tersely. As the oats and bran thickened, she stirred it carefully into a gruel, adding water from the kettle.

When Abby got back to the stable, Jane had got the fire alight. As she dusted the ashes from her hands, and flicked dust from her pinafore, she said, 'This isn't really my job, Mrs Moncrieffe.'

Abby swung on her. '*What?*'

The girl was half abashed, and half unrepentant. 'Actually, I'm an indoor servant.'

'Are ye?' Abby's brogue began to surface, 'well then, get indoors! And when ye see Mick tell him I want him this instant!' Her heart beating furiously, she poured the gruel into a bucket and carried it into Mountain Ash's stall, set it before her, and waited as she began to lap it up. She ran her hand over the horse's back, murmuring to her, 'You'll be all right, you're going to be, we're going to take very good care of you, so just eat up your mash . . .'

Mary's head appeared at the door. 'Oh Mrs Moncrieffe, cook said to tell you, your dinner's ready.'

'Tell her to keep it till I say. This horse needs looking after first.'

Two hours later, Mountain Ash had eaten her mash, Abby had given her some fresh hay, she made up the tack room fire, and eventually at about half past nine, and suddenly feeling very tired, came indoors again. 'Tell cook to serve dinner,' she said wearily.

Mary bobbed a curtsy and disappeared. Abby went to her room, and washed her hands and face. She was too tired to change. She would just eat something and then go to bed.

When she returned to the dining room, there was no sign of dinner. Abby rang the bell. 'Where's dinner?' she asked expressionlessly.

'Cook says she getting it ready as fast as she can, but she's afraid it's ruined being kept so long.'

239

'Tell her to give me a bowl of soup at least. The rest isn't so important.'

Mary bobbed a curtsy again and disappeared.

Eventually, she reappeared, and set the soup on the table. Abby took one mouthful, and set her spoon down. 'Take it away.'

The girl looked puzzled.

'It's burned.'

Timidly the girl took the soup away. Abby sat with her hands clasped in her lap, her eyes closed, her head bowed. Oh Nick, I'm so alone. Why are you so far away? Why did I have to come back alone to this big empty house, which is not my house, and where I have to fight and argue with these strangers, who despise me?

Mary reappeared once more.

'Excuse me miss, but cook says she's clearing up for the night. Do you still want your dinner?'

'No. I'm going to bed. I want to speak to Mick in the morning. I want my hot water sharp at six-thirty and breakfast at seven. You can go.'

She was asleep immediately, and woke at six-thirty feeling stronger, though immensely hungry; her hot water was on the wash stand as the girl drew back the curtains – though it was dark outside. At seven she was eating her breakfast, and twenty minutes later she was in the stable, checking on Mountain Ash. The cough was no better. She checked the tack room fire. It was out. Well, the *indoor* servant couldn't soil her hands with lighting it; Abby was in no mood to argue, and she lit it herself. She brought the bucket of bran mash into the kitchen when – at last – the tousled, yawning figure of Mick, in his shirt, bare feet and braces, made his appearance.

Abby was busy stirring the gruel as Mick jerked into life. 'Oh Mrs Moncrieffe, ye shouldn't be doin' that!'

Without pausing in her stirring, without even looking up, she asked in a terse tone, 'Mountain Ash has a nasty chest cold. How long has she had it?'

He grasped for an answer. 'Ah, 'twas maybe the littlest bit of a tickle, Mrs Moncrieffe.'

'Since when?'

'Oh, 'tis nothing very serious, Mrs Moncrieffe – just the last couple of days or so.'

'The tack room fire was out.' Abby's brogue came out hot and strong. 'Did ye think to leave her to freeze to death – and her with a chest cold on her? While ye was in the kitchen with your feet up drinkin' tea – or worse? Were ye born stupid or did ye grow into it? Get out! Get out of this house. I never want to see ye again.'

She ignored his remonstrances as she stirred the mash, bringing it to consistency, and carried it out of the kitchen as Mick followed her with half-hearted pleas and excuses.

In the stall she fed the mare, stroking her and talking to her as she ate. And at last, an hour later, came inside to wash her hands. She wasn't sure at the moment whether the mare's condition was sufficiently serious to send for the vet. As she was standing in the drawing room, undecided, these thoughts going through her mind, there was a knock at the door.

'Come in.'

Mrs Casey's face appeared round the door. 'Mrs Moncrieffe, if I might—'

Abby waited expressionlessly.

'He's only a bit of a lad.' The cook screwed her face into a look, half a sort of sideways knowing, as if to say, 'You have to make allowances for his youth', and half a cringing, whining, wheedling. 'Won't ye give him another chance?'

Abby had her hands on her hips, facing the cook squarely. 'Never in a million years. If that horse doesn't die of pneumonia it won't be any thanks to him.'

'He knows everything there is to be knowed about horses, missis.'

'Don't answer back, Mrs Casey. I was in that stable for

241

two hours last night. It was freezing cold and the mare had no cover on her.'

'He's a good boy.'

'He's a lazy idle good for nothing who should never be allowed near a horse again.'

The cook was taken aback. She paused to gather her wits. 'Well! I won't stand here to hear me own son spoken of like *that*!'

'No you won't, Mrs Casey.' Abby took her up very sharply. 'You can go as well. I've had enough of your temperament!'

'*What!* Well—'

Abby had no wish to carry on the discussion. She marched to the door and flung it open. As she expected, the two maids were listening, bent forward, and almost fell into the room, as she wrenched open the door. 'And you! You're all fired!'

Mrs Casey was galvanised into action. She came up to Abby. 'Well, I for one won't be sorry to go. I'm used to workin' for *real* ladies, Miss Abby O'Leary!' She leered into Abby's face, her hands on her capacious hips. 'Mrs Hester Moncrieffe, *me arse*!' And bursting into a raucous laugh she waddled out.

Abby shouted, 'And if you want to know, *I* was gettin' tired of *burnt soup*!'

'Yah!' The cook turned, glared at her and, as she turned again, lifted up her skirts from behind to reveal copious layers of dirty petticoats and veined mottled legs before disappearing with a coarse guffaw.

Abby turned and strode violently to the window, looked out without seeing anything, turned and strode to the other, and so on, turn and turn about.

That was the last time any servant should answer back to her! She would have fresh servants, who had never heard of Abby O'Leary. From now on her servants would know her only as Mrs Moncrieffe. There would be no more fraternising with servants. From now on, she'd make them cringe. No servants should ever hear the brogue on her lips. This was it. This was the turning point, the crossing over point, the point of no return. From now on she was a lady. You could be on one side or the other; but you could never be on both.

Her path lay clear before her, and nothing was to be too much trouble. She bought a book of etiquette; she had trembled often at the thought of embarrassing Nick over some trifle of social behaviour. She flicked over the pages: 'How to address a peer of the realm, a bishop, the rules for morning calls, whether and when gloves were to be worn ...' She turned another page: 'Don't drink too much at receptions ... A girl should remember that if in her nervousness she sips too fast, it is likely that her glass will be refilled. Unless you are a seasoned drinker it is wise to keep your glass in your hand at least half full ...' Obviously there was much to learn. She read on: 'Ocean travel ... Fancy dress balls on board are delightful and quite impromptu ...' She tried to imagine herself on an ocean liner with Nick, at an impromptu and delightful fancy dress ball.

'Servants' Duties': This she studied with particular care. There were to be no more misunderstandings. From now on she intended to make sure she knew exactly what was expected of a servant. 'A maid should make a point of ascertaining early in the day whether her mistress will be "at home". Should it be necessary to keep a caller waiting while the point is ascertained, she should ask the visitor in, not leave her outside on the step while she goes to inquire.'

Rules for dining were the worst: 'Apples are held firmly by the fork and peeled sideways.' She put the book down as she tried to visualise this. 'Grapes are placed in the mouth and the skin is lightly withdrawn. The seeds must be removed on the fork which you hold sideways to your mouth to receive them. Place the seeds on the dessert plate.' The dessert plate being which, precisely?

243

She read on. 'A Girl's Engagement ... The Engagement
Ring ... It is the lover's pleasant duty to present his fiancée
with an engagement ring ...' She drew a breath, her eyes
slightly glazed: how wonderful that must be ... Nick
presenting her with a diamond ring. Then she closed the
book: such things were not for humble stable girls.

In the meantime she had other 'duties' to fulfil. She sat
upright at her escritoire, dressed in an elegant winter woollen
gown, lovat green with a design of gold running through it. It
was a sober dress, and made her look older than her age.
Opposite her sat, or rather crouched, a girl of sixteen, clutching in a gloved hand a letter of recommendation, a
'character', from her last mistress, which she now held out.

Abby took it without speaking and without smiling, and
glanced through it.

'It says here you are diligent in your duties and careful
for your employer's interests and welfare.' She glanced
round the room. 'There are some valuable pieces here.'
The girl's eyes followed Abby's, as she took in the Chinese
vases standing on a shelf over the door, the Meissen
figurines ranged on the mantelpiece, the bibelots on a table
near the fireplace. 'Are you careful in your dusting?'

'Oh yes, ma'am – Mrs Moncrieffe, I should say –
mistress complimented me on how careful I was.'

'Very well, you seem a good girl. The wages are eight
pounds a year payable quarterly, together with your keep.
If you are a good girl, and work hard, you will find I am a
fair employer. But I give notice, I shall not tolerate any
sloppiness of behaviour. Do you have a follower?'

'No ma'am!' the girl interjected quickly.

'It's as well. Let me see, how much notice do you have
to give your present employer?'

'I can start immediately.'

After the girl, whose name was Robbins (there were to be
no more Christian names), had left, Abby sat thinking over
the interview. She felt old enough to be the girl's mother,

whereas in reality there was barely two years between them. How extraordinary it was. And how far she had come since she had arrived in London.

A few days after her return she received a letter from her aunt. Eileen had made inquiries with Father McMichael, and Fan was to go to boarding school at the Convent of the Sacred Heart in Meath. According to the priest this was a select academy for young ladies, with a high reputation for good conduct and discipline, and Fan would be well educated and trained – which was what she most wanted, Eileen said: 'Between ourselves, she has become almost uncontrollable at home.' And would Abby please tell Mr Moncrieffe the cheque should be made out to the Order of the Sacred Heart, and fees were payable a term in advance.

Abby told Nick what she had done, and asked him to open a bank account for her in the name of Moncrieffe. From now Abby was to be in charge of her own finances. She paid her servants' wages, she paid the tradesmen; she scanned the housekeeping book, communed with her new cook, Mrs Baker – a different order of servant from the late unlamented Mrs Casey; she ordered refurbishment of the house, renewed pieces of furniture and shopped for household items.

It was on one such shopping expedition, some months later, in a shop in Regent Street, that Abby saw Nick with a young lady on his arm. For a second she turned quite white as she stared at them across the shop; of course she knew about Nick's wife, had seen her once at a distance. This was not his wife. The two of them were bending over a bolt of cloth on the shop counter, the shop assistant respectfully turning over the fabric and nodding in agreement as Nick spoke; the woman wore a hat, turned back from her face, which set her off in a very attractive and stylish fashion. This hat particularly enraged Abby and she stood silent as all manner of conflicting emotions rushed through her. If it wasn't his wife, who was it? Through all the months she had been in Acacia Road it had never occurred to her that he might have other women friends.

In another second, however, her resolution stiffened. Quite casually she approached the counter beside the woman and pretended to make an inquiry about some fabric; the assistant brought a heavy bolt of cloth to the counter and set it before her. She turned it over as she examined it and then quite accidentally let it fall on the young woman's foot. With a cry of pain, she jerked round. Abby knelt to retrieve the cloth, now spilled in yards about their feet, with well-feigned apologies, as assistants rushed to help. As she was making up to the woman, she could see over her shoulder the frown on Nick's face, but a vengeful instinct within was well pleased with her work.

The following afternoon he came to the house in a furious mood, but she refused to be abashed. 'It serves you right for going out with other women – when you won't go out with me.'

'Even when the other woman happens to be my sister who has just got engaged?'

'How do I know she was your sister? How do I know you haven't got women all over London?'

'Are you crazy?'

'Yes, I am crazy! Nick, I'm crazy for company! We never go out together. I'm going mad here alone!'

Months passed, the following summer passed, and Nick was away for six weeks, in the Isle of Wight he told her, for his wife's health. Once and once only he took Abby to Somerset for a week, and they had long walks on the cliffs, and ate their supper in an inn by a log fire, talking to the villagers. It was lovely, but it was only one week.

And so a year passed away, and she was still in Acacia Road, Nick was still coming, and it looked as if it might go on for many years like this, if nothing occurred to change it; and as autumn came on and she had passed the first anniversary of her arrival here, she could not see any reason why it should.

246

Chapter Twenty-five

Through all that time he continued to train her. In their conversations he would watch her pronunciation constantly for any telltale sign of the brogue. He continued to dress her. Nick took a particular delight in her dress, and would pore over fashion plates and turn over fabrics at the dress-makers. She teased him about it mildly sometimes – because she had noticed he was very fastidious about his own clothes too, and wore only the finest, softest fabrics, and everything beautifully tailored; he arrived immaculately turned out whenever he came to see her. 'You're as fussy as a woman,' she said once, and he admitted it.

'It gives me such pleasure to choose your clothes,' he told her. And after all, he had taught her everything about dress; why should she be ungrateful? In fact Nick enjoyed everything about her; he was perpetually interested in her, he loved to watch her dress; he loved to watch her undress; he taught her table manners – and corrected the etiquette book sometimes – 'that's only for people who don't know any better' – and she was relieved to learn she didn't after all have to eat an apple with a knife and fork.

But still, still, she was alone an awful lot of the time.

'We hardly ever go out together.'

'Mm?' After the fury of their love-making he was relaxed beside her and half asleep, in a semi-doze.

She moved slightly away from him. 'I'm stuck here, day after day. You don't know what it's like. You can go anywhere you like. You have all your family round you, you can go back to your wife. You never think of me here.'

'Hester!' he turned, alarmed by her tone.

'It's true. I've been here over a year. Last summer you were away for six weeks. I nearly went mad. Why don't we ever go anywhere together?'

'We went to the opera.'

'Last month. I'm half crazy for a bit of company, only the servants . . .'

After a while, he threaded his arm round her neck, and pulled her back towards him and then as he spoke, gently stroked her hair, down over the pillow and her shoulders.

'I have to be careful, that's all. God alone knows what would happen if the family came to hear of you.' He had explained many times about 'the family'. Nick was a gentleman, and married; and what was she? Abby had to be kept out of sight.

But Nick had been troubled by this conversation, and a couple of days later he returned to the subject. 'I wasn't thinking. I've been very selfish, and didn't realise what it's been like for you. You don't know anyone in London. We must go out more together – go places together. It's difficult in London, of course. But – Paris! We could go to Paris together, couldn't we?'

'Paris?' she turned, leaning on his chest, wondering.

They met on the train. She was in a new travelling coat, made for the trip specially, and in her two trunks were the day coats, the walking skirts, the evening gowns, the stout winter boots, the light evening slippers, the underwear newly bought for the occasion. Nick was taking her to Paris! She must be ready for him, ready to do him justice. Nick liked her to have plenty of clothes, he loved spending money on her; she was clever enough to understand that he did not want her to save his money. It gave him pleasure to see her spend it.

She had her ticket in her glove. This was definitely the right carriage, she was definitely in the right seat. And what a difference sitting in a first class seat, she thought as she sank into the padded seat, and rested her arms on the spacious arm rests. She could relax and watch the bustle going on round her, porters pushing their way through the corridor, as others pushed their way past them. People calling to each other, wielding heavy cases. Hers were in the luggage van. People would look in, notice her and raise their hats, and then realise they had the wrong compartment and move on down the corridor.

She stared out of the window – grimy, soot smeared, and smiled. Paris!

And then Nick was there, looking so handsome, and so beautifully dressed. He sat opposite her, took her hands in his, and they sat for a moment in silence smiling at each other.

'Paris, just the two of us, Mrs Moncrieffe,' he kissed her.

She kept pointing things out, or making comments on the journey. 'I bet you've done this dozens of times.'

'Done what?'

'Oh – travelled on trains, gone to France or other countries. It must seem ordinary for you . . .'

'Ordinary? No, I love travel.'

'Tell me all the countries you've visited.'

'Well, let's see,' he considered a moment. 'France, Spain, Italy, India of course.'

'Why of course?'

'Didn't I ever tell you? I was in the army for five years.'

'Never!'

'Oh yes, stationed all over the place – India, Africa – and so on. Why?'

'Oh,' she was flustered, 'nothing. It just made me think of something, that's all.'

'What?'

'Nothing – go on, where else?'

'Well, Caroline and I went on our honeymoon down through Spain to Morocco.'

He paused and after a moment she said hesitatingly, 'And that's where she – caught the disease?'

'Mm.' He was silent, looking out of the window. She was frightened seeing him withdraw like this, and hurriedly touched his arm.

'I'm sorry, Nick dearest, I shouldn't have mentioned it.'

He raised his eyebrows, thoughtfully, still staring out of the window, and went on at last as if he hadn't heard her. 'She was attacked by some insect – very painful for her, but I thought it might simply be a mosquito – bad enough, you understand, when you're on your honeymoon – and it left her low, knocked her out for most of the rest of our journey. She seemed to take for ever to recover; in the end we took the ship home from Gibraltar, easier for her, and I thought sea air would help. And once we got home I thought she was getting over it, but then this kind of list-lessness, this constant fatigue, poor thing, she was always exhausted. And then, it settled into a loss of weight, constant lack of energy. Sometimes there would be a recovery for a time . . .'

His voice trailed away as he stared out of the window. She was silent watching him until at last he roused himself. He took a grip on himself and smiled. 'Is this your first trip abroad?'

She grinned. 'Depends what you mean. I *am* abroad.'

'Oh yes – I see what you mean. Do you often think of home?'

She nodded.

It was early December, there was a strong breeze from the sea and breakers on the shore as the train pulled into the Marine station at Dover. As they stood on the deck, she wrapped herself securely in her winter coat, and took a deep breath, and as the ship passed the breakwater she

250

caught the first strength of the sea, her bow heaving and then dropping into the trough, and thudding against the next wave. The sea looked something not to be trifled with: the colour of the waves changing, merging, blending through grey, blue, green, ultramarine, the spray whipping from the wave tops and the wind thrumming in the rigging. Looking up, the smoke from the tall funnel was caught and lost in the wind in a second. High above clouds dashed, driven before the impetuosity of the gale.

'It's lovely!' She threaded her arm through Nick's as she stared out to sea.

'Want to go inside?'

She shook her head. She could never tire of this, never tire of the sea in all its primal potency, its eternal power and majesty; mesmerised she stood at the rail, clinging as the ship rose to meet the surge, and plunged again. After a while Nick went inside and she was left alone on the deck, except sometimes for a sailor who would stagger past her in waterproofs.

The ship came at length into Calais, the wind seemed to disappear, stillness descended, passengers appeared from the saloon, and they were on dry land – how reassuring it felt after the rise and fall of the sea. On the station platform there was activity, and Nick was consulting the tickets and then leading her along to the train – which seemed far longer than the trains in England, and higher up too – found the first class carriage, saw her to her seat, and disappeared again to check on their luggage.

And so at last after night had fallen they were coming in slowly through marshalling yards and a wilderness of sidings and shunting engines, the train crossing, heaving and complaining as if it were being hauled unceremoniously from one line to the next, and at last coming under the great shed and slowing to a halt.

'Welcome to Paris.' He leaned forward and kissed her lightly. On the platform beneath the green glare of the gas lamps, the porters were vociferous, aggressively pushing

251

their way through the crowd with their barrows, people were shouting across her in a language she did not understand, and she waited as Nick once more disappeared, and eventually returned followed by an old fellow in a blue smock and battered peaked cap, with their boxes heaped up before him. Nick took her arm, threaded it into his and together they made their way down the platform and through the station to the street outside. Here there was a bewildering crowd of passengers looking for cabs, whistles blowing, cabs constantly jostling past her, the clattering of hooves on cobbles, but now she was being helped into a cab, the boxes were going on to the roof, Nick was calling up to the cabbie in incomprehensible words, and they were off.

Paris was a blaze of light. All the shops were open, and the pavements crowded with people, the shop windows brightly lit, all kinds of things – poultry, turkeys, and chickens, game, hanging in rows, a baker's shop, cakes of every mouth-watering description, and people hurrying in and out with bread. Abby's head hung from the window taking everything in, until eventually the cab drew to a halt.

A doorman in a long red coat was hurrying down red-carpeted steps, opened the door of the cab, and folded down the steps. She stepped down, Nick took her arm under his, they went up through glass doors, into a huge foyer, a vast crystal chandelier overhead, waiters in white jackets hurrying past, managers bowing in black cut-away coats and stiff high collars; they were being ushered forward and were at the reception desk where an immaculate gentleman like a chamberlain she thought, his cravat perfectly knotted, not a hair out of place, placed a thick leather-bound book in front of them, and Nick was skewing the book to her and she saw the words, 'Mr and Mrs Moncrieffe.' She smiled up at him, and hastily scribbled 'Hester Moncrieffe.'

Upstairs, the corridor was silent. The porter opened the door, entered before them, and lit the gas lights. A fire burned in the grate. He knelt at it, adding coal, and gingering it into life.

'*Bon soir, m'dame, m'sieur*,' he touched his forehead as Nick clinked coins in his hand and he bowed out. The door closed, there was silence, and they were alone together.

She turned slowly taking it all in. A pretty crystal gas chandelier hung from the ceiling, which was encrusted with reliefs, flowers, curlicues, classical motifs. Two old-fashioned armchairs, and a pretty sofa with brocade in gold and rose designs in front of the fire. Rare old furniture, beautiful mirrors, thick velvet curtains; she was taking it all in. She turned back to Nick.

'Where do we sleep?'

'I expect they've thought of that,' he murmured dryly, crossing and opening a door. She was behind him, 'Oh Nick! It's lovely, the most perfect . . .'

The most perfect little bedroom in fact, with an awning in lace and gauze over the bedhead.

There was a tiny knock at the door.

'*Entrez*,' Nick called.

A pretty chambermaid, stiff in starched cap and apron holding a jug.

'*Excusez moi*,' she smiled, went quickly by them, and set it on the wash stand in the bedroom, then fussed about the bed for a moment, turning it down.

'*Bon repos*,' she smiled again very prettily as she let herself out.

Abby threaded her arms round Nick's neck, and rested against him looking up into his eyes.

'It's perfect.'

He nodded.

After a moment, and now beginning to feel all the hurly-burly of their journey catching up with her, she turned away.

'I think I'll just have a wash and lie down, Nick, if that's all right?'

'Of course.'

'And then later we can go out.'

*

The next thing she knew, however, as she gradually opened her eyes, was that it was morning. Nick was asleep beside her, but she felt quite awake and perfectly refreshed after the journey of the day before. She pulled herself out of the delicious down bed, padded in bare feet to the window and opened the curtains.

Outside, it was a brilliant morning, the sky a piercing flawless blue. And, spread out before her, the largest open space she had ever seen, a huge square, traffic clattering across it, though the sounds were subdued by the closed windows. In the centre of this vast space stood a tall obelisk, there were trees or gardens on either side, and far away on the other side what looked like a Greek temple. She took some time to absorb this great panorama, and as she stood admiring it all, she heard Nick turning a little in bed, awakened by the light.

He opened his eyes at last and saw her at the window. He looked at her for several seconds without saying anything.

She was conscious of him enjoying her nakedness, and turned, in a mixture of pleasure at showing herself off, and a slight self-conscious modesty.

'What is it?'

'A man might wait all his life for such a sight,' he murmured.

She probably didn't hear this because she turned again to the window. 'What is this enormous square, Nick?'

Awakened from his reverie, he replied drowsily, 'The Place de la Concorde.'

She repeated his words reverently beneath her breath, and then looking out again, murmured, 'Paris!'

There was a wry smile on his lips. 'Some lucky cab driver down there is getting the surprise of his life.'

'What do you mean?'

'You are standing in full view.'

She turned quickly, beaming. 'We must go out! Ring for some water, darling!' and as he leant to reach for the tassel

254

near the bedhead, she ran lightly and perched on the bed beside him.

'Are you glad you came?'

He didn't answer, but only looked up into her eyes, and then almost absent-mindedly, ran his hand up her front and over one heavy breast, pressing it momentarily. She sighed involuntarily, and moved against his hand as a shiver of pleasure ran through her, but then giggled, pulled herself away, and sprang up. 'Come on! I want to go out. And I'm hungry!'

After she had washed, she looked through her clothes, which a maid had hung in the wardrobe the previous evening, and thought, We're in Paris now, and I *must* look nice for him!

And eventually after much dithering and changing her mind, at last dressed as she had never dressed before, from all the new clothes she had brought specially, and conscious of herself in her best finery, she descended with Nick to the dining room for breakfast.

She was glad she had dressed so carefully. Everything was hushed in the dining room. White-jacketed waiters moved between the tables, where ladies sat, upright and stiff in coats and hats, opposite gentlemen in tight frock coats with stiff collars. It was a wonder they could breathe, she thought, they looked so buttoned up. These could be only the very cream of high society – of international society she corrected herself, as she heard the people at the next table with American accents.

As she was still looking about her and taking everything in, Nick spoke in French to a waiter, and he returned shortly with a tall silver coffee pot, and a dish of pastries.

Then, wrapped in her winter coat, with a fur hat pulled firmly over her brows, they stepped out into the square, her arm tucked through Nick's. She stopped to look back up at the majestic façade – the awe-inspiring classical severity of the hotel, and for the first time noticed the name: the Hotel Crillon . . .

As they crossed the square, not hurrying, though

255

sometimes having to scamper out of the way of carriages that came rattling across at them without apparently any rhyme or reason, Nick was telling her things.

'The obelisk is from Egypt – brought back by Napoleon, I think, and that Greek temple over there is the Assemblée Nationale – the Houses of Parliament in France.'

The day was exceptionally clear, the sky was a brilliant piercing blue, intensely cold, the air like diamonds, so cold that it caught the throat, but exhilarating, too.

'We'll take a stroll in the Tuileries.'

And then as they were about to enter the gardens, he remarked, 'This is where the guillotine used to stand you know—'

'Hush!' She placed her gloved hand over his mouth. 'Don't talk of such things. Nothing is going to touch our happiness, no mark, no blot, no shadow. Everything is so perfect . . .'

Later, as they walked between the wintry trees, each cut to shape, rows of them regimented, precise, she became thoughtful. Nick noticed the great interest she took in the well-behaved, respectable couples, families, young gentlemen, moving about them, each going their own way, strolling, hurrying, sitting on a bench . . .

When she failed to answer his question for the second time Nick tightened his grip on her arm slightly. 'What are you thinking?'

'Oh,' she sighed, 'I was thinking how nice it is to be able to walk with you like this without having to fear that anyone might see us together.'

Later they were walking through crowded streets and found themselves in a very wide avenue, crowded with passers-by, and traffic, and they strolled staring into windows, and eventually came to another great square where a vast building stood, like something left over from Ancient Rome. A flight of steps before it, a great dome above, rows of classical columns across its august façade. A temple? The senate house?

'The opera.'

Everything about Paris was so grand, so stately; it was a lot to take in.

And later still they found themselves strolling past a haberdasher's, where ladies' underwear was displayed. She glanced across the wares spread out to view. They had nothing like this in London. She made a mental note to come back later on her own, if she could. They weren't so far from the hotel.

That afternoon as dusk was gathering over the roof tops, as the street lights began to shed their golden radiance over the crowded streets, and as her feet began to ache – and to chafe too – her walking boots were tight – they made their way back to the hotel, where Nick ordered tea and pastries. A silver stand, on which cream cakes and light dainty puffs dusted white with icing sugar, things she had never seen before, were heaped up.

They sipped their tea, transparent, golden brown, served with a slice of lemon, in porcelain so fine the light shone through it and she bit into those confections that were lighter than air, just a cloud of pastry thinner than paper, collapsing under her bite, and the dusting of sugar on her fingers as she licked them. She had never tasted anything so delicious in her life.

'Don't eat them all, we're going out tonight.'

Chapter Twenty-six

They dined in a smart brasserie on the Boulevard des Italiens. Having got over her initial amazement at Paris she was athirst for knowledge, asking about everything. She was also beginning to get a grasp of the geography.

'The Boulevard des Italiens – it's the sort of Piccadilly of Paris, isn't it?'

They were sitting opposite one another, over a little table. Behind her the walls were covered with etched and gilded mirrors which sent the myriad lights from the chandeliers in a thousand directions, so that everything glittered. Tables crowded about them and the air was alive with chatter as waiters in their long aprons hurried between the tables balancing trays over the diners' heads.

Nick had ordered dinner, and as they waited they sipped champagne.

'Nick, you speak French so perfectly.'

'You must learn French too, Hester.'

'Let's start now,' she said impulsively reaching for his hand. 'Tell me something in French ...'

'*Tu es belle et je t'adore.*'

'What does that mean?'

'Well, roughly,' he paused to think, 'did you remember to put the cat out?'

She laughed. 'Liar. Nick – don't tease. What does it mean?'

'Take the number seventeen bus and get off at the Star and Garter.'

'*Nick*! Really what does it – no! Don't tell me! I think I know what it means. But say it again!'

She was imperious, sitting up straight, her hair, abundant again, pinned up in a mass round her head, white lace spilling over the low cut gown and setting off her bosom. She wore no jewellery but a slender back ribbon emphasised her neck. Nick studied her and at last taking her hand again, murmured, '*Tu es belle, et je t'adore.*'

'You are beautiful and I adore you,' she murmured looking into his eyes. He placed his other hand over hers.

Later as they were lingering over their coffee, Nick excused himself for a moment, and went off. She sat, in a glow of comfort and reassurance, not a little hazy from the wine, but suffused in a warm happiness. Her glance strayed idly over the diners about her, all engaged in their own conversations, and tucking in to their own dinners, and she was thinking how nice it was to see people so obviously enjoying themselves, everyone involved in their own lives, how right it was and normal and—

'*Abby!*'

She jerked her glance up, and beheld three men in evening dress. One of them was a plump round-faced fellow whom she recognised instantly as Willie O'Shea.

'Captain O'Shea.' She was quite breathless with astonishment for a second.

'Abby! What in heaven's name are you doing in Paris? By Jove,' he turned to his friends, 'I say, look here you fellows,' and then turning to her again, uncertain where to begin, 'You look magnificent, Abby—'

'Hester,' said a voice behind him. Nick had returned at that moment.

'Eh?' O'Shea turned. Abby could see by now that he was a little drunk. His two friends watched. 'Nick Darke! I say – are you two—'

'Hester,' Nick repeated calmly, as if teaching a

backward child some elementary piece of information. 'Allow me to introduce Mrs Hester Moncrieffe.'

'What, but that's—'

'Mrs Hester Moncrieffe,' Nick repeated in that same kindly tone.

A dawn of understanding passed over Willie's face.

'Oh, I see.' He paused and seemed to sober up. 'I beg your pardon. Yes, I see now . . .'

'Hester, this is an old friend, Willie O'Shea.'

Willie's two friends were also introduced.

'Mrs Moncrieffe's husband died in India,' Nick said as he took his chair. 'He was a chum of mine in the regiment, and I had known Mrs Moncrieffe out there. Then, by the most extraordinary coincidence, we happened to meet again in Paris a few days ago.'

Abby had not spoken till this moment, but she understood instinctively that this was the moment when she must repay her debt to Nick. She raised her hand to Willie, and said in her sweetest, and most English accent, 'Captain O'Shea, I am so pleased to make your acquaintance at last. Mr Darke has often spoken of you. Are you in Paris long?'

Willie was goggling at her in frank amazement. 'Eh?' He made a huge effort to keep up. 'Oh er – well, a few days, y'know – with some chums—' indicating his two friends.

'It has been rather cold for the time of year, don't you find – though none the worse for that? Paris is always so beautiful in the fall of the year, I think.' She enunciated clearly, and smiled at the same time.

'Cold? Yes.' Still stunned with amazement, he nodded vigorously.

'I do hope we may be able to resume our acquaintance in London some time.'

Willie understood this was his cue. 'Yes, that would be very nice.' He turned to his friends and then back to Nick. 'Er, so long, Darke, as you say—' glancing back at Abby – 'we might meet in London . . .'

260

The three men weaved their way between the tables, and Nick turned back to Abby.

He was silent for a long time as they gazed into each other's eyes and he threaded his fingers through hers, but at last he murmured thoughtfully, 'Well done, Mrs Moncrieffe.'

The following morning Nick said he had to call at the bank, wouldn't be more than an hour, and hoped she would be able to keep herself amused in the meantime. Abby told him to take as long as he liked, she was quite capable of amusing herself, and the second he was gone, she was out of the hotel too, and round the corner into the Rue du Faubourg St Honoré and the little haberdasher's she remembered.

There were things here you couldn't find in London, and she wanted to give Nick a surprise. So she spent an hour turning over the finest silk underwear, the lightest and daintiest garments, frilly nothings, lace-threaded chemises, stockings, drawers, things designed rather to reveal than hide, which played a game with a man, teasing, luring him on ... She owed everything to Nick, and she intended to repay him in full.

That afternoon Nick ordered horses and they rode in the Bois. The plane trees were bare now, and the horses' hooves swished through drifts of leaves. Sometimes a gardener in the ubiquitous blue smock she had seen everywhere in Paris would be sweeping piles together and she would catch the pungent scent of burning leaves drifting through the misty air as the afternoon closed in.

An open *calèche* rolled by and she turned to watch. A single woman lolled in solitary splendour, dressed in the most elegant clothes Abby had ever seen and she couldn't help her eyes following. As the afternoon went on, other carriages would roll past, with these single ladies, sometimes with a dog on their laps.

One of them stopped some yards ahead of Abby and Nick, where a gentleman on horseback had been waiting, and he was in conversation with the lady in the carriage for a while. Then voices began to be raised and suddenly the lady slapped his face and, in an imperious voice, ordered her coachman to drive on. The man was looking after her with surprise, and Abby heard him call out, '*Mais je vous assure* . . .'

Abby laughed. 'She gave him his marching orders.'

'Told him to pay up, more likely,' Nick commented dryly.

She turned. 'What do you mean?'

'What do you suppose? I mean you know who she is, don't you?'

'How could I? I'm a stranger here.'

'Even so, one might have guessed,' he murmured.

'How?'

'Hester, she is one of the *grandes cocottes* and, unless I am very much mistaken, that gentleman was her protector. Come on, the horses will get cold.'

He urged his horse forward again, and as she caught him up, she went on, 'But what does that mean?'

'*Grande cocotte?* Can't you guess?'

'Is it, like, a title? A duchess?'

He threw his head back, laughing openly, freely.

'*Nick!* You must explain!' She gave him a playful blow across the shoulders with her riding came.

'No,' he sobered up. 'She is,' he shrugged, 'his mistress, his kept woman.'

'How do you know?'

'Well, I suppose, they're such a feature of Paris life, and at this time of the afternoon, you know, I expect she's just got out of bed.'

Abby looked thoughtfully after the carriage disappearing down the long avenue. 'She lives in very grand style.'

'It is said that Alphonsine du Plessis charged a man forty thousand francs for a night once. But then again, she died at twenty-three.' They rode on for a while then he said lightly, 'A short life and a merry one, I suppose.'

'Forty thousand francs – how much is that?'

'Fifteen hundred – more or less.'

'Pounds?'

'Mm.'

'Fifteen hundred?' she breathed.

They rode on in silence for a while as his words sank in. Because what was she, after all, but Nick's 'kept woman'? He loved her, she knew, so it was different; Nick was the soul of generosity, and she would never argue with him about money, *never* make a scene in public. Still . . .

On the way back, although conversation between them soon sprang up again, there was in her another conversation with herself, as she tried to think out exactly what the significance of this little scene was. She knew what her status was, after all; she had known exactly what she was going into from the beginning. Yet it wasn't the same as that because – why? Well, because Nick and she loved each other, and would be married she was sure if he hadn't been married already – and . . . still, something remained.

Once they were back in London, the situation would revert to what it was before; the hours alone in St John's Wood, and Nick away with his family, his mother, his sisters, his brothers, his wife . . .

And if Nick should ever tire of her . . . A gloom gradually descended, which it became more and more difficult to shift, try as she might, and she did try as hard as she could to hide it.

That evening they were alone together in their room, the fire was lit, and it was cosy and inviting. During her shopping trip of the morning she had planned to show him her underwear now, to have a little fashion parade, as it were; to take him by surprise, to see the look in his eyes as she revealed herself . . . to enjoy the fierce pleasure it always gave her to know she excited him.

263

But her mood of the afternoon would not pass, and the things remained in their tissue wrappings in her trunk where she had hastily stowed them. Eventually, the mood would pass, she tried to convince herself, and an opportunity to show them would come.

The most important thing was not to let Nick see her feelings; she dreaded having to explain to him; it would only make him miserable too, and she wanted at all costs to protect him from unhappiness.

In any case, he did not appear to notice anything.

Yet despite all her efforts, as it drew towards bedtime, she could see that Nick had suspected something. He too had become more thoughtful and, as they undressed for bed, conversation between them was fitful, inconsequential, there were silences, abrupt changes of subject, and she became more and more miserable. Just let them get to sleep, she thought; once we are asleep, tomorrow we will wake up and the mood will have passed, and everything will be back to normal.

Just go to sleep . . .

She had got into bed, snuggled down beneath the great puffy quilt, and could already feel herself ready for sleep, wanting to lose herself in sleep, to forget, as Nick got in beside her. 'Hester,' he said softly.

'Mm?'

'There's something—'

She rolled over half-asleep already, looking up at him where he sat up in the bed, looking down at her. He turned on one elbow looking down into her face.

'A few weeks ago, my wife – Caroline – said something. It's been going through and through my mind ever since.' He paused awkwardly. 'You see, she said—'

Abby was alarmed 'What is it – about us? Has she found out?' She half rose in alarm.

'No, no, of course not. We wouldn't be here if she had. No, what she said was – well, it was quite simple. She said, that since she could not conceive, we ought to adopt a child.'

264

He was looking down at her. She waited for him to go on, but he did not. At last she said awkwardly. 'Well, what did you reply?'

'I told her I agreed with her.' He stopped again.

Still Abby did not understand.

'So – what did you do?'

He looked terribly serious. 'I hardly know how to say it. You see, the thought that went instantly through my mind was – what *we* might do.'

'We? You mean—'

He nodded.

'You mean—' Abby stumbled on – 'you and me?'

He nodded again.

'I don't—' Then she understood. A hot flush went through her, and her face glowed with shock. 'You mean – if I had a baby you could adopt it?'

'If *we* had a baby—'

She pieced out the thought. 'We – you and I – would have a baby, and then you would adopt it. And what would Caroline—'

'She would never know. I would tell her it was an orphan.' He said it without expression.

Abby stared up at him, her mouth dry as she registered the shock. But now Nick went on, more passionately, with a growing intensity.

'Hester, can you imagine what this means to me? That you and I could have a child? The very moment I had the idea, my heart leaped within me. Our child, yours and mine! And that I could call the child by my own name! I would have an heir, Hester! Can you imagine what that means to me? Can you imagine the thousand times I have dreamed of a child, a son perhaps, my own son, and it was a dream, an impossible dream, I would wake in the morning and—' He paused, looking away, 'You would want for nothing. Frankly, I could never repay you, if I gave you everything I possess.'

There was silence as she lay staring at the ceiling. For

265

the moment she did not know what to think. Feelings conflicted – of course, to bear Nick a child, to give him an heir ... but to give the child away, to know it was being brought up by another woman – a woman who could never give the care and love she could give ... Abby couldn't think.

Nick saw the shock in her, and said no more, looking down at the quilt. 'It's been a shock. Don't say anything now. Just think about it.' She was staring away from him, rigid. 'But Hester. There is one other thing.'

Stupidly, she turned to him again. 'What?'

He was looking down at her still. 'Whatever you say,' he spoke very gently, very softly, 'makes no difference to us. Whatever you decide you are still my own.'

She gave a whimper, and, like a little animal, she curled up in his arms, burying her face in his chest, as he held her. 'Hold me, Nick, hold me, never let me go ...'

Chapter Twenty-seven

She could not sleep. The ideas went through her head, round and round. Trying to see it clearly, trying to understand every aspect, every consequence. To have a baby – and not have a baby. At first there came a joyful thought, that she would bear Nick's child, they would make a baby together ... but then the thought would swing again: how could she give it away ...

And in the cold light of the December dawn, sore-eyed, stiff, unslept, she was conscious of Nick awake too beside her, and turning seeing him, his eyes open, and the bare grey light filtering through the shutters, and reaching an arm tentatively towards him ...

Nick took her in his arms, and they lay, light headed with lack of sleep, as the light strengthened.

'Give me time to think, Nick,' she said.

The next day they returned to London. By prior arrangement they parted in the train. They sat, holding hands, both feeling drained, strange. At last he rose from the seat, kissed her forehead.

'I'll come as soon as I can. There's no hurry. Take as long as you like. And whatever you decide will be all right with me. It won't make any difference.'

He went first and sent a porter back for her boxes. Then she was sitting in the carriage which Nick had ordered for her, wrapped in her overcoat, the fur hat tight over her brows, her gloved hands clasped in her lap. She could not think, waiting in a frozen hibernation for a decision to come to her. It was not something she could command; whatever she was to do, the decision would come to her eventually. In the meantime she must wait in this raw, nervous, sensitive state.

The maids knew she was coming – Nick had sent a cable – and they were full of smiles, were helping her off with her coat, she was looking round the hall, and then going through into the drawing room as if she had been away a year instead of five days.

She stood alone in the centre of the carpet, before the fire clasping and unclasping her hands; her thoughts were automatically with Nick, where he would be, what he would be doing, greeting his wife . . .

And she was here, home again, alone. She drew a breath, rousing herself. There were things to be done.

As she was walking in the park, her hands in her pockets, her head lowered, staring morosely at the path before her, she realised at last the most important fact of all, the thing she had overlooked in her preoccupation with herself: that this was Nick's only chance of a child – maybe a son? She remembered the expression in his eyes when he had asked her, in Paris. Did she have the right to take that chance from him? Nick had given her everything; without him she would either have returned to Ireland, where she had no home – or she would probably be a whore on the streets of London. Every day, she reminded herself, every time she looked round the house, every time she rang the bell for a servant, she owed everything to Nick. She drew a deep breath, pulling the collar of her coat tightly round her neck, looking away across the park, sightlessly.

A new thought occurred to her: it wasn't as if the baby would be going away. It would be still in London, still near, and Nick would bring her news – perhaps in time they might find some way she could see him – she persisted in thinking of the child as the son Nick wanted – it must be easy enough – her thoughts raced ahead. Of course they could think of something. It wasn't such an all or nothing decision, was it?

And yet, and yet, how would she behave at the moment she had to hand it over? She walked on, still trying to think it through, trying to visualise the moment, the actual moment . . .

But as the day wore on, and as she went to bed that night, lying in the dark, her thoughts gradually focused themselves again on the central fact: it was what Nick wanted. If she refused, their life henceforward would be overshadowed with this fact. Every time he looked at her she would wonder whether he was thinking of the child she could have given him, but had refused. It would hang over them both. It would destroy them eventually.

It became clear at last. If she refused his request, their relationship could never continue, whatever Nick might say. All that talk about there being no pressure, and whatever she decided would make no difference to them – yes, it would make a difference. Though Nick was the most generous man on earth, loved her, had refused her nothing, had never asked anything of her that she was not overjoyed to grant – nevertheless, it would hang over them, the memory would always be there – the child he could have had, the child he would never have, the son that might have taken his name, the child she could have given him . . .

And there was another thing. Her family. She was sending money home. Fan was at the convent. Eileen was caring for her father. She lived in style here. All this she owed to Nick.

She had no right to refuse.

When he came a few days later, a day in which he had told her he would be able to stay the night, coming in through the door, taking his hat off, unbuttoning his coat, she went to him, reached her arms to his neck, kissed him gently on the cheek, looking up at him, unspeaking, and yet by her look—

'Nick,' she whispered, 'I have decided . . .'

And she kissed him gently, again, on the cheek.

And he, swallowing, almost unable to believe her, as he took her hand and they went into the drawing room where the fire was burning merrily, and muttered something like, 'You have decided?' still unsure whether he might believe her; she just nodded so slightly, bashful, looking down as if she might be a young girl, acknowledging her lover . . .

Then she pulled his face down to hers, imploring him silently, and he kissed her hard now, and could feel the wetness on her cheeks, as he held her tightly.

'Only don't let's talk about it,' she whispered. 'Later perhaps.'

They dined together, talking of anything, of everything, both filled with the consciousness of this huge decision, and all the consequences that must flow eventually from it, but not ready yet to think them all out, because the most important fact had been established, and later would be time enough. She had known at the instant he understood her meaning, had seen the flicker of light in his eye, the concentration on his face, known that this was the right decision.

A candle burnt by the beside. He enfolded her in his arms as she slid down in the bed and then they were kissing, kissing as they had never kissed before, as she knew it was right to kiss, not to think, not to calculate, but just to know this was right, that she had made the right decision.

So she opened herself to him, as if they had not made love a hundred times, but that this was *the* time, not bothering with the usual preparations and precautions, but giving herself to him, wanting him in her, wanting to conceive his child that very night. The candle was still alight beside the bed but before he pinched it, he rose over her, supporting himself on his hands and looking down into her eyes as she

270

felt the force of him thrusting into her, and she knew it was the perfect consummation of herself, the complete knowledge that they were absolutely united, and she arched her back as his long steady strokes pierced her, crying out in wordless cries.

Later they were quiet together in one another's arms, talking about the future, telling her his plans, his arrangements, and she not minding any of that, it didn't matter, and whatever he wanted was right for her.

Later still they were moved, aroused, and were making love again; it was as if there was a fathomless need, a heightened sensuality that made for them an eternity of kissing, of caressing, of touching, of knowing and belonging, that was not any mere physical release, but a holy rite, a consecration of each to the other. They seemed to reach a plateau of sensuality where he could just go on and on, in long, slow, languorous strokes that pierced her through and through till she thought she must die, it couldn't go on any longer, but it did go on, and on, and on . . .

And still they were awake, still talking, still exploring each other, still the need to penetrate the essence of the other, that they might be fused together in this electric furnace of their togetherness . . .

And only as the dawn began faintly to light the room, filtering through the curtains, they fell into a deep sleep, she curled within his arms.

It was late when they woke, she didn't know what time it was, but it didn't matter, and they lay slowly, coming to consciousness, and feeling strange, unreal, not part of the ordinary web and woof of life, but apart for this time, not yet back in the world.

Eventually he turned and saw she was awake.

'Shall I ring for water?' he whispered.

'In a minute.'

'Hungry?'

She nodded faintly, her head on the pillow beside his.

271

He rang, and when the maid knocked, told her to serve some breakfast in front of the fire downstairs.

A little later she could hear a flurry of activity in the drawing room, dishes were set out on the table, the fire was made up, and eventually, pulling on a robe herself, she tiptoed down to find Nick at the little table in front of the fire, heaped with an appetising breakfast. They sat, opposite one another, sitting feeling strange and dreamlike, and not yet of this world again.

She sipped at her coffee, which had never tasted so heavenly in her life, coursing energy through her, always looking at Nick, and he at her. He smiled, 'Sleep well?'

She nodded. She didn't want to speak yet. Speaking implied thinking, involved planning, deciding. She didn't want to plan, or decide, or think – not yet. The time would come for that. But now at this moment, she wanted to *be*, just to be here with Nick – here, in this place, in this moment which she knew instinctively, without thinking, would be the most important of her life.

Much later, like a couple of invalids, or very old people, they dressed each other, reverently, gently, slowly, lovingly, doing up fastenings, lacing boots, fussing round each other, and at last in overcoats and hats and gloves, and arm in arm, they went out in the street, and made their way slowly down and into the park, walking, without speaking, between the bare trees, beneath the clear sharp sky. Not thinking, not planning, not deciding. Just *being*.

She placed her hand over her belly. She knew by now she had conceived. Her period was two months late. It was certain as anything can be. The signs were unmistakable, the queasiness, the morning sickness – oh, there was no mistaking the signs.

As she stared into the garden – a dull cold day in February – she tried to take a grip on her thoughts. There were important things to think out. Things she had purposely put away from her the night they had made love.

272

The night they had made love, she told herself.

She had accustomed herself to the arrangements. She would have the baby, and a few days later, Nick would come for it. A nursemaid had been engaged already. She swallowed, but controlled her thoughts. In any case there were to be no thoughts. The decision had been made, and she was sure it was the right decision. It was time to go down and visit Rory again, too – before she got any bigger. However, before she could do this, there was knock in the middle of the morning, and Taylor brought in a card on a small silver tray: William O'Shea (Capt. Retd)

'Willie! Oh, do show him in at once!'

And as the portly figure appeared in the doorway, she ran to take both his hands in hers.

'Captain O'Shea! You came to see me! Come in, this is such a pleasure. Taylor, bring us coffee!' she led him to the fire – there was a brisk fire this morning – 'Sit down, I was just writing a letter and feeling lonely and bored.'

Willie was very proper, very subdued, a far cry from the ebullient man who had first introduced himself to her in Hyde Park. This was the difference between being a stable girl and being a lady, she thought. He sat, upright, his hat perched on his knees, awkward, tense, until at length she burst into laughter.

He looked alarmed. 'I say, what is it?'

'Oh, for heaven's sake, do relax. We're old friends, you know.'

It seemed Willie had something to get off his chest, and after a few more pleasantries, the words began to come haltingly out.

'Rather embarrassing, Mrs Moncrieffe—'

'Yes?'

'Yes. There's something I wanted to say, hope you don't mind my bringing it up – this girl I used to know – damned pretty one too, pardon the language, bit of a misunderstanding, felt bad about it ever since – been led up the garden path, y'see, meant no harm, I assure you—'

He ground to a halt. Abby had risen as he began this recital and crossed to the window. There was a long silence, until at last she turned slowly and gave him a long curious look. 'Captain O'Shea, what *are* you talking about?'

He stared up at her, as she gazed calmly down at him. Then she smiled, a dazzling smile, like the sun breaking through the clouds, and she saw him visibly relax. He smiled too, a relieved smile like a man who has just been reprieved from a long prison sentence. 'Oh – er, nothing really, I suppose – nothing at all . . .'

She clapped her hands together. '*I* think we should go into the park! Come on!'

Well wrapped in a fur-trimmed coat to her ankles, a fur hat, and gloves, she slipped her arm through Willie's and they made their way into Regent's Park. She dropped her letter into the box at the corner.

During their walk, Willie began to expand on his parliamentary career. 'Damned serious matters afoot, Mrs Moncrieffe, pardon the language. You see, I'm so to say, a secret emissary—'

'Really?'

'Yes, between the Chief and the PM.'

'I beg your pardon?'

'The Chief – Parnell, don't you know.'

'I never read the newspapers.'

'Well, we Irish members have weighty matters in hand. No less than a Land Bill.'

'Really?'

'Oh yes. Ticklish business. The fact is the PM, old Gladstone, needs the Chief on his side – to form a majority in the House. And the Chief – for his part – won't sell his support cheaply. Gladstone's going to have to pay through the nose for the Irish nationalist vote. And that's where I come in.'

'As a secret emissary?'

'That's right.'

'I had no idea you were so important, Captain.'

274

Willie shrugged his shoulders in a gesture of modesty. 'Oh well, you know—'

He was silent for a moment, and a frown passed over his face.

'Is anything the matter?' she asked carefully.

He turned to her suddenly. 'Mrs Moncrieffe, you're a woman, a damn fine woman, and a sympathetic one too, I can tell, and understand these things. I wouldn't tell anyone else.' He was looking very seriously into her eyes. 'There's more to it.'

She waited for him to be ready, and in the meantime, took his arm again and they resumed their walk. Willie was collecting his thoughts.

At last he said, almost under his breath, 'It's my wife.'

She was silent, waiting.

He turned to her. 'You don't mind my talking about it, do you?'

She shook her head, looking sympathetic.

'Well, the fact is,' he cleared his throat. 'We've been married fourteen years, got two children, but over the years we've rather drifted apart, separate establishments, all that. Though I go to see the children every weekend. Well, about two years ago, my wife – Katherine – met the Chief, and they—' he coughed – 'started up a clandestine—'

'I see,' she interrupted, helping him over this one.

'Puts me in a very difficult position. You see Parnell's the Chief, we're at an historic moment for our country, could change the course of history, and I'm crucial to the negotiations – so it's difficult for me – mustn't rock the boat, you see, not just now. Still, you can imagine, can be damned embarrassing, when I go down to Eltham to see Katherine, and there's Parnell, with his carpet slippers on, in my favourite armchair by the fire . . .'

'I see.'

There was a long thoughtful silence between them. At length, she began carefully, 'Have you talked to Katherine about it?'

275

'She won't discuss it. Fact is, she's a rather forceful character ... tells me to mind my own business. She worships the Chief, needless to say, thinks he can do no wrong, the saviour of his country and so forth. I say to her, what about the children – what are they supposed to make of it, having two papas in the house?'

Abby was very thoughtful at this. She remembered hearing Parnell speak, though recently she had taken very little notice of politics, having more pressing matters to attend to. Still, she was intrigued, and now having more time on her hands was prepared to know more.

'And you're afraid of an upheaval – in case the scandal should harm the cause – the Land Bill?'

'Exactly! By jove you understand exactly, Mrs Moncrieffe! That's it! What can I do?'

'Have you spoken to the Chief about it?'

'Hmph!' Willie made a grimace. 'Rather you than me! A bit of a tartar, Mrs Moncrieffe – not that I'm afraid of him, I'm not. But he's not the sort of fellow you can reason with, you see. Got very fixed opinions. Passionate sort of man – holds aloof. Frankly, I have a choice: put up with it, or call him out; appointment in Boulogne – all that. But I can't do that! Think of the scandal – the Chief fighting a duel? It could ruin the Cause – upset the negotiations.' He drew a long and painful breath. 'You see the position I'm in.'

Abby was more and more intrigued by Willie's woes. She remembered Mr Parnell's passionate speech at Westport all that time ago. It occurred to her he must appear in the House.

'Do you see any long-term solution? A divorce?' she said at last.

He shook his head mournfully.

'The scandal?' she suggested.

He drew a breath. 'You see, Katherine has an Aunt Ben – eighty-nine years old – who dotes on her. Aunt Ben has made a will leaving all her money to Katherine and the children.'

'Yes?'

'Well? It's obvious.'

'What is?'

'Look – think about it. If I sue for divorce, and cite Parnell as co-respondent, what's Aunt Ben going to make of it?'

'You mean – she doesn't know about Mr Parnell?'

'I should think not! What? The fur really would fly. Oh dear no, they make quite sure Aunt Ben hears nothing. Katherine goes over to read to the old girl every night before she goes to bed, you know – the dutiful niece!' He snorted.

'So you haven't threatened Katherine with divorce?'

Willie looked craftily at her. 'I've a better idea.'

'Yes?'

'As I said, if I sue for divorce, Aunt Ben might change her will, and then nobody would get anything, except the dog's home, possibly. No, the proper path, the astute thing to do is' – he leaned in closer, and lowered his voice – 'wait till the old bird falls off the perch – and *then* go for divorce.'

Willie looked a model of Machiavellian subtlety at this moment.

They walked on again in silence as Abby turned his words over in her mind. Suddenly she said, 'Do you ever speak in the House, Willie?'

'From time to time,' he said airily. 'Why?'

'I should love to see you.'

'Would you? Really?'

'Really.'

There was another pause as they walked on, and Willie seemed noticeably taller. 'Tell you what, the next time I intend to speak I'll send you a ticket for the Ladies' Gallery.'

'I should love that!'

Chapter Twenty-eight

Dear Hester,

Change of plan, I'm afraid. Caroline unwell this morning and the doctors have been here. Not sure when I'll be able to get away. Will contact you again as soon as I know more clearly what the situation is. As always,

Nick.

These notes always unsettled her. Poor Nick, what he must be suffering! She tried to picture him tending his wife, but it was not easy. She had never seen Caroline close to, never heard her voice. Was she beautiful? Abby always imagined her beautiful simply because she was Nick's wife and Nick's wife must be beautiful. She would be a lady, with perfect manners, and would look so pathetic, stretched on the sofa, pale, delicate like some rare flower – but here some deeper, more brutal, instinct broke through. What right had she to make Nick unhappy? Why should he be saddled with an invalid? It was unfair! Caroline was unfairly keeping Nick from his happiness. That was the honest truth. Of course he was a gentleman and devoted to her – unless it was *because* he was a gentleman that he would nurse her to the bitter end, even if he didn't love her any more. Of course he had been in love with her when they married – but now? How could he go on loving an invalid when he was confronted with her helplessness every

278

day? Surely the love would drain out of their marriage? It must! The natural course of his life was being frustrated. He was denied his children – Caroline was denying them to him, while she – Abby – was giving him what his wife could not. And in this hole-in-the-corner way too, unable to stand proudly before the world as his proper wife, which she should be, in all truth and justice.

Abby stood in the middle of the carpet stiff with indignation and frustration as these thoughts flashed through her mind. She drew a breath, turned away, calmed down. It was unworthy of her, and she knew it. She had understood the situation before ever she came to this house. Nick had explained everything clearly to her. Caroline came first. It was that simple.

But then a new thought intruded. Did she? Did Caroline come first? Even after the birth of Nick's child? Abby was thrown into a frenzy again as new thoughts flashed through her mind: the birth would change everything. She must keep the baby, Nick must send his wife off to the south of France – or somewhere else far away – and they could be together, with their child . . .

For a few seconds she walked about the carpet, her hands clasped rigidly together, her heart beating rapidly. And then she stopped, staring at the window, calmed her breathing again and steadied herself as the truth came into focus once more.

She put away the note into her reticule, set her hat on her head, and adjusted the veil. The hired carriage was at the door, and soon she was seated in it, hatted, buttoned, on her way to Waterloo and Portland.

Rory seemed changed – it was not easy to say exactly how – he had put on weight, and seemed perhaps older? More a man. After all he was twenty-two now – the poor boy had celebrated his coming of age in Portland prison – but there was also, she didn't like to admit it too clearly to herself, something about him, something roughened, something harder.

279

She reached her fingers through the bars.

'Rory—'

But he didn't raise his hand. He was looking over her. 'I scarcely recognised ye, in all this finery, Abby. What's become of ye? And the hat and veil – ye look quite the fine lady.'

She smiled bravely. ''Tis my employer, Mr Moncrieffe, Rory, is the soul of kindness and said I must be decently dressed to visit my brother—'

'Did ye tell him he was in gaol?'

She looked down embarrassed by his brusque question. 'Of course not – 'tis of no consequence to me Rory darlin', but ye know how people will talk, and I have a good place, and should not like to lose it if it became known that my brother—'

'You don't have to go on. I understand.' There was a pause, as they both looked down.

'Rory darlin', are they lookin' after ye?' Her natural speech always came out instinctively. 'They're not treatin' ye too rough?'

He shook his head. 'No, they let me have books now, and I can write.'

'Books, that's good, sure – ye can educate yourself.'

'I do. I educate myself in history – the history of our unfortunate country.'

'Oh Rory, there's to be a Land Bill!'

'How d'ye know about that?'

She hesitated. 'Oh, I read too, you know. 'Tis in the papers. A new bill to give justice to the farmers of Ireland.'

'There'll be no justice in Ireland till the English get out.' He spoke in measured tones, thoughts which had obviously gone many times through his mind. 'What have we ever had from the English, Abby, but contempt, and injustice?'

She looked down. After a moment he drew a breath, 'I'm sorry I spoke unkindly to ye. Ye have been a friend to me, Abby, and that's the truth. I don't know how I'd have borne it this long without your visits.'

She smiled and again reached her fingers between the bars, and this time with a little sigh, he touched her fingers with his own.

'Do ye hear from Fan, Rory?'

He shook his head. ''Tis little she cares for me. Never a word.'

'We had a letter from Fergus! He's in Chicago now – and they've had a baby!'

'A baby?' Rory was thoughtful. 'He's well out. Good for him. Starting a new life in a new country.'

'And I'm able to send money now to help out. That's good anyway. And my employer, Mr Moncrieffe, is paying for Fan to go to school.'

Rory smiled for the first time. 'Little Mother. That's what Da used to call ye, Abby. Ye've been a good friend to us all. Did ye bring Fan's letter with ye?'

'Oh – I left it at home. I'll try to remember to bring it next time . . .'

It was more than a week since she had seen Nick. Surely something bad must have happened? Perhaps his wife was dying?

Then one morning she received his note. 'Shall be able to see you this afternoon.'

He was still very preoccupied when he arrived, and looked tired.

'I think she's past the worst of it,' he began almost at once, scarcely a word of greeting, as he took her in his arms and gave her a little peck on the forehead. Scarcely a word asking about her or about how she felt; straight in about Caroline. 'It's been a bad time. I sat up with her all night for two nights in a row, but she is a little stronger now. The doctors have been in and out of the house all day. I've had every specialist in London – and Edinburgh – to see her. It was a crisis. Still,' they had come into the drawing room now and settled themselves before the fire. He drew a long breath, looking round as if to remind

281

himself where he was. 'Things have taken a turn for the better. She was able to get out of bed today. It's been a week since I've been out of the house.'

Abby fussed over the tea tray, waiting, trying to gauge his mood, and what to say. He looked up at her, stared for a moment as if remembering she was there, and smiled.

'Sorry.' He reached across his hand. 'Hester darling, how are you? How is the little one?'

She smiled. What else could she do?

'Growing,' she said.

Dear Mrs Moncrieffe,
I enclose a pass for one to the Ladies' Gallery. The debate comes on around nine, I believe. If you could arrange to arrive about eighty-thirty, I shall have the pleasure of escorting you to your place.
William O'Shea (Capt. Retd)

She turned the thick card over in her hands as she sat in the carriage. The Ladies' Gallery: how grand that sounded.

And Willie was waiting under the arch as the carriage turned into the Yard. He was looking very stiff and buttoned up, and was nervous as she quickly detected.

'Have you got your speech by heart, Willie?'

He nodded vigorously, then swallowed. 'Don't speak very often, Mrs Moncrieffe – like to keep it for the really important moments.'

'I see, and is this a very important moment?'

He nodded again. They had passed through a gothic portico and were now going up a wide staircase beneath lofty medieval vaulting, almost lost in the night gloom, and supported on slender columns. She could not resist looking about her as they talked. Tall stained glass windows rose, statues of august personages in medieval costume – kings? – glared across at each other from recessed niches in the wall. Coats of arms emblazoned in brilliant golds and reds and blues glittered in rows.

282

All that was ancient, all that was most encrusted in trad-
ition, all that was most surely buttressed by immemorial
custom; here was the very heart, the seat of power and
privilege. She could not help her eye straying about her, as
she kept up her conversation with Willie.

'First reading of the Land Bill.'

'I see.'

'Gladstone has bowed to a superior will, and brought it
in at last.'

'Superior will?'

'The Chief of course.'

'Oh you mean – it's an Irish bill?'

'*The* Irish bill, Mrs Moncrieffe! It's going to transform
the Irish countryside.'

'You astonish me.'

'Oh yes – security for the farmer, compensation for
improvements, fair rents—'

'Really? And you are going to speak – at around half past
nine?'

'Near as I can guess. Of course the Tories are going to
make it hot for us. As far as they're concerned, the bill's
rank communism.'

'So it's going to be a lively night?'

He frowned. 'You could say that.'

They had reached a door, which he opened for her. This
was the Ladies' Gallery. She turned, and took his hand.
'The best of luck.'

'Thanks.'

The Ladies' Gallery was quite small, and there was a
high rail before her, so that she could by no means see all
the chamber. For a minute, quite bewildered, she sat where
she had squeezed in between other women – for the gallery
was full – in the third row staring about her at the chamber,
and scarcely noticing the man speaking below her. There
was a sombre dignity about it. The chamber was panelled in
unvarnished oak, and the benches of the members were in
dark green. At night the ceiling was almost in darkness, the

283

windows rising into the gloom. As her attention gradually concentrated on the activity below she was surprised to find the benches were by no means full. Quite large gaps yawned between those members who were present and who, to her astonishment, lounged in every kind of graceless posture, their hands in their pockets, their hats tilted over their faces, legs sprawling in front of them. A man was on his feet speaking in a low drawling monotone, and her attention quickly wandered. He was quoting from innumerable statistics, and coming as she did in the middle of his speech it was impossible to make sense of what he was saying.

Then as she sat and had begun to feel a little at home here, the significance of what was happening began to impinge on her.

A Land Bill. She knew exactly what was at stake. She understood only too well what a fair rent was about. She and her family had been evicted from their home only for the want of a fair rent. She knew all about compensation for improvements. When Rory had proposed to drain the field above the cottage, what had Da said? 'What's the point of it? Sir George Pelham will say the field's improved – and put up the rent.'

There was a commotion, suddenly a group of men were coming into the chamber, there was a buzz of attention, and the speaker still on his feet with his sheets of statistics had to pause till the commotion died down.

The ladies about her were whispering to each other, and she caught immediately, 'That's Mr Parnell!' She craned forward looking among this influx and presently recognised Mr Parnell as the one they all clustered round; unlike the others, who were in black cut-away coats, he was in a shabby countryman's tweed suit, with a thick woollen cardigan buttoned beneath it, and looked altogether quite unparliamentary. Mr Parnell made no acknowledgement of any one in the chamber other than the briefest of bows to Mr Speaker, and took his seat on the front bench, his head

284

down, and stroked his beard reflectively.

Abby now caught sight of Willie on a bench two rows behind Mr Parnell. It was difficult to tell from so far away, but she wondered whether Willie were nervous. She thought he probably was. Poor Willie, it was really very daunting; what an ordeal!

Especially because, since the entry of Mr Parnell and his phalanx, things had hotted up. The man with the statistics had sat down and another speaker was on his feet, and he was getting a rougher reception. It came as quite a shock to hear a broad Cork accent here in the heart of London. And straightaway, the atmosphere in the chamber had changed. So long as the man with the statistics, who had a bland upper-class English accent had been speaking, no one had paid any attention, but now this man – who she could see was not comfortable here, losing the place in his speech, stumbling over certain words – once he had begun, the benches opposite came to life. No one was interested in what he was saying, and were shouting foolish irrelevant taunts, or mocking his accent, which she admitted to herself seemed as out of place as if he had come from outer Mongolia. Abby felt a hot anger. However, as things progressed, she was glad to see the speaker was giving as good as he got, and at one point she heard him shout clearly, 'One day, God willing, we won't have to come over here at all, but will have our own parliament in Dublin!' to cheers from his friends, and jeering laughter from the opposite benches.

Abby glowed with pride. He had put that supercilious Englishman in his place. She sat up straight, and looked forward to the moment when Willie should rise to his feet.

However, as the current speaker sat down, another man rose to speak, and Abby had the most enormous shock when she recognised Mr J.J. O'Toole. Mr O'Toole, who had defended Rory in faraway Castlebar! She stared and stared at him. Was it him? It clearly was. And that he

285

should be here! She stared at him bewildered, scarcely listening to what he was saying. Mr O'Toole! She kept repeating his name to herself. She had never known he was a politician. But then perhaps he had gone into parliament since the trial?

She began to listen to what he was saying, studying him the while. He was dressed as he had been when she saw him last, neatly, his hair combed, his stiff collar straight, his necktie, his black cut-away coat ... his voice was strong, evenly modulated, controlled, his speech clear throughout the chamber. The barracking from the opposition had died, and to her pleasure she saw that even Mr Parnell had turned round to watch as Mr O'Toole spoke.

But she wasn't taking in what he was saying. The memories of the trial flooded through her mind. It was not that Mr O'Toole had defended Rory, as it might be any ordinary client. No, there was more than that. He had put his heart and soul into it. He had laid himself out for Rory, beyond the call of duty. And he had been the only man in that bad time who had not blamed herself. Abby owed him a debt of gratitude.

It came to her then. Now that he was an MP, perhaps he could do more for Rory? Perhaps he could speak to the Home Secretary or someone who was in charge of such things – ask him to look into his case or perhaps request an early release?

And perhaps too she was now in a position to return the debt? Her mind cleared. She *was* now in that position. She must make herself known to Mr O'Toole.

Chapter Twenty-nine

Mr O'Toole had sat down by the time these thoughts had passed through her mind, and for some time as other men rose to speak, she was only half attentive as the impact remained with her. The fact was, she was expecting a baby; suppose she got Willie to invite Mr O'Toole to her house. How should she be introduced? It was difficult. Perhaps it might be wiser to wait till the baby were born . . .

She noticed with a slight jolt that Willie himself had now risen. Poor Willie, what a contrast with Mr O'Toole! He had some papers in his hand, which he held to his face – he must be short-sighted. His voice was thin and weak; he stumbled in his text. He had written his speech out in full, she realised, and was reading it. This was a fatal error in a public speaker, it was clear. Attention wandered, a faint hubbub was audible, and Mr Speaker, in his wig and robes, had to cry 'Order!' more than once. Poor dear Willie, he was not cut out for public life . . .

She wondered whether he would expect her to wait for him? Probably he would; poor thing, he would need a bit of cheering up. When he finished she made her way with difficulty over the laps of the ladies packed beside her, down the stairs to the door in the windy, shadowy gothic portico, and soon afterwards he joined her.

'It was a very gallant effort, Willie. Everyone was most attentive.'

'You think so?'

'Oh yes. And how proud you must be, to make your contribution at such a momentous time in your country's history!'

He was visibly cheered. 'Rather!' he said stoutly. After a little more of this, he went on, 'Mrs Moncrieffe, I'll call your carriage.' He disappeared for a minute, then was beside her again. 'I suppose – I wonder – whether I could offer you a little supper?'

'That is most kind of you – the fact is, I am rather tired, Willie. I think I should prefer to go home now.'

'Right! Yes, of course!' He helped her up into the carriage. 'Home it is!'

As the carriage rolled out of the Yard and into Whitehall, she sat back to reflect on Mr O'Toole. She wanted very much to meet him, to mention her brother's name – and yet how could she? She would have to remind him of who she was. *Should* she remind him of who she was? Did she want the story getting round the other members – did she want Willie to know?

There was something else. She was expecting a child. If she invited him home, wouldn't he expect to meet her husband? It would be awkward. It was going to take a little thinking out. Because in a way what was her position now? She had been a poor stable girl when he had helped her brother; now her position was – to say the least – equivocal. She could pass herself off as a wealthy widow but once she reminded Mr O'Toole of her brother, how was she going to explain her present position? How could she introduce him to Nick? It might be wiser to wait until after the birth of her baby.

As summer drew on, and she grew heavier, he made a suggestion.

'I'm going to take you to Brighton. Sea air is what you need.'

'Do I look pale?'

'No my darling, but sea air is good for you, and besides Brighton will be more relaxing, more tranquil; it's good for expectant mothers.'

'Will you come and see me?'

'Do you need to ask?'

'I do, Nick! You don't remember, but after Christmas – that time – soon after we got back from Paris – you were away for weeks on end. I was all alone!'

He was thoughtful, and at last drew a long sigh. 'I remember very well. When Caroline was bad.'

'Maybe you should take her to the seaside?'

Those days were often in her thoughts – those few days when their love had been made flesh – literally, she told herself, running her hand over her belly.

'Do you remember Paris?' she asked him one afternoon as they strolled arm in arm along the promenade. It was May now, a bright day, though the wind was fresh. The sea was running, and there were little white caps to the waves. She was well wrapped – Nick had seen to that – and the air lifted her spirits. Further along, past the Old Steine and up towards Kemp Town, a pretty Regency house was theirs, and she could rise in the morning and stand in the window and see how the sea was today.

He pressed his hand on her arm, tucked beneath his. 'Often,' he murmured.

'I think of Paris as ours. Silly, isn't it?'

'Is it, why?'

'Think how many lovers must have been to Paris before us ... and they all thought Paris specially belonged to them.'

'Doesn't make any difference,' he replied after a while. 'It's still ours.' She snuggled against him.

But then he returned to London, and whole days she was alone. She had a housekeeper, and would sometimes sit with her in the kitchen and chat. Otherwise she would walk along the promenade, or sleep in the afternoon.

Then a very strange thing happened. It was a weekend – a Saturday afternoon. Nick had been unable to get down, and she had taken herself out to walk by the sea when as she did so, she saw a man and a woman ahead of her arm in arm, and astonishingly she recognised the man immediately. Even from behind there was no mistaking that back, the shoulders. Unless she were very much mistaken that was Mr Parnell. And that meant the woman beside him, twirling a small parasol over her shoulder, must be—

They were walking very slowly, so she managed to overtake them, and got herself a little ahead to where a promenade shelter offered her a bench. She took her seat and was able to get a clear look at the couple as they came slowly towards her. She need have no fear that they might notice her inquisitiveness. They were quite engrossed in each other, and he appeared the soul of attentiveness to his companion.

The woman was expecting a baby too, Abby realised. What an extraordinary coincidence! Mr Parnell had brought the woman he loved to Brighton for the air, just as Nick had done. She studied the woman, Mrs O'Shea. She was very pretty, vivacious with a good colour, a brunette as far as Abby could tell by the hair peeping from her bonnet, with bright merry eyes, and plump cheeks. She laughed, and prodded Mr Parnell, and he laughed too, in a more modest humouring way; it was quite clear he was devoted to her.

They arrived at the shelter, and to her surprise sat beside her, still arm in arm. Abby made a tiny remark, and moved slightly to one side to make room for them. She sat looking away, dying to listen to their conversation, yet trying not to. In any case, she could not make out their words, which were whispered between them, as the lady sat close beside Parnell, nestling against him, while he leaned in to whisper to her. There were suppressed giggles, chuckles. It was very intimate, and Abby felt more and more embarrassed. Poor Willie! It was obvious that his wife and Mr Parnell were deeply in love and if appearances were anything to go by, she was expecting his child as well.

Abby was about to get up but they forestalled her, and strolled away still in close and intimate conversation. Abby watched them go, and then, as her gaze unfastened itself from their backs, she saw that Mrs O'Shea had left her parasol on the bench beside her.

She snatched it up, and hurried after the couple. They were walking so slowly that it was not difficult; Abby caught them up, was able to compose herself and, in her sweetest tone, present Mrs O'Shea with her parasol. They were both perfectly polite, and Mrs O'Shea thanked her graciously and gave her a smile before they continued their walk.

But in those few seconds Abby was able to get a good look at both of them. They were older than she – how old? In their thirties? She couldn't say. Parnell had a noble, calm countenance – the word seemed appropriate in his case; there was something rather god-like about him. He murmured the few words in a drawling upper-class accent, very genteel. In the meantime the two women had inspected each other, liked what they saw, and politely wished each other the time of day. Abby turned back along the prom. So that was the famous Mr Parnell – and the vivacious Mrs O'Shea.

A few days later, Abby was on the promenade again, leaning on the rail and idly looking down at the people on the beach when she was conscious of someone beside her, and turning saw it was Mrs O'Shea.

'We meet again,' the lady said with a pleasant smile.

Abby was very pleased to make her acquaintance, though she did not of course let on that she knew her as they shook hands.

'We have something in common,' Mrs O'Shea glanced down at their swollen bulks.

'You mean,' Abby took her up quickly in a spirit of play-fulness, 'we have both been abandoned at the seaside by our men-friends?'

Mrs O'Shea was startled by this. '*I beg your pardon?*' She took a step backwards.

'Forgive me,' Abby could have bitten her tongue off. Red in the face, she took Mrs O'Shea's arm and turned them both towards the sea again. 'I wasn't thinking,' she stumbled. 'I should not have referred to it. I do most earnestly apologise.' She paused, but even then could not help continuing, 'But you cannot walk about on the arm of one of the most famous men in the country and not expect to be noticed.'

'Not even in Brighton?'

'What do you mean?'

'In Brighton, there is an unwritten rule. Here one is anonymous.'

'Really?' Abby was thoughtful.

'I think I have been at this game a little longer than you,' Mrs O'Shea said with a small laugh. 'My dear, I am nearly forty, while you are twenty, if that. Am I right?'

Abby nodded, humbled after her blunder. For a moment both women gazed down at the crowded beach.

'You said you had been abandoned,' Mrs O'Shea, remarked gazing now out to sea, 'not for too long, I hope?'

'Oh no, a day or two only.'

'And you rather indiscreetly referred to a man friend?'

Abby looked down, embarrassed. 'It was foolish of me, I'm sorry.'

'Oh that's all right with me, I assure you. I am not going to cast any stones. Is he married?'

Abby nodded.

'And you are carrying his child?'

She nodded again.

'Well,' Mrs O'Shea was brisk, and drew a deep breath of sea air. 'There's life after birth, you know. It's not the end of the world.'

'I think it may be – for me.'

'What do you mean?'

'Oh—' Abby found it difficult to say the words. 'He has

292

asked me to give up our child – so he and his wife can adopt it. She cannot bear children.'

There was a long pause. Neither looked at the other.

'And you have agreed, obviously?' Mrs O'Shea said after some time.

Abby nodded.

'He has money – and position, I take it?'

'Yes.'

'So your child will be brought up respectably, in security; it will be surrounded by every comfort, it will receive a good education, and when it grows up will be in a good position to carve out a profession – or make a good marriage – as the case may be.'

'Yes.'

'That's a lot. That's more than many women can hope for for their children. I take it you have no money of your own?'

'Only what he has given me.'

'Hmm,' Mrs O'Shea thought for a moment. 'Well, just look at it from the child's point of view. It must be better off with its father, mustn't it?'

'You're right. Thank you. I hadn't thought of it like that. You are very kind. I wonder – my house is up there—' she pointed away – 'not far. Will you take tea with me?'

'I will.'

By the time Mrs O'Shea left, an hour later, they had agreed to meet again, and as Abby closed the door behind her, she was deeply pleased to have found a friend – and one who spoke such sense too. She had made her feel much more comfortable about her situation.

'Mrs O'Shea, you may perhaps have wondered how I knew about you and Mr Parnell—'

She set down her tea cup carefully, and turned her gaze out to sea. They were on either side of a low table in the bow window of her little sitting room on the first floor. Outside it was another bright day, with a breeze from the sea. The flags were stretched from the flagpoles along the sea front. 'Yes?'

'It's through Captain O'Shea. He is a friend of Mr Darke – from army days.'

By now Katherine knew all about Nick Darke. She drew a breath, 'Ah yes. Willie. I wondered when he would surface. How much has he told you?'

'Not very much – only he did mention about you and Mr Parnell—'

'Discreet of him, I'm sure. I wonder how many other friends he's confided in? I dare say we're the talk of London.'

Abby was at a loss. 'I'm sorry,' she said, 'I seem to have put my foot in it again.'

'Oh, it's not your fault. I suppose I ought to be grateful. At least I know where I stand.'

'I have never spoken of it to anyone, I assure you. But poor Captain O'Shea – he did seem to need to confide in someone.'

'Poor Captain O'Shea?' There was a twist in her words, as she made a small ironical smile, catching Abby's eye again. 'He has been telling you about the heartless wife, I dare say, who has cuckolded him with the greatest statesman of the age? You had better tell me everything – the evil witch who has ruined his life—'

'Oh no! It was not like that. He is far too gentle—'

'Hmm.' Katherine was silent for a moment. 'I met him, you know – Willie – when he was still in the army. A uniform can do wonders for a man. Why is that I wonder? What exactly *is* the lure of a red coat? And having been brought up in a very sheltered existence I was easily wooed. But then, after we were married, Willie resigned his commission. Instead of a red coat suddenly he was in a tweed suit, and at a loose end. He was wasting his time in racing stables and dubious mining schemes, and finally went into parliament ...' She paused, staring out of the window as the thoughts went through her mind. 'I found I

294

had married one of nature's foot soldiers,' she went on at last. 'I wonder – can you imagine how it feels to be married to a foot soldier – and then be introduced to the general?'

'The general? You mean, the Chief?'

Katherine was silent for a moment biting her lip. 'Please don't misunderstand me. I have nothing against Willie, and we are on the best of terms. He is sincere, honest, and he means well. It's just that, unfortunately, he's – limited. Once I met Parnell, I saw what I had been missing all those years. I saw what a man could be. I had met a man who seemed – well – taller. A man who sees farther than others, made for great endeavours and great achievements, a man marked out, born to shape his country's destiny. I wonder – can you imagine how it feels to be held by a man like that? To be the beloved of such a man?'

'I think so,' Abby hesitated.

'It was *my* destiny to be loved by him, Hester. I could no more turn my back on it, then he could shun his own destiny.'

'You are very ambitious,' Abby said tentatively.

'Am I?' she seemed genuinely surprised. 'I suppose I am.'

Towards the end of August, when Abby was within a month of her confinement, Nick arrived for the weekend bringing with him a clutch of letters which had been piling up in St John's Wood. One was from Eileen.

Even so it was not until the evening that she got round to opening it. There were more pressing matters.

'You can feel him moving Nick,' she said. 'Place your hand here,' and she had watched his face as he placed his hand against the side of her belly. 'It's his feet,' she looked up into Nick's face. 'Isn't it extraordinary? He was kicking this morning, and woke me. He's there – just inside. Isn't that just so extraordinary, to think of him, all ready inside, waiting to be born?' She watched Nick's face as he carefully, timidly, reverently, pressed his hand to the side of

295

her belly, and then looked into her eyes as he registered the baby's movements. Because of this she did not open the letter until the evening:

Dear Abby,
Not such good news I'm afraid. Your da's not been well. I haven't written before because I wanted to be sure before writing, and not alarm you unnecessarily. But it is serious. He's comfortable at the moment, and I've got him tucked up in bed, but he's not the man he was. He's got very weak, and will hardly touch his food, he just seems to have no appetite any more, and every day, I watch him sink lower. The doctor was here, he said there's nothing to be done, just to keep him warm and give him anything he wants. Sorry to have to tell you this. It's not good news; but I think it would be best if you were to come back as soon as you can.
        Your loving aunt,
                Eileen

Reading this she went quite cold, and only after some time could drag her eyes from it up to Nick's face. Stupidly, she looked at him, looked round at the cosy sitting room, the candles, looked down at her swollen belly, as she tried to take in what her aunt had written.

'What is it?' Nick had seen the look in her face.

'It's my father. He's ill.' Her voice was hoarse.

Nick murmured, 'I'm sorry—'

'My aunt wants me to go over.' She started round again, and then back to Nick. 'How can I? Like this?'

'You can't.'

Abby rested her head on her hand. 'I can't—' she repeated stupidly.

'You'll have to write. We'll think about it together, and compose something suitable.'

'You don't think—'

'Hester, you're not fit to travel,' he said calmly.

296

'No. Not fit to travel. And even if I were? How could I appear in the village, like this? Oh Da—'

Nick crossed to her and took her in his arms. 'We'll do it together,' he repeated.

In the morning they composed a letter to Eileen. It was evasive, and did not set out exactly why she was unable to come immediately, but did say that she would be free within a very few weeks, and hoped that Eileen was perhaps exaggerating Da's condition. She would come the very moment she was free and was looking forward to seeing them all again.

She hated this letter, its lies and half lies. In any case it didn't matter because the following weekend Nick brought another. This was quite short. Eileen informed her that her father had died the previous evening; that he had been quite comfortable at the end, and had not suffered; that everyone commented how peaceful he looked; that she had done everything necessary and Abby mustn't worry. The funeral would be the following Friday in the parish church in the morning.

'My father's funeral. Nick, I must be there,' she said white faced.

'You can't be.'

'How can my father die, how can he be buried, and I not there?' She wandered through the room, unseeing. 'I feel completely helpless.'

Again Nick was soothing, held her and reassured her. 'It's God's will, my dear,' he whispered, her head on his shoulder. 'It was meant to be. And there is nothing we can do. You will go to Ireland the moment you can. You must not reproach yourself.'

'It's my fault—'

'It's nobody's fault.'

'If I weren't expecting—'

'Hester.' He took her hands, made her sit beside him on the sofa. 'Listen very carefully. Your father has died. Your aunt has done everything necessary. He was comfortable

297

and not in any pain. There is nothing you could have done if you had gone, that your aunt did not do. Do you understand that? If your father had known why you were unable to come he would have forgiven you; he would have understood. Because you are about to bring a child into the world. Isn't that important too? That is your task—'

She had not been listening, and suddenly it was her Irish self that was speaking. ''Tis little you know of it.' She shook him off, heavy, bitter. ''Twas not you that was set out on the road; not you that had the bayonets of the military in your teeth. My father was thrown off his farm and it broke his heart. What would ye know of that? How can ye have any idea? We were thrown out of our home, that was the home of my father, and his father and his before him. I should have been there! If we had still been in our home I would have tended him – it would have been *me* that nursed him and cared for him. And it would have been *me* that closed his eyes, me that washed and dressed him for his wake! Me that followed his coffin to the graveyard. How can ye know anything of that?' She rose abruptly, pushing him away, crossed to the window and leaned against the window frame as she wept.

Chapter Thirty

'Oh my God, it's getting worse. Mrs Robinson, give me a hand!'

Abby arched her back, and clutched at the banister rail.

'Don't worry Mrs Moncrieffe, everything is ready. We'll just take it nice and steady. Now, lean on me, and we'll get you upstairs.'

With difficulty Abby took the steps one at a time, then stopped when she was still half way up, as another pain shot through her, making her stagger against the midwife. Already the sweat was on her face.

Then she was being helped out of her clothes, the chemise came over her head, she was into a night-gown and being helped into bed.

'Now, there's nothing to worry about, Mrs Moncrieffe. Everything's quite normal. We're just going to let nature take its course.' The meaningless words had their intended effect of soothing her. Mrs Robinson was a wonderfully soothing woman. You felt she had done this a thousand times before – which she said she had – and it was something routine with her.

It was a September evening, and in the bedroom a fire had been lit, the curtains drawn. Beside the bed stood a cradle, baby clothes were in readiness, there were shawls, little blankets, towels, napkins, toys, a rattle.

Abby's breasts were enlarged – engorged, painfully so.

299

She had run her hand over them, inspecting them. They were ready, filled to bursting, aching to give suck. Before her as she lay on her back, rose what seemed a mountain, something over which she no longer had any control.

Nick was not here. He had come down to see her the previous weekend, and told her all preparations were in place. He could hardly contain his own excitement, the intensity of his feelings, fussing about her, loading the house with everything he could think of in preparation for the birth. Caroline knew all about Mrs Moncrieffe – a kindly Scottish lady, Nick had explained, who already had five children, and could not cope with another. She had been vouched for by her minister of religion and her husband's employer had given him a good character. It was a respectable home the baby was coming from, Nick had assured her, and both parents were healthy, no diseases or abnormalities in the family. He had made very careful investigation.

Through the night the pains intensified, until Mrs Robinson gave her a strong dose of laudanum, which gave at least some respite. And then, towards dawn, her son was born. Mrs Robinson held him up as his first cries were heard; she inspected him, pronounced him whole and perfect, washed him, wrapped him in a fleecy shawl, and placed him in Abby's arms as she lay, bathed in sweat, her hair matted about her head, her nightgown clinging to her body. The housekeeper and Mrs Robinson worked round her, changed the bedding, sponged her down, got her into a fresh nightgown, and left her to rest. The baby lay beside her in its wickerwork cradle, and she looked down at it, already asleep and half a second later was asleep herself.

That afternoon she was woken as the midwife gave her the baby, and whispered. 'He's hungry, Mrs Moncrieffe.' With some awkwardness Abby brought the child to her breast, and tried to help him. 'Get it right in, dear, right in That's it.'

Silence fell as the little mite, his eyes shut, fastened on to her, and was sucking lustily.

As she was feeding the baby, she heard the sound of a door below, and a moment later Nick was in the room, overcoat on, hat in his hand. For a moment he looked down at the baby in silence. Abby had never seen such a sight then as she looked up at Nick, seeing the expression in his eyes, and couldn't help smiling with pride.

'He's perfect,' she whispered as Nick came slowly, tentatively, almost timidly, to the bedside, unable to take his eyes from the baby and, pulling up a chair sat beside the bed, still staring in wonder at his son. 'Was it – painful?'

She shrugged slowly and shook her head slightly. 'Just a little,' she murmured, looking down at the baby still.

Later when the baby seemed to have finished, Nick held out his hands. 'May I?' There was between them such a perfect magical moment, together on the bed in which she had given birth to their son. A holy moment; both felt it. 'He's so beautiful,' Nick breathed. As he held the baby he leant forward to kiss Abby on the forehead.

'He's ours,' she said simply.

Later when the boy was asleep, they had tea together, and Nick became awkward. 'Hester, I have to tell you the arrangements I have made. Caroline knows the baby has been born. I told her as soon as I received your telegram. I said—' this was difficult for him – 'I told her I would go to collect the baby in a few days – a week on Saturday. Mrs Hardcastle will come with me. She will have responsibility for him. I shall also bring Mrs Potts, the wet-nurse; her own child is only two months old and she says she has plenty of milk for two. Everything has been got ready at home; he will have his own room. Caroline is very excited about it, I don't have to tell you.'

Abby nodded without saying anything. There was something unreal about this. It wasn't her baby they were talking about – not this little mite beside her bed, the most precious little creature that ever existed, the most perfect baby ever to be born – no, they weren't talking about this one. It was another one that Nick was going to take away on Saturday

301

week. Out of this air of unreality she asked, 'Can you stay till then?'

''Fraid not. Caroline has a touch of something – I'm not sure what – I'll have to get back.'

Abby said nothing. Of course, she understood; everything was proceeding according to plan. This was what they had agreed, what she had thought carefully about, and now it was happening. But if that were so, what was this air of unreality that persisted in hanging over everything they said? Why couldn't she believe it? Perhaps she would wake up the following morning and things would be sorted out. Nick would sort everything out.

Willie came a few days later.

'Willie, will you be godfather?'

'Eh? Of course.' He looked about. 'Where's Nick?'

'Nick can't be here. And I have to hand my baby over on Saturday. But I want him baptised a Catholic. It's this afternoon at St Mary Magdalene.'

So that afternoon at five on a September afternoon, they stood in the tall echoing church the three of them, as long shafts of light reached down from high above, alone in the corner of that great echoing barn, and the priest baptised her son William.

'Thank you, Willie. Come home and we'll have tea.' She had a bright, glacial cheerfulness.

'So, all the arrangements – in place, then?' asked Willie, in his obtuse way.

She nodded smiling.

Why did she have difficulty sleeping? What was this air of unreality that would not go? Saturday was only a few days away and she was in a daze; nothing meant anything. She would forget the simplest things; she would forget the question before it had been asked, and would reply, 'I'm sorry I wasn't listening – what did you say?' And all the time stupid thoughts were going round and round in her head. 'I

302

mustn't forget his little rattle—' which she had seen in a shop and bought for William – 'and now let me see, I must remember to tell Mrs Hardcastle about his feeding hours. I wonder what she's like? She is a mother herself, I expect, so I'm sure she'll be kind, and William had a slight cough this morning – but Mrs Robinson said that was nothing – and I'm sure – it might be this nasty east wind, he must be well wrapped up, of course he'll have his fleecy blanket – and Nick will be there – that's the main thing, Nick will see that everything is all right, I can trust Nick—' and she would find tears trickling down her face, and would go on, gabbling to herself, fussing about the cot now, talking aloud to William, 'Mrs Hardcastle will take good care of you darling, it's a lovely home you're going to, you'll have the best of everything, and you'll be brought up a gentleman's son, and go to boarding school, and have a splendid career—' and then would break down completely sitting on the end of the bed her head in her hands, sobbing uncontrollably.

But she didn't cry the day Nick came with Mrs Hardcastle who, to her unspeakable relief, was a really kind and capable lady – of course Abby knew Nick would choose a good woman – and took to William at once. William was asleep, thank goodness. Everything was packed up – all his things, his little rattle ... she wouldn't think, just do it, everything they had arranged. The boxes were carried out to the cab, but then – and only as they were at the door – Abby took Mrs Hardcastle aside, and whispered quickly, 'Mrs Hardcastle – I was just wondering – you will take William into the park won't you – for some fresh air?'

'Of course, Mrs Moncrieffe.'

'And, you'll think me silly, but I was just wondering ... at what sort of time – more or less – what time of day, you normally—'

'At ten, Mrs Moncrieffe, and again, if the weather's fine, between three and four. I have to get out myself, you

303

know.' She smiled, she seemed a friend, and Abby was greatly comforted, grasping her hand.

'Thank you,' she whispered. 'I wouldn't want Mr Darke to know.'

She must put on a cheerful face for Nick. This was such a great day for him. This was something he had not dared even to dream of; and now it had happened. He had his son. For so many years – he had told her often – for so many years he had dreamed, had not even dared to hope, and now by this miracle it had come true. Hester would never know what she had done for him. It was impossible to express what he felt.

No, she could never allow him to think she was unhappy with the arrangement. She couldn't do that. Nick must be shielded at all costs.

Silence. A most strange uncanny silence. She stood at the window as the cab disappeared towards the Old Steine. What was it? Nothing. She waited, still stupidly expecting something, staring out at the sea, waiting for she did not know what any more. She clasped her hands. How light she felt. Unnaturally light. As if something was missing. Some essential part of her . . .

This was madness. No. She shook her head as if to free herself of her thoughts. She must be busy. There was nothing to stay in Brighton for, the job was done. The business finished. She must get back to London. And she must go to Ireland. Nick would be around in a few days and – but first, she must call on Mrs O'Shea.

'I was hoping we might meet in town.'

'I would be delighted.' Mrs O'Shea's own baby was due in a month. 'I shall be back by Christmas.'

'Mrs O'Shea, I am not a poor woman. I should like to do something for – the Cause.'

'Bravo.'

'But I am ignorant of the formalities, and you are on

such an intimate footing – of course, I would not wish in any way to intrude on your own arrangements, but I would very much appreciate it if I could – well, meet some of the Irish members. I should like to invite them to my house, perhaps give a dinner party.'

'And what sort of help did you have in mind?'

'Money,' Abby said bluntly.

'Ah. Well. I can confidently predict that your help will be appreciated. But I wonder whether you shouldn't speak to my husband. He is more familiar with the MPs than I.'

'Mrs O'Shea – Katherine – there is something else. I have no friends – no women friends – in London. I dearly need a friend.' She hesitated, but the other completed her sentence.

'I shall be happy if you will be *my* friend, Hester.'

In the train she clung on to this thought. She would make friends, busy herself, get involved in politics. And Rory too. She must fix her mind on that. She must write to Mr O'Toole about Rory. This was what mattered.

The following morning at ten she waited in the park, and sure enough saw Mrs Hardcastle pushing a perambulator across Park Lane and through the little gate. Guiltily, like a thief, she stole up to the perambulator, and almost unable to breathe, she allowed herself to peep in. Buried, it seemed, beneath layers of blankets and fleecy rugs, his hands thrown back on either side of his head, he slept. She gazed and gazed till she felt she could eat him, she wanted to snatch him from the perambulator, she could just snatch him up, run to her carriage which was waiting, and in fifteen minutes be at home in St John's Wood . . .

Mrs Hardcastle was kind, and allowed her to lift William out. But afterwards as Abby was carefully replacing the baby, the older woman said, in a gentle voice, soothingly, 'You're only making yourself unhappy, Mrs Moncrieffe. Is it wise?' giving her a look of kindness but also shrewd understanding.

'I feel better about it. I feel I can bear it, Mrs Hardcastle, knowing you are taking care of him. It makes it easier.'

They walked side by side for a few moments as Abby continued to gaze down at William, then spoke with difficulty, 'What does – what does Mrs Darke say?'

'She is an invalid, as you know, and has very little strength. She does not actually touch him at all. Mr Darke brings William for her to see a few minutes each day, and she is very pleased that he has come to live with them. Though I think she is pleased mainly on Mr Darke's account, knowing how much he wanted a son.'

This was clear too when Nick came to see her. She was not yet fully recovered from the birth, so they sat opposite one another before an October fire, she stretched on a chaise longue. His gratitude shone from his eyes, and every five minutes would bring the conversation back to their son and how grateful to her he was, how he could never repay her, and how she would never want. They discussed her allowance which he increased substantially.

'Thank you, Nick,' she hesitated. 'There is something else I have been thinking of, a request I should like to make. You see, Willie took me to visit the House of Commons one night, to hear the Irish debate.' She was thoughtful. 'No one in that building knew better than I what an Irish Land Bill means, Nick, and I want to help. I want to ask Willie to invite some of the MPs here. When I was plain old Abby—'

But here Nick cut her off. 'You're not Abby. I don't know any Abby O'Leary. I only know Hester Moncrieffe.'

'Pardon?'

'You are my own dear Hester.'

'But Nick, it's my past, you know, my childhood.'

'Hester my dear, you have no past. If you want one, I'll make one up for you. Let's see.' He became playful. 'Perhaps you should be the natural daughter of a Scottish peer. Moncrieffe has a kind of Scottish ring to it. Perhaps you should have no past at all. You just appeared, like

306

Venus from the foam. Or best of all, because most accurate, you have created yourself.'

'Created myself? But, Nick, if anyone has created me, it is you.'

'I may have helped, it is true, but the essential work has been done by you.'

They were silent for a moment. She reflected that what he said was true. There was no trace of the old Abby. No trace of her native accent. She wore her clothes as if born into them, she ordered her servants with complete composure.

'So – you wouldn't mind if I invited some of Willie's friends here?'

'Why should I?'

'Thank you.'

She paused, thinking. 'And I can go to Ireland now.'

Chapter Thirty-one

Was Nick right, she wondered, as the train rolled through the Irish countryside. She had recreated herself, it was true. But in doing so, had she cut herself off from her own home, her own country, her own family? Were there now two separate people – Abby O'Leary and Hester Moncrieffe?

She had carefully chosen her mourning clothes, this plain hat, this black fitted coat. She had her story prepared but how she was to tell it, she did not know. How to account to Eileen and Fan for Hester Moncrieffe?

The autumn day wore on as the train pulled its weary way through town after town, village after village, halt after halt, as country folk would be standing on the station, and with her window down she would hear her own speech again, yet how strange it sounded; consciously she told herself it was her own speech, yet it now seemed foreign, distant.

It was dark by the time the train reached Westport. One side car was waiting for the train, and a carman, wrapped in a shabby old caped overcoat, a pot hat pulled over his ears, took up her box and secured it on one side. She perched on the other, the old springs creaking as she stepped up; the carman flicked his whip and they were off, swaying through the town, and then out into the uneven road towards Kilnevin, pot-holed, muddy, splashing through puddles, and the carman keeping up a running commentary on the weather, the harvest, farm prices, the attack on a landlord only a week past . . .

Eventually she was able to direct him up the narrow *bohreen*, between high bramble hedges, the horse stumbling sometimes in the almost complete darkness, and they found themselves before her aunt's cottage. The door opened and a shaft of golden light fell across the *bohreen* as she helped herself down, stiff from the long ride.

There was a moment as they faced each other, then Eileen at last opened her arms, and the two women embraced.

'Aunt—'

'We can talk later. Come in first. You'll be tired from your journey, I expect. Put the box there—' Eileen indicated to the carman, who was behind them.

As they came into the kitchen, into the light from the paraffin lamp hanging over the table, and looking round her, smelling the turf fire, seeing the table, the Sacred Heart on the wall, then her father's empty chair by the fire, worn with long years of handling – 'I wanted to come—'

'You can tell me later.'

Eileen still had not smiled. She helped Abby off with her black coat, her hat, but as Abby was peeling off her gloves, she exclaimed, 'Abby! You're never married!'

'It's what I came to tell you. But later – if you don't mind.'

The room looked strange – empty. She ran her hand across the back of Da's chair. Eileen now crossed to the fire, and fussed over a pot. 'You'll have something to eat – and then you can tell me your news.'

The two women sat at the table and Eileen poured them a cup of tea. As they ate, there was a stillness in the air, and when they ceased speaking a dead silence fell, so that the sound of a spoon on a plate was magnified. In the past the room had been crowded; now the silence weighed upon Abby, oppressive, suffocating.

'Tell me,' she began tentatively. 'How it was.'

309

Eileen raised her eyebrows, thinking a moment, and began in a matter-of-fact tone. 'He was tired. Tired of life. Ever since ye were thrown off the farm, the spirit went out of him. He sat there day after day, ye know yourself, nothing meant anything. And with ye gone, and Rory, he couldn't take the trouble any longer. I guess he was just worn out. It was a shame he couldn't have died in his own bed, that's all.'

'And the funeral, was it . . .?'

Her question hung in the air.

Eileen looked at her. 'Your father had the best send off we could give him. Thanks for the money, by the way. I'll let you have the change, you sent too much—'

'No!'

'No? Since ye weren't able to be here yourself?' She gave Abby a shrewd look, then shrugged again. 'There was talk in the village as ye may imagine, that your da had passed away and you never at the funeral.'

Abby couldn't meet her eye. 'Aunt—' she whispered, but Eileen went on, 'Still, Father McMichael gave him a good sermon, the best. The church was full. The whole village was there, showing their respects, it was good to see so many – and some I hadn't seen in years. We waked him here too.' She looked up at Abby. 'But I'd better warn ye: if ye go into the village, there might be questions – where ye were—'

'Aunt,' Abby interrupted her. 'To think, you know, that Da died here and I never able to be with him, to close his eyes.' She frowned, staring down at her plate. 'There was a reason.' Again she paused, rubbing her hand across her forehead. 'There was a reason, honest, and a good reason, only I can never tell you—'

She was still unable to meet her aunt's eye. 'Please believe me.' She was silent.

'And it's nothing to do with that ring?'

Abby shook her head. 'I am going to explain – only give me a little time.' She paused. 'Shall we go down and see the grave in the morning?'

'Of course.'

That night she slept in the bed her father had died in. The room was bare, clean, neutral; there was no sign, no evidence her father had ever been in it. Nothing to tell her that this was the bed. She stood in the little room, dim in the light from the kitchen next door, looking about it – the crucifix on the wall, the bit of mirror on the whitewashed window sill, her coat hanging on a nail behind the door. Then undressing, and getting into the bed. It took her a long time to sleep; being unable to confide in her aunt was like a heavy weight she must carry: herself and Nick, a secret known to no one but themselves. She could never be honest with her family, and tomorrow she must unravel a string of lies to her aunt.

The following morning they went down to the church. The village was nearly deserted and no one remarked her – or perhaps no one remembered her, she wondered. The grave was new, of course, a grey marble slab, and though she had mentally prepared herself for it, steeled herself as she thought, it still came as a shock to see her father's name, and beneath it the dates. Seeing the date of his death – the closing of his life – gave it a finality no amount of talking could.

Then they walked to what had once been her home, which she had not seen since the day they were evicted, and had never wanted to see. Still, whatever it was, something pulled her. The little cottage stood, a ruin, unkempt in the cold wind. Roofless, the walls half destroyed, weeds already growing in what had once been their kitchen. The two women stood in the *bohreen*, hands in their pockets.

'Our home,' Abby murmured. 'All the years. So many years ...' She walked slowly through what had once been the door; the old paving of the floor already half obscured by weeds, grass, lichen. 'Our house.' She looked about her at the walls, half crumbled. 'Ours, through the long years, ours, grandfather's, his father's, and his father's before him. And now ...'

311

Eventually they turned out into the *bohreen*, glanced back once, and then set off again up the lane.

'For myself I don't mind,' she said after a while. 'I've been lucky. But to think that Da should have been thrown out of his home. You'd think he should have had the right to die in his own bed; it wasn't much to ask. It's the dignity of the thing that hurts me. That a man should be worth only so many pounds, and if he doesn't have them, then get out, and live on the charity of others.'

'I told him what's done is done, and we'd better make the best of it, and he could stay with me as long as he liked. But a day or two would go by and out it comes again, the whole story; he could never get it off his mind. And then Rory in prison, you and Fergus off to the ends of the earth, and only Fan for company . . .'

Abby shook her head, and the two women plodded up the *bohreen* in silence. In a way, she wished now she had not come. It only brought bitter thoughts. Don't live in the past. Forget the past. Ghosts and shadows. Put it behind her.

Later, when they had returned to Eileen's, she went out to the paddock to greet her old friend Starlight. As she was leaning against the rail, communing with the mare, rubbing her nose, feeding her a bit of broken sugar, Eileen joined her.

'She's gettin' to be an old lady,' Eileen commented, coming up behind her.

Abby said nothing for a moment, as she rubbed the mare's nose.

'Aunt, there's somethin' I have to tell you.' She concentrated on stroking Starlight's nose. 'It's about my master, old Mr Moncrieffe. You see, during the summer he died. This is the other thing I came to tell you.' She was awkward, repeating herself as she made up the story. 'You see aunt, he always liked me and would come down to the stable to talk to me, and I would tell him stories you know, about home, and us, and the old tales of fairies and banshees that Da used to tell us when we were little. Then when he fell ill, he asked me to go and sit by him, and talk to him. And then, when you could see he couldn't last much longer, and we thought he must soon die, one day he sends for me.

'The bedroom was crammed with people. The nurse, but also an old gentleman, very respectable, a clergyman and some others. Mr Moncrieffe was very weak, he could hardly speak, just lying there on the pillow. As I went to him he waved towards this gentleman who I'd never seen before and the gentleman turns to me and says that I have been summoned for a very important matter. I couldn't think, you know – I'd been down in the stable. What is it? I was worried, you know, I thought maybe they were about to give me the sack. Mr Moncrieffe has asked you come up this afternoon Abby, says he, to make a very special request. Old Mr Moncrieffe was listening to this, and he smiled and nodded. I am Mr Moncrieffe's lawyer, this gentleman goes on, and Mr Moncrieffe has authorised me to explain everything. I was mystified, as you can imagine. Explain what? says I. Only that Mr Moncrieffe had made me his heir! Aunt only think! But, he goes on, he has a request to make. What is that sir? says I. Now the lawyer went on that old Mr Moncrieffe had explained to him that I reminded him so much of his dead wife when they were first married – well, I knew that, Aunt, Mr Moncrieffe had often told me himself – and old Mr Moncrieffe was nodding as he explained all this, and as he hadn't very long to go in this world, he went on, he asked as a favour to him, whether I wouldn't agree to be married to him, even if only for a few days, and to take his late wife's name!

'Married! Aunt, only imagine; I couldn't think! Married! And him on his death bed! I was struck dumb, but I could see old Mr Moncrieffe was looking at me so pitifully and he whispered, "Only as a favour to me, Abby, in memory of my wife." Well, I looked round at them all. I didn't know what to think. "You won't have long to wait," says he.

Well, in the end, I thought, I'd better go through with it. Mr Moncrieffe had been so kind to me, it wasn't much to ask, and I felt sorry for him. So that's how it is. It was only four days later that he died. And everything was as he said it was. I had to go to the lawyer's, and swear an oath, and now I'm Mrs Hester Moncrieffe.' She paused. 'I've sort of got used to it,' she added, and then after another pause, 'And aunt, I'm rich,' she whispered.

'Why didn't ye write and tell us before?'

Abby swallowed. 'I wanted to come and tell you myself.'

But Eileen pulled away. 'So this was why ye didn't come before, I suppose? Ye were too busy arranging with the solicitors to get your hands on the money?'

'No!'

'No? Well, was it too much to ask for ye to come to your own father's funeral?'

'Aunt! I couldn't come! Please believe me, and please don't blame me – there was a reason I can't tell you what it was – but it had nothing to do with my master.'

'Abby O'Leary,' her aunt turned and snorted. After a moment she went on bitterly, 'I wonder you found time to come back and see your father's grave at all.'

'Don't say that!' Abby pleaded. 'Aunt, I swear on Da's grave, there was a reason, only I can't tell you.'

Eileen thought for a moment then drew a breath. 'Well, what'll ye do now?' she asked coldly. 'Will you come home?'

'The thing is, Aunt,' she was awkward. 'I have this house in London, and I'm used to livin' there now, and know people. That's my home now.'

Eileen nodded. 'And now ye've come into your fortune, you won't want to know us. What about Fan?'

'Aunt, of course I won't forget you! And I'll always come to see you – how can I not? Wasn't it yourself that took us in when we had nowhere to turn?' Eileen was staring away, shaking her head slowly. Abby went on, 'And Fan can go on at school, and then maybe we can think

314

about her later. Now that I'm, you know—'

Eileen turned again and gave her a level stare, and at last slowly nodded her head.

The following day sitting in the train, she felt drained, exhausted. Eileen didn't believe her, it was clear. Their parting had been cool, formal. As far as Eileen was concerned, there was something highly suspicious about the way Abby had come into her money; worse, Abby couldn't wait to forget her family, and get back to her life in high society.

Returning to London, she felt her link with Ireland grow weaker, and she was not surprised to feel a sense of relief as she was admitted again to No. 16 Acacia Road. This was her home now.

That evening as she went down to check the horses were comfortable, she stopped in Dewdrop's stall, her hand resting on the horse's back in the gloom, turning over in her mind the events of the last few days.

'He's at rest, now, that's what matters. Nothing more can harm him. I would have stayed to watch over him, but how could I? After Rory was sent away, there was no staying in the village any longer. And I did make some money, and I have sent money back, regular. I did what I could . . .' Her head fell on her crossed arms on the mare's back, as she wept. It couldn't have been any different, and yet she still felt it was her fault.

The following afternoon she was in her garden. The leaves were thick on the grass, and Abby was out with a rake and thick leather gloves helping the gardener to sweep them up. She looked up at the clouds, high this afternoon, high, racing clouds. It was a great relief to be here, to breathe deeply the autumn air, to catch the drift of the smoke in her nostrils. 'Don't you go soiling your dress, missis,' Marwell the gardener had expostulated, but Abby smiled and wrapped an old sack round her skirt, as they made their way back and forth across the lawn, raking the leaves. She had never had charge of a garden before, and was enjoying her little domain – which was not so little either. The garden stretched back some way and was enclosed by high walls. There was also a greenhouse at the bottom, 'Why not have a vine, Mrs Moncrieffe, that'll give you hot-house grapes,' Marwell had suggested. Hot-house grapes! When she entertained her guests, to offer them grapes out of season! Peaches too.

Kicking her heavy skirt forward with its sacking apron, she renewed her raking. After the few days in Ireland she was happy. At this moment, it was like a window that would open briefly, to let the sun in. Happiness was not a state you could occupy continuously, she realised; we are not meant for that. But occasionally, when everything falls into place, there is a shaft of lightness into our hearts, and just so, then, on that windy light day with the sniff of leaf smoke in her nostrils, Abby was buoyed up from within.

And she had written at last to Mr O'Toole. The events of the last weeks, traumatic though they had been, had left her at last free to think of Rory. She had written, reminding Mr O'Toole of the case, and hoping that he might find time to interest himself in her brother again. Ideally, to petition the Home Secretary for a parole, or ticket of leave for Rory.

'Mrs Moncrieffe!' The housemaid Robbins was at the back door. 'It's Captain O'Shea!'

'I'm coming right away.'

But Willie was behind the girl, and came down the steps into the garden.

'Willie! Come out – only mind, the grass is wet – you'll get your boots muddy.'

'Hester, what *are* you doing?'

She rested on her rake. 'Isn't it a glorious afternoon? The air is so fresh.'

Willie sniffed the air, looking up and round him as if noticing it for the first time. 'For London, remarkably so.' He looked her over. 'You seem very cheerful. And I doubt whether your friends would recognise you.'

'I just feel so full of energy today. I don't know why it should be. Somehow, things seemed to have settled into place, Willie. After everything, you know – the last few months – I don't know how it is, but I feel more at peace now. I feel it was what was meant to be.'

He was silent, gazing vaguely round the garden.

'And at last I have got a real gardener,' she said more quietly, watching the bent back of Marwell further away tending the bonfire. 'That man knows all there is to be known about gardens, Willie; he has been showering me with suggestions. We are to have a vine – and hot-house grapes!'

Willie raised his eyebrows. And then, 'I brought the list, by the way.'

'Oh good! Come in, we'll have tea, and go through it together. Marwell, I'm going inside with Captain O'Shea.'

The old gardener turned slightly and grunted, before continuing heaping up leaves. As they went up the steps and into the house she was pulling off her leather gloves. 'I'll just go and straighten up. Robbins, bring tea into the drawing room,' she said as she went into the hall. The girl turned and went downstairs.

Then they were seated on either side of her fire, with the tea tray between them.

'The members are all back now,' Willie began. 'That's why I couldn't come before, it's taken a few days to contact them all. Though fortunately you can usually find them in the Westminster Hotel; it's a sort of unofficial club for the Irish members. There are eighty odd Nationalists – and obviously you can't invite them all, so I want to go through the list with you – I've shortened it already – or we'd be here all night. Tried to pick out the important ones.'

'Willie, you're so good – may I see?'

She glanced quickly down the list and saw to her relief that Mr O'Toole was on it. But not Mr Parnell.

'No Chief?'

He shook his head. 'Never goes out, Hester. Except to Eltham,' he added lugubriously.

'Has Mrs O'Shea had her baby?' she asked tentatively.

He nodded, looking into the fire.

'You must be – very pleased,' she went on carefully, 'was it a boy or a girl?'

He drew a deep breath. 'Pleased? That's the question, isn't it? It's a girl by the way.'

She was silent too, waiting for him to find the words. Then, as the words were not going to come, she forced a cheerful note. 'And Katherine – must be happy?'

He nodded without smiling. 'Oh, Katherine's pleased all right,' he said on a low note.

'Forgive me, Willie, this is a sensitive subject—'

'You could say that,' he said briefly, then, 'Makes me feel pretty foolish. I can't bring myself to go down there at all. I can't go into my own house, Hester! I want to see my own children. Why shouldn't I? Is there something wrong with that? She makes me feel an intruder in my own home.' He sat hunched forward, his elbows on his knees staring into the flames.

There was a long silence, as Abby tried to think of something to change the subject. At last she said, 'I met Katherine you know—' he looked up – 'it was during the summer, down in Brighton. We met by chance – or not quite; I recognised her, or rather I recognised him, and so – knew who she must be.'

'Did you talk about me?'

'A little. She was very kind about you,' she added quickly.

He shrugged. 'No doubt. They're thinking of moving down there permanently, you know. Out of the spotlight.'

'Willie,' she braced herself, sat up straight in her chair, and reached over for his hand. 'I want you to know you have a friend in me, and I want you to feel you can come here whenever you like.' She gave him the dazzling smile, which always had the effect on him of a strong wind so that he rocked slightly in the force of it.

318

And at last he heaved up from the depths the ghost of a smile of his own.

'Now let's go through the list, and we must fix a date.'

But before she could go on, he laid his hand on her wrist. 'Mrs Moncrieffe – Hester – I can't tell you how grateful I am. I feel you've given me back a little self-respect. Being able to invite colleagues to dinner, and—'

'Willie!' She laughed. 'You are quite wrong I assure you. I am doing this for my benefit! Imagine how grand I shall feel entertaining so many important men, statesmen too, men who are shaping their country's destiny – in my own house.'

After he had gone, she thought, And I shall have a new gown for the occasion. A gown which I shall order, and which I, not Nick, shall design.

Chapter Thirty-two

She waited in the lobby of the Westminster Hotel. Mr
O'Toole had asked her to come at five. She sat, tight, dressed
as soberly as she could, veiled, an umbrella in her gloved
hand, upright, nervous, running the story through her mind.
She had to get this interview right for Rory's sake. It might
be that Mr O'Toole could get years cut off his sentence. But
would he be interested, now that he was an MP? He must
have so many other pressing matters on his hands, matters
concerning the fate of a nation; why should he be concerned
with the fate of one convicted felon? She pulled a glove off.
Her hand was sweaty. She put it on again. On – or off –
which was correct? During the season, she had read, gloves
should be worn at all times. But this was not the season. She
had checked her appearance a thousand times. Her most
serious, darkest clothes . . .

'Mrs Moncrieffe?'

She rose quickly to meet him, offering her hand.

'You asked to see me.' He motioned them both to be
seated, and drew up a chair close to hers. His manner was
businesslike, as if he could spare her ten minutes of his
valuable time, but no more. She grasped this immediately,
and was flustered. 'Mr O'Toole, I wonder—' She raised her
veil. 'I wonder whether you will remember me?'

He stared at her for a moment, and then, 'Yes, I
believe—'

'You will know me perhaps when I remind you of a man you once defended on a charge of attempted murder in Castlebar. Rory O'Leary.'

'I remember him very well. He is serving a sentence in Portland. But—'

She nodded, embarrassed, and murmured, 'His sister' in a half whisper.

'Miss Abigail? You have a sister, Miss Frances. And now – do I take it, you are married?'

'I am now known as Mrs Hester Moncrieffe. I am a widow,' again she whispered.

'I am very sorry to hear it. So young . . .'

'Mr O'Toole,' she wanted to rush on past these formalities. 'You were once very kind to my brother; I have not forgotten. So learning that you are now an MP, I have taken the liberty of approaching you to remind you of my poor brother's situation, in the hope that you might – whether there might be anything—'

O'Toole looked brisk, businesslike. 'I shall have to remind myself of the circumstances.' He thought for a moment, 'He received a fifteen-year sentence, if I remember correctly?'

'That is so.'

He nodded again. 'And he will have served, let me see, it will soon be three years. Yes. I shall have to look at the papers again, but it might indeed be time to make an application for parole. Ticket of leave,' he explained, as she looked up. 'I shall write to the Home Secretary.'

Afterwards, she walked through the park, thinking over her interview. Mr O'Toole had been kind, very thoughtful; and his energy and certainty were infectious. She felt that merely by reminding him of Rory there was a chance that something could be done. Yet he said he remembered everything – she chewed her lip. Everything? Somehow his purity, his goodness were untouched by her grubby worldliness. She thought about him, yet he was almost

321

incomprehensible to her; he dwelt upon some higher plane where he dealt in important matters, matters which affected whole nations, and was upheld by high moral standards. His life was lived openly, freely, before the whole world. He did not descend into the hard world of compromises; Mr O'Toole would have gone to his father's funeral; he would not have to make up stories for his family; he would not have to tell lies to his aunt.

An old rose; it suited her strong colouring and her thick black hair. She went through many a pattern book, she fingered many a swatch of fabrics. There was a fierce pleasure in that – the silks, the brocades, the satins. Hours were spent discussing the fall of the skirt and the bustle; of course she had long since mastered the bustle. She understood now just how to take up a handful of skirt, to lift it, and swing round, to create an effect with the weight of material swirling about her, as she held her fan in her gloved hand – long gloves of course, with a hint of jewellery. Not much. Too much jewellery – it was one of the first things Nick had taught her – merely showed lack of breeding. And then – the tight waist, the stiffly boned bodice, the pearls stitched in rows, tiny pearls, hundreds of them – yet, at a distance, little more than a kind of texture. The shoelace shoulder straps set far apart, and the sweep of the décolleté. There would be no false modesty about this gown. She had wares to show.

In the end it was simple – Nick would approve the silhouette, as he put it – but not too simple. She wanted a hint of metropolitan sophistication. Nick might prefer the simplicity of a young girl, but she wasn't a young girl. She was a woman, a rich one, and one who was going to make a striking affect as her guests came into the house. They would be all men. She wanted to dazzle them. All this she thought out as she was fitted for her gown, and discussing the trimmings with the dressmaker.

And what a blessing to get her out of the house, and take

322

her mind off events in Mount Street.

Sorry shan't be able to make it after all. Doctors here again, they want to talk to me. Shall try to get away tomorrow.

The weak autumn morning light streamed across the chequered floor as she stood in the hallway staring at the note, vexation eating at her, almost a physical irritation. She drew a strong breath and glanced at the clock. She must go.

In the park she waited for Mrs Hardcastle. And at last the lady appeared with the perambulator. Abby was well accustomed to their morning walks together, was accustomed to William: and had been able to absorb into herself their routine. So long as they could meet like this, all was not lost. It was not much, but it was something, and each morning for this hour, she could be as it were alive, and whatever went on for the other twenty-three all was not entirely lost because she did have this. But Nick's note was on her mind.

'Mr Darke says the doctors have called again,' she started, tentatively.

Mrs Hardcastle nodded as they walked side by side towards the Serpentine.

'So, er, what is it – a relapse, or—'

Mrs Hardcastle turned her kindly face to Abby. 'The doctors are always in the house, Hester, coming and going, in and out, every day. The bell is always ringing. At the moment Mrs Darke is no worse than usual.'

Abby hunted for words. 'And they still have no idea what may be the matter with her, have they?' Mrs Hardcastle did not answer. 'I mean, there is no sign of a cure?' Then after another pause, 'Do you think she will decline further – or get better?'

'No one knows. She does not seem actually ill, you know; just frail, and weak. Some days she is a little stronger and walks about the house for an hour or so. At

323

other times, Mr Darke carries her down to the drawing room—'

'He carries her?'

'And she lies on the sofa.'

There was another silence as the two women pondered this.

'And does she take an interest in William?'

'Oh yes. She likes to see William once a day. Otherwise he is in his nursery and Potts and I take care of him.'

'Potts – she is the wet-nurse?'

Mrs Hardcastle nodded.

'And is she kind to William?'

Mrs Hardcastle stopped the pram, and turned to Abby. 'Mrs Moncrieffe,' she said gravely, but as always in her kindly tone, 'you may be sure that Mr Darke will do everything right for his son. He chose Potts himself after interviewing many women.'

'And once he is weaned, but of course—' Abby hurried on – 'that will not be for some months yet?'

'No.'

Abby was relieved, and they continued to the Serpentine, and strolled along the bank, as their conversation gradually turned to other subjects.

A week had gone by before Nick finally came.

He looked exhausted. She wanted to cry out, 'Nick, *where have you been?*' but she saw instinctively that this would be wrong. He was tired and seemed distracted. She helped him off with his coat and, as they came together into the drawing room, took his hand, looking up into his face, desperate to know what had been happening, but even more wanting to be of comfort to him, forcing herself to wait, to smile, till he should be ready to tell her in his own way. She turned to Robbins standing expectant in the doorway.

'Robbins, bring us tea.'

'Yes m'm,' the girl closed the door behind her.

They seated themselves before the fire, in two upright chairs, curiously formal. She reached her hand tentatively to touch his face, moving the hair across his brow, a small unconscious, wifely touch. He had barely touched her when he arrived – a perfunctory kiss on her brow.

'I heard – the doctors—' she began hesitantly.

He nodded, stared into the fire, and then up at her again, searching in her face as if seeing her for the first time. Then he looked away, ran his hand across his face, and abruptly stood up and walked to the window. 'You've been doing work on the garden,' he said in surprise.

'Yes,' she brightened. 'I have found a good gardener at last, and he has been full of ideas – an espaliered peach for the south-facing wall and a vine in the glasshouse. I help too, you know.'

'Hester.' He turned, cutting through her words, 'There is something. I have not been before, I mean I did not come sooner, my darling, because something has happened, something – I hardly know how to tell you—'

'Not your wife – *she's not dead?*'

He shook his head quickly. 'No.'

'Oh thank God, my darling, well then—'

He turned away, trying to gather his thoughts. At last, still with his back to her, he said quietly, 'The doctors say she must go away. Somewhere warm. They say she might not survive another winter in London. They have recommended Madeira.' He looked terribly serious, and seeing her incomprehension, went on, 'It's an island in the Atlantic – warm, mild, temperate ...'

Abby could not believe her ears. 'You're sending her to Madeira – for her health?'

'I'm *taking* her,' he corrected her gently. 'There's nothing else I can do. Believe me, we have talked it over. For days. I have thought and thought about it. But the doctors are absolute. If she is to be saved ...'

'Taking her.' Her voice was dead. For an instant an unhoped-for vision had opened: Caroline would go to

325

Madeira with a nurse, with a hundred nurses, and Nick remain in London – with her and William.

There was a long silence. She could not even understand yet; not take it in. As she was still struggling to comprehend, he went on, 'There is something else. It is time to make good my promise.'

'What promise?' she said in a hollow voice.

'I said I would see you want for nothing.'

'I want for nothing now.'

'No.' His voice quickened, as he felt himself on safer ground. 'From now on you will have money in your own right. You will be more than well provided for. You will have a fortune, and,' he hesitated, bracing himself, 'you will meet another man. Hester, it's only fair that you should have the chance to lead a decent life – to be married openly and to have a family of your own, not to have to live in the shadows for my sake.'

He was going too fast for her. 'But I don't understand. You will go to Madeira – for the winter – and then—'

'We may not stay in Madeira,' he ran on. 'It depends. I shall have to see. Whatever happens we shall not be returning to London. That's why I want to provide for you—'

'Nick!' It was a great cry as she held out her arms. 'I don't want any one but you!'

He came quickly and took her in his arms. 'And I don't want anyone but you!' For a moment they clasped one another, then – 'But I have a duty to Caroline. Hester,' he rushed on through arguments that he had obviously thought through, 'she is my wife! I swore to care for her through better or worse.' His voice dropped suddenly. 'I must keep my oath.'

Her mind had recovered from its first shock, and was now working feverishly. 'But, couldn't I come to Madeira, too? Couldn't I take a house nearby? Who would know?'

He shook his head. 'It's out of the question. In London it's one thing. London is enormous. We can meet, and no one be the wiser. But Madeira is tiny. Our friendship would

326

become known at once. It would be impossible to keep it from Caroline.'

'You don't love me,' she said.

'You know I love you,' Pulling slightly away from her now, he took her hands in his, and looked her squarely in the eyes. 'But my first responsibility is to her. Hester, I swore to love, honour and keep her, in sickness and health. Nothing can change that. Even if, even—' he was perturbed – 'Hester, if I were to leave her to come here with you, she would probably die. Do you think we could be happy together knowing that? It would kill our love, my darling.' Then, stronger, he went on, 'But there is something else. You must have a life of your own; it's not fair you should have to live in my shadow. You must marry.'

The reality was clearer and clearer. 'You're leaving me,' and anger began in her. 'You're leaving me. And taking William! So soon after—' He nodded.

She swung away. 'Oh God, I don't believe it! How can you? How can you do this? *Nick!*' she screamed, 'how can you?'

He was looking so miserable. But she did not see him; her mind was red, she could not see, could not think, there was only this huge hurt, and she turned away, screaming. 'You're leaving me! Oh God, I can't believe it. And William—' and collapsed against the front of the sofa sobbing, her head in her hands.

327

Chapter Thirty-three

She could not sleep. Yet she could not think either. Thoughts would start, then switch, another would intrude, she chased them like fishes' tails, always slipping through her hands. And always a cold fear in her guts, a nasty writhing in her limbs, she was unable to rest, her mind groping for a way out.

She was helpless, she was drowning, and she reached up for Nick, but he was above her on the deck. A beautiful delicate woman was looking up into his face, her arm in his, and he was putting his hand over hers, looking into her eyes to reassure her. Everything was safe, they were going to Madeira where she would be well – and Abby was fathoms deep. The ship's side rose above her and she reached her hands up towards them, but they did not see her. They were so in love, gazing into each others eyes, and Abby cried out, Nick! Nick! but he didn't hear her . . .

She awoke, starting up in the darkness. It had been a nightmare; but still the nightmare persisted when she was awake. She felt restless, exhausted, feverish, her hair wet with perspiration, her nightdress clinging to her body. She wanted to get up to move, to go out and walk – but only fell back on the bed. Nick, oh Nick – it was a sigh, a moan – oh Nick . . .

The dawn came very slowly, just hinting between the curtains, as she turned her head on the pillow, staring at the first faint gleam. Oh Nick ... She dragged herself out of bed, but had no strength and her eyes smarted from lack of sleep.

Robbins, who came and helped her to dress, was in a cheerful mood and began to prattle about some incident in the kitchen, that silly woman Taylor who had forgotten—

'Shut up.' The girl, cowed, muttered 'Sorry, ma'am', and continued with her lacing, and setting out Abby's shoes.

She sat at breakfast. She had no appetite. She drank a cup of tea, and at last glanced at the clock. Mrs Hardcastle: she must go. She hurriedly pushed away the cup, rang for her coat, and in ten minutes was in her carriage, heading for Hyde Park.

The cold morning revived her. She walked between the bare trees down towards Mount Street trying to breathe deeply. Yes, she must breathe deeply, calm herself. She must tell Mrs Hardcastle nothing. Yet she must know? It occurred to her – was Mrs Hardcastle going to Madeira too? There she was now – coming through the gate into the park, pushing the perambulator. She had her winter coat on too this morning. As they greeted each other Abby glanced quickly inside the pram to make sure William was well wrapped. It was a little damp this morning – not nice, a chilly, damp, wind. Unhealthy ...

They walked towards the water.

'You know about Madeira?' Mrs Hardcastle said at last. Abby nodded.

Mrs Hardcastle was silent for a while, only a kindly and sympathetic smile. 'There was no other choice,' she said at last.

'I know,' Abby muttered. Then, 'I've never met Mrs Darke, you know. I don't even know what she looks like.' Mrs Hardcastle did not reply.

'I would never have given him up if I had known Mr Darke would take him away,' she said abruptly.

'You would not say that if you saw Mr Darke with him,'

the other replied. 'Mrs Moncrieffe, you will never know what you have done for that man. You would never take William from him.' Abby was quiet. There was nothing to say. She was utterly impotent, helpless and everything was out of her hands.

Later they were near the public toilets and Mrs Hardcastle asked her to wait while she went in for a moment. Abby pushed the pram to a nearby bench and sat down to wait. There was a slight gurgling from inside the pram; she stood up again and looked in. William had woken and was looking about, clenching and unclenching his tiny fists. Wide awake, he was turning his head on the pillow. He had dark hair – like Nick's – like her own. Mrs Darke was fair, she knew that. It was not Mrs Darke's child, that was obvious. Obviously it was not in its rightful home. She lifted him carefully from the pram, felt his weight in her arms, clasping him on one crooked arm, and arranging the shawl round him, carefully. William yawned. She laughed softly, What a big mouth you've got haven't you, my darling! And such a rush of feeling washed through her, she felt the tears start in her eyes, and had to sniff. She drew a long sigh, and what a weight, you're such a little darling, so perfect, so perfect . . .

She glanced about her. The park was deserted on that cold misty morning. She stood alone, near the lake, the pram beside her, William in her arms. Then an insane idea rushed through her. She could take him. Now. She could go now, run through the trees, and across the grass. The carriage was waiting; in a moment they would be in the carriage, they could drive to a hotel, she could register under a false name. No one would know. Just the two of them together. She would have her son with her – where he should be – with his rightful mother, she would go now, while Mrs Hardcastle was in there – then she could write to Nick: he couldn't leave London, he must send his wife to Madeira, and himself stay in London with her and William – yes she could just go—

330

She waited ... go ... go now! She did not move. William yawned again, and wriggled in her arms as Mrs Hardcastle returned.

'He's woken up,' Abby said wearily. Mrs Hardcastle took him with practised efficiency, adjusting his shawl, smoothing his hair, and settling him again in the pram.

She's more of a mother to him than I am, and she was weeping before she could help herself. 'I'm sorry,' she muttered, as she dabbed at her eyes. 'I don't know,' and then, 'Mrs Hardcastle, I don't think I can bear it if he goes—' and she broke down into sobs. Faraway across the lake, the swans moved with easy effortless grace, and a rider had appeared in Rotten Row.

'Mrs Moncrieffe, about the arrangements for the dinner tomorrow?'

She started. She had been in a doze, still exhausted from her lack of sleep, and staring into the garden. Marwell had finished raking the leaves, and was turning over flower beds in readiness for next spring. She dragged her attention back to the cook. This was another order of cook from Mrs Casey. This lady was all efficiency and order. Maidservants went in fear and trembling beneath her sway.

'I've taken the liberty of drawing up a menu, Mrs Moncrieffe.' She placed a sheet of paper respectfully on the table near Abby.

Abby dragged her attention round, saw the sheet and, like a sleepwalker, reached and picked it up. Words swam up at her meaninglessly and after a moment her hand dropped listlessly, and without even having looked at it, she half held the paper out to the cook. 'That will do nicely.'

'And would you like to discuss the wines?'

'I think Mr O'Shea has taken care of that, Mrs Baker.'

'Very good ma'am. I'll get started then.'

Abby's eyes had turned again to the garden and she did not hear as the cook let herself out of the room. Was this what the rest of her life was to be? Living in this topsy-turvy world,

331

where she would lurch sometimes, like a crazy woman or a drunk, lurch, and have to steady herself against the back of a chair? She tried to draw breath, but she couldn't; a constriction of her chest tightened her, oppressed her, dragged her down.

She stood up, took a grip on her herself. The dinner she had looked forward so much to; she would be a political hostess, that had been her plan. Famous men would gather at her dinner table, serious matters of state would be discussed. She could make her contribution to the cause of Ireland's prosperity – and eventually freedom. She mustn't let them down.

On a dummy in her dressing room hung her new gown, made specially for her entry into society. It was good. Her decisions had all been the right ones. It suited her strong colour and her thick black hair. Oh – and she mustn't forget: a woman was coming tomorrow afternoon to do her hair.

She stared at the dress. On one level, her mind was mentally making arrangements: the seating plan, the menu, the wines. Her gown, her hair, what jewellery – she must choose her jewellery.

And on another level? This was all madness. She couldn't go through with it.

'Can't go through with it?' Willie looked staggered.

She sat on the edge of the settee, leaning forward one hand pressing against her forehead.

'He's leaving.'

'Leaving? Who?'

'Can't you guess? His wife must go to Madeira. The doctors say so.' Her eyes were closed, her head still pressed against her hand.

Willie pulled a chair up close to her, and took her hand away from her face. 'You poor girl,' he whispered, looking into her eyes. 'You poor, poor girl. Of course we'll cancel.'

But then she saw the disappointment written across his simple features. She shook her head. 'I'm sorry – no, of course we shan't cancel. The preparations have all been made, the invitations gone out. Don't worry about me, I shouldn't have told you – besides,' she stood up, 'I have a new gown.'

In a state of suspended hibernation, she would lurch sometimes in her steps. Still, she told herself again, she must go through with it; it was planned, her guests were looking forward to it, Willie would have been disappointed.

She surveyed herself again. She was pale, and her eyes were dark from lack of sleep. She must powder her face. Some distant part of her brain was telling her that this should have been a splendid triumphant moment, her first dinner party! And it was telling her too that she looked very striking indeed in this new gown. Nick would have approved – and as she thought it, she had to steady herself on the edge of the dressing table for a moment before she could regain her composure. The gown was indeed everything she had wanted; her hands on her hips, she swung round, taking in the effect of the ensemble.

And her hair – the woman had rearranged it to give her a fringe, making her face look quite different. It was extraordinary: she realised the transformation that could be wrought in a woman's appearance by the rearrangement of her hair. This fringe was the latest style.

She sat at her dressing table and lethargically opened the powder box, and began dabbing it here, there, trying to hide the shadows of tiredness.

A butler had been engaged for the night. Strangely she had never had one before. She must think about it. A butler certainly gave one – whatever it was – but as he announced the next guest, Mr Timothy Healey, she was able to go forward, flashing a smile, and greet him, extending her arm in its long glove. 'Mr Healey, I am so glad you were able to be with us!'

333

Already half a dozen men were standing about the drawing room sipping glasses of champagne, and engaged in low conversation. As yet the atmosphere was subdued. She hoped they weren't in awe of their surroundings. One or two of them were examining the Chinese vases and the Dresden figurines on the mantelpiece. But then, she reflected, being Irishmen it would not take them long to liven up.

'Mr J.J. O'Toole!' intoned the butler.

'Mr O'Toole!' She turned from where she had been in conversation and crossed to the door. She smiled. O'Toole was in evening dress – they all were – but there was no doubt that, unlike some to whom it was clearly not customary, he wore it well. He had a natural elegance – an economy of movement, a physical containedness. He took her hand, spoke quietly, yet confidently, thanked her for inviting him.

'No word from the Home Secretary?'

He shook his head. 'We have to wait for the meeting of the Board.'

Willie was being Willie. Affable, loud, chaffing people, thumping them on the back, and her attention was distracted by the arrival of other guests.

Then they were at the table – fourteen of them, and the talk was all of politics. The passing of the Land Act had been a tremendous victory, and the talk now was all of a Home Rule Bill. This was what the Chief had his sights on. This would be their greatest achievement. Yet the party refused to take off; there was no lightening of the atmosphere. She sat at the head of the table ordering the hired butler discreetly, and the maidservants as they came in and out, encouraging her guests to help themselves to a little more of this or that – and seeing that the glasses were replenished, and at the far end of the table, Willie was doing his best to be affable.

It didn't work. She sat like a tragedy queen, unable to smile. She would start, make another effort, yet a moment

334

later her attention was gone and she was staring across the room, still unable to believe his words, still running the scene with Nick through her head, trying to rephrase it, make it different, make it something it wasn't. Someone was asking her a question. She turned slowly, like a sleep-walker.

'I'm sorry, did you say something?' Yet even before he had finished his question, her attention had wandered. How had she ever got herself into this situation? How had it begun? She would run the whole story of their love through from the beginning – how it was so clearly meant to be from the first encounter in the park, when Nick had been with Willie. Willie had been a bit of a clown, but Nick had instinctively understood her; then again at that awful party of Thady's Nick had understood everything, and had been solicitous for her even then, taking her arm, and protecting her from the gross attentions of that drunk . . .

She turned, as if waking from hypnosis, and said, in a faraway manner, 'Do forgive me, I wasn't concentrating, what were you saying?' Her mood communicated itself throughout the table; despite all Willie's efforts, the guests were unable to unbend and enjoy themselves. She could see, intermittently, when she dragged her attention to them, looking round briefly before her own thoughts intruded, looking at their polite smiles, but being aware of their constrained conversation, the gaps, the awkwardness, the exaggerated deference, as if she were the queen, for heaven's sake.

Eventually, as soon as she could she rose, 'Gentlemen, I am sure you would like to be left to your port and cigars. When you are ready, coffee will be served in the drawing room,' and swept out as the butler opened the door for her. She could hear behind her the conversation audibly pick up as she crossed the hall to the drawing room. How hot it was. She turned in the empty room, checking that every-thing was in place.

'Shall I serve coffee now, ma'am?' Robbins asked. Abby

335

shook her head imperceptibly, passed her to the fireplace and looked down into the flames, resting her hand on the marble mantelpiece; then restlessly turning again through the room, unable to be still. Feeling all the time an intolerable burden pulling her down, as if she wore a gown of lead, no strength in her limbs, only this numbing futility . . .

Pushing through the French windows she went down the two or three steps into the garden, and stood staring into the darkness. The trees were barely illuminated by light from the window behind her as she stood, seeing nothing, only forcing herself to breathe deeply. Just breathe, don't think, no need to think, just breathe, be calm . . .

It was a chill, damp night, and within a few minutes she shuddered. What of that? What did *she* matter anyway, she had done what was required of her and now there was no longer any need for her . . .

'Mrs Moncrieffe, is there anything the matter? Are you unwell?' She started slightly at the voice, and turned. Mr O'Toole came down to her. 'You'll catch a chill. Please come inside.'

His voice was low, calm, reassuring. She looked into his eyes, for a moment desperate, then checked herself. His face was serene, noble, unclouded – yet full of understanding and compassion. He was like an old-time saint, pure. Still staring, almost like a mad woman, she thought, I could trust this man with my life. He would be a rock of strength and security for me. Yet, a split second later, she thought, How? How could *I*, used, cast-aside – how could *I* confide in this good man? What would he say if he knew my story? And yet I so need him, I must make him a friend, to help Rory.

As these thoughts flashed through her mind, she took a grasp on herself and held out her hand. 'Thank you. You are right.'

He offered her his arm, she put hers through it and they mounted the few steps together.

Chapter Thirty-four

'You realise, Mr Darke, this is a considerable sum of money?'

'I only wish it were more.' Nick's voice was barely a croak, and Abby squeezed his hand. Poor Nick was almost in tears. Outside, she could see, through the grimy window behind the old gentleman opposite her, the bare elms that filled the square. Somewhere too in that dull late autumn afternoon, she heard the cawing of rooks. Gray's Inn; they had met by appointment at the gate, both buttoned up against the cold; he had offered to come and fetch her, but she had said, 'No, Nick, I don't think I could bear it. Let's just meet at the solicitor's.'

And now they sat, like two children, holding hands, facing two elderly and grave gentlemen, as one of them, the one who had been reading out the settlement, finally placed the sheet of parchment on the desk before him, and looked up at Nick over his pince nez.

'You would wish us to act for Mrs Moncrieffe in the future?' he went on.

Nick nodded.

'Very well.' The pince nez were adjusted. 'In that case it merely remains for you to sign . . .' He raised again this unwieldy parchment document – like some relic of the Middle Ages, as if the king were about to declare war, or raise someone to a peerage – skewed it round and proffered

337

it across the desk, already crowded with other documents and papers, while his colleague took up a pen, dipped it into the ink well, and offered it to Nick.

Nick took the pen, and glanced across to Abby before signing his name, with a determined and quick motion. Then he smiled a bleak, wintry smile, and took her hand again. The old gentleman turned to his colleague. 'Now Mr Montague, if you would be so kind—'

The two solicitors took it in turns to witness the document.

The solicitor had noticed the look between them, and turned at last to Abby. 'Perhaps, Mrs Moncrieffe, it might be convenient for you to call at another time, and we can go through the provisions with you in more detail, and make arrangements for transfers at your banker's?'

She nodded.

'In that case, would you care to make an appointment with my clerk as you leave?' What else was there to do? Nick had signed this great sheet, which the solicitor had carefully blotted, and was now rolling up and securing with a red ribbon. Her future, signed and sealed.

They were in the square again, the light thickening among the tall elms, and the rooks wheeling above them among the bare branches. They walked along the gravel path, hand in hand. There was nothing to say. Everything was arranged – she did not want to know the details. No doubt passages had been booked on a liner, the house was shrouded in calico, the blinds down, windows shuttered, servants dismissed, travelling wardrobes planned, travelling companions detailed – Mrs Hardcastle detailed too – she did not want to know the details. They were at the gate, and Blake pulled forward from where he had been waiting. 'I'll take you home.'

She shook her head slightly, looking down, unable to meet his eye at this moment, for fear what might follow.

'My darling,' he breathed. 'I'll write—'

'No!' she interrupted. 'Don't write. I couldn't bear it!

338

Having letters from you – watching the post every day, living in hope, and having no hope. I couldn't—'

He turned away his head muttering, 'I can't stand it.' Then, in a strangely matter-of-fact tone, 'I don't think I can live without you.'

'Please Nick, don't speak.'

'Get in, I'll drive you at least—'

'No.' Again she was firm. 'Let's say goodbye here. It's best. Let us shake hands, Nick, and then you can get into your carriage, and—'

'Have it. Have Blake. I've already spoken to him. Then you won't need to use those livery people any more. I wish I could give you everything I have.'

She glanced back at Blake waiting a few yards further along the pavement. Then looking back said quickly, 'Goodbye, my darling. God bless you and keep you, and take care of William. And remember me. I shall never forget you.'

They embraced, hugged tight pressing, pressing, a universe of feeling in one short embrace, she kissed his cheek briefly, turned and climbed quickly into the carriage. She did not look back, as the carriage swung into motion.

At her door as the maid opened it she walked through into the drawing room. 'Shall I light the candles, madam?'

She shook her head, turned once in the middle of the room, as the girl went out, then collapsed wordlessly on to the sofa, sobbing as if her heart would break.

When her sobbing eventually grew to a close, she lay, a dry-eyed useless husk, staring at the window, where the grey afternoon had closed almost to darkness. There was a light tap at the door. Taylor the maid stood before her holding a candle. Abby viewed her as a stranger. 'What do you want?'

'Mrs Moncrieffe, are you unwell?' Abby gazed up looking round her as if not recognising the room.

'Shall I light the candles now?' the woman went on tentatively. Abby said nothing, did not move and Taylor went

339

across to the mantelpiece, and lit two candles. Abby pulled herself with great difficulty upright, sitting with her hands beside her staring at the fire.

She stood up, crossed to the mantelpiece, where her gaze had been fastened, took up a pretty little Dresden figurine, a shepherdess in pastel colours – one of a pair – and, turning with deliberation, hurled it at the wall opposite where it smashed and fell to the floor. She turned and taking another, hurled that. Then bolder, took another and threw it with all her strength, and suddenly incoherently screaming – a wild, wordless yell – picked a Chinese vase from a side table hurled it against the marble fireplace, and now screaming again, ran to the shelf of other Chinese vases, hurling them about her, here, there. The maid-servant, dodging one of these, watched with terror, as Abby pulled and wrenched at the curtains, trying to pull them down, hanging on them, and then turning again, swept her hand along the mantelpiece, as items flew in all directions, swinging round and overturning a little occasional table where a candelabrum stood, screaming, and at last hurled herself on to the sofa again, burying her face in a cushion and sobbing uncontrollably.

As dawn at last filtered through the curtains she turned again in her disorganised bed, shivered, and tried for the hundredth time to organise her thoughts. But a leaden apathy had settled over her. She did not blame Nick in any way: he had been honourable always, always, and he loved her, she knew it. She would never blame him, never dream of it, but still – she had lost. That was it. Nick said she must marry. She didn't want to marry – she wanted Nick. She wanted to follow him; he wouldn't let her follow him.

Sometimes sitting alone in the afternoon she wondered where they must be now. They must have arrived in Madeira long ago. She knew nothing of the island, could only imagine palm trees and monkeys – except that there must be hotels and so on, towns and shops probably. It

340

would be beautiful, that was obvious, otherwise Nick would never take his wife there, and perhaps – as her imagination flowed on – perhaps it was like Brighton, and Nick would push his wife along the promenade in her invalid carriage, while Mrs Hardcastle followed carrying William?

Her loss was absolute; she just didn't see what there was for her to do any more. How could she ever have another relationship – even if she wanted one? Her future was in Madeira, not in London in this big empty house. Futility rose about her like a tide, a sea. What had it all been *for*? Why was she getting up in the morning? Why go through all that effort, why bother to pick her dresses, why brush her hair? Why wash herself? Why eat? What was it all *for*?

Winter passed. Months went by as she remained in a state of hibernation, and it was almost the end of winter. March weather, occasional blustery days, and a hint of warmth in the sun and, with the return of life to the earth, she too felt a rebirth.

One morning unexpectedly she said to herself, 'I need exercise – that's what it is. I'm getting morbid in this mausoleum,' and she sent a message to Blake to bring the carriage to the door.

Half an hour later he saw her at the door, in her full riding habit, all in black, the pert little top hat perched forward on her head, a cane in her hand. As she climbed into the carriage she said, 'Sussex Square, Bayswater.'

In the corner of the square as she descended she told him to come back in an hour and turned into Bathurst Mews.

Nothing had changed, and in fact she saw Jenkins in a stable doorway. 'Have you still got The Baron?' He had.

'Saddle him up for me.'

'Yes ma'am.' It was only as he was turning away that he recognised her. 'Stone the crows, Abby! What on earth?'

She stood expressionless. 'What are you waiting for?'

'Abby, it is you?'

341

'It looks like it, Jenkins. Are you going to bring out The Baron, or shall I ask someone else?'

After a moment he dragged himself round and disappeared into the stable, as she waited in the mews, on the wet cobbles, breathing the old stable smell she knew so well.

Then she was on The Baron, walking him through the square and into the park, just like old times. The horse was as over-fed and under-exercised as he had been the day she first rode him. He would enjoy a good gallop, and so would she. As they came into the park, she let him take up a nice easy canter, to get into the swing of it, and warm himself. In ten minutes they had reached the far end of the Long Water; she crossed to Rotten Row, turned his head west, and bending over him, whispered in his ear, as she loosened the reins. 'Sss . . . sss.'

The Baron took off, jerking her back in her saddle by the force of his impetus, and a thrill of joy shot through her. At last, this was where she could be at home. Oh, the exhilaration, the thudding of his hooves beneath her, the force, the strength of that huge body, those powerful thighs thrusting her forward, the wind in her face. A smile broke unconsciously on her face, she could feel the heat in her cheeks, the unaccustomed pounding of the blood in her veins. Why hadn't she done this before?

She came to the Albert Memorial, turned him and headed back eastwards, lashing him into a gallop, urging him on. She only wanted to go on galloping, riding, never have to stop, never have to go home, never – she lashed The Baron forward.

And it wasn't until they had been galloping for half an hour up and down, until the horse was well winded, and so was she, that she slowed The Baron to walk for a spell. Only now did she look about her, and take in her surroundings. The park was quiet at this time of year, a few riders were about, the birds among the elms, traffic in Kensington Gore; otherwise she was alone. It suited her mood, to be

342

alone with The Baron. She turned his head, and began walking him comfortably eastwards again towards the barracks.

She returned to the stables in a very much better frame of mind than when she had set out. 'Jenkins – forgive me – I was so short with you just now.'

'Feeling better now?' She nodded, smiling.

Then out of another stable came Thady O'Farrell. Before she could turn away they had seen each other. His astonishment was complete. '*Abby!* Is that ever yourself? By Jesus, and the fine lady too!' He came towards her, wiping his hands as if in preparation to shake hers. She braced herself. Thady was in filthy breeches, a torn and greasy shirt, his hair disarranged – a ragged groom.

She took a step backwards, her hands on her hips where it was clear she had no intention of letting him touch her.

As he saw her retreat, he slowed, and stood looking at her. 'Aren't ye going to say hello to old Thady?'

She stood there surveying him a long minute, shaking her head slowly.

''Twas me brought ye here, Abby – ye owe it all to me.'

'All what?'

He raised an eyebrow. 'I don't have to tell ye, surely?'

She wanted to change the subject, and looked about her. 'Still here, then?'

He came closer, looking miserable. 'I'm still paying off the debt, Abby,' he confided.

'What debt?'

'How did ye think we was able to take the house, and buy all them new clothes? 'Twas the colonel lent me the money, and if I don't work to pay him off, 'tis the gaol house. He's got me over a barrel, Abby – I'll be workin' for him till the crack o' doom – there's the interest, ye see.'

She could not feel any sympathy, staring at him again. 'You should have thought of that before you took the money.'

'Don't I know it!'

343

She turned away impatient. 'You took me for granted. Do you expect me to feel sorry for you?' Thady was behind her; the last thing she wanted was him to remind her of things she would rather forget.

But sitting in her carriage, and later by her drawing room fire, his ugly face returned to haunt her. That wretched Thady! What a fool! He had thought to use her, to make her his whore. He deserved everything he got. But behind this lay another nagging thought, a thought she did not like to confront but which, as the evening drew on, gradually forced itself into her consciousness. Yes, but she had asked him to bring her to London. Only with Thady could she ever have come here. She owed him something too.

The following morning, back in the colonel's stable, she took him aside. She did not smile, and her speech was brief. 'Don't say anything, just listen. There's a job for you – if you want it. The money's better than here, and it's clean – you'll be working for a rich lady. Write this down: 16 Acacia Road, St John's Wood. Ask for Mrs Moncrieffe. Go and see her this afternoon. Now saddle up The Baron.'

'Yes ma'am!'

This was better. She felt lighter. If she could be out like this, enjoying a hard gallop, things weren't so bad. She had slept better too. Perhaps in time she would be able to establish a new way of life; simpler, healthier, and memories and thoughts would retreat, grow less intense. She put The Baron into a gallop, and felt again that unspeakable thrill, to be on a such a huge, such a powerful beast. She lashed him up and down the Row several times, and only at last slowed and allowed him to walk.

She heard the thudding of hooves behind her, and took no notice, until she was aware of a man reining in his horse beside her.

'I thought it was you.' She turned in surprise. She did not recognise him.

'We were watchin' you yesterday.' He set his horse to

344

walk beside her. She said nothing.

'Yes,' he went on, in an aristocratic drawl, quite at ease. 'But afterwards there was a bit of a dispute, you see. My friends claimed it had been a trick of the light. I maintained you were a real woman but they were convinced you were a vision – a will-o'-the-wisp. No woman could ride like that or be as beautiful as that, they said. But I am glad to see that I was right. You are a woman.' He was studying her. 'You made quite an impression.'

She looked sharply up at him. And as she did so, she recognised him. It was Lord Morton, who had once embarrassed her with a twenty pound note. It was obvious, however, he did not recognise her. 'And what sort of impression are you supposed to make on me?' she said without expression.

'An agreeable one, I hope?' He leaned forward a little in his saddle, and smiled. What was he – about forty? There was something worldly about him, something cynical, something lean and wolfish. He looked used.

She studied him calmly. 'You aren't a will-o'-the-wisp, that's for sure. There is something decidedly earthbound about you, I should say.'

'A man of flesh and blood. Lucas Morton – at your service.'

He had black hair, a dark-shadowed lantern jaw, heavy eyebrows, with deep-set penetrating eyes. A determined, cold man, used to having his way; used to being obeyed. She gave him another considering survey, and at last murmured, 'What kind of service do you think you could render me?'

'I was wonderin' just the opposite.'

She turned her head away and they rode in silence for a second. There was something intrusive, domineering, about this remark, with its obvious innuendo. She felt an unfamiliar beating of her heart, a mixture of fear, anticipation, and something else, a sort of fierce, cynical recklessness. Two can play at that game, she thought.

345

'*I* wonder,' she said at last, casually, 'whether you could afford it,' and gave him a direct look.

He pulled his horse to a halt beside her, holding her look. 'I'll be blunt with you. I'm a man accustomed to layin' a thousand guineas on a horse or the turn of a card. Put a figure to it.'

Without speaking, she pulled a visiting card from her glove, scribbled on the back of it, and handed it to him. He glanced at it. And looked back at her.

'That does not buy me outright, you understand,' she said distinctly, 'that is only the down payment.'

'Supper first?' he said softly. She was conscious how her manner had subdued him. He was like a dog, excited, waiting for a sign from its mistress. Her power over him at that moment gave her an exultant thrill.

'Come around nine,' she said as she set the spur to The Baron's flank.

All the way back to the stables she fought to control herself. She had beaten him at his own game. He had thought to domineer over her, and he had had a shock. The figure she had written on the back of the card had been so preposterously high that she had not imagined for a moment he would have agreed. It give her a powerful sense of triumph; she understood instinctively that this was a matter not of pleasure, not of mating, but of one thing only – power.

Chapter Thirty-five

When she got home, she changed out of her riding habit, stripped off and washed herself all over; she had got quite hot and sticky after the ride, and especially after her interview. She needed to cool down, clean herself up, change into lighter clothes. She needed to calm down and think out what she had done.

But even after all these preparations – which took nearly an hour – and even after lunch, nothing had changed. She was calmer about it, cooler, certainly, but she did not intend to change her mind. In fact, when she took time to examine her own thoughts and motives, she could see that there had been nothing surprising or shocking about her interview with Lord Morton. It was exactly what she wanted; she held the cards, she had the whip hand. She could deal on her own terms. It was that last image of Morton, and his palpable excitement, though he worked hard to conceal it, that she had perceived and relished. She was in charge, and she would make him pay dear for his pleasures.

She was turning through her drawing room thinking these thoughts, when there was a distant knock at the front door. She heard Taylor cross the hall, and a whispered conversation. A moment later the maid reappeared at the door. She looked embarrassed. 'There's an Irish groom at the door, madam, says he was sent.'

Abby had completely forgotten him. 'Show him in here.'

She stood in front of the fire, her hands on her hips. Thady appeared at the door, a hat in his hands. He looked about him for a moment in undisguised awe. Then, as he saw her, 'Abby!'

'You found your way, then?'

'You said to ask for a Mrs Moncrieffe?'

'She's in her drawing room.'

There was a long silence. Thady looked about him, more and more uncertain, gradually taking everything in, the tall French windows with their swagged curtains, the pictures on the wall, the lovely French furniture . . .

'The drawing room?' he gestured vaguely, 'but, isn't this?'

She waited unsmiling.

'Abby, I don't—' then understanding dawned. 'You don't mean, ye never, ye mean, *you're* Mrs Moncrieffe?'

She crossed the room to her escritoire, sat and studied him severely as he came gradually, timidly, closer. 'You don't deserve it. However, I've a job for you.'

'Abby, but *how*? All this—' he looked round again.

'There's a job for you, O'Farrell. On one condition. If one word ever gets out – one word mind, one hint, one smile, one nudge, one wink – you'll be back working for Colonel Wilkes.'

'But I owe him money.'

She shook her head. 'You owe *me* money.' He looked mystified. She drew a long-suffering breath. 'I bought your debt.'

'Oh Abby!'

'Mrs Moncrieffe.'

His excitement grew, and he stared down at her in undisguised awe. 'Mrs Moncrieffe! Glory be! Mrs Moncrieffe – well, if that doesn't beat all! Abby – and now raised up to be a lady! By Jesus, did ye ever see the like!'

'Get used to it, O'Farrell, if you want the job.'

He humbled himself immediately, gripping his hat in

both hands, his shoulders hunched. 'Oh yes indeed, Mrs Moncrieffe.'

'I need a man in the place; you're by no means ideal but I'll try to train you. There's a lot to learn, O'Farrell. And the first thing is never to call me Abby again. Ever. This is a good job for you – it's the best chance you'll get and if you've a head on your shoulders – which sometimes I doubt, you'll seize it with both hands.'

'Mrs Moncrieffe,' Thady breathed in accents of undisguised awe. 'Trust me! Trust old Thady – he'll never let ye down—'

'We'll see.' She rose with an ironical expression. 'Settle your affairs with Colonel Wilkes, pack up your traps and report back here on Saturday.' She handed him a piece of paper from her desk. 'Go round to these people and get yourself a uniform – it's all written there.'

She dabbed the scent behind her ears, at her wrists, patted a little over her bosom, set the bottle down and inspected herself again in the glass. Yes, Lord Morton should get his money's worth. In fact, she was going to leave Lord Morton panting for more. He was probably panting already; he was downstairs in the drawing room and she had kept him waiting twenty minutes. She slipped on a pair of dainty evening slippers, set the diamond earrings in her ears, turned her head to judge the effect, went into her bedroom, and inspected the bed. All was ready. The fire was lit; the curtains were drawn, the bed turned down.

As she picked her way carefully downstairs, taking up the fullness of her gown in one hand, she called, 'Robbins, the sable,' and the girl, who had been waiting in the hall, returned a moment later with this ankle-length fur coat. Morton was at the drawing room door. She had not yet acknowledged him, but as the girl helped the fur over her shoulders she glanced across at him.

'Ready?'

'For anything.' He came forward.

'Well then, my lord, let's see what you have in mind for supper.' As she saw him about to take her in his arms, she walked past him towards the door which Robbins had now opened. 'You had better wait up till I return – and make up the fire in my bedroom later,' she called over her shoulder.

'Yes, madam.'

The restaurant was crowded, and the food was good, probably she thought, the best that could be obtained. But she didn't take much notice of the food, or the conversation – of which she scarcely remembered a word the following morning. What did it matter what they talked about? She sat, her elbows on the table, looking at Lord Morton, and Lord Morton sat looking at her, and there was one thought between them.

But, apart from that thought, she had others. Oh yes I'll give him his money's worth – but I'll pay myself back too. Morton may be only flesh and blood – but what am I? I deserve it. Why shouldn't I please myself?

In the cab afterwards they were already hectically exploring each other. He had her face in his hands kissing her violently, roughly; he was a coarse man, and took his pleasures coarsely, whatever veneer of breeding he might possess. But she was not inhibited by the slightest modesty either; pressing a hand into his groin, she found him in a massive state of readiness. Her breath quickened.

And when they were in her room – she sent her maid to bed immediately – he was at her before she had even undressed – had splayed her across the bed, kissing her bosom, trying to pull the dress off her shoulders.

Still, there were one or two little formalities to complete first. She pulled herself away, sat up, and whispered, 'Get in. I'll be with you in a moment.'

In her dressing room, she huddled quickly out of her gown, picking her way down her back through the hooks and eyes, treading it on the floor, a heap of white, lace and fine lawn petticoats, as she quickly pulled her chemise over

350

her head, pulling off her stockings, her drawers, and then taking the box from the top drawer. With practised fingers, she took out a little piece of sponge, soaking it in the preparation from the bottle, and setting a foot on a chair, inserted it with a finger.

As she came into the room, a single candle burned on the bedside table. She paused for a moment naked in the doorway. Morton's eyes were fastened on her. He said nothing, but threw back the bedclothes and snuffed the candle. The fire was alight, and threw a warm glow through the room. Morton was strong; there was nothing delicate or considerate about him. He was not concerned for her feelings – she had seen that the moment she first spoke with him. But the point was, she didn't care; this was what she wanted. She *wanted* to be handled roughly, she wanted his weight bearing down on her; wanted him in her, thrusting, gripping, smothering her face, her neck, her breasts with his kisses. She wanted him sliding down her body after a while, covering her belly, her thighs, with his kisses, and licking her between her legs, like an animal; she exulted in it, she only wanted him to go on long enough – and she had an idea that he was not the man to tire easily. She didn't care what he did: let him have her from the front, and from the back, let him have her any way he wanted so long as he had her long enough. What she wanted above all was oblivion, and Morton was the tool. That was all.

She was awake and could hear distant voices at the front door; she lay concentrating, trying to hear. Morton still slept beside her. Outside it was a grey day and she had no idea of the time – but it must be late. The conversation finished and she heard the door close. Curious, she rose, pulling a wrap round her, and crossed to the window. Through the lace curtain she saw a man cross the road and walk away on the other side. It was Mr O'Toole. She watched him until he disappeared round the corner and, then pulling the wrap tight about her, went out on to the

351

landing. She could still feel the shock, the sudden rush of blood in her face as she tried to control her breathing.

'Taylor, who was that?'

'A gentleman, ma'am; I said you were not at home, and he left a note.'

'Bring it up. What time is it?'

'Half past twelve, ma'am.'

'And bring me some hot water, please.'

'Yes, ma'am.'

She turned back into her room, went again to the window and looked up the street in the direction Mr O'Toole had taken. Resting her hands on the window sill, she hung her head for a moment, trying to gather her thoughts. She should have been downstairs welcoming him, asking him about Rory – she glanced round at Morton still asleep. And instead . . .

Then she noticed the money on the mantelpiece. She crossed quickly, took the notes and, going into her dressing room, thrust them into a drawer. She didn't need to count them. She didn't need the money. She had only named the figure to put his lordship into the proper frame of mind.

He was still asleep when Taylor knocked. The maid came into the bedroom, saw the man in her bed, and glanced at Abby as she handed her a small envelope, and set a jug of water on the wash stand.

'Thank you. That will be all.'

She turned again to the window and ripped open the letter. It was quite short. Mr O'Toole had had a reply from the Home Secretary. Unfortunately, the Board was not minded at the present time to consider Rory O'Leary for parole. Mr O'Toole went on to express his disappointment, and to assure Mrs Moncrieffe that he would continue to press the Home Secretary and, if a suitable occasion should arise in the future, to raise the matter in the House.

She clutched the little note to her for a moment, as Morton stirred.

'You had better get dressed and go,' she said, folding the

note again, and slipping it into a pocket. 'I have business to attend to.'

He sat up slowly as he came fully awake. 'How are you this morning?' he asked after a moment.

'I'm perfectly well. And I have an appointment this afternoon.'

He was not put out by her businesslike manner. A moment later as he moved, he made a grimace, and reached his hand awkwardly to feel his back. 'These scratches on my back – how am I supposed to explain them to my valet?'

'Tell him you were attacked by a wild animal.'

He raised his eyebrows. 'I think I was.' He lay back in bed and watched her brushing for a moment. 'Are we goin' to meet again?'

'Maybe.'

'You don't sound too sure.'

But she remembered Mr O'Toole's call, and in a moment of bitterness, said casually, 'Oh yes. Come again. Why not? Bring your friends.'

'They're on your bed. Try them on and then come down to the drawing room.'

She stood in the doorway, pointing. Thady went forward into the little room and looked about him. 'And this is for me?' he breathed. 'All me own?' He looked about.

They were in a room on the third floor. It was small enough, partly under the roof, and the ceiling sloped towards the little window overlooking the garden. A narrow iron bed, a small bit of carpet on the bare boards, a wash stand with a bowl and jug.

'I'll tell Robbins to bring you your hot water at six, and I'll expect you to be on duty from seven, to serve breakfast.'

Thady had put down his bag, picked up the black swallow-tail coat from the bed and was looking it over. 'Serve breakfast. Very good, Mrs Moncrieffe!' He gave her a wink.

'As I said, no winks. From now on I'm Mrs Moncrieffe to you, and never forget it. Get that on, and come down to my drawing room.'

'I will, Mrs Moncrieffe.'

Five minutes later Thady appeared in his butler's uniform. She stood back, and looked him over. The uniform fitted; if she could just get him to stand upright, instead of that servile cringe, and learn to keep his hands out of his pockets.

'Come down to the kitchen and I'll introduce you to the other servants. Then you had better go and get a haircut. There's a barber's on the high street.' She looked him over again. 'You need a shave too. You're an indoor servant now, O'Farrell. If you want to stay one, you'll have to smarten yourself up.'

'Leave it to Thady!'

She had the gravest doubts about 'leaving it to Thady'. 'When you come back we'll make a tour of the cellar.'

It was over a year later, on an April afternoon, that she sat at her escritoire studying her list of things to be done, and playing with a pencil. She was giving a party for Lord Morton and his friends on Saturday. She rested her chin on her hand, thinking. It was extraordinary how her life had changed, and how she had changed, in the year since she had met Morton. She felt so much older, so much more mature and, in a way she didn't like to contemplate, so much harder too. Sometimes she wondered how she would appear if her younger self were to walk through the door.

It seemed her life had settled into a new pattern, and for the time being she was prepared to let it continue. She didn't know how long it would go on and she didn't care. She had enough confidence in herself now to know she could handle whatever might turn up. She was rich; and Morton had made her richer. She had no qualms about taking his money and she considered she gave him good value for it. She wasn't in love with him – that was obvious

– but neither was he in love with her. It was a convenient arrangement, that was all. Morton was a countryman and even when he was in town there was a flavour of the hunt about him; they spent a lot of time together at the races or a meet. He admired her courage on horseback, and she gave him what he wanted, a bold and witty companion in the field or at a party – and a good time in bed. She had her freedom and plenty of money. What more did she need?

But as all this clarified in her mind, she had to remind herself – she did not need the money. If all else failed she had money enough to live in considerable style; Nick had seen to that. She was not doing this for the money. She gave a small cynical laugh; but perhaps she was? What was her real motive, if she were to be honest with herself?

The motive was deeply hidden – not easily to be teased out; and it was not one of which she could be proud. It was the part of herself she kept hidden – a dark part hidden deep beneath the surface. Because to say, 'Why should I give it away when I can be paid for it?', to say that sexual allure gave her power, to say that she relished that power, the power to grant or to withhold, to say she could translate that power into money – these were not worthy thoughts, not thoughts she would like to bring out and parade in the noonday sun. They were miserable thoughts, associated with loss, disappointment, frustration, a picture of herself which she did not wish to acknowledge.

Oh Nick. Why did you have to go away? And she clasped her hands together as the heart within her ached, a bitter ache, as she remembered Paris, she on his arm, looking up to him. Nick so gentle, so funny, so loving ... She remembered when they first met in Hyde Park with Willie. Afterwards it had seemed inevitable; it was obviously meant to be. She remembered when he first made love to her, so tender, so loving; remembered the first time he held his son in his arms – their son – that holy moment when they had been together, the three of them for the first time.

To remember that and then to see her now – Lord Morton's whore. She felt heavy in her body. Suppose Nick were to return now? To see him in the doorway with her little boy? 'William, this is your mama.' But Nick would not return. She knew it and at last shook her head slowly, painfully, as the truth burnt through her like acid, corrosive, scalding, bitter.

Anyway, she mustn't think of all that – love and the thoughts of a family, children – she had shut all those things away. That was for other people, not for her. She forced herself to sit upright and took a deep breath. She was content as she was, and the important thing was that she could look after her brother and sister. They would be her anchor.

The guests started arriving around ten. They were mainly men, of course. She knew Morton's friends by now; they were a very masculine clique. Very much the sort of men who had come to her first party years ago in Connaught Square, Thady's 'entry into society'. Wives, if they had any, were left at home, and any girls you might see were either like herself, of, shall we say, equivocal status, or else picked up for the night in dance halls, casinos or various insalubrious 'divans' – she didn't inquire too closely.

By midnight the rooms were crowded, there was talk, laughter, the piano was open. Thady was opening the door as they arrived, in white gloves; Taylor and Robbins circulated with trays of champagne. Abby glanced round the room. That plump fellow with the beard was de Souza, a Jew who played the stock exchange; that bald middle-aged man, who looked as if he should have been at home with his wife and children was Ackroyd, who owned paper mills and was very rich; she glanced round and noticed a youngish, rather short man – Smithson – he was on the board of six railway companies, and had done very well for himself. All of them in their different ways were buccaneers, gamblers by instinct.

'Who's he?' she tapped Morton on the arm, and pointed out a red-faced man standing in front of the fire.

356

'The Earl of Romsey – owns half of Hampshire.'

At one o'clock a supper was announced. Things were getting rowdy, it was impossible to hear a conversation, difficult to push through the crush in the dining room where a buffet was laid out. Abby gradually became aware that there had been knocking at the door for some time and as she came out of the dining room, she saw Taylor opening it to admit two more guests.

A moment later she caught the woman's arm. 'Where's O'Farrell? Why isn't he doing that?'

'He's in the drawing room, madam,' Taylor said with a significant look.

Abby marched across the hall and into the drawing room. The room was deserted at this moment except for Thady who was helping himself to a glass of champagne from a tray on a side table, and forcing a canapé into his mouth. She took the little morsel from his hand.

Thady did not seem unduly alarmed to see her. His gaze was unfocused. 'Mrs Moncrieffe–' he laid a hand on her shoulder – 'though I say it meself–' he hiccuped. 'The catering is of the very *highest* standard. Me compliments to the chef–'

'You're supposed to be at the front door!' she muttered venomously. 'Thady, I told you before. I said—'

'Ah! Ye called me Thady!' he became maudlin, and his arm slid round her shoulders. 'Ye haven't forgotten old Thady – though reduced to a butler's humble station—' he gestured round to the empty room with his other arm. 'She knows her old Thady.'

'You're drunk! Again,' she hissed.

He waved his hand vaguely in the air. 'The merest drap – a modest elevation proper to the occasion.'

She shook herself free. 'Listen to me, O'Farrell, if you still want to be here tomorrow morning. Get out there and do your job!'

Thady adjusted his bow tie, and attempted to assume his

butler's manner. 'Very well me lady. I shall endeavour to give satisfaction.' He hiccuped again, and staggered towards the door.

She walked quickly past him. 'On second thoughts, get down to the kitchen, and don't let me see you again tonight. That's an order.'

A little later she retired to her room to straighten her hair. She took out her tiny scented handkerchief, dabbed at her nose, drew another breath and checked her appearance. Gazing at herself in the glass, adjusting her hair a little, dabbing on a little more perfume, she composed herself.

As she was coming down the stairs, just opposite the front door, there was another ring at the door. After a moment Taylor went to open it. Three men came in, more revellers, talking loudly among themselves and, as she reached the foot of the stairs, one of them turned. It was a friend of Morton's whom she knew, Colonel Meredith.

'Hester, my dear!' He was another red-faced, outdoor man. 'I brought a couple of pals – allow me to introduce—'

One of the two others had been shrugging off an opera cloak and now turned to face her. She recognised the man. It was Randolph Pelham.

Part Three

Chapter Thirty-six

She did not give herself time to think as she went forward and extended a hand. 'I'm so sorry gentlemen, my butler is elsewhere—'

Meredith introduced them as they crowded round her and Pelham smiled warmly as they shook hands.

'How do you do,' she gasped at last, her face frozen into a smile. She was waiting for him to say something, but after a formal greeting as if to a stranger, he turned to his friend, who was eager to be introduced. They shook hands and, recovering herself a little, she went on, 'You're just in time! Do come in – supper is being served.' Without thinking she led them into the dining room, crowded with people round the buffet table. 'I expect you have plenty of friends here,' she gestured, 'Lord Morton is somewhere, Lord Romsey's over there – I'll send the maid with something to drink.'

She was able to leave them helping themselves as she turned back into the drawing room, trembling still as she understood what had just happened: he had looked her full in the face and had not recognised her.

She stood a long time with one hand on the mantelpiece to steady herself, looking down into the fire, yet seeing nothing as the shock of it still of it still rang through her. At last, as her breath steadied, she turned again to the door, seeking him through the crowd.

She saw him now. He was as she remembered,

good-looking, slim in figure, with that slightly worn quality she remembered and had remarked when they first met, a man who had been in Africa, which had etched its marks on his face, matured him. She remembered him so clearly as she studied him, fascinated in spite of herself, fascinated in spite of everything. He was talking to a woman; he laughed, she laughed. He was leaning over her, looking close into her eyes. He touched her arm, and made a small intimate gesture, smiling as he talked. He was flirting with her, obviously; he couldn't help it. He was probably like that with every woman he met.

Suddenly self-conscious, she was turning away from the dining room, as Robbins came out with a tray. Her hair was disarranged, the cap in her hand as she hurriedly tried to straighten her dress. Seeing Abby she giggled, 'Sorry miss, only the gentlemen getting playful,' and hurried past.

'De Souza!' someone shouted at that moment, and a bread roll flew through the air. It missed its target. 'Goin' to Newmarket this year?'

'Of course. Morton's got a filly in the Two Thousand Guineas. What about you? Lookin' to buy?'

'We'll make a party of it, like last year?'

Near her there were shrieks and turning she saw a girl with a soda syphon in her hand directing a jet of spray across the table. Things were beginning to warm up.

'Nelly! I'll get you for that!' a man shouted, and snatching up an empty lobster shell hurled it at her. It missed her but caught Mr de Souza. Another girl had a soda syphon now and by chance as she sprayed it about her, it caught a man on the back of the neck. He spun round, astonished for a moment, then grinned, and with a devilish expression, boldly snatched it from her hands. 'You saucy—'

The girl shrieked, attempting to flee but the crowd was too thick about her, and in a second he had caught her by the waist, and kissed her. She was happy to respond. The men round him cheered.

The noise had become tremendous; people seemed bodily

transformed, whooping and yelping. For a long time Abby could not respond to the fun; like a ghost, her mind was still elsewhere as she checked that refreshments were circulating, that the fire was made up regularly. But some time later she heard his voice – she recognised it easily over the noise.

'I'll teach you a jig!'

Inevitably she felt herself dragged to the drawing room door where she saw Bessy – Mr de Souza's *chère amie* – at the piano striking into a tune Abby hadn't heard for years, and Pelham, who was obviously a natural for this sort of thing, a born party-goer, was arranging sets of four, and coaching them in the steps of an Irish jig. It didn't take long before men and women were whirling about, swinging each other wildly, until one of the men let go unexpectedly and a girl crashed into the arms of Lord Romsey and sent them both flying on to the sofa amid shrieks of laughter. Clearly Pelham was an asset at any festivities.

Then another blade, in officer's dress, suggested tobogganing down the stairs on tin trays, and in a moment, two of them were careering down, spilling over, rolling on top of each other, cravats undone, collars at all angles, food and drink stains on what had been spotless shirt fronts, shrieks and hoots of laughter. Bets were being called, men shouting across each other ... and in the drawing room a man was on top of a girl on the sofa, wildly kissing and caressing her ... The party was a decided success. Morton was getting his money's worth.

But all the time Abby couldn't help herself, drawn, fascinated, looking about for him, and saw Randolph Pelham again across the room, talking with another woman and, as Abby watched him, he glanced up and saw her. But instead of continuing his conversation he seemed struck by a thought, staring at her through the crowd. It was a nasty second before she could break his look; her heart beating, it took all her strength to drag her eyes away.

She did her best to keep out of his way but, some time later, in the early hours when things had quietened down, she found him at last beside her.

'Mrs Moncrieffe,' he spoke in the caressing and intimate manner which she remembered vividly. 'I've been staring and staring at you; I hope I didn't embarrass you – but you know, I've an idea we've met before.'

'Not to my knowledge, Mr Pelham.'

'Are you quite sure? There's something, I can't put my finger on it, something familiar about you . . .' he shook his head. 'I could be sworn—'

She smiled. 'I am afraid you must have me muddled up with another of your lady friends,' and added, 'you're not supposed to flirt with the hostess, you know.'

He laughed politely.

'You're not a Londoner, Mr Pelham?'

'No. Irish actually – just over for – well, a few months.'

'Ireland? Ah, I'm afraid I was never there. It's very beautiful, so they say.'

'Beautiful?' He nodded. 'I suppose it is. Never thought about it.'

'And what has brought you to London?'

'Oh, business – and personal,' he said in an offhand way, looking about him at the other guests.

She wondered what this business – and personal – might be. However the longer she talked to him the more likely he was to remember who she was, and as soon as she decently could, she made a polite comment, and moved away. As she turned her back on him, she had an idea his eyes were following her.

Later she found Morton, and after a few words was able to introduce the subject of Pelham. 'Who is that man – is he a friend of yours?' She pointed with her fan.

'Pelham, isn't it? Friend of Meredith's.'

'Does he lived in London?'

'Not so far as I know. Why?'

'I want to get to know your friends, that's all.'

'Well, don't get to know them too well, will you?'

She turned sharply at this. 'Why not?'

'What do you mean, why not? You know damn well.'

'You forget yourself. I told you the first time we met, I didn't belong to you.'

'You've cost me enough.'

She gave him an impudent smile. 'I hope you got your money's worth?' she said softly but provocatively, looking into his eyes.

'Oh yes,' he murmured, drawn in spite of himself into her concentrated gaze, 'I get my money's worth.' And then, as if making an effort to hold his distance, he glanced away to where Pelham was talking to a woman. 'Anyway why are you so interested in Pelham?'

'What made you think I had designs on him?'

'Have you?'

'Ah!' she laughed, 'Wouldn't you like to know?'

'I hope for his sake, you haven't.'

'What on earth do you mean?'

'I leave you to guess.' He turned away. He was angry.

Later, the guests were making their adieus, drunken, sleepy, girls on their arms, carriages and cabs were being summoned, and she was shivering in the cold night air from the open door, tired.

'Mrs Moncrieffe.' It was Pelham again, in his cloak and silk hat, 'I wonder if I might have a word?'

She turned to him. Morton was away talking to someone else. 'Mr Pelham?'

'Don't think me impertinent, but—' his head was bent forward close to hers, 'I wonder if we might meet sometime? Would you care to have dinner with me?' He looked quite as assured as he had the first time she ever met him. A look, a manner, which was confident she would say yes.

She appeared to be taken by surprise. 'Mr Pelham, how very kind—' she glanced helplessly about her at the crowd of departing guests – 'though I am afraid now is not a very good time—'

'Do say yes. I should very much like to talk. There are

365

things—' He spoke caressingly under his breath, looking away as he spoke.

'Heavens!' She seemed flustered, unable to think. 'Mr Pelham—' and then appearing to collect her thoughts. 'Not today – let's see it's Sunday, isn't it, already? So – Monday. No, Monday won't do—' she was hurriedly making it up – 'Tuesday? No. Wednesday? Shall we say Thursday in the park at three? I ride almost every afternoon.'

He repeated her words in an undertone, again glancing away, and took his leave. The guests had gone, and she dismissed the servants. 'You can clear up in the morning. Tell O'Farrell he can go to bed now – if he's still awake.'

Morton had returned to the dining room, and she caught a glimpse of him through the door, tossing back a glass of brandy. He would be after her in a moment. The man was made of iron.

Her maid was following her up stairs, but Abby turned. The woman was clearly dropping on her feet. 'It's all right, Taylor. You go to bed. I can undress myself. Thank you for everything.'

'Thank you, madam.' Taylor turned gratefully away.

Abby was exhausted herself as she undid drawstrings, hooks and eyes, dragging things off her, drew back the covers and slumped into bed. Soon afterwards Morton came in, throwing his clothes about the room, and a moment later he was getting in heavily beside her and taking her in a passionate embrace.

'Not tonight, in the morning—' she murmured.

'It is the morning. What's the matter, tired? It's not like you.'

She turned over to face him. He looked at her for a moment with a satisfied smile and kissed her hard. She disentangled herself and murmured, slipped out of bed, and into her dressing room, to equip herself for his attack.

Tired she might be, and her mind full of thoughts about Pelham, but Morton was not to be denied, and made love to her roughly, selfishly, fully. The first time, it had suited her

366

need; tonight it jarred on every nerve. But the truth had confronted her long ago: Morton had paid. And so long as he was paying she must give him what he had paid for. He had paid a lot, too. She had long since realised that this was not a game. At their first meeting in Hyde Park, she had triumphed over his lordship's vanity and egotism, visibly triumphed, as she thought. But of course, she had done nothing of the sort. This was not a sport or hobby; it was a profession. She had hired herself out; Morton must be satisfied.

Later, alone in the dark, she was helpless to prevent the dark hurt, that wound in her mind, from flooding back into her consciousness. The man whom she had watched this evening, that amusing, light-hearted man, full of fun – that shameless flirt – had looked at her and had no idea who she was. She was powerless to stop the scenes running through her mind again: the afternoon in The Goat when she had taken that terrible leap into the unknown, when she had opened herself to him in defiance of everything she had been taught, everything she knew from her family, from her friends, from every family in the village, from Father McMichael himself. She had broken this greatest rule of her life because Randolph had promised to help her family. And afterwards? Brushed aside as if she were nothing. And worst of all – even now she could scarcely allow herself to think of it – the day of her riding accident – to remember the day her baby had died.

And Rory too. She wondered: could Pelham understand what it meant to have your brother waste his youth, his energy, his promise, all the fairest days of his life, the days of love and pleasure and laughter, to lose all that, to sit in a foul and noisome prison, day after day staring at the sky through a tiny barred window? And to come out at the last a tired, hurt, bruised, wasted man in his middle years?

Randolph Pelham had been face to face tonight with the one woman in the world who had more cause to hate him than anyone alive.

367

Chapter Thirty-seven

> Wonersh Lodge, Eltham, Saturday 8 April
>
> Dear Hester,
> It is an age since we spoke. I would not be surprised if
> you had completely forgotten me. But I have often
> thought of you and wondered how your son is. Will you
> come and see me? I have great need of a friend just now,
>
> Katherine O'Shea

This note drove all other thoughts out of her mind. She
wandered through the house as the servants cleared up after
the party. The stink of cigar smoke was rank in her nostrils.
Morton had gone. She had been thinking of Pelham, still
uncertain what to do about their hasty assignation. She was
unwilling to meet him again until she had a clear idea of
how to proceed in the business.

'Where's O'Farrell?'

'Mr O'Farrell hasn't left his room yet, Mrs Moncrieffe.'

'Hasn't left his room? What does he think this is – a
hotel? Tell him the mistress wants him downstairs in five
minutes.'

'Yes, ma'am.'

She was still wandering about the rooms overseeing the
clearing up when the tousled unshaven figure of Thady
slouched into the dining room, hastily buttoning his shirt, the
collar hanging from its stud, his tie hanging over his arm.

368

'I hope it's not getting too much for you, O'Farrell? But this is not a rest home. I expect you on duty when I tell you.'

'I'm awful sorry, Mrs Moncrieffe, 'twas me alarum clock never went off.'

'Alarm clock? Didn't Taylor bring you your hot water at ten? I gave you an extra lie-in as it was.'

''Twill never happen again, don't you worry, Mrs Moncrieffe.'

'I'm not worrying. I'm not the one who has to worry, O'Farrell.' She folded her letter, slipped it into an envelope and licked it down. 'See that this is posted immediately.'

'I will, Mrs Moncrieffe. Leave it to Thady!' He snatched up the letter, and two minutes later she heard him calling. 'Taylor, get this to the post box this instant!'

The following afternoon she was in the train to Eltham, just outside London, and half an hour by train. At the station she took a cab to Wonersh Lodge, which she found stood in fine and spacious grounds. She had not really grasped until this time that Katherine was wealthy.

'I'm not, my dear,' Katherine said as they kissed cheeks. 'The grounds belong to Eltham Lodge – over there – which is the residence of my aunt.'

'Aunt Ben?' Abby was removing her gloves as they passed into the house, which was a pleasant villa of the previous century.

Katherine turned and raised an eyebrow. 'Willie has told you all, I see.'

'He did tell me a great deal. How are things between you?'

'Not easy. You'll see why in a moment. Come with me straightaway.' She took Abby by the hand and led her up a broad staircase, with a dull red carpet. Above and around them rose sombre oak wainscoting; portraits dark with age hung above. At the top, Katherine stopped, held her finger to her lips, and opened a door carefully. As she went into a

369

large light bedroom, a maidservant rose from a chair near a window where she had been reading, curtsied and came towards them.

'She's asleep.'

Katherine, still holding Abby's hand, led her across to a cradle beside a high canopied bed. 'Do look.'

Abby bent to examine the sleeping baby.

'Sophie. It's the name of Charles's sister.' She made a small grimace of excuse. 'She has been registered in Willie's name, of course, but Charles and I wanted her to have something of him about her – and that was the nearest we could manage.'

Abby was unable to speak for a moment, taking in the scrap of humanity bundled beneath the covers. Sophie was a slender child, with finely moulded features. Abby studied the thick eyelashes on her cheek, a cheek almost translucent in its perfect smoothness, the little rosebud mouth, a tiny hand thrown back on the pillow beside her head ... 'She's beautiful,' she murmured at last.

'We won't disturb her,' Katherine merely allowed herself to rearrange the coverlet slightly. 'Sophie hasn't been in the best of health, and I want her to sleep all she can. The doctor came yesterday.'

'The doctor?'

'She is delicate, and seems to have a slight trouble breathing.' Katherine was still fussing over the covers, and would not look at Abby as she said these things.

'*Trouble breathing*? My dear, you must be worried to death!'

Katherine straightened herself, though still looking down into the cradle. 'It has been a trying time. I hope you didn't mind my little cry for help? Things have been rather getting on top of me,' she said quietly.

Abby took her hand. 'I hope you'll tell me everything,' she said gently.

'Come downstairs, and let me give you tea,' Katherine braced herself. The maid curtsied again as the two women left the room, descended the gloomy staircase and entered a broad drawing room, with windows at both ends, though heavily shrouded with swagged curtains. On this chilly afternoon in April, a fire burned beneath an old carved wood mantel, with a tall mirror over it. As they approached the fire, Katherine unconsciously glanced at herself in the glass and put a hand to her hair. She looked pale and worried, a contrast to the woman Abby had first met.

'Charles is in prison, as you know,' she said abruptly.

'Prison! I didn't know.'

'But surely – it has been in all the papers.'

Abby sighed. 'I never look at the papers. Why is he in prison?'

'Gladstone couldn't handle him – all the agitation in Ireland, the land war as it's called. Charles was accused of inciting the farmers to refuse their rents. So last October Mr Gladstone had him thrown into Kilmainham Gaol. In Dublin. There are quite a few of them there, Dillon, O'Kelly, O'Brien, others. Fortunately, despite what one reads in the press, they are being treated quite well. Charles has his meals brought in from a restaurant – almost anything he wants – and is comparatively comfortable. But he is delicate and never in the best of health – Sophie takes after him – and the thought of him in prison—' she uttered a short nervous laugh – 'if you could see the parcels I have sent him, the socks I have knitted, his cardigans, his thick underwear—'

'So he wasn't here for the birth of Sophie?'

Katherine shook her head. 'He has never seen his daughter.'

'He must be feeling the strain terribly.' There was a silence as they both thought of the Chief in prison. Finally as they sat in two old brocade armchairs opposite one another, Abby asked tentatively, 'What did Willie say when Sophie was born?'

Katherine was crouching forward, her hands clasped. Without looking up she said hesitantly, 'He believes Sophie to be his daughter.'

There was a pause as Abby tried to take this in. Still not looking her in the face, Katherine went on, 'So of course he had Sophie baptised a Catholic.'

'What did you say?'

Katherine shrugged. 'It didn't seem much to ask. Charles could never have attended a christening in any case. Charles is Protestant of course.'

'And – you?' Abby was still struggling to take in what Katherine has just revealed.

'I'm nothing really. It's of no great interest to me. I did take instruction from a priest when I married Willie but I couldn't warm to it, and gradually dropped away.'

'Are you – seeing Willie at the moment?'

'Oh yes. He comes down to see the children. Though the boys are away at school just now.'

There was another silence as they both stared into the fire. At last Abby said tentatively, 'My dear, you have got troubles.'

Katherine nodded. 'It was kind of you to come.'

'I am very glad I did. You see, I—' she hesitated, 'I thought I had troubles enough of my own, and it is a relief to me to know I am not alone.'

Katherine looked up at her. 'I'm sorry – I never asked after your son. I have been so engrossed in my own problems. How is he?'

'I don't know,' Abby said simply.

'What do you mean?'

Abby paused, unable for a moment to phrase her thought correctly. 'He has gone away from me,' she said at last.

'Gone away?'

'I didn't want to say, taken away – because that would suggest that I was unwilling.'

'I don't understand.'

'It's very difficult to explain.'

The maid entered at this moment with the tea tray and, while it was being set on the little table between them, and Katherine was fussing with the teapot, she was able to run her mind over events which she had little thought of over the last eighteen months – little thought of consciously by day, that is, always seeking to put them behind her. By night of course it had been another matter.

'I can't remember what I told you.'

'You told me how much Nick had wanted a son, and had no hope of one, unless you—'

At last Abby began, uncertainly. 'Nick took William ten days after he was born. Back to London – he has a house in Mount Street, Mayfair, and I returned to London too. I used to wait in the park every morning when the nurse brought William out for a walk. I could be with him for half an hour and sometimes in the afternoon too. I thought we could go on like that, you know. It wasn't much but it was something. But then, only two months later, Nick told me that the doctors had advised taking his wife to Madeira for her health, and there was nothing he could do. He had to go if her life was to be saved. They said she could not survive another winter in London.'

She stopped. Katherine read the expression in Abby's face and reached for her hand as Abby sought for words to continue. 'Nick was very kind. I have my house, I want for nothing, a carriage—' she stopped again, staring into Katherine's face.

'My dear girl,' Katherine murmured, 'will you never see William again?'

Abby shook her head. 'I was so glad you wrote to me. I thought I had been abandoned, you know, completely, and now – now I know I have a friend.'

'Yes. And Hester, what will you do?'

Abby raised her eyebrows, thinking again. What would she do?

'I mean – do you think anyone will ever take Nick's place?'

'No one will take his place.'

'Perhaps eventually?' Katherine said softly at last.

Abby shrugged. 'Perhaps,' she said in an offhand tone.

373

As she was leaving, she asked, 'Have you any idea how much longer Mr Parnell will be kept in prison?'

'Not too long, I hope. There are negotiations going on behind the scenes.'

'Willie?'

'Yes, the trusted emissary. A pawn between two kings,' she added on a slightly sarcastic note.

'You said there were a number of other Irish MPs in Kilmainham with Mr Parnell.' She hesitated and tried to sound as offhand as she could, 'I believe – do you know if Mr O'Toole is there?'

'He is not.' Katherine turned to her as they stood together in the doorway. 'Why?'

'Oh, a personal matter.'

Katherine raised her eyebrows. 'A personal matter? Am I to be allowed to know?'

'Mr O'Toole has been very kind to my family. I should like to find a way of repaying him.'

Katherine kissed her on the cheek. 'I shan't pry any further – yet. Though, I give warning, I have a rapacious curiosity. I shall worm it out of you some time or other.'

Abby shook her head, looking solemn. 'Not this, Katherine. It goes back too far. Goodbye. Let us meet soon.'

In the train she thought over what they had said, and at the way Mr O'Toole's name had come unexpectedly into her mind. Perhaps this might give her an excuse to invite him to the house. It was a long time since he had called. A long time since she had woken up in bed with Lucas Morton, a scoundrel, if the truth were told, not fit to clean Mr O'Toole's boots. But she felt she had to cling on to Mr O'Toole, for Rory's sake and, in a strange way, for her own. Could she invite him to dinner? Would that seem too forward? What did he think of her? It was impossible to tell; he was always immaculately polite, always considerate, always concerned. The real man behind this shining exterior – him she had not yet found.

That evening, she took a sheet of her embossed, headed notepaper, and began to write,

Dear Mr O'Toole,
It is a long time since we spoke. But I often think of you with gratitude for your efforts on behalf of my brother.
I wonder whether you would care to dine with me? Next Thursday or Saturday would be convenient – or if neither of these suits, perhaps you would name another day?
Yours very sincerely,
Hester Moncrieffe

Yet how could she invite a single man to her house? Not any single man – not a Lord Morton – but a gentleman, a man of delicate scruples who might feel compromised. It was difficult. She stood up, stretched her back, screwed the note up and threw it away. Mr O'Toole was not for the likes of her.

Chapter Thirty-eight

Her instinct was against it. She wandered round the garden in a thick skirt and heavy overcoat as the thought cleared in her mind. Something in her hesitated. She was not afraid he would recognise her; she was certain now he wouldn't. And even if he half guessed, she was sure she could carry it off.

No, that was not the problem. It was a question of tactics. To go might seem too forward; but, if she failed the appointment, it might seem as if she didn't care at all. Which? She wanted to draw him on, but also to hold him off; to keep the reins in her own hands at all times. Mr Pelham must be drawn in so delicately that he was unaware of what she was doing.

At first, in a reaction after the shock of seeing him, she had had scruples. And by day, there did seem something sordid, something underhand, about revenge; in a way, it was beneath her dignity. Why drag it all up again? Why not just put it all behind her? Even if she did achieve some sort of triumph over him it wouldn't shorten Rory's sentence by a day. So why not just forget him?

But by night she remembered. Forget him? Just let him walk away as if nothing had really happened at all? As if it were perfectly all right to seduce an ignorant girl who was totally dependent on him to save her family? And it occurred to her too that there must be others. Was she to let him go free – to ruin other girls? Didn't she at least owe it them to stop him?

As these thoughts had clarified in her mind, she felt herself stiffening. Oh no Mr Pelham, you're not getting away; you're going to pay – even if not for my sake, then for Rory's. And if not his, then for all the other girls he might entrap.

She crossed to the kitchen window. 'Taylor! Please tell Blake I shall not be needing the carriage this afternoon after all.'

She heard a distant chime from inside the house. Three o'clock. Good. And for some time she thought of him in the park riding up and down looking out for her, in vain.

A note arrived the following morning:

> Army & Navy Club, Pall Mall
>
> Dear Mrs Moncrieffe,
> You have left me bereft. I looked for you, but you were not there. Have I been abandoned? Or was there some mistake? I do hope no accident prevented you. Please reassure me that all is well, and that we may be able to arrange another, more secure appointment soon.
>
> I remain, in trepidation, torn between hope and fear. You won't fail me?
>
> R Pelham

She drew a certain bleak satisfaction as she perceived the hint of desperation imperfectly disguised. She had achieved one other thing also – she now knew his address in town. She composed a letter in reply.

> Dear Mr Pelham,
> Thank you for your note which arrived this morning. I am so sorry we were not able to meet. It was as you correctly surmised a previous engagement, which in the hurry of our last conversation I had overlooked. But as I had not your address I was unable to warn you. I am

377

distraught and can only hope you were not too greatly inconvenienced. Please don't lose all faith in me; I should like us so much to be friends.

I shall be at the opera on Friday next; my box is on the Pit Tier. Shall you be there? Perhaps you might call on me then and we could have a little chat. I must make you some amends, mustn't I? We must talk over how best to do that.

Yours very sincerely,

H Moncrieffe

This seemed to hit the right note.

The box at the opera dated from Nick's time. It had been a part of his programme of education for her, and she had enjoyed going with him. More for his company at first – because in those early days merely to be with Nick was enough for her – and if it pleased him, then it pleased her too. But by degrees he began to educate her, and the more she listened and watched the more she learned – she was always a quick learner, so that she was now a tolerable authority in the opera house, and could comment on the singers without making a fool of herself.

Still, tonight that was scarcely the point of the exercise. She surveyed herself in the glass. What an expert she had become in her dress and deportment. This gown – white satin, glowing against her fine skin, beautifully fitted round her bust, boned to the waist, and with a bustle. She made a superb silhouette, as Nick used to say, as she turned and surveyed herself in the glass. That name stopped her. Nick – where was he now? And her thoughts were miles away as Taylor worked round her, helping to adjust the fall of the gown over the bustle at the back.

'Ma'am, if you wouldn't mind—'

She came back to the present, drew a little sigh, and sat at her dressing table.

Taylor threaded the tiny flowers into her hair as she

378

herself fitted her diamond ear pendants, and dabbed a little powder over her bosom. No point in thinking of that, no point of thinking of her son, no point in thinking of what might have been.

There had been one more letter to write:

Dear Katherine,
I am planning a night at the opera – on Friday next. I wonder – would you be my guest – and stay the night? Perhaps it would give you a pleasant break from your cares? Come a little early so we can have dinner here before setting out.
I was so glad of the chance to renew our acquaintance.
Very sincerely yours,
Hester Moncrieffe

Over dinner they discussed her daughter. Sophie had not been at all well; and Katherine's health was suffering under the pressure of broken nights and worry.

'There was one good thing. Charles was able to come briefly to see her. He was given parole to attend his nephew's funeral in Paris, and called at Eltham for a few hours. Sometimes, Hester, I look at Sophie and wonder whether she is going to – survive. It is such a horrible prospect – normally I don't allow myself even to contemplate it, but over the last few days I have been disciplining myself to accept that she may—'

The words hung in the air unfinished. What could either of them say? But gradually, over dinner, Abby had been able to cheer her a little – even by the simple expedient of listening sympathetically – and by the time they set off for the opera, Katherine had been able to compose herself and was trying to forget her woes for a few hours.

So the two women wrapped themselves snugly in warm coats and bundled themselves into the carriage, which rattled through the suburb. In the darkness Abby could not see Katherine's face. And after a little while, Katherine said, 'It was what I needed – I have been too much indoors. Your letter came at the best moment, my dear.'

Arriving in Bow Street was always a headache; it was crowded with carriages and cabs, and there was a line of them at the covered entrance to the opera house. Eventually the carriage reached the opera house steps; the door was opened by a footman, they were assisted down and went through into the foyer. Their coats were taken, and they took the opportunity to vanish into the ladies' room for a moment to adjust and arrange their gowns.

Katherine now took in the full extent of Abby's preparations. 'My dear,' she said, 'you look quite superb tonight. What a pity you've only got me to keep you company. In all that finery you need someone – well, I am sure you must know many men who would have been better company than me.'

'You are quite wrong,' Abby said quietly, taking her arm. 'Now let us go and find our box.'

The box was taken by the season, and Abby showed her ivory ticket. She also had a sixpence ready in her gloved hand as the footman unlocked the door of the box, and they found themselves inside. Katherine advanced to the front and looked out at the auditorium, filled with people finding their seats, and their eager chatter. The orchestra tuning up, the dark red curtains, the gilding, the ornate painted ceiling, the great chandelier ...

'It is an age since I was at the opera! And you have made yourself very comfortable! My dear we could be royalty!'

'Nick got it for me,' Abby said quietly, taking a seat, her elbow on the balustrade. She did not look about her; not once did she glance round to see who else might be there, but concentrated her attention on Katherine. In the light again, she could see more clearly the effect her daughter's illness had had on her. Abby remembered the summer when they had strolled arm in arm along the sea front at Brighton, how plump, how vivacious her friend had been then, witty and charming. Now, though she made frequent attempts to sparkle, it was obvious what a strain she was under. Abby placed her hand over Katherine's. 'Perhaps for one evening you will be able to forget your troubles?'

As for herself, she was not able to concentrate very much on the singing. She found herself continually running through her mind all the possibilities; what he might say, what she might reply. How friendly she should be, or how cool; she had to adjust the amount of line to a very fine degree – not too friendly, and not too distant. Just enough to hook him.

It was only a few minutes after the lights had come up for the interval that, as she had expected, there was a knock at the door; she called, 'Come in', and Pelham presented himself. He was in evening dress.

'Mrs Moncrieffe, good evening.'

'Mr Pelham, I am so glad we meet again.' She raised her hand to him. 'You cannot imagine how I felt when I realised I was unable to keep our appointment! And not being able to reach you in time to let you know – can you ever forgive me?' She gave him her dazzling smile, and a look of sweet complicity, as if he were the only man she knew in the world, and she had waited all her life only that they should meet. He held her hand a moment, unwilling to let it go, turned and at last noticed Katherine, as Abby introduced them. He pulled up a chair. The three of them were at the front of the box, and all around, in the great bowl of the auditorium, people were chattering, there was movement, vivacity and talk. Katherine was about to rise, but Abby begged her by a tiny motion of her head to remain in her seat. Pelham was visibly constrained by Katherine's presence, making an effort to include her in the conversation and, as he turned to say something to her, Abby was able to study him in comfort for a moment. It was really a most bizarre affair, she thought again. He had completely forgotten her, it was that simple. Only the arrogance of a man could do that. Oh yes, she would play very hard to get.

'Katherine, would you like Mr Pelham to fetch you an ice-cream?'

She turned on him her dazzling smile again, and he leapt up as if he had received an electrical shock. 'My pleasure!'

'Who is he?' Katherine asked as he went out.

'Oh,' she looked idly about her at the auditorium, half filled at this moment. 'I scarcely know him. A friend of a friend.'

'I think he's very interested in you. I am feeling decidedly *de trop*, I assure you.'

'Don't go, whatever you do.'

Katherine gave her a hard look. 'What is this?'

Abby didn't answer this, but went on after a moment, casually, 'What do you think of him?'

'How can one tell? He seems very charming. A woman could do worse, I dare say. Has he any money?'

'I've no idea.'

'You'd better find out. You might be wasting your time, otherwise.'

'I'm not wasting my time, I promise you.' Abby gave her a level look.

'Hester? There is more to this than meets the eye. Is something going on?'

'I'm not quite sure. Yet.'

'I really don't understand you.'

'It's too complicated to explain—'

Pelham returned at that moment with a tray which he set on the table in the back of the box, and handed the ice-cream dishes to the two ladies.

'Are you in town long, Mr Pelham?' Abby asked.

'A few months, for the season.'

Later, as the bells were ringing, and people were returning to their seats, Pelham rose. Though his self-command was total, she had detected signs of strain. He glanced at Katherine before leaning over Abby and murmuring with a smile, 'Mrs Moncrieffe, you promised—'

'Our ride?' She looked up brightly. 'I hadn't forgotten! Why don't you drop me a note? Then we can fix a time. I should enjoy it very much. You cannot imagine how much I enjoy riding! Do write.'

Pelham was looking uncomfortable as he murmured a reply. At that moment Abby let fall quite by accident the little bouquet she had been trifling with. Pelham knelt instantly to retrieve it for her, and in front of both the women, pulled a flower from it. 'If you will permit me?' he put it to his nose for a moment, and went quickly out.

The two women looked at each other.

Abby could not prevail on Katherine to stay the night. In the carriage as they at last got free of Bow Street and were in the Strand, Katherine told her, 'I must get back.'

'My dear, you cannot possibly travel down by train at this late hour! Do come home with me.'

'I couldn't. If anything were to happen – but thank you for a delightful evening. And I shall expect to hear all about Mr Pelham.'

They parted at Charing Cross Station, and Abby bade her a very unwilling farewell.

As she sat alone in her carriage on the way home, rolling through the dark suburban streets, she thought over the scene in the opera house. There had been a note almost of desperation in Pelham's voice as he asked her for a meeting. On the whole she was very contented. But she still didn't know much about his present situation. She would have to step up the pressure a little, or endeavour to track down some friends of his. Perhaps Morton? Except that Morton was jealous. She didn't want to discuss Pelham with Morton – or did she? Perhaps it might not be a bad idea at all?

Nevertheless after she had thought this out, she was left with a rather unpleasant taste. There was something degrading about revenge, after all – something profitless, and she was left depressed – especially when she thought about Katherine and her troubles. Katherine who was prepared to return home in a draughty cold train at midnight so anxious

383

was she about her daughter's health. Compared to that, what did Abby's vendetta against Pelham amount to?

The carriage drew up before No 16 Acacia Road, and, feeling weary, she waited as the door was unlocked. The servants had of course heard the sound of wheels in the quiet street; there was seldom any need to knock at her own door.

It was a few minutes after Taylor had let her in, and was helping her off with her coat, that there was a knock at the door. They looked at one another. It was late for visitors, and she was certainly not expecting anyone. Abby waited uncertainly in the middle of the hall as the woman went to answer the door.

Randolph Pelham walked quickly in, pushing past the maid, and was looking at Abby before she could speak. 'I have to speak to you.'

Chapter Thirty-nine

'Is this your usual style of visiting – to force your way into an unprotected woman's house after midnight? It must make you very popular.' She remained cool, outwardly at least.

He glanced round at the servant. And then back into Abby's face. 'I beg you to spare me a few minutes.'

She turned away and said carelessly over her shoulder, 'It seems I can hardly refuse. Taylor, see that we are not disturbed. Don't go to bed. I shan't be long.' She paused in her drawing room door, and turned with a small impudent smile. 'Well, come along then,' and went in. He followed her, closing the door behind him.

She crossed to the fireplace, knelt and pushed the poker into the remains of the fire, which had sunk low and threw out a ruddy glow. A pair of candles burned on the mantel, otherwise the room was unlit. She sat back on the rug, gazing into the fire. She said nothing.

'I'm sorry to burst in on you like this,' he began more calmly. 'No doubt it's very rude. But it seemed you were deliberately putting me off; I was afraid I would never get the chance of talking to you alone.' She was still looking into the glowing embers of the fire. He had hesitated. She imagined he must be close behind her, but she would not look round.

He sounded calmer now, more in control of his words.

'Ever since we met, I have been obsessed with the idea that we have met before.'

'I told you we haven't.' She still didn't look up.

'I know. And yet, I can't help it, I have been racking and racking my brains, trying to remember where it might have been, or if it wasn't you, as you say it wasn't, who it could have been.'

'Yes,' she said carefully, 'no doubt you have confused me with someone else.'

An armchair stood close to where she sat, and he now sat himself on the edge of it, leaning over her. 'I haven't been able to forget you. I have thought of no one and nothing since I saw you. That first time – here in this room – when I saw you, you looked so lovely, and it was, I don't know how to put it very easily ... it was like a shock of recognition ... it was that I knew you ... I tell you I couldn't understand it myself – I knew you and yet I didn't know how I knew you. And then when you didn't turn up in the park, you can't imagine the effect it had – I felt I had been shut out of paradise.' He paused. 'I can't imagine what you must have made of my letter. I was desperate; and tonight, with your friend there I felt you were playing with me, taunting me. I couldn't stand it. I just had to be near you, be with you together, even for a moment.'

She had no answer to this. At last very slowly she looked up into his face. He was leaning forward, bending over, close to her. Without speaking he leaned forward and kissed her. She received it stoically, unresistingly, unresponsively.

'You are very forward,' she murmured.

He was staring into her eyes. 'You are the most beautiful woman I ever saw.'

She leaned away from him, still saying nothing, then rose to her feet and crossed to the door. She opened it, and called, 'Taylor, Mr Pelham will be leaving now.'

He rose and crossed quickly towards her. 'I have offended you.'

'Oh no. You have not offended me. Only – I am rather tired just now. I am sure you understand?'

He was clinging on to his self-control, seemed confused, and quite unlike his normal self. 'I don't know what you must think. Frankly, I don't know what to think myself. I'm sorry.'

She shook her head very slightly. 'Really, there is nothing to forgive.'

The servant had reappeared in the hall.

'Is there a chance—' he muttered, scarcely able to look into her eyes, and embarrassed by Taylor's presence. 'Might we – could we meet again?'

'Of course,' she said lightly. 'It would be a pleasure – and in the meantime you must go on trying to remember who it is I remind you of.'

He tried to laugh, a short nervous laugh. And then blurted out, 'When?'

'Ah.' She appeared to think. 'I must consult my engagement book. This week will be difficult.' She became brisk. 'Let me look in my book, and I will send you a note in the morning. You are staying at your club?'

'Yes. You will write – tomorrow? Without fail?'

'Without fail.' She held out her hand. 'Good night Mr Pelham.'

'And you forgive me – for bursting in on you like this?'

She studied him calmly. 'You are forgiven,' she said at last. He was still holding her hand and on an impulse brought it to his lips.

'God bless you!' he blurted out, and the next moment was gone.

Who would ever have believed it? Randolph Pelham infatuated with her – and on such a short acquaintance? It was more than she could possibly have imagined. Fortunately she was strong enough to handle him. But how they should work it out – she would leave that to Rory to decide.

*

On her journey down to Portland a few days after this, she was still thinking over Pelham's late-night visit. She still had not quite fathomed what her own feelings were about it, and in a way, she didn't want to know. It seemed at first as if heaven had played into their hands, had handed Pelham to them in an extraordinarily vulnerable condition. She could do anything she liked with him, it seemed. Whatever she and Rory might decide between them – and ultimately Rory must decide for them both – Pelham was helpless. All the years since those events in Ireland, all the years Rory had rotted in Portland Prison they had always had this thought between them: Randolph Pelham – and how one day he would be punished. And now the day had come; all that was required was to decide how it should be.

Rory seemed changed yet again when she saw him. Older, more mature, stronger. But also – and it was something she was attempting to work out during the early part of their conversation – more settled, as if, God help him, he had grown used to prison. It occurred to her that he must scarce remember what it was like to have been free; those days were receding ever further into his past, overlaid by the life he had lived since he had come to this place. Prison had become his life.

'I've done so much work on the garden Rory,' she was saying. 'Once you're free again you'll be able to see it. You'll be able to come and stay with me as long as you like.'

He was subdued. 'Better not to talk of freedom, Abby. 'Tis still too far off.'

'I told you in my letter about Mr O'Toole. He wrote to the Home Secretary about you.' She paused. 'It was a pity about the ticket of leave.'

'I never expected any different.'

There was silence for a moment as they thought of the years still ahead.

'I had a letter from Aunt Eileen,' she started again. 'She's well, and says Fan is doing very well at school, too – quite the little lady, she says.'

388

'You're quite the lady yourself, Abby.'

'Oh!' she chuckled, 'I'm still only the same old Abby, Rory. I'll never change – not for you – whatever the world might think.' She reached her fingers between the bars, and he reached his to touch hers. After a moment she went on, more subdued. 'Rory there's something important has happened – which I've come to tell ye.' She paused.

'What?'

''Tis about Randolph Pelham.' She sensed his alertness, his concentration. 'I've seen him,' she went on, 'in London. 'Tis most strange Rory – and ye'll never believe it – or maybe ye will, I don't know – 'twas at this party, I went to—' she stumbled here – 'I saw him but he didn't recognise me.'

She paused as this piece of news sank in Rory said, 'Never recognised ye? What, well, I suppose, well, now that ye've become the fine lady, Abby—'

'That's it! And can speak in an English accent but isn't it the strangest thing ye ever heard of? He was right there as close as ye are to me, talking to me, and never knowing who I was. And Rory – he wanted to see me again. He followed me home one night, came bursting in and said he had to talk to me. It was as if he was in love with me.'

Rory was staring into her eyes. 'And ye're sure he never knew ye?'

'He said I reminded him of someone – only he couldn't think who.'

'All his tricks no doubt. What did ye say to him?'

'I let him know I liked him, just to keep him on the line, like, while I came to talk to you. Until we decide what to do.'

'What to do?' Rory murmured. 'Yes. What to do. What to do with Mr Randolph Pelham. Thanks be, there is justice after all,' he whispered to himself, covering his face with his hands. 'Who would have thought it?' He looked up. 'God! If I wasn't in this place! To think that Randolph Pelham is walking about a free man while I sit in here! To

389

think he is free to insult me own sister – again! Oh God!' he brought his fist down into his palm, as the thought came to him.

'It's all right, Rory,' she hastened to reassure him. 'Ye've no need to worry on my account. I'm well able to keep him in his place. He won't dare talk to a lady like me the way he talked to Abby O'Leary.' She laughed, though still carefully watching her brother. He seemed to be thinking furiously.

'It'll drive me mad. In a way I wish ye hadn't told me. Pelham – out there! Pelham – intrudin' into your very house, insultin' ye with his lies! Jesus!'

'Rory! Stop! I'm outside! I can be your arm – you don't have to wait till you get out: I can act for you.'

'I wouldn't ask it of ye. It's not woman's work. Would I ask ye to risk yourself, maybe risk the gallows—'

'The gallows?'

He fixed her. 'D'ye think I could let him escape that time, do you think I could waste all these years in here, and be satisfied with anything less than his life? It'd be a mockery. Look at me! I'm twenty-four now. I'll be thirty-four when I get out! Thirty-four. I can't even imagine it! Me life, Abby, gone! What'll I do at thirty-four? Who will I know? Where can I go, that have no home? And you – how would ye ever welcome me into your home, me that was lagged fifteen years, broken in this place – I wouldn't ask it of ye. I'd rather be an outcast, rather go to Australia than be beholden to your charity. And to think that all this while, Randolph Pelham should be a free man, should enjoy himself making up to me own sister, that was responsible for her downfall in the first place. I can't stand it, I tell ye! It'll drive me mad.'

She watched in appalled fascination, in horror. Rory could scarce contain himself, a hand across his face, writhing. 'Rory darling,' she implored through her tears, 'please, darlin', don't, don't! Ye'll always have me, I'll always be here, and we'll always be together, even though you're in here, and I'm outside. I'll always come to see ye, ye know that, and I'll never change. And when ye do come out, why – we'll be together again, just like before – and if ye want to emigrate, we can emigrate together, can't we and start a new life, where no one will ever know ye was in this place. I beg ye, Rory—' she could scarce control her tears, – 'I beg ye not to be unhappy, I can't stand to think of ye unhappy.'

There was a long silence. Rory was looking down at the rough stone sill before him, as she studied him, drinking him in, trying to remember every hair of his head, everything about him. He drew a shattering sigh. 'It's bad enough I'm to be shut away in this place but I can't bear it should make ye unhappy too.' He drew another long sigh, and spoke quietly, as though exhausted. 'What will be, will be. Just promise me ye will have nothing to do with Pelham, that's all. I can't bear that he should even talk to ye. Leave him to his conscience.'

She shook her head. She too had sobered up. She wiped her eyes. 'I'm not leaving' him to his conscience. He has no conscience. I'll find a way. I don't know yet what it is, but I'll find it.

Rory was watching her closely. 'What?'

'Do you think I can leave him another eleven years to wait for ye? No, Rory. No.' She looked round. 'It's time for me to go,' she said briefly. 'I can't even bid ye to cheer up, my darling.' She looked again between the bars at his thin gaunt face. 'There's no comfort I can bring except one thing.'

'Abby—'

She said no more, giving one last searching look before turning away.

In the train she sat tense, would up like a spring. The meeting with her brother, the memory of him in his misery had cleared her mind and she could see her way ahead. Rory need have no fears for her; she could handle Pelham with no difficulty. The only thing was to decide exactly what to do with him.

When she arrive home that night a note awaited her on the hall table. It was Lucas Morton's calling card with a message scribbled on the back:

If you are free on Thursday, and are not yet tired of me, I am at your service; usual arrangement?

LM

She turned the card over thoughtfully. Lord Morton? She sat down to write a short note – not to his lordship, however. This one was for Randolph Pelham.

Chapter Forty

When Robbins brought the post to her breakfast table the following morning, she found among her other correspondence a letter from Fan:

Dear Abigail,

I thought I would write to you as I shall be completing my studies this summer, and shall need to discuss my future with you. The nuns have been very obliging but of course one cannot remain at school for ever. Please can you give this matter some thought? It is quite out of the question that I should return to Aunt Eileen's. The very idea of living on a farm now fills one with horror. I had to go back at Christmas, it was so muddy and dirty, and there is no one there one can know any longer. I saw Susan Gilhooley who is married now, and has a little boy. I scarcely recognised her she has changed so; and her accent! I cannot believe I ever spoke like that.

I shall need some money: when I am to come to London, I shall need at least a travelling coat, two day dresses, and two evening gowns, as well as shoes, stockings and gloves. I should think fifty pounds sufficient.

I will write again nearer the time to let you know exactly when I shall be coming, and remain in the meanwhile,

your loving sister,
Francesca
PS Please note I am never to be addressed as 'Fan' in
future; it is an odious nickname, and I detest it.

It occurred to Abby for the first time that perhaps it hadn't
been such a good idea sending her sister to boarding school.
She had always been a lazy, selfish little baggage, and now
there was an imperious tone as well: *Francesca*, indeed.
Fan was obviously going to be something of a handful. And
she was coming to London: she would have to be accom-
modated.

Abby was indeed going to have to give the matter some
thought. As far as the clothes were concerned, that was
easy: she could send a cheque. More importantly, she
would have to think about Fan's future. What was the girl
going to do with herself: did she intend to remain in
London? Did she intend to live off Abby? Quite possibly.

After breakfast she went down to the stable to see after
the horses. Blake was having his mid-morning break with
the stable boy.

'Blake, would you give Dewdrop a good dressing down?
I shall need her at half past two.'

She was about to leave when she noticed a picture postcard pinned to the doorpost: a holiday postcard showing the
tree-lined promenade of some foreign watering place. The
name 'Funchal' meant nothing to her, but she turned to
Blake.

He was momentarily embarrassed and said it was from
Madeira. This gave her a huge jolt and, taking a moment to
control herself, she smiled knowingly, at which Blake
admitted bashfully that it was from Mrs Hardcastle.

'And does she say anything? Mr Darke – is he well?'

Blake unpinned the card and handed it to her.

Dear Ted, just a line to let you know all is well here. The
climate is lovely, the air good, and we have very

comfortable lodgings – makes a change from London! Regards, Nancy.

She muttered something and handed the card back. Blake grinned. 'Lucky for some, eh ma'am?' as he pinned it back on the doorpost.

Afterwards she tried to extract some meaning from this message for herself, but eventually realised there was none. Everything had gone exactly according to plan. 'All is well here.'

That afternoon she dressed carefully in her black riding habit, her little top hat perched forward on her head. Mounted on Dewdrop, a shiny black boot in her stirrup, a pearl-handled riding cane in her hand, she made her way through the streets to Hyde Park, and at three o'clock was galloping along Rotten Row. Making her way through the busy throng she found Pelham, also on horseback, waiting for her beneath the trees near the Albert Memorial. The plane trees were now fully out, and with all the fresh spring green, the view through the park was lovely; if she hadn't been concentrating so hard on her forthcoming meeting, it might have lifted her heart, and she might have been enjoying her ride.

However, as she drew up to him, Pelham saw the serious, distracted expression on her face, her efforts at self-control, and heard her disjointed replies as he greeted her.

They turned their horses back eastwards along the Row. She was silent. He had more to say, though he spoke hesitantly, uncertainly at first, his words muffled and forcing themselves out. 'I don't know what you must have thought. Bursting in on you the way I did. Honestly, I thought you'd never forgive me, never thought you'd speak to me again.' He fell silent, awaiting an answer.

She was silent too until, 'Oh Randolph!' she burst out wretchedly, miserably. 'Be thankful you are not a woman!'

'What do you mean?' he said in alarm as she turned an anguished face to him.

She shook her head. 'I should not have come.'

'Why?'

'I—' she corrected herself, looking down, painful thoughts obviously going through her mind. 'I have to be so very careful.'

He pulled closer, leaning towards her. 'What on earth is the matter?' he said tenderly.

She was looking away from him. 'It's not fair on you,' she said gravely, turning back and looking him deeply, questioningly, in the eyes.

'Hester, you can tell me.'

'After you came that night—' she was intensely serious – 'after you came, I realised the danger . . .'

'Danger?'

'Can't you guess? Oh, I feel so ashamed.' And at last, in a bitter whisper, 'Lord Morton.'

'Morton – why?'

She went on with difficulty, 'You were so kind to me, and he – oh you have no idea. He is a very jealous man.'

Randolph relaxed away from her. 'Is that all?' He laughed. 'I'm not afraid of him.'

'Of course not my dear. But you see—'

'What?' He began to understand. 'You don't mean – he hasn't threatened *you*?'

She nodded silently.

'He hasn't – he hasn't – beaten you?'

She was unable to answer this.

'I don't believe it.' He was hoarse with shock, and then, 'I'll thrash him,' he said coldly.

'No!' She turned quickly. 'No, you mustn't say that! You mustn't! You don't know him. He is a violent man.'

'For heaven's sake, if he beats you why don't you leave him?'

'It would be difficult,' she hesitated, uncertain how to go on and then, awkwardly, in a low voice, 'He has been very good to my family.'

He took a moment to digest this. 'You have accepted

money from him – for the sake of your family?'

She nodded. 'You don't mind me telling you this?'

'Of course not.'

'Two years ago my brother, my darling younger brother Freddie, fell into debt, gambling. He was still so young and very foolishly got into Morton's set. You don't know it, but they are all hard gamblers, and immensely rich. Before he realised it, Freddie found he owed Morton an enormous amount of money – money he simply didn't have. He came to tell me – we have always been very close and I am the only one in the family he can confide in. He told me he would be ruined and would have to resign his commission. He knew it would break papa's heart – and all because of the money he owed Morton. He begged me to go to Morton and plead with him. Of course I went, and you may imagine the scene. Morton – oh, I cannot bring myself to tell you—'

'Don't, if it distresses you . . .'

'Yes, I must, it's only fair to you—' she drew a long breath and dabbed at her eyes with a tiny handkerchief, and forced herself to go on – 'I went to Morton and pleaded with him; I told him how young my brother was and—' again she had to stop to regain her strength – 'Morton was relentless, he said Freddie was old enough to know what he was about, and if he had been fool enough to get into debt – oh, he was heartless! I begged, I pleaded. Oh Randolph, I feel so ashamed! At last Morton told me he would cancel the debt if I—'

'Yes?'

She spoke in a whisper, so quietly that Randolph had to lean in to hear her words, 'He said he would cancel it if I consented to become – his mistress . . .'

Randolph was silent. 'You poor thing,' he breathed after a long pause. 'You poor thing.'

'So you see,' she turned a tear-stained face to him, 'when you said those things to me the other night, it put me in a terrible position.'

'You mean, you weren't offended?'

She gave him a mournful smile, sighing wistfully, a tear glinting on her cheek. 'Offended? Oh my dear – no! No!'

He was searching her face, still uncertain whether to believe her. 'I thought you must have been terribly offended.'

'Oh, you can't imagine . . .'

'Hester,' he drew near and took her hand. 'I can scarcely believe this. It's like a dream. You're just so beautiful.' He raised her hand to his lips.

'It's been so long, so long,' she murmured allowing her hand to remain in his, 'since a man was kind to me – touched me like that, spoke to me like that. When you spoke those words to me the other night, Randolph, so tender, so loving, it was as if Heaven had opened and I had seen—' She looked deep into his eyes, still speaking low. 'I treasured your words. Only, my dearest, for Freddie's sake, you must never betray, not even by a flicker, what is between us.'

'What is between us?' He still seemed incapable of taking it in.

She started suddenly in alarm. 'You did mean it?'

'Oh yes, yes. Oh God yes. I can't tell you how I've thought of you.'

She looked round and withdrew her hand from his as if suddenly afraid. 'When I think – oh, I am the unluckiest of women!'

'Don't say that! Anything I can do—'

'There is nothing you can do. Believe me.' She sighed.

'But surely, my dear – I mean – your brother, shouldn't he take responsibility for his own debts?'

'You don't understand. He is so young. Perhaps in a few years . . .'

There was a pause.

'Look,' he found the words difficult, 'we must talk. There must be something we can do. Isn't there somewhere we could be together? It's confoundedly crowded here. Couldn't we go—'

She looked up at him not understanding.

'Couldn't we go – to your house?'

'To my house?' She looked about her in bewilderment and fear, before turning again. 'And yet perhaps – oh my darling – perhaps it would be safe—' she murmured, 'perhaps for a short while – briefly – oh—' she swallowed – 'do you really wish it?'

'You have no idea! Hester, I'm dying for you—'

'No! Surely not that – you must give me your promise. Oh, what am I saying? I cannot think, you have so confused me.'

'Hester dearest, I swear you need have no fear. Oh, if only we could be alone together even for a short while.'

After a moment she murmured, 'Very well,' and a moment later, smiling mournfully, murmured with girlish modesty, 'You see, I cannot refuse you.'

As they were making their way back across the park, she caught sight of a man riding towards them at an angle, coming from her side. At first she scarcely noted him, but as he drew closer she recognised the man as Lucas Morton. He had recognised her too, and at fifty yards or so, as she rode past, stopped his horse, and watched her. She was acutely aware of him, though she gave no sign of recognition – and neither did he. Pelham saw nothing. He had eyes only for Abby.

She led the way into the drawing room, and rang the bell. A moment later the maid appeared.

'Taylor bring us some tea, please. And then leave us alone.'

'Yes madam.'

She turned back to Randolph. 'Give me two minutes to change.'

As she left Randolph in the drawing room she caught the maid as she was going downstairs. 'Taylor my dear, I want you to interrupt me in about twenty minutes' time. Say there's been an urgent message for me.'

Upstairs she got out of her riding habit and into a loose afternoon tea gown, a something and nothing in pale pastel blue and white, a sort of negligée or wrap that needed only a pull at the girdle to fall open – the sort of thing that hinted she was wearing nothing beneath it. She also let down her hair, which had been stiffly pinned up beneath her riding hat, and bound it casually in a ribbon, so that it partly cascaded about her face and shoulders. Checking her appearance in the glass she was pleased with her preparations.

She was not mistaken. Coming into the drawing room she saw the effect of her ensemble on Randolph immediately, but crossed to the tea tray as if quite unconscious of it.

'I'm sorry, the tea will be getting cold.'

She fussed with the cups and saucers apparently ignoring Randolph. 'Do you take milk with your tea?'

'Hester.' He was breathless.

She turned as she handed him the cup. The front of her wrap hung open naturally as she leant forward to pass him the cup so that he caught a glimpse of her bosom.

'For God's sake—'

'What is it?' She looked up at him in wide-eyed innocence.

He dashed the cup down on the little table, and half rose from his chair. 'Can't we go upstairs?'

'*Randolph!*'

'Forgive me!' He sat down again, taking his cup. 'What must you think?'

For a moment they sipped their tea in silence.

'It's just that you're,' he began again, hesitantly, 'you're so very beautiful. I've thought of nothing else since we met, there's never been a woman like you, never—' He moved to sit beside her on the sofa.

'You said I reminded you of someone,' she murmured, looking down into her cup. A lock of hair hung down beguilingly over her cheek, and he could not resist reaching forward and running his hand down it, and touching her cheek. She did not appear to notice.

400

'I've thought and thought,' he murmured as he caressed her cheek, 'racking my brains to remember where we might have met before, your face always before me. The fact is, Hester, I've been going round in a dream, wondering what you were doing, whether you were happy or sad, awake or asleep, what you were wearing, whether you were at home or out somewhere. I'd be sitting at breakfast, and think you might be having breakfast too. Here I am at table, I'd think, and there, across town, you might be at your table too—' He took the cup from her hands, and then took her hands in his own. She continued to look down as if afraid to meet his eyes.

'Hester,' he whispered, 'look at me.'

At last timidly, she lifted her eyes to his. They were large, dark, luminous, searching his own. 'What is it?'

But he bent over her face and kissed her gently, thoughtfully. 'Oh my darling,' he whispered, as his mouth explored the hair above her ear.

'My darling,' she echoed. 'It's such a relief to have found a friend.'

They kissed again, then she pulled away, suddenly afraid, 'You do mean it?'

'Oh yes, yes, you're everything to me, can't you see it? So beautiful, a goddess—' This time he kissed her passionately, and she met his kiss, her head forced back, as he dominated her. As they broke she let out a gasp. 'Oh, you will kill me, oh Randolph my darling!'

He kissed her again, and as they embraced fiercely, he broke the kiss, and stretching her back on the cushions, ran his lips down to her bosom, wrenching open her gown and kissing her breasts, open, exposed, kissing and caressing them as if any second might be his last. She lay back passively, her eyes closed, sighing, as he rained a storm of kisses on her face, her neck, her breasts, kissing her as he had never kissed a woman in his life, kissing her as if his life depended on it.

At that moment there was a tiny knock. Abby started up

401

in terror. 'Oh my God! It's him. Wait—' She went to the door hurriedly covering herself, opened it an inch and whispered, 'What is it, Taylor?'

'A note madam, just came for you – said it was urgent.'

She took it – it was a blank piece of paper. 'Thank you, Taylor. You may go.'

She shut the door and hurriedly studied the note, still breathing hard, and turned to him. 'Oh my dear, I'm so sorry.'

'What is it?'

'Can't you guess?' She was staring down at the note then crushed it in her hand. 'Oh, I curse the day I was born! Oh!' She flung her arms round his neck and kissed him passionately. 'Now you must go – you must – don't ask, it's better not to ask. Oh Randolph, why is fate so unkind – but you must go!'

'Oh my darling!'

She had pulled her negligée straight, opened the door and was hurrying him through the hall. 'It would never do, you cannot imagine,' she was muttering half to herself. 'You *must* go—'

'When shall I see you again?'

'When?' she was all distraction, 'Ah, I'll write—'

'Promise?'

'I promise, my darling!' Again she flung her arms about his neck, kissing him passionately. 'Oh my darling, oh—' He saw the tears on her cheeks, the wanton disorder of her hair, the heightened flush of her cheeks, her eyes bright with tears. 'Oh my God it will kill me – but you must go, you must!'

'Hester, for God's sake, tell me we'll meet again!'

'Yes, oh yes, my darling but we must be so careful!'

After he had gone, she walked about the house in the spring evening, walked out into her garden, back up the steps, back and forth in the drawing room, eventually changed her clothes and went out into the street, and walked down to the park, walked across the park to the

402

pond, over the bridge, back across the park. It took her a full hour to cool down.

A letter was waiting for her when she returned.

You are playing a dangerous game I suggest you decide who it is you really want; I cannot answer for your friend's health otherwise. I am not accustomed to being trifled with. I await your answer.

LM

She stared at this card for some time, but again did not answer it. In any case, all thoughts of Morton and Pelham were driven out of her mind by another note which arrived later that afternoon. It was from Katherine

Hester,
I hardly can see to write this, yet write it I must. My dearest child, my angel Sophie passed to her eternal rest at four o'clock this morning; I held her in my arms as she breathed her last breath. She was not in pain, and knew that she was going to a better place. Willie has been here, and brought in a priest to give my little darling the last rites.

Could you bear to come down? It would be so good to see you,

Katherine

As she approached the house, she could see all the blinds down, and as the door opened it was Willie himself who admitted her. The hall was dim, the house silent.

'Katherine is upstairs, Mrs Moncrieffe.'

They went up together and, as Willie opened the door, she entered alone. The room was in almost darkness. Two candles burned on either side of the great canopied bed. Katherine was crouching at one side of the bed, while on it, Abby saw as she approached the child laid out in a white dress, as if asleep, her hands folded on her breast.

403

Before Katherine could rise, Abby was beside her, and they knelt together as she took Katherine in her arms.

'Don't say anything,' Abby whispered. And Katherine wept helplessly against Abby's shoulder, as Abby held her tight.

'I knew, I knew,' she began at last, drawing slightly apart. 'I did know Hester, that she was going. I had prepared myself.' She stared at the coverlet, almost as if afraid to raise her eyes to the cold white form of her daughter. As she held her arm round Katherine's shoulders, Abby looked closely at the form of Sophie. The young child was perfectly still, perfectly in repose. The thick dark eyelashes against the alabaster cheek, the rosebud mouth, the little hands crossed on her breast.

'She wasn't strong enough for this world,' Katherine said, heaving up a shattering sigh. 'So little time; I don't understand it.' She turned to Abby. 'I don't understand it, Hester. When I think back over her life. When I think of her – I mean when I think of her making, of how much Charles and I wanted a child, of how we had both prayed for a child, how glad I was when I knew I had conceived her. And then to carry her in my body for nine months, to know she was growing within me every day, and then to go through the pain of her birth, all of which I gladly underwent for her sake! And now, my little darling is taken from me so soon. What was it for, Hester?' She was silent again, her head down on the coverlet beside the child, as she wept.

Later they went downstairs. Willie was in great difficulty, poor man, he felt it as keenly as she did, but he had no means of expressing his feelings. He was dressed in black, all buttoned up, and as they sat together later in the drawing room, Willie still seemed tense, still unable to express his feelings.

Katherine sat opposite Abby, white, her face drawn, haggard with tiredness. 'I haven't slept for three nights. Perhaps tonight I may be able to ... Now that it has happened, now that no further harm can come to her. She is at rest, and perhaps I may be able to be too. Willie has been a great comfort to me,' and she reached a hand towards his as it lay on the arm of the chair.

Willie smiled awkwardly.

When Willie was out of the room she asked about Parnell.

'He is still in Kilmainham, though I believe talks are going on with Gladstone – Willie has been travelling between them, as I told you before. With any luck he should be released soon. Of course he will not be allowed to attend the funeral . . .'

Chapter Forty-one

Abby was very subdued in the train that afternoon. The terrible fate of Katherine's child inevitably reminded her of her own son. At least she had the consolation of knowing that 'all was well' in Madeira. William had been a robust boy; he was certainly heavy enough, he had cried lustily at his birth; he had taken her milk readily, sucking greedily at her breast . . . he was normal. She stared out of the window at the dreary rows of dirty brick houses, with their tiny yards, and lines of washing, at the narrow suburban streets, and rows of chimney pots, and thought, I will never see him. All my life to live, day following day, and I will never see him again. As she stared out of the window sightlessly, she confronted the simple truth. He is twenty months old, and in September he will have his second birthday. I wonder whether Nick will have a little party for him? Of course he will. And then – he will grow, he will become a toddler, and learn to speak. It occurred to her, I will never hear his voice. And then one day he will be five, a little boy, and go to school, and then ten, and then . . . all the years of his life and I will never be there to share them.

As she entered her own house again, Taylor met her.

'There's a gentleman waiting, Mrs Moncrieffe,' she whispered.

'Who is it?'

'Lord Morton, madam.'

406

'How long has he been here?'

'Half an hour, I think.'

Abby drew a long breath, squared her shoulders, and advanced to the door.

'Open the door,' she whispered. Taylor opened both wings of the double doors and Abby swept into the drawing room. Morton was standing at the far end of the room, still in his overcoat which hung unbuttoned, his hand on one hip. He was wearing riding boots, and even in a London drawing room there was a flavour of the turf about him. He looked at her unsmiling and they studied one another in silence for a long moment.

'Morton,' she said at last.

'You did not answer my note,' he said in an expressionless voice.

'I have had a lot on my mind.'

'And I've had a lot on mine. I don't like the game you're playin'.'

'Lord Morton, before you say anything more, I should just like to say that I have returned this minute from the home of a dear friend, whose little girl died this morning.' She still had not moved.

He was brought up by this. His manner changed, and he said, 'I am sorry for your friend, then.' She came towards the fire-place and gestured to the armchairs. He did not move. At last he said, 'I will say no more. Obviously this is not a good time. I know what it is to lose a child.' He gathered himself. 'Another time – in a day or two – I will call again. You know what about.' He moved towards the door,

'No, it is quite all right. Let us talk.' She turned, quite composed.

'I've said what I came to say.'

'You think I am carrying on with Randolph Pelham, is that it?'

'Aren't you?'

'Why do you think so?'

'Don't play with me. Are you or aren't you?'

407

She moved across to the fireplace, turned and faced him. 'Randolph Pelham means nothing to me. You have my word.'

'Good.'

'But I will add this, Lucas. I will not be followed, I will not be spied upon, and I will not be questioned about my actions. I told you the first time we met, I am a free woman. If you are unhappy with our arrangement, you have only to say so.' She stood upright, confronting him.

He surveyed her in silence, and at last said, heavily, 'I told you before, I won't answer for his health if I see him in your company again.'

She waited a moment then crossed to him, and stood close beneath his face, looking up with a small smile. 'Have I given you any cause for complaint so far? Hmm?' She ran her hand down the front of his coat, still regarding him wonderingly. 'What's the matter? We're happy together, aren't we?'

He was watching her, clearly uncertain.

'I can't help it if Pelham stops me in the park. What am I supposed to say to him? Go away, Morton won't like it? He pesters me. That's all.'

He grunted, still unconvinced.

She repeated, coaxingly, 'That's *all*,' and reached up to kiss him. He was unable to resist her. 'In any case,' she broke away. 'I thought you were here to talk about something else.'

'What?'

'There was some talk about Newmarket, I recall.'

He responded to this. 'Are you game?'

'What do you think? I'm bored in London. Let's get out. I'd give anything for a gallop on the heath. Let's go to Newmarket and have a really *hard* ride.' Unexpectedly she burst into laughter. He took her in his arms, laughing too. 'I'll give you a hard ride . . .' and gave her a playful smack on the bottom.

'So, when are we going?'

'Tomorrow if you like. Meredith's taken the house for the week.'

'Good. I can't wait.'

'And we've entered Ashanti for the Two Thousand Guineas.'

'Ashanti?'

'The prettiest three-year-old filly you'll ever see. She's been in hard trainin' for a month.'

'Ashanti.' She turned away, musing. 'What an interesting name. Perhaps she'll bring us luck.'

'Why do you say that?'

'What are her odds?'

'At the moment, they're givin' seven to four.'

'She's the favourite?'

'Second favourite.'

'Why didn't you tell me this before? Let's go immediately! Let's go *now*!'

'All right,' he laughed. 'That's really what I came to see you about.'

This could not have come at a more opportune moment. After Morton had gone she took up her reticule, opened her purse, took out Randolph's medal and studied it for a moment: 'Ashanti Campaign', turning it over in her hand; it was an omen. Then she sat and wrote a short note:

My dearest,

The most wretched luck, my dear, I have to go to Newmarket for the Two Thousand Guineas – I need not say with whom – and I shall be away a week or ten days. Can we meet when I get back? Keep faith, my darling. I live only to see you again.

Hester

And to Thady, 'I am going to Newmarket tomorrow morning, O'Farrell, as the guest of Colonel Meredith at Cheveley Hall. I've written it down. If anyone should call, you can let them know where I am. I shall take Taylor and Blake with me.'

'Blake, me lady? You're takin' Blake to Newmarket, and leavin' old Thady behind?'

'I'm taking Dewdrop.' She studied him for a moment. 'What's the matter? I thought you preferred an indoor job? I thought it suited you better? No more mucking out at seven every morning? Do you want to go back to the stables?'

'No, me lady,' he drew a sigh.

'Blake is very good at his job. Let's leave things as they are.'

'Very well, me lady.' Thady turned away.

'And O'Farrell,' she stopped him. 'You can cut out all this "me lady" nonsense. I'm not aristocracy. Yet. Just say "ma'am" like everybody else.'

'Yes, me lady.' He shuffled out of the room. She raised an eyebrow at the familiar and unlovely sight of his back.

Cheveley Hall was a recent building, a large gentleman's residence, bright red brick in the Dutch style, with gables sprouting in every direction, large windows, and tall chimneys. It had ten bedrooms, a drawing room, a dining room, a library, a billiards room, a morning room, a smoking room, stables and broad lawns to the west. The drawing room was filled with afternoon sunshine. In a word it was very comfortable, and perfectly constituted for a party of friends to enjoy a week at the races.

Abby arrived with Morton in the late morning, saw Dewdrop settled comfortably in the stables, and was in time for lunch. Many of Morton's friends she knew by this time. Colonel Meredith was red-faced and affable; she had learned a little about him since their last party. He owned forty thousand acres of Wales – 'mostly mountains', he told her – had been years in India with his regiment, and as a young man was known as a polo player. De Souza was always slightly overdressed, expensively suited in a way

410

that disguised as far as possible his pot belly and the bent shoulders of a man who spent too much time at a desk; a bearded man with a gold rimmed pince nez, and a shrewd brain, a gambler by instinct, and owner of a share in Ashanti.

It was not by accident that when she was shown to her room, she found it was next door to Morton's. Two servants deposited her trunks, and as Taylor was hanging up her gowns and coats, her tweeds, and arranging her underwear in a chest of drawers she stood at the window, turning over her thoughts.

She was still uncertain of her plans with Randolph, and up till now had played things moment by moment. The fact was, there was very little *she* could do to harm Randolph Pelham – unless she were simply to buy herself a pistol and finish off the job that Rory had started. But that was something she could never bring herself to do; however badly he might have harmed her family, she could not bring herself to kill him. On the other hand, Lord Morton was a man, and a very jealous one. Suppose he could be persuaded – or goaded – to do the work? Not to kill Pelham but – here her thoughts grew uncertain. What exactly did she want him to do? Thrash him, perhaps? That might do.

At lunch she met most of the rest of the house party. There were two other women. Neither of them were married to the men they appeared to be with. The atmosphere in this respect was rather strange, since outwardly at least proprieties were observed. Ladies were accorded separate rooms, though presumably everybody knew who was sleeping with whom. One of these women, Jessy Milbanke, was a slender quiet creature, domestic, and when she returned to the house late in the afternoon Abby found her in the drawing room working at petit point. She spoke little – in a Lancashire accent – was demure, and never initiated a discussion or offered a point of view. She was the mistress of Mr Oakroyd the manufacturer. The other

411

was Bessy and Abby knew her of old; she was Mr de Souza's *chère amie*, and was quite the opposite, a loud noisy over-blown woman, a one-time barmaid who erupted unexpectedly into shrieks of laughter, and jabbed people in the ribs if they hadn't got the point of her jokes – of which she had a great many. The other men had come alone, so that the three women were outnumbered seven to three. This was perfectly agreeable as far as Bessy was concerned, and for most of the time, for Abby too, though none of the men particularly attracted her.

After lunch she went with Morton, de Souza, Smithson and Colonel Meredith – members of the syndicate – to inspect the filly. The stables at the course were crowded. Everywhere jockeys and trainers were busy, and horses were being led in and out of loose boxes; everywhere the familiar smell, a compound of fresh hay, oats, straw and urine. She felt at home.

The jockey Fred Archer was tiny, with a strange child's face on a man in his forties; a child's face, yet aged too. He was a cockney, bandy legged, and respectful to Morton.

'I was out this mornin', me lord, took her down the Rowley Mile and back. Lovely mornin' it was too, me lord; she went beautiful. A couple more days, take it nice and easy, and she'll float in on Saturday.'

Ashanti was led out, and Abby's heart almost missed a beat. A glossy chestnut coat, a white star on the forehead, a finely made, light-boned, high-stepping creature, the body in perfect proportion; a thing of air, all energy, all grace and speed. Abby ran her hand over the horse's withers, down over her flanks, down one foreleg, feeling the fetlock, and lifted the hoof.

'She's light,' she murmured, 'has she got the stamina for it? She won't blow too soon?'

'She'd go another two furlongs, miss, and not tire. She was bred out of Millbrook – look at that chest – got the depth, see? She'll hold the distance, never fear.'

'What are the odds today?' said Morton.

412

'Still seven to four, me lord.'

'She's a winner,' Abby said, straightening. 'I can feel it.' Still examining the horse, she walked round her, and ran a hand across her rump. 'So long as the going's firm,' she murmured.

'There's muscle there,' said Fred. 'Feel that? Hard as a rock. She's a lovely little runner – never rode a finer.'

'You'll be out tomorrow early?'

'You bet.'

'Good, we'll go too, shall we?' She turned to Morton.

As they walked back, she looked round her at the buildings, the grandstand, the offices, the paddock and the ring. Marquee tents were being erected, there was the sound of hammering, carts were being backed, barrels of beer unloaded, and trestle tables erected. Flagpoles already carried brightly coloured pennants, stretching in the breeze.

Abby stood a moment as they inspected all the preparations, and looked beyond them across the vast expanse of the heath, bright green with the first summer grass. She took a deep breath, and was filled with anticipation; the mixture of the fresh greenness, the air, and the excitement of the race to come; she turned spontaneously smiling at Lucas Morton and slipped her arm through his. 'Thank you for bringing me.'

Tea was served late that afternoon in the drawing room, but Abby found herself alone with Jessy. Bessy was with the men playing billiards and drinking whisky.

'You're not interested in horses, Jessy?' Abby asked as she poured tea.

Jessy smiled, and shook her head, as she concentrated on her petit point.

'But you've been before?'

'Oh yes.' Jessy had a ready manner, smiling easily, quite inoffensive.

'It's not boring for you, I hope?'

'Oh no.' She bit off a length of wool, and lifted her work

413

basket on to her knee. 'It's an opportunity for me and Oakroyd to get away. Have a few days together.'

There was a pause as Jessy sorted through various skeins of coloured wools in her basket. She seemed quite nonchalant about it, so Abby felt emboldened to continue. 'Mr Oakroyd, he's a manufacturer, I believe?'

Jessy nodded, and was threading a new skein of wool through her needle.

'And you?'

'It's all right. I know what you're thinking. I've known Oakroyd seventeen years. We see each other once a week. Twice sometimes. He's been very generous. There was no other way I could have supported my mother, Mrs Moncrieffe; I have every reason to feel grateful. It's peaceful too, at home, and I think he enjoys that. It allows him to get away; he can relax and unwind. I keep his carpet slippers by the fire, ready; it's very cosy really. And then, every so often we manage to get away for a few days together.'

'I see. I take it then –' she paused – 'Mr Oakroyd's married?'

'Oh yes,' Jessy went on quite tranquilly, 'he has a wife and five children. A big house in Bayswater.'

There was a silence as Abby drank her tea, and glanced into the garden. 'Seventeen years,' she murmured at last. 'It sounds like a lifetime.'

Jessy laughed softly. 'You'd be surprised how quickly they passed.'

'And he's never –' again she hesitated. 'He's never – looked elsewhere?'

Jessy smiled at her across her petit point. 'No so far. I know him, Mrs Moncrieffe, you see – that's the secret. I know what he wants. I studied him.' She worked at her needle. 'You have to study a man, that's the secret.'

Although Jessy was such a sweet-natured, gentle little woman, there was something in this conversation which stuck in Abby's throat. The talk of 'studying' was not entirely to her taste. Yet when she thought it over, and remembered Jessy's mother, it occurred to her that very likely Jessy had had no choice. What else could she have done? Work in a shop? But if she had an elderly mother, which she appeared to have, how could she have worked the twelve-hour day, the half day on Saturday, that being in a shop required?

In any case, Abby herself was in no position to criticize Jessy. Had not she herself studied to please Nick? Of course – but she had been madly in love with him. Jessy, by contrast, seemed so much older – as if the days of hectic fumbling, of blind driving need, must have long passed, and she had settled into a comfortable routine. It was the complacent, settled nature of Jessy that had taken Abby by surprise, the mention of carpet slippers which sounded so incongruous. She sipped her tea and watched Jessy's patient fingers over the tambour.

De Souza was sharing the hospitality with Colonel Meredith, and he entertained in opulent style. Dinner was served that evening on eighteenth-century Georgian silver plate, the choice wines poured into Venetian glass, the coffee later in the drawing room was served in paper-thin Sèvres porcelain. Around eleven the gentlemen decided for cards.

'We're gettin' up a baccarat table,' Morton turned to Abby. 'Are you in?'

She shook her head. 'I'll watch a while. But I want to be out early tomorrow.'

Ever since seeing Ashanti and glimpsing the open space of the heath she had been looking forward to an early gallop on Dewdrop. Still, she followed Morton into the library.

A long narrow table had been covered by a green baize cloth, and there were about a dozen chairs about it. Mr de Souza was at the centre of one side and was shuffling four packs of cards together. Around the table were the men, Morton, Mr Oakroyd, Mr Smithson, Colonel Meredith –

these she knew – as well as Bessy, and two others who had arrived during the early evening, one an older man, another soldier, Major Pickering, and the other Mr Sandys, a friend of de Souza's from the City, also a member of the syndicate. Jessy had excused herself and already gone to bed.

De Souza was the sort of man who possessed his own personal set of baccarat counters, leather discs in different colours, and embossed in gold with numbers – twenty, fifty, a hundred. These were purchased at the start of play. There was no limit of liability. Acquaintances of Morton had been known to stake – and lose – a horse, a house and, on more than one occasion, a mistress. This was what made the game interesting. All the men round the table had at various times staked everything they had on a hazard – soldiers who had risked their lives, stock exchange gamblers who had mortgaged their houses to finance a hunch, women too, sometimes, who sought to recoup their finances after reckless expenditure – or to impress a man. There was something about a reckless woman – whether on the hunting field, or at the gambling table – which excited men of Morton's sort.

It had, however, never appealed to Abby. She knew baccarat – there had been many a game played in her house – but the novelty had long since worn off. She no longer had anything to prove – or to show off, and baccarat certainly could not compete with the prospect of an early ride on Dewdrop over the heath.

'Betting at twenty pounds minimum?' de Souza looked around.

'Twenty?' called Mr Oakroyd, 'what is this? A children's tea party?' He had been drinking, it was clear. They all had, but it was an unspoken rule in Morton's set that it shouldn't show.

De Souza turned. 'What do you propose?'

'A hundred.'

Abby who was behind Morton's chair glanced round. The men looked at one another.

'Keep it to twenty,' said Smithson.

Oakroyd turned to him jocularly, 'Short of tin, old boy?'

'They say the Prince of Wales bets in five-pound stakes,' Smithson said coolly in his dry, nasal voice. The others looked at one another with raised eyebrows. Smithson was a man of few words, but looked as if he meant every one of them. Abby was slightly surprised to hear the aggressive tone in Oakroyd's voice but, after hearing Jessy talking about him, she decided this might be only bluster – or the wine speaking.

'Smithson moves in higher circles,' de Souza said ironically, looking round the table. 'Twenty pounds minimum it is.'

'Well the Prince of Wales ain't supposed to gamble,' Oakroyd insisted. 'Let's make it a hundred, it ain't worth the time otherwise.'

The others assented.

'What about the white line?' said the young Mr Sandys. Again there was a pause. De Souza glanced up at Abby. 'Would you mind ringing the bell, Mrs Moncrieffe?'

When the butler entered, de Souza said, 'Walters, bring us a stick of chalk, will you? And set the brandy there.'

And shortly afterwards a chalk line was drawn round the table on the green baize about a foot in from the edge of the table.

'Stakes over the line, everybody.'

Play now commenced. De Souza dealt two cards to the man on his left, two to Bessy on his right, and two for himself.

After half an hour watching the game, Abby left them to it. She had told the servants she wanted to be called at half past six with a cup of tea, and that Dewdrop should be ready by seven.

Chapter Forty-two

Since Morton did not appear that night, she slept soundly, and as she woke the following morning a happy idea came into her head. Without bothering to ring for Taylor, she dressed as quickly as she could in her riding habit, the tightly fitting coat, and breeches, but she left off the over-skirt or apron which was customarily worn over them, and when she reached the stables she asked Blake, who was waiting with Dewdrop, 'I'm sorry to trouble you, Blake – would you mind putting a man's saddle on her?' The stables were already busy as grooms mucked out and fed the horses. It didn't take Blake long to fit Dewdrop with a man's saddle, and she mounted him astride. She could see the effect she had on the groom.

'It's early. Who's looking?' she grinned, and turned her horse's head towards the gate.

'But Mrs Moncrieffe, what about your hat?'

'Don't need it!' she called over her shoulder. She had secured her hair loosely by a ribbon and it hung long down her back.

She glanced at the house she rode by. It looked deep in slumber. No doubt the cards had gone on long into the night. As she came out on to the open heath, the cool air of the morning hit her; she sat taller in the saddle, and breathed deeply. This was why she had come. All the rest, even the race itself, couldn't compare with this. The heath stretched away, gently undulating to the horizon; she glimpsed a clump of trees where the sun hovered a little above the horizon, rose pink yet in the early light, with pockets of mists hanging in the hollows, and horses and riders scattered across the great expanse.

Lifting her head and sniffing the rich early morning air, Dewdrop was ready for a gallop. She had realized immediately that her mistress was mounted in a different fashion but by the time they had arrived on the open heath, she had become accustomed to it, and it needed only a touch of the spur to set her off.

'I know you're not one of these paragons,' Abby whispered, 'but we can show them all the same, can't we?' and she leaned forward, crouching like the jockeys about her, and letting Dewdrop have her head.

There was never a moment in her life quite like that – free alone on the open heath, with only Dewdrop beneath her in a perfect harmony of movement – the thudding of the hooves, the easy rise and fall of Dewdrop's flanks, the cool morning breeze in her face.

It did not come entirely as a shock, forty minutes or so later, as she was riding into the stables, to see a carriage at the door, and Randolph handing out a couple of grips to a footman. She reined Dewdrop in and waited as he came up to her. 'You're here!' she seemed astonished.

'Are you so surprised?' he sounded a little crestfallen.

'Oh, no! But surely—'

'I had to come.' Randolph spoke in an angry undertone. 'Hester, I've thought of what you told me – thought and thought – I've thought of nothing else. It's barbaric, the hold that man has over you. You must break free, you must!'

'You don't know what you're saying.' She spoke tersely, seemed much more in control of herself this morning, and almost angry with Randolph.

'Yes, I do. And if you won't do it, I will.'

'You?'

419

'I'm not afraid of him. I tell you, it's driven me mad! I can't stand the thought of you and that man. The thought of you and him together, it's gone round and round in my thoughts.'

'You are very kind,' she said calmly after a moment. 'But I fear I said more than I should when we spoke before – I had no right to burden you with my troubles. It was just such a relief to be able to speak.' She seemed in command of her feelings now. 'Please Randolph, I am all right now. Really.' She smiled. 'It's not as bad as you think, and I'll get through somehow. But you should not have come. It could be dangerous and I could not bear it if –'

'What?'

'Promise me you will say nothing.'

'I can't'

'Randolph, I insist. Promise! You are so brave – but you must be careful! I beg you to do nothing rash.'

He smiled grimly. 'We'll see whether my Lord Morton will change his tune while I'm around.'

'Randolph,' she was insistent, 'I implore you, command you! Say nothing! Do nothing! You cannot know the consequences for me. I warn you. If you do not promise I shall leave myself.'

He laughed openly at her anxiety, reached his hand and placed it over hers. 'Don't worry about me, Hester,' he said, 'I would do nothing to harm you.'

At that moment she glanced up over Randolph's shoulder and saw Morton's face at her bedroom window. He had seen but he had not heard. Her expression did not change, but she nudged Dewdrop into motion and Randolph accompanied her round to the stable. Paradoxically, the atmosphere now lightened between them and Randolph became relaxed, even cheerful.

'Do you know, Hester,' he said as she dismounted, 'I don't believe I ever saw a woman riding the way you are – like a boy. It's rather—' He couldn't find the appropriate word; the sight of her in tight-fitting breeches left him

420

temporarily at a loss. As she led the mare into the stable she glanced over her shoulder.

'Never?'

She wasn't looking at him, so she couldn't see his face, and was waiting for the answer. She still didn't know quite what she was going to do when the penny finally dropped – if it ever would.

He leaned against the stable door watching her as she unbuckled the saddle. At last he spoke as if from very far away, dreamily, 'Well, there was someone once, now I come to remember. Many years ago.'

'Really? Who was she?' She was studiously offhand, as she turned to place the saddle on the partition.

He shook his head slowly. 'Oh, no one; no one important.' As she turned she found him staring into her face. She held his gaze.

'Extraordinary,' he murmured.

'What is?'

'Mm?' He was still in this strange thoughtful mode. 'I couldn't begin to explain.'

'Well! You are a tease, and no mistake. "Couldn't begin to explain"? What am I supposed to make of that? What a man of mystery you are, Randolph, to be sure.'

He was still staring at her, but she boldly held his gaze, with a small smile on her lips, and tapped him lightly on the chest with her crop as she walked past him. At long last he shook his head slowly, and murmured, 'No. No. It couldn't be.'

'What's goin' on? Randolph Pelham's been invited to stay.'

'So he told me.'

'Do you mean you had nothin' to do with it?'

'I? Why should I?'

'I've told you before – don't play games with me, madam. There's something goin' on, I can feel it. Hark 'ee, Hester – you know me by now – I won't be fooled with. If you prefer Pelham take him, and be damned to you. But I warn you, he hasn't a penny.'

'Lucas, I keep telling you, it's all your fancy. You're man enough for me – man and a half, I'd say. By the way, what time did you get to bed last night?'

'Three.'

'Three? That's no good to a woman. I was asleep by half past eleven. What was I supposed to do? Read a book? Why on earth were you wasting your time on cards when there were so much better things to do?'

At last his face broke into a small smile. As he was leaving her room, he turned, and remembered why he had come. 'But I warn you – I know you're a damned clever woman. Don't overplay your hand, that's all. Because if you do, you'll find it'll come down round your head like a house.'

'Not my head, Lucas,' she murmured as he left the room.

That night at dinner, to her surprise, Randolph proved to be the life and soul of the party. She wondered about this as she watched him and concluded that perhaps it was the soldier in him – the prospect of danger brought out an insouciant, devil-may-care side. And she had, after all, commanded him not to betray her. He kept the table, especially the women, agog with tales of his campaigns in Africa. Abby was conscious of the fact that many of the other men, pale, physically out of condition, had spent their lives in offices poring over account sheets, studying to make money. Randolph, with his open-air complexion, and breezy tales of adventure, wasn't entirely to their taste. Then, after dinner when Bessy opened the piano, and after she had sung a couple of songs, he volunteered to give them one, and kept them in fits of laughter with 'Miss Houligan's Christmas Cake', an Irish patter song with a tongue-twisting chorus:

> There were plums and prunes and cherries,
> And citron and raisins and cinnamon too,
> There was nuts and fruits and berries,

422

And the crust it was nailed on with glue.
There were caraway seeds in abundance,
Sure, 'twould give ye a fine stomach ache.
You would kill a man twice
After eatin' a slice
Of Miss Houligan's Christmas cake!

While enjoying the song, Abby also kept an eye on Morton who was beside her. Clearly comic songs were not his cup of tea. His face expressed nothing, except perhaps a super-cilious sneer.

'Come on Morton,' she nudged him. 'Your turn now.'

He turned calmly. 'Sorry, never was much good at makin' a fool of myself.'

She raised her eyebrows in a faint *moue* of amusement which he caught.

Abby went in the morning with Morton to inspect the mare again. Morton had been up till after two the night before, he told her, but it didn't seem to affect him. He was dressed as he always was, as if he was just off for a ride himself, in top boots and a long old riding coat. Fred Archer had been out with Ashanti already, and was fussing over a bridle when they arrived. A boy had been giving the horse a rub, and was now wiping her down with a soft cloth. The stable smelled of fresh hay, and Ashanti had an indescribable smell, compounded of strength and energy and sweetness.

'We was out for a run this morning, me lord, and she went as sweet as you could wish,' he told Morton. 'If I don't win Saturday, it won't be for want of trying.'

'The odds have shortened. Three to two.'

As they were turning away she remarked over her shoul-der to Randolph, 'Ashanti – you'd better have some money on her, Pelham – should be a lucky horse for you.' Then walked on arm in arm with Morton before he could answer.

Two days later, Abby was at the ring watching the parade

423

of runners and riders, with Morton and the others. They
were in dove-grey morning suits, accoutred with bin-
oculars, top hats and cigars. Morton had gone silent,
concentrated. Randolph was also with them, and she kept
up a studiously off-hand banter with him. Morton's threats,
and Randolph's light-hearted chat, provoked in her an
impishness to which she was inclined to give free rein.
However intent Morton might be on Ashanti, however, he
had time to notice what Randolph was up to. From time to
time inevitably there would be moments when Randolph
would touch her, or she might take his arm to point out
something. All her antennae were out.

Then out came Ashanti with Fred Archer on her back in
the syndicate's colours, purple and white.

'She's jumpy,' Morton muttered, as he saw Ashanti shy
at a little boy who was creeping under the rail, and waving
a paper flag. He pushed the boy away harshly, and the
boy's mother turned to him indignantly 'You mind what
you're at!'

'Keep your brat out of the way! Didn't you see the mare
shy?' Morton said harshly. Abby had never seen him so
concentrated, willing his horse to win. He didn't hear her
when she addressed him, kept his hands in his pockets,
frowning later as he made his way through the crowd to the
stand. She and the others glanced at each other and
followed him. Morton was the leader of the syndicate, and
Ashanti had been bought on his recommendation.

About them swirled the whole world in its finery, ornate
hats on the ladies, men red-faced and beery, waistcoat
buttons undone, children everywhere under their feet.
There had been a shower during the night, which lent an
indescribable freshness to the air. It left the ground softer,
though, and the turf was chewed up by the thousands of
feet.

'Have you placed your bets?' she took Morton's arm,
trying to keep up with him. 'We've only got half an hour.'

'Of course I've placed my bet.'

'How much?'

'Three grand.'

She turned to Randolph. 'What about you, Pelham?'

He had his card in his hand. 'Just engaged in a little last-minute computation.'

She let the others go ahead and stood with Randolph amid the swirling noisy crowd, as she stared for a moment in annoyance. 'None of them know how to have any fun!' she said. 'They've spent all that money on Ashanti, and all they can think of is their investment. She's just money to them.'

'Hmm?' Randolph had his nose in his card.

She turned her attention to him. 'Well? Do you have some inside knowledge?'

'Intuition. Besides, I have my lucky penny.' He winked at her.

'What?'

'My lucky penny. Given to me when I was a little boy.'

'Go on.'

He laughed. 'My aged grandmother – God rest her soul, she's gone to a better place. The first penny she ever gave me – the way grandmothers do – she wrapped my fingers round it, and said, "Keep this Randolph. One day it'll bring you luck."'

'And has it?'

'Oh yes.' Then shook his head uncertainly. 'Mind, I don't use it too often – mustn't push my luck. But today, I don't know, I feel—' He gave her a happy smile, and she couldn't help responding. Unlike the others, Randolph was really entering into the spirit of the thing.

'So, what is your fancy?'

He gave her a conspiratorial look, then studied the card again. 'Well now. There's Jericho in the two o'clock at seven to one. She did well at Cheltenham last autumn, and Teddy Francis is riding her. He's a pusher. So we'll have a hundred on her.'

She raised her eyebrows. 'Sure you can afford it?'

'It's the system. Now Jericho wins the two o'clock, so the winnings go on Irish Mist in the two-thirty at eleven to one – long odds I grant you, but Irish Mist is a lovely little creature – I'd back her against the world. Then after she's won—' he was still studying his card '—the money goes on to St Blaise, favourite in the three-thirty at seven to four against. What does that make?'

She laughed. 'I don't know! What does it make?'

'A lot of money, my dear!' he clasped her by the arms for a moment in sheer enthusiasm, then broke away with a tiny frown. 'Which I need, if truth were told.'

She followed him to the betting ring. Randolph was absolutely fascinating company at this moment. 'Any you recommend?' She looked round at the bookies, Major Bagstock, Tommy Wood, the Old Firm.

Randolph drew in a sharp breath as he studied the odds chalked up on the boards. 'Ooh, Irish Mist has shortened. Nine to one. I thought she might. Better not waste any more time.' He looked around the betting ring. 'Well, here goes for Major Bagstock.'

She waited while he paid over his money and returned two minutes later with his paper slip. He gripped it tightly, gave it a little kiss, and shook it in the air. His eyes were alight. 'You're going to make me a very happy man!' He stowed the paper in his pocket and turned to her.

'Now, what about you?'

She shrugged. 'All my money has gone on Ashanti, obviously. Morton wouldn't like it if I'd backed any other.'

Randolph was silent now as they turned back towards the stand. The crowd was thick, and he solicitously squired her through the heaving and pushing, the belching and laughing, the children squawling, the turf ground into mud by the thousands of boots, bits of paper strewn about, the remains of food.

'I noticed you didn't?' she said.

Randolph made a tiny grimace. 'She's a lovely little horse – and a tryer. Has Fred Archer ridden her before?'

426

'No.'

'That's what I thought. Between you and me, Hester – do you think she'll go the distance?'

'Don't you?'

'She's delicate. May not have the stamina.'

Abby was thoughtful. She frowned. 'The thought did occur to me. The going's soft ...' she murmured after a moment. There was a hundred of her own money riding on that horse. 'She's a lovely creature,' she said again. 'If she's ridden right.'

'You've got it! We'll trust to Fred Archer. He's the best. Come on. Those hogs will have cleared the luncheon if we're not quick about it.'

Instinctively she took his arm and they hurried on.

'By the way,' he said after a moment, not looking at her as they negotiated the crowd, 'Something's been puzzling me. Yesterday you told me to have something on Ashanti – because it would be a lucky horse for me. What did you mean?'

She shook her head vaguely. 'Did I? I don't remember now. Nothing, probably.'

'It's rather a coincidence, you see ...'

They went into the stand and up into de Souza's box. The luncheon was indeed spread out, and the others were busy with knives and forks, and fingers too, wrenching at the remains of lobsters, sucking cracked claws, tearing cold chickens to pieces. The table was crowded as well with pigeon pies, cold sides of beef and lamb, a tongue, a Stilton, eggs, salads. After these days in the air, after her early morning gallops, Abby had a healthy appetite. She was ready too for the popping of corks; and the festivity of the occasion was enhanced by the picnics being laid out all about them in other boxes.

'Hester! Take this!' De Souza thrust a glass of champagne into her hand. 'Come on – move up there Romsey, look here's a chair. Pelham – make yourself comfortable on the ledge there. Here's a rug.'

427

As she took her glass Pelham glanced across and caught her eye. He raised his glass and winked at her and she couldn't help smiling in return. As she did so something moved inside her, and suddenly awkward she looked away. They had an uninterrupted view of the entire ground and the course below them where whole families, and parties of young men and jolly girls garish in their finery and fancy bonnets, perched on the roofs of carriages and chaises, their luncheon spread out between them.

Thousands upon thousands of punters enjoying a day out. But she was scarcely aware of them because exactly at that moment a terrible thought had struck her. Perhaps she had been mistaken? Perhaps after all there was a reason why Randolph had not been able to save them? Perhaps it had not been entirely his fault . . .

Chapter Forty-three

The mood as they returned was not good. Ashanti had come fourth, and Morton and the syndicate were taciturn. Smithson even had the bad taste to suggest that Morton's judgement was not all it might have been.

'We bought the nag on your say-so,' he said in his blunt way. They were crammed into a carriage with Abby, who had a headache.

'Ssh,' De Souza cautioned.

There was silence for a moment, then Morton said coldly, 'You knew what you were about. No one asked you to put your money in.'

'She's a lovely little horse, Morton,' Abby said, trying to lighten the atmosphere, 'and you know what they say: fourth in the Guineas, first in the Derby!'

'Listen here, Smithson,' Morton abruptly leaned forward, 'I won't take your cheek. If you want to sell your share I'll buy it off you.'

'Done.'

The rest of the journey was made in silence.

Later, as they were drinking tea before separating to dress for dinner, Randolph was cheerful. 'A lovely day out, de Souza and I'm indebted to you, man, for your hospitality.'

'I don't know what you've got to be so cheerful about, Pelham,' Abby couldn't help turning to him. 'You lost your money. Whatever happened to your lucky penny?'

'Lucky penny?' Morton overheard them.

Randolph frowned. 'It's not guaranteed,' he said carefully, then brightened. 'But it's the thought that counts. It reminds me of Grandma; she was very good to me.'

'Not guaranteed?' Morton laughed coldly. 'Whoever heard of such a thing? A lucky penny that's not lucky?' He laughed even more loudly, 'I've never heard of such a thing. How Irish!'

Pelham's good humour was imperturbable, though he was clearly aware of Morton's hostility. He turned again to Abby. 'You see, Mrs Moncrieffe, Irish Mist is the sweetest little filly, with a heart too big for her – but the going was too soft. Great shame. She'll win again, don't you worry.'

That evening the men sat down again to baccarat. This time Randolph was present. His eyes had been on her throughout dinner and he was always finding amusing remarks for her; she knew Morton had noticed. But now, instead of relishing the situation she felt a nervous anticipation, and as she saw Randolph passing into the library, where the table was ready for cards she turned to him as if in surprise.

'Are you a card player, Mr Pelham? It's baccarat.' Randolph did not seem to notice the anxiety in her voice.

'Well,' he said cheerfully, 'I've never played the game – French, isn't it? But I'll try anything once.'

'They do play for high stakes ...' she murmured; she didn't want the others to hear, but as the men were assembling round the table, she did not dare to raise her voice, and she wasn't sure he had heard.

De Souza took the bank, and the coloured counters were issued.

'Are you in, Mrs Moncrieffe?' Morton looked up at her as she stood behind Randolph's chair.

'No, I'll just watch.'

She gave Morton an uncertain smile. Unconsciously she had stationed herself behind Pelham's chair, and Morton had noticed. 'She can be your lucky mascot, Pelham,' he said cynically. 'Maybe she'll bring you more luck than your "lucky penny", eh?' And he laughed sarcastically. He and Pelham were sitting face to face. Randolph glanced up at Abby behind him and said lightly, 'You know what they say – unlucky in love . . .'

'Poor boy, has someone let you down?' Oakroyd, who was next to Pelham, helped himself to brandy.

Pelham glanced across at Morton. 'I'm not sure. Yet.'

'Well, we shall see. Come on, de Souza, dish out the cards.'

She had detected a gradual hardening in Morton since dinner. Obviously he suspected her by now with Pelham, and it was true she had been around him all evening unconsciously in little wifely ways, and now found herself lighting a cigar for him as he sat at the card table. However, these were all things which might, or might not, be interpreted as indicating something deeper. Morton was clearly unsure, and was in a raw mood after Ashanti's loss; he adopted his usual taciturn, cool air.

'So, just remind me, de Souza,' Randolph called, 'the cards must add up to nine, isn't that it? And if I win, it's double my money? Bit like Vingt-et-un? And court cards and tens don't count?'

'Hundred pound stakes. That all right with you, Pelham?' Morton glanced casually across the table.

Abby was watching Pelham closely as Morton said this. He had to take a moment to digest Morton's words, but then gave a little shrug and smiled up at Abby. As de Souza dealt the cards she tried to busy herself, to take her mind off the game, and went round the table with the brandy decanter, in case any of the players wanted a refill. Several of the men lit cigars, and as the night progressed, the air gradually became blue with the smoke. Inevitably though she found her gaze drawn back to Randolph, and as he caught her eye, he smiled and, on an impulse, doubled his stake on the tableau in front of him: it was a four and a two.

431

'Let's see a third card here, de Souza,' he called.

De Souza dealt one – an eight. He now turned his own cards, a king and a nine. 'A natural,' he murmured and scooped up Randolph's stake together with the others who had bet on Randolph's hand.

However, Randolph won the next coup. He left the winnings on the table, as he noticed Morton had lost. 'Double your money,' Randolph said cheerfully glancing across to him. He looked up at Abby. 'It's my system, Mrs Moncrieffe. Always double your stake after you've lost.'

He lost this coup.

Later in the night Morton took the bank. He took less and less trouble to hide his hostility towards Randolph now. Randolph however reacted by assuming a cheerful reckless-ness towards him; it was obvious to Abby that he was inspired by her presence behind his chair, and it only made her watch with greater anxiety. Morton, who saw every-thing however, did not lose his control, and seemed if anything to grow colder and colder, more and more super-cilious, as he watched Randolph begin to lose heavily.

It was after two o'clock when Randolph had to pause. He scribbled a few figures into a pocket diary and studied them. 'I'm out of funds for the moment. Will you take an IOU?' he said casually to Morton. Abby felt a tightening inside her; despite having been up since dawn, she felt no tiredness and was watching with intense concentration.

Morton who seemed made of steel, glanced across to de Souza. 'Do you want to accept Pelham's IOU?'

De Souza looked between them thoughtfully, but before he could reply, 'You're a younger son, ain't you, Pelham?' Morton went on in an insolent drawl, leaning back in his chair.

Pelham looked taken aback. The other players waited as the two men confronted each other across the table.

'What the devil's that got to do with it?'

'Quite a lot, I would have thought.'

There was another pause. The hostility between them

432

was now frank and open. 'What do you mean?'

'You ain't got any tin of your own,' Morton went on coolly.

Randolph blushed. 'Confound your impudence! Will you take an IOU or won't you?' He half rose in his seat.

'Don't know that I will,' Morton replied in his leisurely way. He looked round the table. 'Any other fellow want to take a chance with Pelham?'

'Take a chance?' Pelham was furious. 'What are you implying?'

'Oh,' Morton looked up at the chandelier, and the clouds of cigar smoke hovering above them, then glanced across at Pelham. 'Suppose you welshed on me? Put me in a devilish pickle, wouldn't it?'

Pelham threw back his chair, and was half way across the table before he was pulled back by Oakroyd and Smithson on either side of him. 'You'll take that back, or I'll beat you within an inch of your life!'

'Truth hurt, do it?' Morton stood up, and turned coolly. 'Look here, Meredith, what's he doin' here anyway? I don't recall he was one of the party originally. Seems to have crept in somehow.'

Meredith also retained his self control. 'Your remarks are uncalled for,' he said coldly. 'Pelham is here as my guest. If you don't like it, you know what you can do.'

Morton raised his eyebrows, and suddenly burst into laughter. 'Well, bless me, that's put me in my place! Meredith, I apologise for disturbing the calm of your house. Now I'm for bed.' He stubbed out his cigar, and scooped up his winnings. 'We'll cash up in the morning, all right?' As he stuffed the counters into his pocket, he glanced across at Pelham on the other side of the table, and still hemmed in by the two men who had restrained him. 'I dare say one of these fellows will take your IOU, Pelham.'

'Don't you walk away from me, Morton!' Pelham shouted. 'Don't walk away, you scoundrel!'

But Morton had already gone. The others were clustered

round Pelham trying to soothe him. 'We can settle this in the morning when heads are clearer. Relax man, surely you know Lord Morton by now.'

Randolph was white hot, trembling. 'He'll apologise for those words or I'll call him out!'

Abby followed Morton hurriedly and as she expected found him in her bedroom. Before she could open her mouth however, he crossed behind her to slam the door, then took her by one arm and thrust her hard so she fell backwards over her bed.

'I won't have you makin' a fool of me,' he said in a tight undertone. She was so taken aback that for a moment she couldn't think. 'Do you think I couldn't see?' he went on in a quick concentrated low tone. 'Every fellow in the room could see what you were up to. You came here as my guest! And he followed you here. It's obvious. He's been sniffing round you since he arrived.'

She was trembling as she pulled herself upright.

'You behaved like a cad,' she said at last attempting to regain her self control. 'There is such a thing as decency and manners.' She stood up to confront him. 'Things you know nothing about! You deserve a thrashing. If you don't apologise to him in the morning I'll never speak to you again.'

Morton gave a short contemptuous laugh. 'Let him do his damnedest. He'd be a fool to call me out, I can tell you.'

'You're a brute.'

'And you're a whore. I'm done with you. I've stood enough of your games. You'll not make a fool of me again, madam. Good night to you.'

She stood silently, still quivering, as he took up his coat from where it lay on her bed, and went to the door. She waited, her arms crossed, her heart still beating painfully, till, only a few seconds later she heard a shout, then a sort of thump, a crash, a woman's scream and more shouts. She rushed out on to the landing, and saw below her at the foot of the stairs, two men struggling, and as she came round the landing to the head of the stairs, one of them threw the other from him, stood briefly glancing round, and she saw it was Lord Morton. He glanced up and saw her, as the other – who was obviously Pelham – scrambled to his feet, squared up to Morton, but was immediately knocked flying across the carpet, slipped, fell, hit his head against a large mahogany sideboard standing against the wall, and lay still. De Souza and Bessy, who had screamed before, ran quickly to him.

'You've killed him!' Bessy screamed.

'I doubt it,' she heard Morton say in a casual tone.

'You'll leave this house first thing,' Meredith stood after a brief examination of Pelham's inert body and turned to Morton.

Morton raised his eyebrows. 'For heaven's sake, he attacked me! Fair's fair. What did I do?'

Meredith knelt and he and Bessy managed to get Pelham into a more comfortable condition, and as Abby arrived at the foot of the stairs, Smithson appeared with the brandy decanter from the library, and kneeling beside Pelham and supporting his head as best as he and the others could, they managed to tip a mouthful down his throat. With a great spluttering, Pelham opened his eyes, and made an effort to sit up. He put his hand to his head.

Morton made his way nonchalantly upstairs as they managed to get Pelham into a sitting position. Abby knelt by him, among the others.

'We'd better get you into your room. You've had enough excitement for one day,' she said as she examined the bruise on his head. 'Nothing broken, thank goodness. But you've got a shiner here too,' as she saw the bruise already beginning to rise round his right eye.

Two of the men got him upright, and the whole party escorted him up the stairs and to his room, which was on the floor above the others, among the servants and where he was laid out on his bed. Abby fussed round him, getting his shoes off.

'Walters,' she turned to the butler, 'would you tell one of the maids to send up a jug of hot water.'

The butler went out, and she stood up. 'He'll live. I suggest we leave him in peace.' She turned to Pelham again. 'Get yourself into bed, and get a good night's sleep. You'll feel better in the morning.'

He grinned sheepishly up at her. 'Thanks,' he whispered.

Twenty minutes later as she was about to get into bed, there was a timid knock, and a diminutive maid whispered, 'Oh Mrs Moncrieffe, Mr Pelham asked me to give you this.'

It was a scrap of paper on which was scrawled, 'Can you bear to come and see me? R.'

'Are the others all in bed?'

'Yes, miss.'

'Very well. You can go to bed too if you like. God knows it's late enough.'

'Thank you, miss.'

She pulled a wrap round her, and went out; fortunately the corridor was deserted. And since Pelham's room was on the floor above they were unlikely to be disturbed. She found him still lying on his back as they had left him, and staring at the ceiling. She stood over him, studying him; the eye had come up badly.

'Sorry,' he said after a moment. He seemed embarrassed – had a guilty look, like a schoolboy caught out.

'An exciting night,' she murmured.

He grinned awkwardly, and after a moment she sat on the side of the bed, smiled slightly too and murmured, 'Lucky penny . . .'

He laughed slightly too, and their eyes met. 'My own fault,' he said. 'After all, I followed you here.' He was still looking at her. 'Couldn't stop thinking about you, you see.'

She was silent.

'After, you know—' he paused. 'I mean, after that afternoon in your house. That was special – for me anyway. And then the sight of you and Morton – it drove me wild,

436

watching him touch you or whisper to you, I couldn't help
myself.' He paused. 'I'm glad I hit him. Made me feel
better.'

She laughed softly. 'Didn't do you much good, though.
Have you looked at yourself in a mirror?'

He shrugged. 'Don't matter. I've had some knocks in my
time, Hester. I'm used to it.'

After another moment, she said, 'I'm through with
Morton.'

The various noises in the house had gradually stilled, and
the house was asleep at last. There was a silence that
lengthened, and then it seemed to go on and on, and at
length, their eyes met. She was deeply conscious, conscious
all through herself, of their being alone together ... then
some instinct warned her against staying any longer and she
forced herself to stand and turn away.

'I'm going back to town in the morning.'

'Me too. Shall we go together?'

'If you wish.'

'Hester.'

She turned at the door.

'Good night my dear.' He was staring at her intensely. 'I
found out something today.'

'What?'

'I'll tell you. Soon. As soon as I can. Thanks for
coming.'

At first she walked about her room; she drew back the
curtains and stared out into the darkness; she closed the
curtains again and got into bed waiting for sleep to come.

Randolph had been fighting Morton for her, that was it.
And try as she might to control her feelings, the effect on
her had been quite unforeseen. Seeing him lying on his bed
just now with his absurd black eye, how could she help
feeling for him? How could any woman remain unmoved?
Morton was heavier, and had a hard callous way – knocking down someone like Pelham was nothing to him. Yet

Randolph had not counted that, he had not calculated, not weighed it up; he just struck out. She thought back over the day, Randolph so light-hearted, so merry – he made the others look like what they were, cold, calculating, men who spent their waking hours thinking only of money.

And there was something else. It had come to her when Morton had scoffed, 'How Irish' – about the lucky penny business. It occurred to her now, that Randolph was in truth as Irish as she was. In the past, years ago, men like Randolph, rich, living in large and beautiful houses, Protestants and speaking with an English accent, travelling the world, they hadn't seemed Irish – not like her, as if the poor people, the Catholics were the real Irish. But from this end, from the English end, standing outside her native land, she could see that he was as Irish as herself – only in a different way, that was all. It gave them a link that she had not seen before.

And now she remembered the extraordinary thought which had come so unexpectedly at the grandstand that afternoon. Suppose there were some other explanation for what had happened all those years ago? What if Randolph had attempted to save them but had been unable to? After all, it had been his father who had evicted them – and then he had not actually been responsible for Rory's imprisonment, had he? But still – still, there was the afternoon in the Goat, and once her thoughts went back, she remembered the terrible day she had lost her baby. She tried to associate her loss with the light-hearted man she had just been talking to, that devil-may-care manner, the smile that made her stomach turn over . . . it was impossible to sleep.

Chapter Forty-four

They travelled back to town together, but the atmosphere was subdued. Pelham now had a bandage over his eye.

'Makes you look like Lord Nelson,' she remarked; it was meant to sound funny, but in reality it was a cover-up for the tender feelings the sight of him now aroused in her. She was confused. She had gone to Newmarket with the intention of luring Pelham to his destruction, and instead she found herself returning to London, half in love with him. What was she doing? They sat mostly in silence as the train made its way through the early summer countryside; the wheat and barley showing green in the fields.

The atmosphere was still awkward between them, and when they parted at Liverpool Street station, it was difficult for their eyes to meet. Her plans had been working well; in a way, they had been working too well. He had lost all his money, and he had a black eye; she could not have asked for more. Except that she could feel his attention on her, the intensity of his feelings, and the effect they were having on her. She tried to fight it.

'How are you going to explain that?' she asked casually as they stood on the platform.

He shrugged. 'Walked into a lamp post, I expect. The usual.'

'Have you got a reputation for this sort of thing,

Randolph? It won't come as a terrible shock, I hope. Your mama won't faint?'

'Mother's in Ireland. Are we going to meet again?'

'If you wish,' she said uncertainly, looking down.

'You know I do.'

She hesitated. 'I'll send you a note.'

'Notes! You're always sending notes – then you change your mind. Look, what about Thursday?'

'Very well. Thursday.'

'Shall I come to your place?'

She nodded and repeated, 'If you wish.'

'*If I wish?*'

She was flustered; honestly, she no longer knew what she wanted. 'Come on Thursday. Now, I must see to Dewdrop. Goodbye, Randolph.' She turned away hurriedly to find Blake and her horse.

Then she was home again, Thady was helping her off with her coat, she was giving instructions for meals, and at last as she sifted through a sheaf of letters, she found one in her sister's hand several days old, to inform her that she would be arriving at Euston in a week's time by the night train.

As she was climbing the stairs to her room, she thought, Thank God I've seen the last of Morton.

On the following Thursday, despite her misgivings and uncertainties, Randolph did come to dinner, and did stay the night. It seemed inevitable. During the evening as they sat opposite one another in the candle light, as she tried to remind herself of all the reasons why she should not do it, she knew they were being drawn closer and closer – the looks between them grew more and more intense, the silences longer and longer. And when they were on the sofa supposedly drinking coffee, all she could be aware of was his presence beside her, his masculine presence, that faint smell of him she remembered from before, from that afternoon in the Goat, she remembered it so clearly. Now here he was again, his face nearer and nearer; all pretence that she was in charge of the situation had flown out of the window, she was helpless as he took her in his arms to kiss her, and she was straining up to him, returning his kiss. . .

Was she falling in love with him? When he saw her naked in bed for the first time his admiration was so apparent, he approached her so reverently, touched her, explored her so tenderly; the heart was tight in her throat as he took her in his arms, yielding to him with what seemed a sigh of relief that she didn't have to fight him any more, or plan or scheme, but could just let him do with her what he would.

That night she had a dream. She was on a ship and was sailing over the ocean to Madeira, a beautiful mountainous island covered all over with tropical vegetation. As the ship approached this island, she saw the natives run down the beach to their canoes and paddle energetically out to the ship as it dropped anchor in the bay and, as she stood at the rail, she could see in the foremost canoe, standing and stretching his arms to her, Nick, with garlands of flowers round his neck. Then she was stepping into the boat, he was twining the garlands round her neck, and somehow the garlands were about them both and bound them to each other, so that they were wreathed together by these brilliantly coloured and sweetly smelling flowers. They were reclining now in the boat as the natives rowed them ashore, singing to them as they rowed, singing to the rhythm of the oars, a song of unbearable sweetness and longing, so that in herself she seemed to melt, yielding to all her longing, reaching her arms about Nick's neck as he smiled above her . . .

As she awoke in the dim light of dawn, her dream melted away, and only that indefinable longing, that fathomless yearning remained in her body as she gradually returned to consciousness and understanding that she would never have Nick now.

In that moment of intuition Abby understood that Nick's wife must have died long ago, but that he had never come to claim her. That he was somewhere off in the world far, far away, and she would never see him again. And coming to clearer and clearer consciousness this terrible sadness grew in her, and she wept in bed in the half light, wept because she would never see Nick again.

As her weeping drew to a close, she remained, as it were at the bottom of a deep well, looking up at the sky high above her, and unable to climb out. Utter despair was closing over her and she was drowning, drowning . . .

She had slept with Randolph Pelham. How could she have fallen so far? She looked back, or tried to, over her life; her dream showed her how far she had gone astray and she was filled with a lethargic, cold bitterness. She glanced across at Randolph asleep. How *could* she? All her plans and her schemes to punish Randolph Pelham – and how could she ever explain to Rory? 'Rory, I have been in bed with Randolph Pelham – *again.*'

She turned over again and drew a long sigh. Oh Nick! she murmured, why did you go away? Ever since you left I've gone all wrong. I don't know where I am, or what I'm doing. First I was Morton's whore, now I've slept with Randolph Pelham. What am I doing? Oh Nick, you're the only one I've ever wanted. Why am I in bed with Randolph Pelham? I'm so confused – why can't you come back and take me away? I gave you William, didn't I? And I'll never see him again. Without you I'm nothing. I feel utterly lost.

The atmosphere between them was strained that morning. She felt nervous – and wondered whether this communicated itself to him. In any case he was evasive, and when he left after breakfast, was vague. For the first time since they had met in London, he was unsure of his plans. He didn't know what he would be doing over the next few days, and there were various matters . . .

'I'll write,' he said as he kissed her briefly, and she was left standing in the hall as he hurried away wondering at the

442

change in him. After her own uncertainty she had been looking to him for reassurance.

The station was crowded as always, strangers hurrying in a bewildering and confusing muddle past each other, each intent on their own journey, their own priority, concentrated, distracted by their own thoughts. The strange loneliness of such a crowded place, she had often noticed it. And in the air, the hissing of steam, the whistles, and distant shouts, all echoing up in the spacious vault overhead. It was an early summer morning, and strong sunlight looked down through the dirty windows. A few stray pigeons fluttered from one beam to the other, as Abby huddled her coat round her, chilly at this early hour. How typical of Fan to arrive at an awkward time. Abby tried to focus her thoughts on her sister; she hadn't seen her since before Da died.

Fan was eighteen now and grown up; marriageable, and with a mind of her own. What were her plans? She would have plans, that was certain. She was a wilful little thing, always had been; selfish too, if the truth were told. As a little girl she had been spoilt by their father. Abby might be 'Little Mother' – very convenient when it came to cooking dinners and washing clothes – but Fan had been Da's little darling, something slightly different.

As the train was coming in she caught the shoulder of a passing porter.

'Follow me,' she said briefly, as she walked forward on to the platform. The train came to a halt, puffing steam, doors were opening, and people spilling out on the platform and hurrying past her, dividing like a river round a rock.

'Fan,' she checked herself. 'Francesca!'

Fan was in a tweed travelling coat – obviously made for the occasion by some provincial dressmaker. She was taller of course, very pretty, and wore a flowery hat over hair which was piled up behind her head. Even in that split second, Abby thought, quite the little lady.

443

'Oh Abigail! There you are. Listen, I cannot find a porter anywhere. Will you be an angel and find one for me – my box is in the luggage van.'

'I found one,' Abby said dryly. 'Well, aren't you going to give your big sister a hug?'

'Oh, yes, of course.' She turned to the porter. 'It is a blue trunk, clearly labelled O'Leary.' She turned back to Abby as the porter went off. 'Oh don't crush me!' She stood back after this perfunctory hug. 'How are you, Abigail?'

'How do I seem? You look very well.'

'I don't know about that.' She reached her hand to adjust the back of her hair. 'Is my hat on straight? It's impossible to care for one's appearance after such a journey. I'm sure I look a perfect haystack. I've had the most trying time; the journey was a nightmare. I nearly lost my trunk in Liverpool. The porters were most ungrateful.' Her old Mayo accent had been refined to a genteel tone.

'Glad to be done with school, eh?' Abby said breezily.

'Oh! Don't mention it!' Fan looked round for the porter as they still stood on the platform. 'I've had quite enough of *that*! I assure you I never want to see another nun as long as I live.'

Abby made a small grimace but said nothing. The porter now appeared with her box. Fan started forward. 'Be careful!'

When they were outside the station, and Blake was at last able to get the carriage close to the kerb among the confusion of the other carriages and hansoms, their horses clattering on the cobbles, even Fan couldn't restrain her astonishment. 'You never have your own carriage, Abigail?' Abby smiled, and Fan was covered with confusion as Blake lowered the step and helped her up.

As the carriage pulled away, Abby took Fan's hand, and kissed her on the cheek. 'I'm really glad to see you; it's been such a long time. And we're going to do everything to make you enjoy yourself while you're here. And we've got to talk about your future. Have you any idea what you want to do now – Francesca?' Abby asked tentatively.

'Well, I shall stay with you for a while, I think, then decide. There's no question of going back to Mayo. The very thought!' Fan's attention was caught by something she had glimpsed through the carriage window. They were driving at this moment up the carriageway beside Regent's Park, and the elegant façades of Nash's terraces gleamed white in the morning sun. 'Who lives here?' she said after a moment.

'I don't know – various people, I suppose,' said Abby vaguely.

'It looks like a palace.'

'No. They're private houses.'

'*Private houses*? You mean, ordinary families?'

Abby shrugged. 'I don't know how ordinary they are. But families, yes.'

Fan was silent as she continued to stare at the colonnaded façades, the urns, and classical motifs, the occasional servant glimpsed at a door.

As the carriage pulled up outside the house, and Fan stepped down, she looked up in frank amazement. 'This is your house?'

Abby nodded. 'Come on in.'

The door opened as they reached it, and Fan turned to Abby again in surprise. Abby took her arm, and they went in together. Thady was waiting, and was at his most butler-like. He helped them out of their coats.

'Darling, this is O'Farrell the butler. O'Farrell, this is my sister Francesca.'

Thady bowed gravely as Fan was gaping about her at the spacious stairwell, the elegant wrought iron balustrade, the gleaming white walls, the paintings, the chandelier hanging above them. 'A gentleman is waiting for you, me lady. In the drawing room. I told him I didn't know when you were returning . . .'

'Who is it?' Abby whispered as he helped her off with her coat.

445

'Mr O'Toole, me lady.'

Abby took Fan's arm, and led her towards the drawing room. Fan turned once to glance back at Thady who was disappearing through a door.

'A *butler*?' she mouthed.

O'Toole was waiting. He was dressed in his best parliamentary coat, looking spruce and neat. She advanced towards him at once, and shook his hand, then before he had time to say anything, she turned to introduce her sister. 'She has come to stay for a while.' Fan curtsied prettily. 'Mr O'Toole is our MP, Fan – Francesca. He has very kindly interested himself in Rory's case. Won't you sit down, Mr O'Toole? And let me offer you a cup of coffee.' She moved to the bell pull by the fireplace.

O'Toole did not sit down. 'I may have good news, Mrs Moncrieffe.'

'About my brother?' Abby said.

He nodded and took from his pocket a letter. 'This came from the Home Secretary this morning.' He handed it to Abby.

Her eye skimmed down the letter, which was quite short. The Home Secretary had been in conference with the PM, who was minded in the near future to reconsider the cases of certain Irish prisoners currently serving sentences in English prisons. 'I must go down and see him.' Fan snatched the letter from her hand and read it.

Mr O'Toole was watching her with a sympathetic face. She reached for his hand and gave it a squeeze. 'Thank you for coming to tell me yourself. It's wonderful news.'

There was a silence as Fan handed the letter back to O'Toole but he offered it to Abby again. 'You may keep it if you wish.' She took it gratefully. 'I knew it was worth while to keep up the pressure on the Home Secretary,' he went on. 'The unrest in Ireland has caused the government enormous embarrassment in England. After the years of coercion, the PM is bound to wish to make some conciliatory gesture towards the Irish, perhaps in the not so distant future, and releasing prisoners is always popular. In which case your brother will stand a good chance. His case being of a political nature.'

'Political?' Abby murmured thoughtfully.

'Obviously, Mr O'Leary was gravely provoked by your eviction from the farm. I made this point very forcibly in my letter to the Home Secretary. And at a time when Irish politics are so strongly affected by the agricultural question—'

Fan was staring hard at Abby, and Abby could feel it. She reached for Fan's hand and held it firmly. 'We're very grateful for everything you have done for our brother, aren't we, Francesca?'

'Very.'

'Especially as you must be so busy. We are very conscious of the other calls on your time.'

He relaxed a little and smiled. 'Fortunately at this time of the year, things are winding down for the summer recess. One is able to relax slightly.'

It was on this note, that soon afterwards as he was about to take his leave, Abby said, 'Mr O'Toole, would you do us the honour of dining with us one day soon? Next week perhaps?'

He looked genuinely pleased. 'I should be delighted.'

'Is there any day that would be especially convenient?'

He brought out a pocket diary. 'Wednesday would suit.'

'Wednesday it shall be. We shall look forward to it, shan't we Francesca?'

But as soon as the door was closed behind him Fan turned on Abby. 'I don't think you needed to remind Mr O'Toole we have a brother in gaol, Abigail.'

'You don't understand! He's been very sympathetic to Rory's case. He always was, right from the trial. And think Fan – Rory might be released soon!'

Fan scowled. '*Francesca*! And he can stay there for all I care. Do you tell all your friends about him?'

'Of course not.'

447

'I'm sure.'

'Come on, I'll show you the house!' Abby tried to cheer them both up. 'It'll be fun having Mr O'Toole here, won't it?'

Fan was shown into her room. Her box had already been brought up and was standing at the foot of her bed.

'Robbins will put away your things. And she will bring you your hot water in the morning. Will seven be convenient?'

'Convenient? *Convenient*?' Fan's mood could turn on a pinhead, and she now pirouetted about the room, and struck a lady-like pose and a sort of English accent. 'Eau yes! Thet will be maust convenient! Abby, it's wonderful! I'm sorry I said those things about Rory. And to think – an MP is coming to dine with us! It's paradise!'

Abby rang the bell and when the servant arrived she introduced Fan. 'You can call Robbins when you need help dressing.'

'Help dressing?'

'For special occasions, you know. I expect you can do up your dresses most of the time.'

'Help me dress?' Fan was almost in a trance. And as the maid went out, she threw her arms round Abby's neck. 'Oh Abby isn't it wonderful to be rich! I never want to be poor again! And all thanks to Mr Moncrieffe!' She looked round breathless with awe. 'You must go down on your knees every night to give thanks to him!' She knelt in mock prayer by the bedside. 'Oh Mr Moncrieffe, wherever you are, and I am sure you went straight to heaven, how can we ever thank you.'

Later it occurred to Abby how very fortunate Fan's arrival had been in one respect. At last she had been able to invite Mr O'Toole to dinner with perfect propriety. Now she had a chaperone.

As they came downstairs again, Fan was still in ecstasies. 'Our MP coming to dinner! Only imagine!' Her mouth hung frankly open in amazement. 'And to have our

448

own butler, and our own carriage. Abigail, it's heaven! What would Susan Gilhooley say if she knew – I only have to ring and the butler appears! And Abigail, you have an English accent, I mean – no one would ever know—'

'Well ring now, and we'll have some lunch. And after lunch we'll go out.'

'I'm dying to see London!'

Abby beamed. 'By the way, Francesca, you'll remember I'm known here as Hester. It'd be best if you called me that too. In front of others, anyway. You don't mind? I'm used to it now.'

That afternoon, the two sisters went shopping. There were no doubt many interesting and important sights to see in London, and many wonderful places to visit, but the shops came first.

As they walked arm in arm down Regent Street, Fan's eyes stood out, and she constantly stopped to point at some gown or coat or hat in the window.

'We can get you some things. Would you like that?'

'How can you ask?'

'I have a very good dressmaker, and she can make you up a few gowns. I'll drop her a note.'

'A *dressmaker*?' Fan's cup had finally run over, and she stopped in the street, her eyes filled with tears. 'Abby, I've never been so happy in my life. It's simply paradise.'

Chapter Forty-five

She had never been more nervous of anything as she was that night. Mr O'Toole was expected at eight. Of course she had entertained other men: she had entertained Nick, she had entertained Morton and his louche companions; Randolph had been in her house, and in her bed. This had been her life hitherto; irregular was perhaps the kindest term for it.

Mr O'Toole knew nothing of this. Like her family he had been told about the late Mr Moncrieffe and the marriage, of how Abby had risen from stable girl to fine lady in one leap. Mr O'Toole must never know the truth. This was why she was so nervous.

Because Mr O'Toole was different. He represented things she had never had in her life: open honest dignity; he was a man who stood four-square in the world; he had principles; people depended on him, distressed farmers wrote him letters; he took up matters with the prime minister. Besides this, there was another thought that she did not allow to press too far forward in her mind – it smacked too much of calculation, and she detested calculation. But just sometimes she wondered to herself, vaguely, whether Mr O'Toole might be a lifeline, an escape route for her to respectability, a chance for her to put her past behind her . . .

She spent the previous day fussing with the cook over the details of the menu: the *foie gras*, the asparagus, the salad of sorrel, which she remembered from a dinner in Paris with Nick, served after the soles *à la Normandie*. It was too late in the season for game; she dithered over *poulet aux cressons*, or a *canard pressé*? Or would he prefer meat? Perhaps a veal *à la daube* to follow? Or cutlets? Then there was the question of desserts . . .

'How are your soufflés, Mrs Baker?'

'As good as anyone's, ma'am,' said that lady confidently.

'Perhaps a meringue as well?' Abby was turning over a cookery book. 'What about a compôte of oranges?'

Mrs Baker looked dubious. 'Oranges are not at their best just now, madam.'

Abby flicked through the book more nervously. 'None of these look very exciting – charlotte russe, cabinet pudding, blancmange – oh, I need something more interesting than this, more – somehow *different*!'

In her dressing room, as Taylor dressed her hair, teasing the fringe, and setting the heavy coils of her shining black hair against the nape of her neck, so that her neck and shoulders were revealed freely, she adjusted the diamond necklace to her satisfaction (the diamond necklace had been bought with Morton's money), drawing on her long evening gloves, slipping her feet into the embroidered evening slippers. With all her preparations, she was still extremely nervous.

Fortunately she had Fan as chaperone; everything would be pleasant and she would not feel under pressure. Briefly, as she was about to go downstairs to inspect the dinner table, she stood in her bedroom, looking down at her bed, and was suddenly thoughtful. Mr O'Toole was undoubtedly a once-for-a-lifetime man, the antithesis of someone like Morton – or Pelham. He was the real thing, proper, upright, the genuine article, it was obvious. She bit her lip. Lucky girl, whoever got him, she thought, and turned away.

She looked into Fan's bedroom. The little features were

451

turned up in annoyance, as Robbins attempted to set her hair in place. 'Oh Abigail, this girl's useless! Look at me!'

Robbins turned a harassed face to her mistress as Abby came in and inspected her sister in the glass. 'You look very pretty, and your hair is lovely. I always envied your hair – you were the only girl in the village with blonde hair—'

'Oh don't talk such stuff! Look at these curls!'

Abby turned to Robbins. 'What happened?'

'Oh miss,' Robbins turned half away whispering. 'Miss Francesca set them in papers last night but they got a bit mussed up.'

'*Mussed up*! That's only her excuse!'

'Well, why don't you scrape the hair back, and pin it up with a fringe – that's the style now – curls went out years ago in London, Fan dear.' Abby smiled sweetly at her sister in the glass, as she sat hunched forward in her new pink gown. 'And the gown looks perfect on you.'

The storm clouds lightened. 'Do you think so?'

'Certainly. Stand up and turn round.' Fan pirouetted across the room. 'Hangs very nicely on you, love. Now sit down, and Robbins will put your hair up. Wait—' She ran back to her own room and fished in her jewel box for a tiara set with pearls – not the gruesome thing of glass Thady had bought years ago, but a really expensive and beautifully made one.

This'll cheer her up, she thought, and handed it to Robbins. 'And here –' a gold necklace with a white sapphire pendant (a gift from Nick).

The effect was more than satisfactory; Fan was in ecstasies. 'Abby, they're wonderful! Wherever did you get them?' She raised her hands in mock prayer. 'Oh Mr Moncrieffe, however can I thank you!'

'Now, I must get down to see about the dinner. Hurry up, Mr O'Toole will be here at any moment.'

The table was set, and she went round adjusting minutely the relation of knife and fork and spoon, the champagne in its bucket, the claret decanted on the sideboard. There was a distant sound of the doorbell, and she took a deep breath, and cast a last quick glance in the mirror.

Thady was at the door in white gloves, and she was advancing across the wide hallway to greet Mr O'Toole, the fullness of her gown taken up in one hand.

How handsome he looked. There was something – what was the phrase? – clean cut, about him; his hair was neat, his features firm, his skin clear, his eyes bright, and he had a pleasing smile – perhaps just a shade hesitant? A little shy? Her heart was beating. Before she could speak, however – 'Mr O'Toole!' Abby looked back. Fan had appeared at the top of the stairs, descended graciously, advanced across the chequered floor and held out her hand. 'I am so glad you were able to be with us.'

Abby turned in amazement at her sister's complete assurance. Fan was really looking quite lovely; Robbins had managed to do a last-minute job quite satisfactorily on her hair, and the pearl tiara set it off very well. Fan had a neat slim figure, and the sapphire pendant dangling above her pretty young breasts drew attention to them in a very happy fashion. Abby was almost non-plussed for the moment. However she adjusted, and led them into the drawing room. O'Toole glanced about him as she asked, 'Sherry?'

'Thank you.'

A decanter had been set on a silver tray on a side table, and she poured three glasses. She was handing them about and was about to speak when again Fan began, 'Oh Mr O'Toole you cannot imagine how delighted we are you have been able to come tonight.'

'Oh, as a matter of fact,' he gave a small awkward laugh. 'My dear Miss O'Leary – and Mrs Moncrieffe – you have rescued me from a very dull evening in my rooms.'

'I always imagine you fearfully busy,' Abby waved him to a chair, and they sat. 'Sitting till two or three in the morning, and with so many committees to attend. Then I

453

imagine you must often have to travel back and forth from Ireland.'

He nodded without replying, and she raised her glass. 'To Home Rule.'

He raised his glass and, after taking a small sip, glanced round. 'Are we – I mean – are we awaiting other guests?'

She shook her head with a smile. 'I hope you don't mind – it's just us three tonight; will that be convenient?'

'Convenient?' He echoed. 'I feel honoured. I hope I may be able to do justice to the occasion.'

'Why should you not?'

'Oh Mr O'Toole,' Fan burst through this rather stilted conversation, 'you will never guess, we were at the opera last night – to see *Lucia di Lammermoor*. It was wonderful – have you seen it?'

'No, I—'

'Oh you must go! I could go to the opera every night! The settings, the music, the acting, the singing – it was simply perfect. And Madame Patti is quite marvellous – she sang Lucia, you know. Oh it is the most affecting story; I cried buckets, I declare, so did everybody. Really, we were weeping out loud weren't we, Abigail – Hester, I should say – you could hardly hear the singing for the sobbing in the audience!'

O'Toole burst into laughter.

'And the music is quite ravishing! Do you like music Mr O'Toole, I declare I adore it. I am so glad I learned to play—'

Abby turned at this. Fan hadn't opened the piano since the day she arrived.

'It is so nice when one has guests, to be able to entertain them – and when one is alone too, it is so pleasant to be able to soothe oneself and smooth away one's cares. I should think every wife ought to play, do not you?'

'Oh – certainly.'

'I do, I know. What can be nicer when a man returns from his work – when he has passed a hard day grappling with his business affairs – or as it might be, a man like yourself, Mr O'Toole, who has been attending to important matters of state – to be able to come home to a loving wife, and for her to soothe away your troubles and worries by the gentle touch of her fingers on the keyboard. Would you like me to play for you after dinner?'

'I should like it very much.'

Abby was amused by Fan's ready prattle, the flow of her chat; relieved too that it had broken the ice, and helped Mr O'Toole to unwind in a way she herself hadn't anticipated.

Soon afterwards she suggested they go into dinner, and they took their places at one end of the long table. A candelabrum stood on the polished mahogany, and the silver glinted in its flickering light; a decanter of claret waited on the sideboard and, in the meantime, in an ice bucket there was also a bottle of champagne. Everything was as she had arranged it.

'May I ask you to do the honours?'

O'Toole opened the champagne bottle. 'It is a long time since I drank champagne,' he murmured. 'I am afraid I do not have much of a head for wine.' He glanced at the label. 'It is a terrible confession to make when I am offered such choice wines as yours.'

'I assure you I could not agree more. I drink very little myself. Still –' Abby smiled awkwardly – 'it is nice to be convivial once in a while, all the same. In your profession I think you are entitled to unwind every so often. Let the cares slide from your back?'

'Do you not drink champagne, Mr O'Toole?' Fan burst in again. 'Neither do I, if the truth were told. I am afraid it will go straight to my head, and then I shall say all sorts of foolish things, I am sure! I do hope neither of us will be betrayed into an indiscretion!' She gave him a huge conspiratorial grin, and he could not help responding.

Abby raised her glass. 'Here's to you, Mr O'Toole.'

They drank. 'You know, ladies, before we go any further, you really must call me J.J. All my friends do.'

'Here's to you, J.J.,' said Fan. Thady was now hovering

about the table, and as Robbins brought in the *foie gras* on a silver tray, he took the plates and with butler-like condescension, set them out on the table. 'Do tell us about yourself, J.J.,' Fan went on. 'We'd be fascinated to hear, wouldn't we, Hester?'

Abby smiled; she was extremely relieved that Fan had taken the weight of the evening as it were, off her shoulders. She herself had not really known how to approach a man like Mr O'Toole, and here was her younger sister fresh from the convent prattling artlessly, and charming the man without any effort at all.

'My family?' J.J. raised his eyebrows. 'It is not something I ever talk about. The fact is, I have not spoken to my father in years.'

'Oh how sad. Do tell us, J.J. – I am dying to know all about you.'

Abby frowned and touched her sister's foot under the table. Fan did not notice.

J.J. paused, as if making a decision, and went on, 'My father owns fifteen hundred acres of Mayo and I have been familiar with our tenants since my childhood. They were all around me. He is not a good landlord. He hates and despises the tenants, and has never had a shred of sympathy for them. I am an only son; my mother died when I was quite small so I was brought up by a housekeeper, a Scottish lady. My father does not employ Irish servants, if he can help it. It sounds disrespectful of me to say this, I know, but the fact is he is a cold, distant man. Already by the time I was fourteen or fifteen, I was able to see him for what he was, a tyrant – to me and to them. I think my sympathy for the tenants derives from that. I naturally identified with them against my father.'

'You must have been very lonely, having no mother, and your father being so distant?' Abby said sympathetically.

He shrugged. 'It made me want to make my own way in life – and not to be dependent on him, if I could help it. It made me work very hard, at school, and then at the bar.'

456

'You must have made friends?'

'Not many,' he said after a moment. 'Of course I have dozens of colleagues in the movement, and my life is crowded. I am surrounded by people every day, but friends – that is another matter. Perhaps it is as you say – having no women in my family, no sisters, no mother – I am not boasting of this, Mrs Moncrieffe. I believe I am only speaking out on account of the champagne – which by the way, is very good, as is the *foie gras*. You are doing me proud tonight. I can hear myself unwinding most indiscreetly, boring you with my private affairs—'

'Not boring at all,' murmured Abby.

'Not at all!' cried Fan, 'it is really most interesting, I do assure you!'

'You are kind.' He drew a long breath, leaned back in his chair and looked about him. 'This is very nice, really very nice. I have endured some dull dinners in my time, in Kensington and elsewhere, some glacial dinners, if you follow me. And I have heard many a flunky snigger behind my chair when he heard my accent too. I have made more than my fair share of small talk – but with you tonight, I feel I can say anything.' He laughed. 'And I am saying anything! You must put it down to the champagne.'

'Please don't say that! What you tell us is most interesting. I am so sorry you never knew your mother. That is a terrible loss,' Abby hesitated, and repeated thoughtfully, 'never to know your mother; I do sympathise. And to have no sisters either. You have had to make your way with no support from anyone.'

'No sisters, J.J.!' cried Fan, 'that is very sad. I cannot tell you how grateful I am to Abby – Hester. She has been so kind to me, more like a mother than a sister.'

She leaned forward over the table as she gave Abby a great smile.

'You are fortunate to have each other,' he said quietly after a moment.

Abby was suddenly reminded of her duties. 'O'Farrell,

you may remove the plates,' she murmured.

'Very well, me lady.' Thady, so stiff with dignity he could hardly move, took up the plates, handing them to Taylor who piled them on a silver tray, and carried them out.

The asparagus soup was served. Then the cutlets were brought in.

'Where are the soles?' she whispered to Thady.

'Soles, me lady?'

'The fish course, you remember?'

'The fish, me lady?'

Abby glanced across at J.J. 'Do excuse me a moment.' She rose from the table and hurried out of the room. Thady followed.

'You know perfectly well the fish comes after the soup.'

'There's been an accident with the fish, me lady,' whispered Thady.

'And stop calling me "me lady". It sounds ridiculous! What accident?'

'Abby, me lady.'

'What do you mean, Abby?'

'The cat, me lady.'

'*The cat*?'

'The kitchen cat.'

'Since when have we had a kitchen cat?'

'Months now, I forget when. 'Tis very useful, me lady – to keep down the mice.'

'O'Farrell,' she narrowed her eyes, 'are you telling me that the cat got the fish?'

'Yes, me lady.' Thady looked down in embarrassment.

This conversation was going on in whispers in the hall. At that moment she heard a peal of Fan's laughter and J.J. joining in. Thank God, she's keeping him entertained, Abby thought.

'Why wasn't I told before?'

'I only just found out this minute.'

She drew a breath, and muttered, 'Very well, you may

458

continue to serve the cutlets.' She was about to turn away. 'Why is the cat called Abby?'

Thady looked down lugubriously. 'I only wanted a little Abby of me own to care for, me lady.'

She gave him a look, took a deep breath, straightened her dress, and entered the dining room graciously. 'So sorry to keep you waiting. I think we'll go straight on to the cutlets. There's been an accident with the fish. O'Farrell, the claret.'

'Very well, me lady,' Thady intoned at his most solemn, and poured the wine.

Later, as they took their coffee in the drawing room, J.J. glanced several times towards the piano, and at last turned to Fan. 'I wonder if I might prevail upon you, Miss Francesca?'

She beamed him a smile. 'It would be a pleasure, J.J. But you will have to turn the pages for me. Will you do that?'

He seemed only too willing. Fan opened her piano book, which just happened to lie ready on the instrument, and set it up before the keyboard. Then glancing up again, as J.J. positioned himself behind her shoulder, she began to play. There was nothing remarkable about her performance; she did not hit any wrong notes; on the other hand the piece was undemanding. It was pretty, it was easy to listen to, it was perfectly suited to after-dinner entertainment. The sort of thing practised precisely for these moments. J.J. knew his part too, leaning forward reverently to turn the pages for her.

Abby sat and watched the two of them. Fan in her juvenile way, had been a real friend to her tonight. All through the evening Fan had made an effort to keep the atmosphere light, always ready with some bantering conversation, some light silly chatter, exactly suited to lighten the mood. J.J. was such a serious man; Abby hoped he would remember this evening at her house, as her guest, as a welcome diversion from his work. And Abby was particularly pleased that he didn't condescend to Fan, that he responded to her childish prattle with genuine interest. It was very good of him, a man who had conferred with prime ministers – a man who must have spoken to Gladstone scores of times – taking the greatest pains to be nice to her little sister. Abby was very pleased. The ice had been broken perfectly, and no doubt there would be many occasions in the future, many opportunities for their friendship to ripen.

Chapter Forty-six

The following morning Abby woke feeling cheerful. She looked into her sister's bedroom as she went down to see to the horses. Fan was fast asleep, her clothes thrown about the room, and Abby stood looking down at her for a moment, feeling an almost maternal affection and protectiveness, and kissed her gently on the forehead as she went out.

A few days later, Abby was alone at breakfast. She did not normally expect Fan to appear at this hour; her sister was young, and would probably sleep awhile yet. And, especially on a day when they were intending to go out in the evening, Fan would be in no hurry to get up. Abby herself was exalted with a sense of pleasurable anticipation, mixed with not a little nervousness; tonight she would be seeing Mr O'Toole again, and it would be her privilege to invite him to share her box at the opera. She pictured him in her mind's eye, handsome, distinguished in evening dress; eyes would turn up to the box – he would be noticed – who is that young man? they would whisper. Oh that is Mr O'Toole, you know, the Member of Parliament. She wondered whether he liked music? There was so much she did not know about him, so much to find out. She gave a small delicious shiver and turned her attention to her breakfast.

What a relief, too, that she had heard nothing from Randolph Pelham. Having Fan in the house had revealed to her the depth of her own folly; if her sister were ever to get wind of what had been going on between them ... if Fan were to find out about Newmarket, if she knew that Randolph had been here, in Abby's house, in her bed. The idea made her cold; she could see clearly now how far she had gone astray at Newmarket, and afterwards. She had better write this morning; she should have written before.

She steadied herself, and turned to her breakfast. As she sipped her coffee, she picked up the morning correspondence which Robbins had set beside her plate and looked through it casually. Among the various letters was one in a hand she did not recognize, on a thick and expensive paper and bearing a London postmark. She opened and read it.

27 Queen's Gate. SW

Mrs Moncrieffe,

You do not know me, and I do not know you, but your name has been mentioned to me in connection with Mr Randolph Pelham. I have no idea what is going on between you, but I think it best that whatever it is, it should cease at once. It is only fair to inform you that Mr Pelham is engaged and will shortly be married to

yours faithfully,

M. Thorpe

Engaged? Randolph engaged to Marianne? Shortly to be married? But then – still she struggled to order her thoughts – but then what had he been doing with herself? Why had he followed her to Newmarket? Why had he said all those things to her, those intimate, seductive things ... Why had he taken her to bed? She turned, rising from the table, crossing to the window, seeing nothing as she struggled to take it in. Randolph? Was it possible he had been deceiving her all this time? The letter was postmarked the previous day: *yesterday* Marianne had believed Randolph to be

462

engaged to her. She sat again in her chair and rested her head on her hands – there could be no mistake.

At last her head began to cool and she felt more calm. She sat up straight and took a deep breath: well, there was no need to be surprised after all. She sipped her coffee, and started on her breakfast. The letter required an answer. And that shouldn't be difficult.

But as her carriage clipped through the park on its way to Kensington, the significance of the letter grew in her and her calm determination gradually swelled into a monstrous anger. She sat, her hands folded on her lap, attempting to control her breathing, to set her thoughts in order. The interview need not take very long.

The carriage turned down from the park into the broad tree lined boulevard with its high white fronted terrace of aristocratic residences. Blake pulled up a little short of number twenty seven. Abby got out, and walked down the street on the other side of the road.

There was nothing to be seen. It was a house – just like any other. She was about to cross the road when a carriage turned the corner further along, came up and stopped outside the door, and as Abby stood beneath the trees on the pavement opposite, Marianne Thorpe and her mother issued forth from the house and into the carriage, the coachman clicked the horses into motion, and in a moment they were off. Abby hurried back to her own carriage. 'Follow them.'

The two carriages made their way up to Kensington Gore, past the Albert Hall, and turned into the park, clipping through it and over the bridge. The park was looking lovely now that the trees were in full leaf. But they continued to the other side, turned along the Bayswater road, and eventually found themselves outside Whiteley's department store.

'A morning's shopping,' Abby thought as she got down in time to watch the two women go inside. 'Come back in an hour, Blake, please,' as she hurried after them.

Whiteley's was the largest and most elegant shop in London, a long imposing frontage. Marble columns heralded the way in, huge bronze doors were opened by uniformed men, chosen for their height and imposing bearing, ensuring that no undesirable elements might stray inside. Abby was in time to catch sight of the two women as they were seated examining gloves, and she was able to study them at her leisure. They were both very much as she remembered them and Abby stood for some time watching them as thoughts and memories passed through her mind. Her anger had subsided, and a doubt arose. Was this after all the right thing to do? Marianne Thorpe was about to get married. Was Abby really intending to ruin that; the girl was harmless enough – why should she be sent back to Ireland in tears?

At that moment, it appeared a small contretemps had arisen between the two women; Abby caught words hissed in vexation; a tone of annoyance. Marianne stood up, speaking in a low angry voice to her mother who was looking up at her with a frown.

Pre-wedding nerves? Most likely. A pair of gloves was not much to get worked up over. Marianne turned abruptly and her eyes were fully on Abby but she wasn't seeing her; thoughts were obviously hurrying through her mind, and a moment later her mother rose, and embraced her daughter, and there appeared to be a reconciliation. Marianne sniffed, and dabbed at her nose with a tiny handkerchief. They moved on, arm in arm.

Of course Marianne had always been something of a spoiled darling; it was inevitable there would be spats between her and her mother from time to time. Especially at this time. Abby followed them from room to room. They went upstairs and were a long time inspecting beds, prodding them, sitting on them. Abby watched with a sinking heart, and a streak of bitterness rose in her. Marianne Thorpe was choosing the bed in which she and Randolph Pelham would disport themselves. The bed in which she would conceive his child; which symbolized a long and fruitful life – a life of

464

happiness and fulfilment for Marianne and Randolph. At this thought her bitterness overwhelmed her and she had to turn away for a moment to get a grip on herself. Her dear brother was in Portland Prison, and Marianne Thorpe was choosing the bed in which she would share the delights of love with the man who had put him there.

Eventually she was able to get her feelings under control again, still watching them. She took a deep breath. She must not rush into anything, do nothing in a hurry. Then she saw the mother saying something, and go off – probably to the ladies' room. Abby drew a deep breath and approached as if inspecting beds herself. Marianne was sitting on a chair staring into space. Abby strolled past her, then looked down. 'Miss Marianne Thorpe?'

Marianne looked up. 'Yes?'

'I wonder whether you'll remember me?' Abby couldn't help smiling now as she looked into the familiar face.

'I don't think so,' Marianne said doubtfully.

'And yet I remember you so well. I remember you in your bottle green riding habit, Marianne; you looked so pretty. Riding on Cannonball – surely you remember?'

Marianne was looking extremely puzzled. 'I beg your pardon – I don't think I've had the pleasure.'

Abby couldn't help bursting into laughter. 'Oh Marianne – you can't imagine – it's such a pleasure to see you again! Surely you recognise me?'

Marianne was staring at her, but it was clear she still didn't recognize Abby.

'Abby O'Leary!' Abby burst out, spreading her arms. 'Your Abby, that used to ride with you – and you flying like the wind – up to the monument and back – and to think you should be here. You're looking so well!'

Marianne stood up, still gaping, and at last recognition dawned. 'Abby O'Leary? You can't be.' She drew herself in and rescued her dignity, somewhat dispersed by her amazement. 'It really is – Abby O'Leary. I remember now. You were sacked.'

'It was the saddest day of my life. Oh Marianne—' Abby tried to take her hands, but Marianne pulled them away.

'You were sacked,' Marianne went on, colder now as she regained control of herself, 'and afterwards I found out why.' Abby looked uncomfortable, her exuberance checked. 'I found out why you were sacked, O'Leary,' Marianne got into her stride. 'I must say, you have a nerve to address me at all. You wormed your way into our house under false pretences.'

'What?'

'You were nothing but a low common harlot! My father took you in and gave you everything. And all the time you were hiding your shame. You knew he had a soft heart and you hoped he would excuse you and shelter you, no doubt.'

'But how did—'

'Oh everyone knew it, after you were gone!' She was contemptuous. 'It was common gossip among the servants, and didn't take long before everyone else knew too. We were well rid of you. My God, you have a fine nerve to speak to me! Who on earth do you think you are?' Marianne looked her over. 'And I wonder what you're doing in London now? You seem well enough turned out. Though on second thoughts it is easy to guess. Good day to you.'

'Marianne – don't be so hasty! There's something I have to tell you. Wait!'

'I really don't want to speak to you. You deceived me. Good bye.'

'Marianne, you don't understand!' Abby followed her. 'You must hear me, it's very important! You must hear me!'

'I do *not* wish to hear you.' Marianne turned on her, cold, haughty. 'I understand well enough, and looking back, one should not have been surprised. I was only sorry for papa who was so cruelly misled.' Her mother reappeared at this moment. Marianne took her arm, and firmly directed her into the adjoining room. Abby stood

466

staring after her, white with shock. A moment later, Mrs Thorpe reappeared briefly in the doorway looked her over and turned back.

Abby wandered slowly through the shop. She was quivering; Marianne's coldness, her open hostility, had come as such a surprise – and yet, as minutes passed, and she tried to control herself, and think it out, it was inevitable.

In her carriage, her head sunk on her breast, she felt bruised and shrunken; cold and tired. It was the nastiest few minutes she could remember. How could any woman behave like that to another? Did the girl have no imagination? Could she not conceive any situation in which she might find herself in such a plight? By the time Abby reached her own home her mood had settled into anger and bitterness and she could feel a headache coming on; what a fool she was! Always ready to find excuses for the likes of Randolph and Marianne, to see their best side. Not any more.

It occurred to her she only had to write a letter to Marianne setting out what had been going on between herself and Randolph and there would be no wedding. Perhaps she should write the letter before the bed was bought? she thought bitterly.

The result of this day's work was that the headache grew worse, and by four o'clock, she could scarcely stand upright. She was forced to go to bed, and was lying in her darkened room as she heard the usual clatter, the exclamations and petulant rebukes, from across the landing as Fan was being dressed by the long-suffering Robbins.

Eventually Fan was at Abby's door. 'Aren't you getting ready?'

Even turning her head on the pillow sent a shiver of pain up through Abby's neck. She opened her eyes for a second to see Fan arrayed in her finery.

'Abby! Come on! Why are you lying there? Mr O'Toole will be here soon! Hurry up!'

467

Abby had closed her eyes again, but at last she made a supreme effort and attempted to sit up. It made her dizzy and the throbbing in her head was a million times worse, as if her brain were bulging and about to split her skull open. She fell back with a groan.

'For heaven's sake, what's the matter with you? Hurry up, Abby!' There was no reply and Fan came to her bedside. 'Are you ill?'

Abby turned her head slightly on the pillow again. 'In my reticule—' she gestured towards her dressing table — 'you'll find the ticket,' she whispered. 'You'll have to go without me.'

'What, why?'

Abby made a vague gesture. 'Just go without me.'

Fan now understood, and perked up. 'Oh. Very well.' She lost no time fishing for the ivory ticket. 'What shall I tell Mr O'Toole?'

'Just apologise for me, that's all. Enjoy the opera.' Abby murmured, and turned her head away.

'Right! Leave it to me!' Fan bounced out of the bedroom, and downstairs two steps at a time.

The following morning Fan came bursting into her room, and flung herself onto the end of Abby's bed.

'Oh Abby I had the most wonderful time! It was bliss! Utter, utter bliss!'

Abby propped herself up. The headache was gone, but though she had had a good night's sleep, she still felt weak. 'What did you see?'

'*Il Trovatore*. It was so sad! Manrico was the gypsy's son – only he wasn't really – because the babies had been separated at birth. He was really the Count of Luna's brother, only they didn't know it! And they were both in love with the same woman, only she loved Manrico – he was so handsome – and hated the other brother, the Count of Luna – but then the Count of Luna captured Manrico's mother – except that she wasn't his mother – and

468

condemned her to be burned at the stake—'

Abby laughed. 'All right! I think I get the idea.'

Fan rolled over, pulling a pillow on top of her. 'It was wonderful,' she murmured.

'It sounds it. How did J.J. like it?'

Fan cooled a little. 'Oh Mr O'Toole quite liked it, you know. I don't know whether opera is really to his taste. He's such a serious man; but he was very polite and brought me back after, very proper you know. Oh that reminds me – what happened to your headache?'

'It's better now.'

Fan glanced round the room. 'It must have been bad; your bed is awfully rumpled.'

A moment later and she had forgotten Abby's headache. 'Oh I do love the opera. I should like to go out every night. Why don't we go out more often, Abby?'

Later as Fan wallowed in her bath, Abby lay in bed remembering her conversation with Marianne the previous day. Now she knew why she hadn't heard from Mr Pelham.

Chapter Forty-seven

On the Tuesday morning she received a letter from Rory. The familiar grey envelope, the familiar post mark, HM Prison Portland, the familiar address: Abby O'Leary, c/o Mrs Moncrieffe.

> Dear Abby,
> Thanks for your letter – it does me good to hear from you, and I don't know how I would have survived these years without you. And I'm glad to hear Fan is with you now; it's good the family is sticking together. Da would be pleased if he knew. You have done well by her, and I hope she is grateful for everything you have done for her.
> As for the ticket of leave – well, it's all right for Mr O'Toole to talk so cheerful and sure, but I've learned never to expect anything. It's not very likely they're going to let *me* out of gaol! I try to put a brave face on it, but at night it gets me down. I lie here, counting the days, counting the nights more like, staring at the stone wall till I could burn my way out with staring. The thing about prison is you never get used to it. Every day when you look up at the sky, you think of the life going on all around outside, the people walking down the street, going into shops, stopping in the pub for a friendly pint. You think of them going in and out of their houses – the

very thought of it drives me mad – to think they can just walk in and out whenever they like, instead of waiting for the clang of the bell, and the screws shouting 'slops out!', the banging on the door, and the exercise yard, or the quarry, where there's never the sight of a blade of grass. I have this dream, sometimes, I'm with you and Fan just like we used to be when we were children, and we're in the field behind the house, playing in the grass, rolling in it. I can remember the smell of grass and the damp earth, it was so good.

Sorry, sometimes my thoughts run away with me. It comes of being alone so much and nothing to feed on but my thoughts. But I am so grateful to you – without you I really don't know what I would have done. Topped myself long ago, I expect. Men do, in here you know, often. But I have always been able to hold on, because of you.

Take good care of yourself and our little sister,
All my love,

Rory

She read this through with difficulty, as Fan watched from the other side of the table, and only at last wiping her hand across her eyes, handed it across to her sister.

That afternoon she spent mostly in the garden. Since her meeting with Marianne she could not get out of her mind the horrible scene in Whiteley's: how could the girl have been so cruel? Abby had been coming to help Marianne, to warn her, to save her, and instead – she squatted, pulling up weeds in a random, desultory way – instead, the girl was going to marry Randolph Pelham. Well, let him have her – they deserved each other. As for herself, she had been tricked – and worse, because she had really known what she had been letting herself in for. She could have driven her head into a wall. How could she have been so naïve? How? Had she *really* believed a man like him could change? She stared across the garden and felt very stupid.

471

Fan sensed that something was amiss and questioned her, but Abby shrugged and said nothing.

At about five there was a knock at the door. The two sisters were in the drawing room drinking tea and they heard Taylor's footsteps as she crossed the hall and opened the front door. They heard words and a moment later Taylor appeared at the drawing room door.

'It's Mr Pelham, madam.'

Fan's glance shot up and a second later Randolph himself appeared at the drawing room door. Abby did not move. He gave her a broad smile.

'Sorry I haven't – oh sorry,' He took in Fan – 'am I interrupting—'

Trying to control herself, Abby did not look up from the table. 'Francesca my dear, would you be very kind and leave me alone with this man for two minutes? Go up to your room.'

Fan stared between them mesmerized, and then squeezed past him and through the door. The moment the door closed he came quickly to her, and would have taken her in his arms. 'God, how I've missed you. It's been an eternity, but I've had so much to do, I don't seem to have had a moment—' Abby still did not look up, and said nothing. He noticed this and hesitated. 'Hester?'

She looked up now, square in the face, then rose from her chair, crossed to her escritoire and returned a moment later with Marianne's letter. She handed it to him in silence.

It took him a long time to read, as if it were in a foreign language.

'Goodbye, Mr Pelham,' she said lightly.

'No,' he began at last, as if coming out of a trance. 'There's more – I mean, there is unfinished business—'

'Unfinished business? I think you have unfinished business, certainly, as that letter makes clear. I on the other hand, do not. Now that I know who I am dealing with.'

She opened the door and stood with her hand on the handle. 'As I said, goodbye.'

They were still looking at each other in a frozen state,

472

staring into each other's eyes. Then Abby became aware of Fan in the hall behind her listening; she glanced back to her, and gestured to her to get upstairs, out of the way. Fan did not move. Abby closed the door again.

Randolph who had not moved either began at last in a low hoarse voice. 'About the letter—'

He seemed unable to go on. Abby calmly prompted him. 'Is she rich?'

Silence. Randolph was intensely awkward. Abby on the other hand was not; the knowledge that she was in complete control of this conversation calmed her wonderfully. 'Well. Let's try another tack,' she went on in a level tone. 'Do you really love her?'

Silence. 'This is very awkward, Randolph, isn't it? Let me see. How soon are you getting married?'

'Six weeks.'

'At last an answer. Six weeks. And you have been in bed with me so recently.'

Silence.

'Let's try again. Do you love her?'

He shrugged. 'In a way.'

'In a way.' She paused. 'And what am I?'

'You're different.'

'Am I?' She moved away from him a little, considering, clearly sensing her power over him, and careful to tease every nuance of it out. She looked at him shrewdly; he could not meet her gaze. 'How can I trust you?' she went on reasonably. 'How do I know whether to believe you? How do I know there isn't *another* woman to whom you've said all these things – for all I know, there could be an infinite succession of women stretching back over the years – right back to your little village in Ireland – isn't that where you come from? Right back to the first milkmaid you ever seduced? Why should I be any different?'

'Because you are.'

'I can't be so very different if you are about to marry Marianne Thorpe.'

473

He glanced up. 'How did you know her name?'

'It's written there.'

'No. It only says M. Thorpe.'

'Well,' she shrugged. 'I expect someone must have told me. *Randolph*,' she went on with heavy irony, 'does it make any difference?' Silence. 'What did you think you were doing?' she insisted. Silence. 'You must think me a common little whore – like Morton? Though I haven't asked you for money, have I? Not so far.' She paused, and then continued lightly, 'Why do you think that is?'

'I thought you liked me.' He stumbled on, 'It seemed you did.'

'Ah. So you think I have feelings?'

'What are you getting at?'

'I want to know what you're getting at – or up to. I want to know why I should ever speak to you again. In a few seconds I am going to tell you to walk out of that door, Randolph.'

'No!'

'Why not?'

'No! I am not going.'

'Give me a reason why I should not ask you to leave now.'

'Because I love you.'

Silence.

'Are you sure?' she said at last softly.

There was another long silence as they looked at each other, then he said, very softly, 'Try me.'

'You realize what you are saying? You will break off your engagement? For me?'

'Yes. If you'll have me.'

'You scarcely know me.'

'I know you well enough.'

'I don't believe you have thought this through. Have you any money? Why are you marrying Marianne Thorpe? Isn't she rich? You're not thinking, Randolph.'

'I've thought of nothing else.'

474

She was struggling now to stay in charge; could feel the ground again beginning to slip from beneath her feet. The game was going her way, but she *must* stay in control.

'You're right,' he went on. 'I *was* marrying Marianne for her money. But from the moment I met you, I understood what was missing. Marianne's charming and pretty. But you – you're a real woman.'

'Never mind that. Marianne will be a real woman too one day. What were you proposing to live on if you don't marry her?'

Randolph was silent. She had been looking out of the window as she awaited his reply. At last she turned. 'Randolph?' He was staring down, awkward.

'I see,' she murmured. 'You were depending on Marianne, weren't you?' He did not reply.

'You're in debt?' He nodded embarrassed. 'Much?' Again he nodded. 'How much?' she went on, implacable.

'I'd be ruined if I weren't getting married.'

Abby raised her eyebrows. 'Bankruptcy?' He did not reply 'Oh dear Randolph, this is very awkward, isn't it? What are we going to do?' He gave her a weak smile, and suddenly he was like a little boy looking to his mother to get him out of a scrape. They studied one another for a moment, then she went on softly, 'There is another possibility.'

She paused. He waited. She was gazing out of the window, considering her words very carefully. 'You see, Randolph, I may not be as rich as Miss Thorpe – on the other hand I'm not exactly poor, either. And they do say, two can live as cheaply as one . . . though I have no intention of living cheaply.'

'Are you serious?'

'Look around you. Isn't it big enough for two?'

'I should say.'

'Only – there must be no more two-timing. You have cheated Miss Thorpe, but you're not going to cheat me. Are you? So you see, my dear, you have got to let her know that you've changed your mind.'

Randolph was galvanized at last. Suddenly he crossed the room, took her in his arms and kissed her hard. She sighed and whispered, 'Randolph my darling, I am yours for ever – or as long as you want me.'

'You really mean it?'

'But only after you have explained the situation to your fiancée. That's fair, isn't it?' He was at a loss for words and could only nod his head vigorously. 'Now – you go off and do that and then we can begin to make plans.'

Randolph was still holding her in his arms. He was still trying to take in everything she had said. As he held her he looked about him. 'Do you really mean it? Seriously? That I should come and live with you?'

She nodded and smiled. 'What are you afraid of – that we might not get along?'

'And you don't mind – I mean, you forgive me for not telling you?'

'I will forgive you, after you have told your fiancée what you intend to do.'

He shook his head in happy bewilderment. 'Oh God, my darling. You can have no idea the way you have filled my thoughts; I have thought of you night and day, wondering where you would be, and what you might be doing.'

'I wonder your fiancée didn't notice.'

A tiny frown crossed his face. 'Things were a bit difficult – explaining why I disappeared to Newmarket so suddenly – and so on.'

'I must say, if it had been me, Randolph, I would have expected you to be at my side every day. This is the most important time in a woman's life; she wants her fiancé where he can be shown off.'

'Hester,' he interrupted her brutally, 'will you marry me?'

'Of course I will. But I warn you now, I am *very* jealous.'

Randolph, still bewildered, left soon after. As she went

476

with him to the front door, she caught sight of Fan lurking in a corner by the stairs.

The door closed and Abby turned as Fan came forward, her face contorted, red with amazement. 'You're going to marry Randolph Pelham?'

Abby did not answer but crossed past her and into the drawing room.

Fan followed her. '*Abby!* Answer me!'

'It's complicated—'

Fan came round energetically and confronted her. 'You just offered to *marry* him! What are you doing?'

Abby turned away from her. 'Don't ask questions. You'll see in the end.'

'What end? Abby, what's going on? How do you know Randolph Pelham – and what is he doing here – and why did you say you were a whore—' she suddenly had a flash of inspiration. 'Unless that was why your bed was so rumpled – *Abby*! You were *in bed* with Mr Pelham! You only pretended to have a headache to get me out of the way, so you could go to bed with him!'

'That's not true – and anyway – oh shut up with your questions!'

Fan had turned away stunned, struggling to comprehend. 'I don't believe it! You were in bed with Mr Pelham, and Rory in gaol, and now you're going to *marry* him?' She turned harshly. 'You are a whore! You are—'

Abby turned sharply on her. 'Well, if I am, who do you think paid for you to go to school?'

'Who?' Fan was astonished. 'Well, Mr Moncrieffe of course—'

Abby stared into Fan's eyes. There was silence between them for a moment, then Fan began slowly, 'You mean?' Abby waited as Fan pieced her thoughts together. 'So there was never—' the girl swallowed, 'he was just—' Again she struggled to join the story up. 'So you were just a whore?' she whispered, 'all along?'

'I made a lady out of you.' Abby said quietly, then, 'I

477

can't explain now, but it's not what you think.'

'And I thought you and Mr O'Toole—'

Abby bit her lip, then suddenly made up her mind. She took Fan by the wrist drew her quickly to the sofa and made her sit down beside her.

'You want to know what I'm doing? All right, I'll tell you. About two months ago I met Randolph Pelham here again, and he did not recognize me. I set out to seduce him, and I've made him fall in love with me. Now he is going to break off his engagement, and we are going to elope together to the continent. And when we are there and I have spent whatever money he has left, I am going to explain who I am and what I have done. And leave him.' She paused. 'Rory wants to kill him. But this way he'll have more time to think over what he did.'

'And do you think you'll be able to carry it through?'

'Yes.'

Chapter Forty-eight

The following morning Fan and Abby sat without speaking at the breakfast table. Abby now realised that the revelation of her secret had shocked the convent girl more than she had expected and was annoyed with herself; she should have been more guarded. Fan would look up every so often with a heavy expression until at last Abby was exasperated.

'I'm sorry you're shocked, Miss O'Leary. But it's paid for you to go to school; it's put those clothes on your back, and that breakfast in front of you. Just try to get used to it, please? In any case, it isn't quite what you imagine.'

'What do you mean?'

'I'll explain one day. It's a long story.'

'I don't see there's very much to explain. You go to bed with men you're not married to, for money. What could be simpler?'

'Don't be such a little prude!'

Fan stood up abruptly. 'I'm sorry if you're offended, and I suppose I ought not to complain since I'm your guest. But I'm also your sister, and I must say what I think.' She turned away, but at the door a thought occurred to her. 'I wonder what Mr O'Toole would say if he knew?' With a malicious smile she left the room; Abby sat with a displeased scowl on her face.

Later she heard the front door shut with a crash. Fan had gone out to look in shop windows – by far her favourite pastime, surpassing even visits to the opera – and Abby was alone, still thinking over that bruising little scene and the hurtful reference to Mr O'Toole. Fan was not stupid – she had been able to work out why he was a guest in Abby's house. These and other profitless thoughts were going round in her mind when there was a distant knock, and after a moment, Robbins appeared at the drawing room door.

'It's a Miss Thorpe to see you, ma'am.'

She rose quickly. 'Miss Thorpe?' and took a turn hastily through the room. After a moment she compressed her lips, straightened her dress, and said calmly, 'Show her in.'

As the door was opened Marianne swept grandly in. She was dressed in fresh clothes, light, summery, expensive – newly purchased for her marriage no doubt – and wore lilac kid gloves and a broad-brimmed hat, set back to do justice to her hair. She had clearly taken care with her appearance this morning and intended to impress.

She stopped as she saw Abby, and for one second they looked each other over. 'What –' she paused, and then louder now, straightening her back. 'I wish to speak with Mrs Moncrieffe. Be so good as to fetch her.'

'That won't be difficult,' Abby said dryly, relaxing a little. 'Take a seat.'

Marianne was affronted. 'I *beg* your pardon? Fetch your mistress immediately.'

'It's all right, Marianne. Sit down. You're talking to Mrs Moncrieffe.'

Marianne was silent as she took this in. 'I see.' She turned away, it seemed, to gather her thoughts. 'I think perhaps I might have guessed. I won't inquire by what means you have acquired this house, these servants. And I will not ask either why you have deliberately set out to seduce my fiancé. This is obviously a vindictive plot against my family – some nasty plan of revenge—'

'Not against your family, Marianne. In fact I believe I may be doing you a service. What has Randolph told you?'

480

Marianne ignored this. She had a speech prepared, which she now proceeded to deliver. 'I wrote you a note,' she began, 'which you ignored. I am here therefore to have this out finally. Mr Pelham has asked me to be his wife, and I have consented. It has been painful to me to hear of his liaison with you, but I was prepared to tolerate it for a while, men being what they are. I was unwilling to make a scene. But when I heard he had been seeing you at Newmarket, I had had enough. It has got to stop. I have spoken to him, and now I am speaking to you. And I mean what I say. I warn you, I will go to any lengths to protect my marriage. I will not allow some low street walker –'

Abby raised her eyebrows. '– I say, some street walker, some common harlot, to jeopardize my future happiness. And I shall not leave this room, until I have a clear undertaking from you that you will never see him again.'

Marianne gave her a strong level look. All through this speech Abby's mind had been working furiously. If Randolph had not spoken yet, then how had Marianne heard about herself at Newmarket? Surely not through Morton?

'And he hasn't told you?'

'Who?'

'Randolph'

'Mr Pelham? What are you talking about?'

Abby turned away, thinking. It seemed Randolph had told her nothing.

'How did you hear about Newmarket?'

'I was informed.' Marianne said loftily.

'But not by Randolph?'

'What does it matter? But I repeat, Mrs Moncrieffe – or Abby O'Leary, or whatever else you call yourself – that I am not going to allow you to spoil my marriage plans.'

'Marianne—'

'Miss Thorpe.'

'Very well.' Abby was quite cool. 'I think it's time I explained a few things. Let us go back a few years. You

481

may remember, I was sacked by your father. I imagine you know why.'

'Certainly. It was the common gossip of the stable hands.'

Abby raised her eyebrows, 'But I wonder whether you can guess who it was that caused my ruin?'

'What does it matter? You allowed yourself—' She hesitated. 'What are you saying?'

'Marianne,' Abby went on gently, 'I want you to think very hard and guess who it was. It's really not difficult.'

Marianne was white. 'Are you suggesting—'

'You won't know this, probably – it's not the sort of thing that would interest you – but Randolph's father was our landlord. We, my family, were in great difficulties owing to the bad harvest, and behind with the rent, and I – foolishly – went to see his father in the hope of persuading him to reduce the rent or allow us time to pay. Instead I met Randolph. Randolph promised to speak to his father on our behalf, and in that hope I allowed him to – have his way with me.'

'I still don't understand.'

'Isn't it clear yet? Why was I sacked by your father?'

Marianne was puzzled. 'Because of your reputation.'

'*My reputation*? You don't understand, do you! Marianne, the day I fell off my horse, I had a miscarriage; I lost Randolph's baby.'

Marianne's voice was hoarse with shock, and she gasped instinctively, 'You're lying.'

Abby shrugged, and did not reply. But she was looking Marianne full in the face.

There was a long silence, as Marianne without thinking slumped on to the sofa. 'Randolph,' she whispered, staring at nothing.

'The man you are about to marry.'

'Why are you doing this? Why should you want him?'

'I don't.'

Another silence as Marianne stared at Abby. The silence

went on, and on. And even when she spoke, Marianne could only gasp, 'What—'

'I'm not proposing to marry him, Marianne. I only want to prevent his marriage to you.' Marianne was still white with shock. 'I see he hasn't spoken to you,' Abby went on, 'which he promised me he would do. And since he hasn't, and since you are here, I will tell you exactly what the situation is. Randolph does not love you. He is deep in debt and only marrying you for your money. He has actually told me as much. He has also told me he loves me. And he promised to tell you so. Only it appears he has not done so yet.'

Marianne was silent, still huddled on the edge of the sofa. Then in a small voice, she began, 'I knew he wanted my money. I mean, I suppose I knew; I didn't exactly want to admit it to myself, but I suppose I knew. Papa said it. It was partly because he warned me against Randolph that I fell in love with him. I knew he was attracted to women, I could see that – any one could – but he was so flattering, so funny, and being older that me, and knowing so much, and having been everywhere, I suppose I was prepared to over-look—' Marianne reached a tiny handkerchief from a sleeve and dabbed her eyes, looking at the carpet.

'You're entitled to someone better,' Abby murmured.

'There's one thing I still don't understand,' Marianne said at last. 'After what happened between you, why should Randolph want you?'

'Ah. Well, you see, there is a rather strange thing. Randolph has not remembered me.' Marianne jerked a look up. 'No,' Abby went on. 'He actually does not connect Mrs Moncrieffe with Abby O'Leary – though he has spotted a resemblance.'

'Do you mean it?'

'Men are not very observant.'

'So he has no idea what you are up to?'

'None.'

'And when you set out to entrap him did you give no

483

thought to me? Did you hate me as much as you hated him?'

'I don't hate you. I told you the other day I was broken hearted when I had to leave your home. It was the happiest time of my life, Marianne. Everything I told you was true. When we rode out together, I can't tell you how pretty you looked. I worshipped you.' She sat beside Marianne on the sofa and took the girl's hands in her own. 'I thought we were friends.'

Marianne did not withdraw her hands. She looked hesitantly up at Abby. 'So did I,' she murmured at last. 'I hated to hear the story about you after you had gone. Mama and Papa forbade me ever to mention your name again. Of course that made me curious to know what you had done. But it was only the stable gossip, nudges and winks.'

There was a pause as they continued to sit hand in hand on the sofa, then Abby roused herself. 'It has been a shock for you. Let me get you something.' She rose and moved to the bell pull. 'Would you like a cup of coffee?'

Marianne did not respond, and continued to stare at the carpet. After a moment she could only repeat in a bewildered whisper, 'Randolph.'

The silence lengthened as they waited for the coffee, and even after the tray had been brought in and set down between them, even as Abby fussed with cups and jugs, speech was impossible. Until as Abby handed Marianne her cup, she whispered tentatively, 'What will you do?'

'I am thinking of Mama,' Marianne replied in a curiously matter-of-fact tone. 'I don't know how she is going to take it.' There was another long pause. Abby waited for her to go on.

'It is of course impossible for us to be married now.' Marianne shook her head slightly as she continued to stare into her cup. 'When I think—'

Abby stretched a hand to her arm, 'You poor—'

But Marianne shook her off, still looking down. 'When I think—'

484

'Yes.'

Marianne stretched herself, and sat more upright. 'I shall return to Ireland. I could not face him again.'

'What will you tell him?'

'I do not intend to see him again.' She set down her cup with an unexpected clatter on the low table. 'When I think—' She stood abruptly, and took a couple of paces towards the window. Abby could see the thoughts working in her more and more quickly, at first disjointedly, and then becoming more coherent. 'When I think that he could have been – all these weeks – when we were going out together, and with mother too – and all the time he was with you, and less that two months to our wedding.' She pulled a handkerchief from her sleeve and dabbed at her eyes speaking more and more quickly, and moving about restlessly in front of the window. 'Only last Monday, after dinner, when mother was indisposed and had gone to bed early, we were together on the sofa, and he was kissing me and telling me how he couldn't wait for the wedding, and wanting me to – oh God, when I think! There at home! With the servants at the door as like as not, and mother upstairs, and Randolph all over me, pulling at me, imploring me not to keep him waiting any longer and how he was dying for me, and I was within an inch of giving way too. I wanted him so badly, Abby! I did! I was ready to give myself to him. I think I would have done so only I was afraid the servants would hear something or come in suddenly. How could he!'

She burst into tears, holding her little handkerchief over her face, her shoulders hunched as she shook with the force of it. 'How could he!' she repeated in a muffled voice.

Abby waited. She was uncertain whether to tell Marianne what she had agreed with Randolph. Perhaps it would be unnecessary now. As Marianne's sobbing drew to a close, Abby asked tentatively, 'So you don't intend to speak to him again?'

The girl simply shook her head slightly, her face still covered by the handkerchief. 'I couldn't.'

'Would you like me to break the news?' Abby said softly. Marianne nodded. 'What I propose, Marianne, is to take him abroad before I tell him. This will give you plenty of time to return to Ireland. He may come after you, in spite of all.'

'He wouldn't dare. Not once I am home.'

'No.' Abby drew a breath more decisively. 'Leave it to me. You won't have any more trouble from him.'

'Thank you.'

After Marianne had left, Abby sat and wrote Randolph a note.

My dearest,

I think for the sake of appearance it would be best if we were to disappear for a while. It would not be pleasant for you here once the breaking off of your marriage becomes known. Will you book seats for us on the Friday night train to Paris, then come and collect me around nine? Bring plenty of things; once we are abroad there will be no great hurry about returning to this country and we could spend the whole of next winter travelling. By next summer the fuss will be long forgotten.

I am so looking forward to our being alone together.

In haste,

Hester

It was now Wednesday evening.

Chapter Forty-nine

When she woke the following morning she felt stronger; the way lay clear ahead of her now, and her head was filled with plans; it came as something of a jolt therefore to hear Fan, as they sat at breakfast, still unable to resist her spiteful jabs.

'Am I inconveniencing you? If you want me out of the way at any time—'

'Why should I?'

Fan raised her eyebrows. 'For your gentlemen friends . . .'

'Fan – Francesca darling – you remember what I told you, about Randolph Pelham?'

'Yes, Hester?' Fan replied silkily, in a tone of heavy irony. 'Mr Pelham? I haven't forgotten him. How could I?'

'You remember – I said I had a plan to take him abroad.'

Fan waited. Abby took a breath. 'We're going tomorrow.'

'Have a nice trip.'

Abby bit her lip. 'I explained to you—'

'Oh you don't have to explain,' Fan wouldn't let her go on. 'You're going to take Mr Pelham off to the south of France, I suppose, to a nice hotel and you're going to punish him thoroughly, I'm sure, wining and dining and enjoying yourselves. I expect he'll be sorry he ever laid eyes on you by the end of it.'

'You know that's not what I intend,' Abby tried to keep calm.

'Well, that's what it sounds like to me,' Fan spat out. 'Punish him! You must think me a great fool to believe such a story.'

Abby tried to ignore this. 'I don't expect to be away long. Probably only one night. Two at the most.'

'Don't hurry back on my account,' Fan cut in.

Abby stood up abruptly and went towards the garden door. Her head was ringing with Fan's taunts, and it wasn't until she had walked up and down for a quarter of an hour that she could restore her calm.

She spent the rest of the morning trying to concentrate on the following evening, making arrangements, and sorting out things to put in boxes – it occurred to her that she had better have plenty of luggage in case Pelham suspected anything.

Later in the morning after Fan had gone upstairs, Abby was at her desk staring at her list of things to do. Robbins who had been dusting at the further end of the room, had stopped work and was staring through the net curtains of the front window.

'Ma'am—' Abby looked up. 'It's that man again.'

'What?'

'He was there before and then went away. Now he's back. I don't like the look of him.'

Abby put down her pen and crossed to join her. Standing in the shade of a tree on the opposite side of the road and watching the house stood a raggedly dressed fellow, with a moleskin cap pulled down over his face. They studied him for a moment, then Abby turned away.

'Just a tramp, I expect.'

Mr O'Toole called and stayed to lunch. This took Abby by surprise – and pleased her too. He had intimated to her, that first evening at dinner, how pleasant it was to get away from Westminster and relax in the company of two such charming sisters – and who could resist such a hint? Abby told him he would always be welcome, and he had begun to drop in from time to time. After lunch the three of them walked in the park. Although she was always glad to see him, however, Abby now felt more than ever constrained in his presence, always conscious of Fan's eyes on her, and frightened at what she might say. However, Fan made no mention of Pelham and babbled on in her girlish way as usual, which made J.J. laugh. He had quite lost his stand-offish manner, and joined in their laughter and jokes with almost childish glee. During their walk Abby was thinking, By next week, all this business will be over, Pelham will be out of my life, and I shall be free – to do what? To concentrate on Mr O'Toole? She bit her lip. Fan had just made Mr O'Toole laugh again, and Abby glanced across at her. So long as Fan was in the house, she would be like a guilty conscience always ready to remind Abby of her past, or drop some hint into a conversation. And if Mr O'Toole ever got wind of the Pelham story . . .

After he had gone, and as Abby was preparing to go out to the shops for a few last-minute purchases, the maid said, 'That man's there again, miss.'

They both looked out. The man, after staring at the house for a while turned and made his way along the street in the direction of the park.

Abby pulled on her gloves. 'I've got to go down to the High Street. I'll mention it to Constable Hawkins if I see him.'

And, as she was going out, she said to Thady, 'O'Farrell, there is a strange man who has been hanging about in the road all day. Keep an eye open and make sure you lock up well tonight.'

But she had forgotten him a moment later as she set off. It was a bright early summer afternoon and Abby was dressed in a muslin frock. She was light-hearted; it was such a pleasure to go out in summer when she did not have to dress up in overcoats and woollens, but could sally forth

489

with a little basket over her arm, dressed only in this flimsy frock and light summer shoes to do a little shopping in the High Street – an eight-minute walk.

But as she turned into St Anne's Terrace she was aware out of the corner of her eye of a man on the opposite side of the road, who now crossed and came up behind her. It was a hot afternoon and quiet, and it occurred to her now that the street was deserted. A moment later she heard footsteps behind her, and automatically quickened her stride. Obviously there was nothing to be alarmed about yet she did not want to look round; she was about to hurry even faster when she felt a hand on her shoulder, and swung round in a shiver of panic.

'Would ye run away from your own brother?'

Rory was grinning at her. She placed her hand on her breast, for a moment unable to speak.

'It's all right, Abby, no need to panic,' he went on, 'I've been watching for ye to come out. Didn't like to knock on your door. Nice house ye have, by the way.'

'Rory!' At last she caught her breath. 'What a shock you gave me! Oh my darling, how wonderful – you're free!'

'I'm free all right.' He was still smiling broadly. 'And the air smells sweet. I've been breathin' it all day. The air of freedom.'

'But why didn't you write and let me know about your release?' She was still struggling to regain her breath.

He chuckled. 'Release? Well I suppose you could call it that.'

'I don't understand. You mean you haven't been released?'

'You'll read it in the papers. We broke out last night. I came up by the late train. Been hanging about London all day.'

She was dizzy as she heard this. 'You *escaped*?' He nodded. 'Oh my dear, you must be in terrible danger! Come back with me now!'

'Not such a good idea, Abby,' he said in a matter-of-fact

tone. 'Best thing would be if I came back at midnight. The fewer people see me the better, eh?'

'You mean you're just going to hang around till then? But someone—'

'Actually it's the safest. London – see – no one takes any notice of me. I'll just go off to the park and have a sleep. It's a lovely day for it.'

'Yes. We can talk later when I see you.' She tried to arrange her thoughts. 'Yes. Come back at midnight then I can let you in without anyone knowing. But I still don't understand,' she couldn't help continuing, 'Mr O'Toole said there was a chance of an amnesty—'

'We'll talk about it tonight,' he winked, and turned away down the street as she watched him.

That evening she told Thady, 'There's been a strange man hanging about in the street today, O'Farrell, so I'm taking extra precautions. I'll lock up tonight. You can go to bed.'

After everyone was in bed, she waited in the drawing room, all lights extinguished, sitting, pacing up and down, peering through the window, waiting.

At midnight, stiff with nerves, she opened the front door, and waited on the doorstep, and after a few minutes there was a movement among the laurels, and a figure was on the steps.

'Come in quick,' she whispered, and in a moment they were inside and she was locking the door. 'Don't say anything, just follow me.' She led him soundlessly upstairs and into a spare back bedroom. Only after she closed the door, she relaxed. 'You're safe now darling. Wait till I light a candle.'

A moment later she was able to look at him. 'Oh God, Rory but it's good to see you.' Rory took her in his arms and they clung to one another for a long moment. 'Are you hungry?'

'Starving,' he grinned.

'I'll get you something, and – oh, do you want to have a wash? There's a bowl and a jug of water there.'

491

Rory stripped off the ragged jacket he was wearing and pulled the shirt over his head. She watched him – watched the lean, muscular back as he leant over the basin and washed himself. As he took up the towel to rub his arms, his shoulders and chest, he stopped for a moment to examine it.

'It's a long time since I held a towel like this. I'd forgotten the feel of anything so soft.'

She sat on the end of the bed watching him. 'It's a miracle, darling, seeing you. But – do they know you escaped? Are they after you?'

He nodded. 'Three of us made it – we'd been sent down on a temporary job to the docks – Portland Harbour – and a group of the lads – there's a good network set up Abby – well, they had a boat. So we were out on this breakwater, heaving stones, with only a guard you see, and the lads came sailing up – just getting towards evening, when the guards were changing over. They pretended to be having trouble with the sails, as if they were unused to it, and drifted up to the breakwater – it was a brilliant plan – and managed to overpower the guard, and get us on the boat. It was an hour before the warning was given, and by that time we were across the bay, and after dark we put into Swanage; they had everything planned – they got the irons off us while we were sailing; they gave us a change of clothes and, by the time we put into land, it was as if we were a party of anglers. We split up, and I got on the train for London; got in this morning.'

He had dressed himself again. Abby was thinking furiously as he had been speaking. 'Stay here. I'll get you something to eat.'

'Thanks.'

She tip-toed in the darkness down to the kitchen. There she found some bread and cheese in the larder; there was also half of a leg of cold mutton, and she cut off several slices, and set the things out on a tray with a jar of pickles. She carried this up carefully in the darkness to the room.

'Make a start on that, darling, while I go to find you something to drink.'

In the drawing room she unlocked the tantalus, took out the brandy bottle, and brought it back with a glass. Rory was devouring the tray-full, and glancing up saw the bottle. 'Brandy! It's been long years since I tasted brandy, Abby,' he whispered.

She closed the door behind her, and squatted on the end of the bed to watch Rory as he ate and drank. The first mouthful of brandy made him choke. 'Hush darling,' she whispered.

'Sorry!' His eyes were watering. 'I've got out of the way of strong liquor. Took me by surprise.'

'Rory darling, they'll all be after you, won't they? By now, I mean, they must all know you've gone? There'll be a hunt?'

He nodded grimly. 'Let them hunt. They'll not find me.'

'We've got to think out what to do.'

'I've thought it out, Abby, don't you worry.'

'What do you mean?'

'You don't imagine I've lain those many nights in my cell and not thought it all through?'

'So what are you going to do?'

'Do?' He echoed. 'What else? I'm going to settle scores with Mr Pelham. I'll get him, Abby, if I swing for it.'

'No!'

'What do you mean, no?'

'Rory, we must talk about it. Not now – when you're tired and hungry. Tomorrow, when you've rested, we'll talk it all through and I'll explain the plan. I think I know what to do.'

'Abby,' he set down his knife, and looked at her carefully. 'I know exactly what to do. There's nothing to discuss.'

'There is! Really, Rory! Tomorrow my darling we're going to talk it all through. But let's not talk now. It's so nice having you here. I just want to enjoy being with you

493

and watching you, I don't want anything else, truly.'

Rory finished his supper. Abby had already made up a bed for him. 'Sleep now darling, and we'll talk in the morning. I'll explain everything.'

But she did not go back to bed herself. She stole upstairs to the attic and into Thady's room. In the gloom she shook him gently. As he started awake, she whispered, 'Thady, listen, it's me, Abby. Hush now—' He was about to speak. 'Don't speak, only listen. My brother is here from Ireland. He's just arrived. It's all right – just stay where you are. Only, tomorrow morning, I don't want any of the other servants to see him. If any one asks, just tell them he's a relative arrived late, and is not very well, and is going to stay in bed for a couple of days. I have put him in the back spare bedroom. You are the only person to see him – do you understand? I want you to take him his meals. Don't disturb him tomorrow morning – he'll want to sleep late – he's very tired. I'll tell you when to bring him his meals.'

'Your brother, Abby, but surely—'

'Don't ask questions now, Thady. Have you got it? I'm relying on you.'

'Trust me, Abby – trust old Thady!'

'I must.'

She crept back to Rory's room and stood over his bed for a long time watching him before she returned to her room, got into bed, and considered what to do . . .

Chapter Fifty

But as she woke she remembered Randolph, driven completely from her thoughts by all the previous day's excitement. Tonight she was supposed to be going to Paris with him. She dressed quickly, went down to her escritoire, wrote out a telegram and sent Robbins to the post office with it. It had been a foolish plan anyway, now that she had thought about it, quite unnecessary, and liable to misinterpretation too, as Fan had made clear. Simpler to let Randolph find out the situation at his leisure. Marianne would be safely on her way to Ireland by this time.

Then she stole into Fan's bedroom. Her sister always rose late – but Abby woke her.

'Fan listen to me—' she sat on the edge of her bed. 'I have some wonderful news. But don't say anything till I've finished.'

'What is it?' Fan was still waking up, her hair disarrayed, rubbing her eyes. Abby took her hand.

'Now don't say anything, or cry out. Something very important and wonderful has happened.'

Fan sat up straight, as Abby leant forward and whispered,

'Rory is here.'

'Here?' Abby nodded. 'What – but when did he arrive?'

'Late last night.'

'Why didn't he tell us he was coming?'

'Fan darling – this is the important part – please be calm and listen carefully. Rory has escaped from prison.'

'*Escaped*!'

'It's true! Isn't it wonderful? But we have got to think very carefully, and plan what to do.'

But Fan wasn't listening. '*Escaped*! You mean – but the police—'

'Of course they'll be after him – that's why we have got to think very carefully.'

'But why did he come here? The police will come here, Abby!' Her voice rose. 'This is the first place they'll think of – they're bound to find him – and then they'll arrest us for helping him. We'll be sent to prison!'

'Hush! I told you to keep your voice down!' Abby grasped Fan's arm tightly.

'Where is he now?'

'He's in the back spare bedroom and he's still asleep. Now listen, the first thing is – I want you to get dressed, and go down to the newsagent's on the High Street and buy all the newspapers you can find. You know it?'

'Me?' Fan sat up, pouting.

'Yes, you darling. I've got to stay here in case Rory wakes. Hurry up and get dressed. I'll order breakfast while you're gone.'

She returned to Rory's room, but found him still deeply asleep. Returning to the drawing room, she encountered Thady O'Farrell.

'Was I dreaming, Mrs Moncrieffe? I dreamed ye woke me in the night and called me by me name, Thady, and said it's Abby—'

'Thady, you are in a position to do me a favour.'

'Just name it, Abby darlin',' he took her hands and pressed them between his own. 'Trust old Thady.'

'Only, don't forget, never call me that in front of the other servants.'

'Never fear, me darlin'.'

'Very well. My brother is still asleep. He arrived very

496

late last night, so we'll just let him be. I'll tell you when I want anything sent up to him. In the meantime say nothing to the others.'

'Very well, Abby. You don't know how good that makes me feel to say your name after all this time.'

Soon afterwards, Fan returned with an armful of newspapers, and as breakfast was served the two girls looked through them. Sure enough, in *The Times* on an inside page and low down, there was a short paragraph, 'Convicts Escape from Portland Prison.' She was relieved that it looked a fairly unimportant item, and she was certain none of the servants would notice it. The two sisters looked at one another as Abby showed Fan this column.

'But why did he have to come *here*?' Fan whispered. 'If he's caught *here* – they'll arrest *us*!'

'Fan!' Abby whispered, 'how can you be so selfish? We must do everything we can to save him. Everything.'

Fan's face was screwed up now in fear. 'But if they arrest us?'

They looked at one another in silence. Abby's face settled into a determined frown. 'They will come here. And when they do, I am the only one who will speak to them. Do you understand? Under no circumstances are you to say a word.'

It was nearly midday before Abby went back to Rory's room. She judged it wiser now to wake him. He was much refreshed, and luxuriated in the comfortable bed. 'You can't imagine how it feels to be in a bed like this,' he grinned. 'I could have slept till Judgement Day.'

The mere sight of Rory made her emotional for a moment. 'Seeing you, darling, in my own house – to have you under my own roof to care for.' She sniffed, then became brisk. 'Fan's downstairs. I'll send her up in a moment. Now listen: I have spoken to one of the servants – Thady O'Farrell – and he'll take care of you. He knows nothing of what's happened. Do you understand?' She stood again. 'It'll be best if you stay in your room so the

497

other servants won't see you. Are you ready for some breakfast?'

'Starving!' he grinned.

'Oh darling Rory, I'm that pleased to see you, you can't imagine! Wait now and I'll get you something to eat and I'll bring up Fan to you.' She hurried out of the room, gave orders to Thady to bring up Rory's breakfast and in the meantime brought Fan up to Rory's room, where he was still in bed.

Fan had little to say, standing uncomfortably, her hands together looking down at Rory. Abby sensed her awkwardness, so she sat on a bedside chair between them, and outlined her plans.

'We have to get you out of the country as soon as possible, darling, to America. You can go to Fergus!'

He smiled. 'You've been thinking hard.'

'I've thought all night. Ever since you came.'

'That's good.'

At that moment, Thady entered with a tray.

'Thady, this is my brother Rory; Thady is from Westport, Rory. He brought me to London all that time ago.'

After Thady had gone, and Rory had eaten his breakfast, he drank a last cup of tea. He sighed. 'The lap of luxury. It was worth breaking out, just to lie here and be waited on. I should have done it years ago.' After his long sleep and the breakfast Rory was stronger and more alert. 'It's grand to see you, and you're treating me like a sultan, but before you go any further, I've got to tell you, there's a piece of unfinished business. You know what it is. I haven't come this far to be put off now—'

'No! Just leave it to me.'

'What do you mean, no? You said that last night! What do you mean?'

'Rory, you're in enough trouble as it is. Darling, you're in deadly danger! We must get you out of the country. Forget Randolph Pelham.'

He sat up and grasped her wrist tightly. 'Abby,' he said

498

under his breath, between clenched teeth, 'I've said it before, and this is the last time I'll say it. Randolph Pelham is going to pay. What's the matter with you? Why are you trying to stop me.'

'For your own sake, darling!'

'Or for his?'

She tried to sound calm and practical. 'You don't understand, Rory; it's complicated. He's been punished.'

'How?'

Abby glanced at Fan, conscious of her accusing eyes on her. Rory saw this and glanced between them.

'What do you mean – punished?' he repeated.

'Abby went to bed with him! That's how she punished him!' Fan spat out. Abby spun on her.

'What does she mean?'

Abby was staring at her sister. 'How could you?' she whispered.

'It's true!'

Abby was between the two others who were waiting for her to speak. She swallowed. 'I will explain. There was a plan, trust me, and Fan should never—'

'You went to bed with Randolph Pelham – *again*?' he breathed, still staring at her. 'Is that what you're tellin' me?' His voice was breathless with shock.

'*Fan*! How could you?' She turned quickly to Rory. 'Honestly honey, it's too complicated I –' she stumbled over her words – 'you see, I had this plan – to lead Randolph on, to –' she swallowed, 'to seduce him, as it were, and then to go abroad with him, but now—'

Rory was staring at her, as if turned to stone. 'He seduced you once. And you let him do it again?'

'No! It was the plan,' she buried her face in her hand and burst into tears. 'It wasn't what you think, and Fan should never—'

'I went to prison for you.' Rory wasn't listening to her, as he continued in a low hollow voice. 'To protect your good name. I wouldn't let your name be mentioned in

499

court. I told the lawyers not to say it before the judge, because you were my sister, and I wouldn't have your name tossed about between 'em to be mocked. Four years I sat in a cell for ye. Six weeks in solitary. *Four years*, Abby, breakin' stones!'

'I wanted to speak!' she burst out. 'I told Mr O'Toole! I said I wanted to explain to the judge it was my fault. But you wouldn't—'

'Do ye hear what I'm sayin'?' Rory wasn't listening, speaking like one mesmerized. 'Four years! I only broke out to get Randolph Pelham. That's what I've done, Abby – risked me neck only to punish him for abusing ye!' She nodded, her face in her hands. His eyes were burning into her. 'And now ye're tellin' me ye were willin' all along? Is that what ye're tellin' me? *Abby*!' He seized her arm and dragged her hand from her face. She looked up at him terrified, her face smeared with tears. Rory was possessed at this moment, shouting in her face. 'Is that what ye're telling me? That ye were a whore all along?'

'*No*!' It was a lamenting cry.

Rory threw her violently from him so that she fell from her chair across the floor. He got out of bed, and began to put on his clothes. Fan was watching terrified.

'What are you doing?'

'What does it look like? Do you think I'd stay here?'

'Rory! You must stay. You must! It's the only safe place.'

'What does it matter? Oh God, I could top meself to think I was in that cell, and you were enjoying yourself with Randolph Pelham all the time.'

'No! It's not true.'

'It is true!' Fan interjected.

Rory was dressed now and was crossing to the door when Abby who had half risen, tried to catch his arm. He shook her off, turning harshly on her, as she knelt before him, her face wet with tears. 'I'd rather be anywhere on earth than here! Jesus, I can't even think it.'

500

She tried to catch his arm again as he made for the door. 'Rory!' It was a dying despairing cry. 'Don't!'

Before he could reach it, however, there was a light knock. They froze, and Rory looked down at Abby. She struggled to her feet, straightening her hair. 'What is it?' she called in an uncertain voice. The door opened and Robbins looked in. The three of them stared at her. 'What do you want?' Abby said at last.

Robbins swallowed, looking round at them, and said, 'There's a gentleman to see you, miss. Says it's urgent. From Scotland Yard.'

There was a moment of frozen silence, then Abby took a huge grip on herself. 'Very well, Robbins.' Her voice was still uncertain. 'Thank you. You may tell him I'll be down in a moment.'

The maid curtsied and closed the door behind her. Abby looked between the other two, and before they could speak, said, 'I must go down.' She swallowed, trying to think it out, her mind racing as she sought to cover all possibilities. 'Wait here. There's nothing you can do. Wait!' Rory had crossed to the window. There was a fifteen-foot drop below it into the garden.

'No! Rory! Don't. Do nothing. I'll go and speak to him. Fan, wait here with Rory.'

Abby was desperately wiping the tears from her cheeks and straightening her hair in the glass. Then, assuming her most regal, gracious bearing, and without looking at the other two, she went downstairs.

A policeman was waiting in the hall. He saluted respectfully as she paused outside the drawing room door, took another long breath, and went in.

A thick-set man in a heavy ulster, a bowler hat in his hand, was waiting for her. 'Mrs Moncrieffe?'

She nodded. Her whole body was still quivering as she struggled to control her voice. 'How can I help you?'

'Detective Inspector Travers, ma'am, Scotland Yard.' He consulted a notebook. 'I believe you have a servant

501

by the name of Abby O'Leary?'

Abby clenched her hands as she tried to think out her answer. Her voice was still a little quivery. 'I had, Inspector. She has left.'

'Oh.' He looked at his notebook again. 'According to my information a letter was sent to her at this address less than a month ago.'

'Really? I have no idea.' A little steadier now, she crossed to the bell, and they waited a minute in silence until Thady appeared. 'O'Farrell, do you remember the girl O'Leary?'

Thady's face did not flicker. 'Yes madam?'

'When she left, did she leave a forwarding address?'

'She did not, madam.'

'Thank you, that will be all.'

'Thank you, madam.' Thady backed out in his best imitation of a butler.

'So you have no idea where she might be now?'

'None. I am sorry I cannot help you, inspector.'

He frowned. 'There is no chance she might return here? Do you think any of your servants might know where she went?'

'I doubt it. You heard my butler.'

He chewed his moustache for a moment. 'Yes. Thank you, madam. Sorry to have disturbed you.'

'That's all right. Why did you want to speak to her?'

'She has a brother who was a convict in Portland Prison. He escaped the night before last.'

'A convict! I had no idea.'

The inspector now had a thought. 'If you do see any suspicious characters about, would you contact me immediately?' He took a calling card from a bulky leather pocketbook. 'He's armed and may be dangerous. They shot a guard as they were escaping.'

'Good lord!' she breathed.

A moment later the inspector was shown out and instantly Fan was at the door. She darted into the room and closed the door carefully behind her. 'He's armed! You heard him. They shot the guard.'

The two sisters stared at each other for a moment as the implications sank in. 'If they catch him . . .'

'All the more reason to make sure they don't,' Abby said decisively.

Rory was still in the room as she and Fan returned, and they looked at each other without speaking. Rory sank on to the edge of the bed. 'I never had a gun . . .'

There was a long pause, then Abby roused herself. 'I must go out. There are things to get . . .'

She spent the afternoon shopping: bootmakers, shirt makers, hosiers, hats, a suit, and arrived home with a carriage full of boxes and packages. There had also been a visit to her bankers.

When she went upstairs again she found Rory sitting on his bed, reading a newspaper. He glanced up at her but there was no flicker of recognition. She bustled about with her packages, hoping somehow to ride over his mood. Rory had had returned to his newspaper. 'Rory darling,' she swallowed. 'I've brought you some clothes.' He continued reading. 'Rory—'

He dropped the newspaper, but remained staring at the floor until he began speaking in a low sullen voice. 'When I think,' he began in a monotone. 'I was in that cell, in C17, all those years, all those years,' he repeated, shaking his head slowly, 'I just can't believe it, and you were away all the time whorin' with Randolph Pelham . . .'

'Rory!' she threw herself on the floor before him, taking his hands in hers. 'I swear on our mother's grave, that was not the way of it. I swear! Rory darling, you must believe me, you must!' Still holding his hands she bent her head over them, her eyes filled with tears.

Rory slowly, carefully disengaged his hands as if she were polluted, stood, and moved across to the window. 'I should have known,' he went on in that same low voice,

503

staring out. 'If I'd thought about it, if I'd really thought about it, I should have known. You were rotten from the start, dashin' about the village on them horses and showin' yourself off. You're a whore by nature.'

Chapter Fifty-one

The house was silent.

Rory was in his room, Fan was lying down, and Abby sat alone in her drawing room. As she stared into the empty fireplace, time seemed to have come to a stop; everything had come to a stop, frozen dead. There was a stone wall between her and her brother. He had no more to say to her, and she seemed to herself now to be completely paralysed, every sense atrophied, incapable of motion, of thought, unable to plan.

In the silence she could even hear the clock in the hall; in the silence the emptiness grew and grew in her mind, the feeling of the geography of this house, of herself here, unable any more to do anything, and upstairs in his misery her beloved brother, unwilling to bend, or make any move towards her at all. He had disowned her and everything she had done, everything she had striven for over so many years had been for nothing. He would accept no explanation, no excuse, he refused to make any effort to understand her situation whatsoever.

She was even beyond weeping. After those terrible things he had said she had fled down here, thrown herself onto this sofa, and wept until she could weep no more. Now, as the summer evening gradually lengthened, and dusk was creeping through the room she sat upright, still, unmoving, unthinking.

There was a distant sound of the front door bell, and soon afterwards the sound of Robbins' shoes on the marble of the hall. Abby remained unmoving, indifferent. Nothing, and nobody that might call could make any difference to her now.

A second later the door burst open and Randolph was standing over her. 'Again! You've done it again! What game are you playing? Do you realize I've made all our plans? Why aren't you ready?' She was still staring up at him. 'Hester! What's going on? Why aren't you ready?'

She rose, still shaking with shock, and turned away a step struggling to gather her thoughts. 'Didn't you get my –'

'Your telegram – yes, I got it twenty minutes ago. I've been out all day making preparations. Hester, don't you understand, I've done everything, I've got everything ready. We're going! Tonight! So get your things together!'

Her mind had abruptly come to life and she was now thinking furiously. 'Tonight! Yes – of course –' She swallowed, and turned away again, her mind was blank, as she searched furiously for an answer. Still trying to hold him off as she organized her thoughts, she turned back to him. 'And you really mean it? I mean – you really want us to go away together?'

'What are you talking about? Of course I do! It was all agreed! Hester I've been dashing about all day – you can't back out now. It's all done – so come on – we've got a bit of time. Get your things together –'

'Yes –' She was still trying to think straight, but gradually somewhere in the recesses of her mind she glimpsed something. 'And you've spoken to Marianne?' she asked tentatively. Then as she saw him hesitate, she was strengthened. 'Randolph, have you explained to Marianne?' As she waited for his reply, her mind was racing furiously. There was just a possibility. 'You haven't spoken to her, have you?'

'I haven't seen her.'

'You haven't seen her?' She picked her way carefully

506

now through the argument, looking him in the eye, and speaking softly. 'You simply wanted to disappear? Leave her with no idea what you were doing?'

She could see how uncomfortable he was. He coughed. 'Darling, that doesn't matter. Let's just go! Now call your maid, and start packing.'

'You haven't even written to her?' Silence. She placed her hands over his. 'Randolph,' she said gently, 'this is what I was afraid of. This is why I was uncertain. I did say, did I not, that you must tell your fiancée. It is only fair.' She was looking at him straight.

There was an embarrassed silence. 'Come,' she went on soothingly drawing him by a hand towards the escritoire, and opening it. 'We have time. If you would just like to do it now?' She glanced back at him with a smile.

'Hester, I really don't think it matters.'

'But you see, my darling,' she said vehemently, 'I do! I am a woman and I understand what it means to be cheated by a man. I cannot allow you to do it to her. Come –' she softened – 'it will not take a moment. And then we can be off.'

He gave a shrug, glanced at her and sat at the escritoire. He took a pen, opened the ink-well, and looked up at her again. 'What do you want me to say?'

'Just tell her the truth. It is simple enough. You realize now that you do not love her, and that it would be unjust to her to continue with the marriage. That you regret the unhappiness you have caused her; and hope that she may find happiness with another.'

Randolph stared down at the sheet of paper for a moment, still hesitating, finally took a breath, and quickly wrote out the few lines.

'Here is an envelope,' she handed it to him. 'You had better address it.'

In a moment he had addressed the envelope, folded the note, enclosed it and stuck it down.

'I have a stamp,' she said lightly. 'Give it to me.'

With a slightly puzzled look he handed it to her. She had taken a stamp from her purse and affixed it to the envelope. Still quite calm it seemed, she undid a button of her dress, slipped the letter into her bosom, and buttoned it again.

She looked at him composedly and suddenly smiled. 'There,' she said lightly.

She could see he was puzzled. He rose from the desk, looking at her. 'What is it?'

She now appeared thoughtful, took a turn away from him, and said casually, 'There is something else, Randolph, something I've been meaning to give you. I wonder if you'll recognize it?'

'Hester, surely that can wait. Call your maid, and let's get ready. I've got my things.' He was trying to regain command of the situation, and took a step towards the door.

She did not appear to hear this as she opened her purse and took something from it. She held it out to him. He came a step to her and took it.

'Do you recognize it?' It was the Ashanti medal.

'Yes,' he said doubtfully, 'I had one like it myself.'

'I don't suppose there are many of them about,' she said thoughtfully, watching him. 'The Ashanti Campaign – something very special, I imagine.'

He looked up from the medal. 'Where did you get this?'

'A man gave it to me once.'

He was staring at her, and at last, almost choking, he gasped hoarsely, 'Abby?'

'You've remembered at last?' Her tone remained light.

'Abby? Really – is it you?'

She was looking closely in his eyes. 'Have I changed?'

'What? Well, of course – you've got me confused. How? I mean – here – like this?'

She waited.

'But look here, why didn't you tell me before, why have you let me go on all this time?'

'I could ask you the same question, Randolph,' she said quietly, still looking closely at him. 'It wasn't very courteous, was it, not to recognize me? I recognized you the moment I saw you.'

'Did you?'

'You weren't easy to forget. Not for a seventeen year old farm girl. But then, perhaps you had me muddled up with the others.'

'Others?'

'Surely there must have been others?'

He looked down again at the medal. 'This is terrible,' he gasped at last.

There was a long silence as he struggled to put his thoughts together. 'Actually,' he managed to speak at last, 'actually, I did think – I remembered you that morning at Newmarket when I saw you on horseback astride like a boy – it was so unusual – it just triggered the memory and then afterwards I remembered everything.'

'Everything?'

'Yes.' He struggled on. 'But I still couldn't believe it was you. I studied and studied you, but I couldn't believe it. It was you and it wasn't you.'

'It didn't affect your enjoyment of the races at any rate.'

He was silent, but struggled on at last, 'It's complicated. You see, I didn't want it to be you.'

'Oh, you didn't?'

'No.'

'Why?'

'Why do you think?' He tried to pull himself together, recovering a little now from his shock. 'That fact is, Hester – or Abby – I don't even know what to call you – I didn't come very well out of that episode. It was on my mind after. I did try to speak to the governor – you know, after what happened – about your family. But he just brushed me aside, didn't want to hear. And the agent, Scott, he was dead against giving an abatement. Give a reduction to one and they'll all want one, was his line.' Randolph was tense, clutching and unclutching his hands, staring down awkwardly. 'I did try, Abby.' He went on, struggling to get

509

the words together. 'And afterwards I thought of coming to see you. But I couldn't think of what to say. You know, it would have sounded so lame. You being evicted, after – what had happened. I went once to see your cottage, after the bailiffs had finished with it. I thought of you,' he repeated. 'The fact is, I'm not very proud of what I did.' His voice tailed away, and then as an afterthought, he added, 'I thought of sending you some money ...'

'Why didn't you?'

'Well, I thought, how would she explain it to her family?' He came to a standstill again. 'So in the end I did nothing. Sort of hoped for the best.'

Another long pause and then he started again. 'But I still don't understand – why are you here? Why have you let me go on so long without saying anything?'

Abby was feeling so bitter at this moment she could hardly speak. Randolph seemed indescribably weak – he was scarcely worthy of Rory's wrath.

'You should have come,' she said.

'I know.'

'If you had come, if I had known you cared – even a little – if I had known you had at least tried to speak to your father, it would not have been so bad. But to say nothing – never to send a message or anything – just to leave me quite ignorant, that was unforgivable.'

'So why have you been seeing me? I don't understand.'

'No. I suppose you don't.' She shook her head sadly. 'You don't understand anything. Randolph, your way of life was so far removed from mine, you could not even conceive what it meant to us to lose our home. My father never recovered from it. Never. My brother went to prison.'

'I felt bad about that too.'

'My brother went to prison for attempting to defend my honour, Randolph.'

'I know,' he whispered.

'So do you still want to know why I allowed you into my house? Why I went to bed with you?'

He waited.

'I wanted to punish you, of course.'

'Punish me?' There was a note of alarm in his voice, and she could see he was thinking quickly. 'How? You mean – what – our trip?' Then he seemed to grasp the point. 'That letter?' He was quick now, active, alarmed. 'The letter? Do you mean –?'

He took a step towards her, and she stepped back. Now he seemed to get the idea and was angry. 'This *is* a trick – you trapped me! Give me that letter!' He came rapidly towards her, as she retreated rapidly to the bell-rope and gave it a tug.

'By heavens, you'll give me that letter! This is a trick, isn't it? You pernicious little –'

The door opened, and Thady appeared. 'O'Farrell, ask Mr O'Leary to come down – at once!'

Randolph swung round. 'What?'

Then as Thady went out, he advanced rapidly again. 'You'll give me that letter. You'll give it to me by God, or I'll take it!' He was over her, took her by the shoulders, and a moment later she had fallen backward on to the sofa. He knelt over her and attempted to seize the neck of her gown.

'Rory!' she screamed.

Pelham wasn't listening, and was trying to get his finger into the tight high neck of her dress in an attempt to rip it open.

'*Rory!*'

At that moment she heard quick steps on the stairs and Rory appeared at the door, Fan behind him. 'Rory!'

In a second Rory had taken Pelham by the neck and hurled him to the floor. He sprawled on his back a couple of yards away and looked up in a daze at the three of them, as Abby straightened herself and attempted to get her breath back.

'*You!*' He was staring up at Rory. Shaven-headed, Rory still had the look of a convict, though he was dressed now in the clothes Abby had bought. 'You're the one who went to prison!' He pointed up at him. 'I read about you. You're the one who escaped!' Pelham scrambled nimbly to his feet, looking round at the three of them. 'I see now. This is a trick, isn't it, a sneaky trap! Well! We'll soon see – yes, oh yes,' he spoke quickly, disjointedly, as he straightened his jacket.

Rory glanced at Abby, clearly mystified.

Abby now stood, straightening her dress, and regaining her breath. 'Mr Pelham is quite right. It is a trap, and he has fallen into it.'

'I don't think so.' Pelham made a move to the door. 'The police will be very interested in your brother.'

As Rory made a move to stop him, he jerked back. 'Don't touch me!' but Rory contemptuously took him by the shoulder and threw him roughly across the sofa. 'Shut up.' He turned to Abby. 'What are you up to?'

Abby tried to control her voice, but still felt somewhat shaken. She was rubbing her neck, where Randolph's rough handling had bruised it. 'As you must realize by now, Mr Pelham, you are not going to Paris tonight. But my brother is, with your ticket.' She waited for him to say something, as Rory turned sharply. 'Now,' she went on, more in control of her voice. 'The thing is, as I told you, Marianne Thorpe knows nothing of this. Unless she receives your letter. Once she receives your letter, Mr Pelham, all chances of a prosperous marriage fly out of the window, and you face the bankruptcy court.' She paused and continued quietly. 'Once my brother is safely in France, you shall have that letter.'

Rory turned on her, and spoke in a fierce undertone, 'And you're just going to let him off – like that? Let him go?'

'Trust me,' she said quietly, 'It's for the best.'

'For the best? I'll thrash him first!'

As he made a fierce move towards Pelham, Fan screamed, and Abby cried out, 'Rory! Leave him! This is the best way. Believe me!'

'You've done some deal between you, haven't you?'

512

Rory was looking between them. 'I can smell it! Some deal to get me out of the way, so you can go on with your fun and games!'

'No! I swear it. This is for the best! And it's our only chance. We have to get you out of the country tonight. Darling if we don't do this tonight – now – you'll be arrested again, and once you're back in prison you'll never get out. You'll be in for the rest of your life. You know it!'

'Rory, you must do it!' Fan unexpectedly screamed out. 'Now Mr Pelham has seen you!'

Rory stopped, thinking, still breathing hard, and looking down murderously at Pelham, who was sprawled across the sofa and staring up in terror.

'Darling, you've got to do it. We haven't much time left!' She could almost have stamped her foot. 'Fan, tell Blake to bring the carriage to the door. We still have an hour. And there are some things I bought for you – they're in your room. I'll tell O'Farrell to bring them down.'

She turned to Pelham. 'Are you thinking, Mr Pelham? Do you seriously want that letter to be delivered? Keep very quiet.'

She now heard the front door open. Thady looked into the room. 'The carriage is at the door, madam.'

'Good.' She ignored the look of amazement on Thady's face. 'We are almost ready. There are some cases in my brother's room.'

'Yes, madam.'

She was carefully adjusting the cravat for Rory, and stood back. 'That'll do.' She turned briskly to Randolph who was at the door. 'Where are the tickets?'

He fished in an inside pocket and brought out a pocket book, and with a heavy look, pulled the tickets out.

She took them and handed them to Rory. 'Now let's go.' She turned to Pelham who was still extremely uncomfortable. 'And you. I'm not letting you out of my sight, Randolph.'

*

513

It was dark as they arrived at Victoria, and the station was nearly empty. The gas was now lit, and threw the corners and recesses into shadows, as sounds and voices echoed in the high roof. Abby was intensely nervous by now, looking about her, watching everyone; her elation had deflated, as she had had time to think through what they were doing. It was a huge gamble – a word, a sign, from Randolph and Rory was lost. There would certainly be police detectives on the lookout at the port. She glanced at Rory as these thoughts flashed through her mind, but he was silent, concentrated.

'Better not to speak darling, if possible,' she whispered, as they made their way along the platform. Four years in Portland had done nothing to take the edge off Rory's accent.

A porter followed them with the boxes.

'Come along, Pelham, we can get you a ticket on the train. Let's find our seats.'

Once they were seated in their first class compartment, Abby looked between the two men. Neither were speaking. She looked Randolph up and down then patted the top of her bosom, in an absent-minded way. 'Really Pelham, everything considered, you've got off extremely lightly.'

It was midnight when the train pulled in to the Dover Marine station. Continental travellers, porters and their luggage were all around them on the dark platform, and the press of passengers filed slowly through the barrier onto the quayside, where, her funnel smoking, the cross Channel steamer was waiting.

Abby supervised the porters unloading the luggage van.

'Pelham, give the porter a hand with those boxes.' He said nothing, and the two men were loaded with the cases and grips she had arranged for Rory. Abby turned towards the barrier, and threaded her arm through Rory's. Glancing up at him, she smiled nervously; she was glad the soft tweed hat disguised his shaven head, and its brim threw much of his face into shadow. Under a dim paraffin lamp an

514

inspector was checking the passengers' tickets, and behind him, as Abby quickly noted, two men in plain clothes were carefully scanning the faces of the passengers as they came briefly into the light, and then out again.

As they approached the barrier, she began to speak, glancing back over her shoulder.

'Oh come on man, don't dawdle! And do be careful! Good heavens, do you know what those cases cost? How many times have I had to tell you – hold it upright! There are bottles inside.'

At the barrier Rory held out the two tickets, and the inspector clipped them without even looking up. In a moment they had passed the barrier, and were on the quay-side, beneath the high black side of the steamer, the air was filled with its hissing, and she could smell the sea. It was an exhilarating moment, the relief exquisite.

'Did you book a cabin, Pelham?'

'You've got the tickets there,' he said gruffly.

'Have we? Rory?' Rory pulled the various pieces of paper from his pocket again, and together they scanned them by a distant light. 'Ah yes.' She turned to the porter. 'Cabin 57.' And as he carried the bags up the gangplank, she turned to Rory again. 'We'd better say goodbye here, darling.'

'You're not coming with me?'

'No.' She was busy opening her reticule, and took out a paper packet. Glancing at Pelham she went on quickly. 'There is a reason. Now Rory darling, don't say anything, but here's a little money. You can pay me back one day. But it's enough to book you a passage to America. You take the train from Paris to Cherbourg – it's easy enough.' She opened another envelope and took out papers. 'These are letters of credit drawn on the New York City Bank, for a thousand dollars each; you'll be able to cash them once you're in America. There are ten of them so take good care of them, darling. The cases are all yours' – there were seven of them – 'clothes mostly, and a few other things.

515

They're labelled in the name of Moncrieffe. Write as soon as you can; I shan't be able to relax till I hear you've arrived safely.' She fished again in her reticule. 'And here are a thousand francs, in cash. This'll cover all your expenses until you're on the liner. It'll probably be a French ship – don't worry, they'll speak English – but you'll need French money for expenses. The meals will be all included.'

Rory stared down incredulously at these pieces of paper. 'Ten thousand dollars?' he whispered. 'Abby, where did you get all this money?'

She shrugged. 'Well,' she grinned, 'don't worry about that, I've enough.'

'All this money –' he looked up into her face. 'Was this – I mean – all this, from –' He glanced across at Pelham. 'Did this come from Randolph Pelham?'

'No!' She took his hands, crushing them round the documents and notes. 'I swear! Never a penny.'

He was looking her full in the face. 'Ye whored with him for free, is that it?'

She was weary, unable to face his accusing look, and at last said quietly, 'Like I said before, it's not what you think. Rory darling, don't let's talk any more of that. It's all in the past.'

They stood for a moment in silence. He could not look at her, still holding the various papers and documents in his hands. He had never looked so bitter, heavy in his face, as she studied him. He looked down at the money with distaste, as if it were dirty, as if he were profiting from her sin. She read his mind, and went on hurriedly, desperately trying to keep the tears back.

'Look, you can pay me back one day, if you want. I don't mind – but if you want to –'

'You're not coming,' he repeated stupidly, looking again between her and Pelham. 'I understand.' With a sudden effort he thrust the handful of papers at her. 'Take them.' His face was black with bitterness. 'You don't have to

516

explain.' He glanced again at Pelham. 'It's clear enough. Take your money. I'll make do without.'

'Rory!'

'Don't say anything, Abby, just don't!' He turned away towards the gangplank.

'Rory, it's not what you think!'

'I don't want to hear!'

'Rory!'

Already he was making his way up the gangplank. He did not look back.

'*Rory*!'

Chapter Fifty-two

She could scarcely make him out through her tears, searching in vain for him as he disappeared up on to the ship. At last, her head hanging, she turned away, one hand over her face.

'How could he? How could he?' Her voice was muffled.

Around them passengers were hurrying past to make their way on board, there was movement on the quay where sailors were preparing to cast off, and shouts from the ship's side above her. She had quite forgotten Pelham who hovered beside her. His eyes were more closely focused on the scraps of paper clutched carelessly in her hand, and when one fell, he hastily retrieved it for her.

'How could he be so cruel? Surely he could have understood – I was only thinking of him,' her words were incoherent, half speaking, half sobbing. She had taken a step, not looking where she was going, but after a moment turned and looked longingly again up to the ship's rail. 'Only for him,' she repeated, and in a last despairing cry, '*Rory!*'

Her only answer was a long crude blast on the ship's hooter. Ropes were being cast off from the bollards, the huge paddle wheels of the ship began to turn, and the water churned to a white froth beneath them.

At last Abby turned away, and Randolph, who had been watching her all this time, carefully took the papers from her hand and helped to stuff them back into her reticule. He tentatively took her arm, steering her towards the railway platform.

'Abby – Hester –' he began. 'About my letter—'

She did not hear him, and he did not repeat the request.

Even when she was sitting in the train, she could only hear those last few words from Rory, as if everything she had tried to do had been worthless, as if she herself was worthless. Now she would never see him again, and he would go all through his life believing her to be no better than a whore.

Pelham sat opposite without speaking. Her weeping drained to a close, she heaved a shattering sigh, and then suddenly felt terribly tired. She could feel her head nodding and nodding, and after Pelham had crossed to sit beside her, her head fell on to his shoulder and she fell asleep.

He woke her as the train came in to Victoria, and then as they came out to the taxi rank, and he was helping her into a cab, he repeated, 'Abby – can you give me the letter now? Your brother's safe.'

She had settled by this time into a cold lethargy, but she took the letter out, and handed it to him. He seemed pathetically grateful.

'Thank you.'

She closed the cab door and looked down at him from the window with a heavy look. 'Do you really think you can write a letter like that, and then tear it up again? Randolph, you were prepared a few hours ago to desert her without even saying goodbye. Can you honestly believe you will be able to carry on as if nothing had happened?' He said nothing, so she went on in a dull voice, shaking her head, 'It will make no difference, in any case, because you will never see Marianne again. She came to my house last week and we talked it all through. She knows everything, Randolph; she has left London and returned to Ireland.'

He was clutching the letter to his chest, and she could

519

barely make out his face, turned up to her in the distant light of a gas lamp.

'I loved you,' he said bitterly after a moment. 'And you tricked me.'

'Goodbye Randolph.'

She sat back in the darkness, rapped against the roof of the cab, and the cabbie clicked his horse into motion. The cab was rolling out of the station forecourt before he had time to say any more.

It was almost dawn when she knocked at her own door and, after a long wait, was admitted by Thady in his nightshirt and a pair of trousers hastily pulled on.

'Abby?' he whispered, almost afraid, as his head appeared round the door, a candle held high.

'It's me,' she said wearily as she came in past him.

'Did your brother get away safely?'

Thady set down the candle on the hall table, and helped her out of her coat.

'Yes, he's safe now. He'll be on his way to Paris. What's the time?'

''Tis nearly four, Abby.'

She unpinned her hat. 'In an hour and a half he'll be in Paris.' This cheered her as the thought sank slowly into her tired mind. 'He's safe now, Thady, and that's all that matters. Rory's safe. He'll be able to go to America to our brother in Chicago.' She paused. 'Yes. And I can write to him at Fergus's. I can explain everything. It'll be all right.'

'Will I get ye something to drink, Abby? A cup of tea?'

In her half asleep state it took her a moment to drag up a decision. 'Mm? Yes, perhaps I will, thank you.'

Thady went into the drawing room and lit two candles and, as she followed him, she saw her sister stretched out on the sofa, fast asleep.

'Wait. We'd better get her upstairs.'

'Right ye are, Abby darlin'.'

'She was waiting up for me,' Abby went on thoughtfully,

as they arranged the sleeping girl between them, Thady taking her under the arms, and Abby lifting her feet.

'She said she was going to sit up for ye, poor girl, but it was too late for her, after all. Ah, what it is to be young,' he shook his head as they were carrying Fan upstairs.

They got the girl laid out on her bed. 'You make the tea, Thady, and I'll get her tucked in.'

'Right ye are, Abby darlin'.'

As Thady went out, Abby threw back the bedding, and with a bit of heaving and pulling managed to get most of Fan's clothes off, and finally got her under the sheets, and arranged on the pillow. Fan slept soundly throughout.

'I still have you, darling,' Abby whispered, kissing her gently on the forehead, then taking the candle, she returned to the drawing room.

As Thady brought in the tray she asked, 'Did you bring yourself a cup?'

Thady chuckled. 'I did, me darlin'.'

He poured the tea, brought her a cup, and then took his own and sat opposite her, perched forward on his chair. 'So, tell me, Abby, how was it? Was the peelers after ye? I was that worried for you and your brother.'

'It was dark,' she began after a moment, 'so it was difficult to see properly, and Rory was well dressed and had me on his arm. We looked like a respectable couple, and with Pelham carrying the boxes.'

Thady chuckled. 'Mr Pelham fetched up the rear, did he?' He chuckled again at the thought. 'I bet he little thought to find himself carrying your bags, Abby. Where is he now?'

She shrugged. 'He's nothing to me now, Thady. All finished. All done with. Thank God.' She laid her head back against the cushion, closed her eyes and let out a long sigh.

Thady shook his head, then sipped his tea. 'I mind the first time he ever set eyes on ye, Abby. When ye rode Emperor through Westport, a queen ye looked, like Queen Maeve

521

herself. And I could tell by the look in his eye he fancied ye. That very first time.' He chuckled. 'Not a man in the square but didn't have his eyes on ye that day, Abby.'

'And if he hadn't set eyes on me—' she murmured.

Thady was watching her. She opened her eyes, her head still reclining back on the cushion. 'If he hadn't seen me that day, Thady,' she repeated.

He shrugged, and was thoughtful. 'Ye might be in Mayo still, with your brother and sister.'

'My father might still be alive,' she went on in a dreamy murmur.

'Ye might have married a rich farmer. Ye might be a mother by this time, Abby, with your wee ones running in and out at the door, and your trap to ride to market, and your cows to milk and butter to churn.'

There was a long silence, a deep silence of the night that stretched between them as they thought of home.

'Do you ever think of going back, Abby?' Thady said softly after a while.

She roused herself. 'I have no home there any more. Our home was taken from us. This is my home. Our home – my sister and I.'

'Ye'll always have me, Abby.'

She smiled wearily. 'And you, Thady O'Farrell.' She stood up. 'I must go to bed.'

She slept late the following morning, and woke heavily, still very tired from the previous day. Late though it was when Abby woke, she found Fan still fast asleep when she called at her room. After a long bath she sat down to a late breakfast, suddenly finding in herself a raging appetite, as if it were a week since she had eaten, and as if the events of the previous day were already in the distant past, sealed off behind the night's momentous happenings. She sat, still tired, but feeling curiously relaxed, all unwound after the tension of the night, as Fan appeared abruptly at the door in her dressing gown.

'Abby! You're back! What happened? Did Rory get away? Is he safe? And what happened to Mr Pelham?' rushing to the table and hastily pulling out a chair, leaning across the table, her hair all untidy about her face, her eyes alight with curiosity.

Abby smiled wanly. 'I'll tell you everything. Just let me eat my breakfast.'

Later that afternoon, she sat down to write to Rory. The letter covered many sides. As she set herself to remember the story of herself and Pelham, as she thought through all their scenes together, she paused many times, her pen hanging uncertain over the paper, biting her lip and staring into the garden, uncertain how to phrase it, and setting down her pen, still unsure. Finally, hanging her head, clutching her hands tightly together she faced the fact: she was not wholly innocent – that was the truth. At first perhaps – but even then? Could she lay her hand on her heart and say that she had not been attracted to Pelham – even that first afternoon in The Goat? Did she do it only for her family? Was there not in all honesty some corner in herself that had desired him?

And again at Newmarket? Seeing him with his black eye – she knew there were feelings in herself she could not be comfortable about. And it was so easy for Rory! she exclaimed to herself. For him everything was straight-forward. Rory was upright and honourable, that was sure – but he saw things only in black and white and in a way, being in prison, being out of temptation, it was easy for him. She twisted in her chair, confused again.

Still, in the end she realized she must tell the truth, all of it. She must try to explain how it had been for her, and that, for all her own weakness, she had done it for the family, and had always, thought first of him and Fan, and she could only beg his forgiveness, if sometimes she had been weak. And she begged him last of all, to reply to her letter, to reassure her that he had not cast her off for ever.

523

Fan had gone out. She was often out; the door would slam behind her, and Abby would have no idea when she would be seen again. The fact was that Fan loved London; she could never have enough of its attractions, its variety, its excitements. She spent freely, too; the money that Abby allowed her was quickly gone, and she was frequently begging for more; there was a pair of shoes, or a bonnet she had seen – and couldn't they go to theatre tonight, she was bored . . .?

Abby walked in the park. The letter was posted; and all she could do now was to wait, and pray that Rory would answer, that she was still his sister, and that they could plan to meet up again one day. And now she felt curiously free. Nothing lay before her; her life suddenly seemed quite empty, and casting about in all this new-found emptiness, she remembered Katherine O'Shea. This gave her an impetus, and when she got home she sent off a short note suggesting they should meet; would Katherine like to come and stay? Or a theatre visit? And to please tell her all her news.

Three days later she had a reply to her note:

36 Bedford Square, Brighton

Dearest Hester,

Your note has reached me here. My dear, I could not have wished for anything more. I am installed here for the summer, and need only your company to make everything complete. I have often thought of you, and have much to tell you, and much to hear from you too, I am sure.

Please say you will come immediately, and stay as long as you like.

With kindest regards,

Katherine

Abby sent off a wire to Brighton, and that afternoon when Fan returned, clutching various parcels as she usually did,

524

told her she would be going down to Brighton the following day.

'How long for?'

'I have no idea.'

'Can I come?'

'Not this time, darling. Look, I'm only going for a few days; we can go together another time. Anyway, I'm sure you'll be able to keep yourself occupied. It's a very old friend whom I haven't seen for months, and we shall have a lot to talk about.'

Fan's eyebrows rose maliciously. 'What about, I wonder? Or can I guess? Is this another of your *gentlemen friends?*'

'It's a woman.' Abby said shortly.

'Oh, another lady of easy virtue, no doubt?'

Abby was about to reply when she had to stop and think about this. Fan noticed her hesitation and nodded. 'Are there more of you? Is there a whole club? Do you discuss your conquests, compare how much you make?'

'Shut up!'

'Oh sorry, have I embarrassed you? Feeling ashamed of yourself, are you – now that I know where you got the money?'

Abby felt hot in the face. Having this unforgiving younger sister spitting questions at her continuously – 'Fan I have been in London a long time, and a lot of things have happened.'

'Doubtless.'

'I will explain everything, eventually.'

'Eventually? You mean when you've made enough to retire? And you can suddenly become wonderfully upright and moral, and put your past behind you? Become a pillar of society?'

Abby did not reply.

The following morning, Abby received an unexpected visit from Mr O'Toole. Fan was still in her room.

For a moment, as Abby showed Mr O'Toole in to the

drawing room, she wondered whether he had heard anything about Rory.

'You have heard about my brother?' she asked tentatively.

He nodded and after a moment went on quietly, 'Although I cannot approve of what he did, I do sympathise with his situation.' He drew in a breath. 'If it had been me, I dare say I would have tried, too. You have no idea where he may be now? Has he tried to contact you?'

She shook her head non-committally. 'He may not even be in the country.'

At that moment Fan entered the room; she was prettily dressed in a flowered summer frock, her golden hair bound up with a ribbon, and was holding a bunch of fresh flowers. She looked as dainty as a porcelain shepherdess. She brightened as she saw Mr O'Toole.

'J.J.! You came after all! Have you told her?'

He had glanced up as she entered the room, and broke into a spontaneous smile of recognition. This darkened immediately. 'I don't think at the present—'

'What is it?' Abby turned, looking between them.

'J.J. has something to ask you, Hester,' Fan smirked.

J.J. looked uncomfortable. 'Perhaps another time—'

'Oh go on! You promised.'

'Mr O'Toole, what is it?' Abby crossed back towards them. 'Is anything wrong?'

'Oh, no, nothing at all. I had intended to ask you – but this is not a suitable—'

Abby smiled. 'We're friends. Please say whatever's on your mind,' she said soothingly. Fan perched on the edge of a chair, smiling broadly. 'Go on J.J.!' she said encouragingly. J.J. took a deep breath as Abby seated herself between them. 'The thing is Hester, you are Francesca's elder sister. She is under age as yet, and since both her parents are dead you stand as guardian to her.'

'Yes?'

526

'Well, what I want to ask you is—' he hesitated. 'I realize this is not the best time—'

'Go on!' Fan insisted

He took a very deep breath indeed. 'Your consent to marry Francesca.'

Fan beamed magnificently on Abby who felt as if a bucket of cold water had been emptied over her. She could only say, 'Well, of course, of course, I wish you both every happiness . . .'

'I wouldn't have mentioned it today, what with the news of your brother.'

'Oh, that's all right,' Abby said faintly, still struggling to keep her balance.

'Hadn't you guessed, Hester?' Fan said teasingly. 'Not even slightly?'

'Never! You really have been very sly both of you.'

Fan crossed to where J.J. was sitting, and placed her hand on his shoulder, looking down at Abby from behind him with a proud smirk, as if to say, 'Got him!'

Abby was still struggling to keep control of herself. She stood up. 'Let me offer you some refreshment. It's a bit early in the day for champagne, but would you care for coffee?'

Later as the door closed behind J.J., Fan was able to indulge her satisfaction uninhibitedly.

'Did it come as a shock? You looked as if a cannon had gone off in your ear.'

Abby could think of nothing to say.

'You must admit, Abby – sorry, *Hester* – it's not bad going, is it? An MP's wife?' She twirled round the room in an orgy of satisfaction.

'Better than a tart, you mean?' Abby said sarcastically as she watched her.

But afterwards the full impact of this news hit her. Mr O'Toole and Fan – who would have thought it? Fan had returned to her room, and Abby sat looking over the list of tasks she had drawn up before her departure that afternoon.

527

But as she sat, she couldn't help thinking over the scene. What of her own wishes? Fan knew very well why Mr O'Toole had been invited to the house. The girl had not allowed that to stand in her way, however; she had had not the slightest hesitation in setting out to catch J.J. for herself and he was netted and landed before he had even noticed.

Chapter Fifty-three

As the cab rolled along the promenade, Abby feasted her eyes on the sea, the afternoon sun glinting on the vivid dark blue with its white wave caps turning in a light breeze. As she watched the flags stretched at the flagpoles, saw the holiday crowds, arm in arm, hand in hand; the bathing machines standing in a row at the water's edge, the fishing boats drawn up, their nets drying; breathing the heavenly air, her heart lifted a little, and she was able to forget that very nasty scene with Fan.

For the whole journey down, it had run round and round in her head. Why was the girl so vindictive? Yet a little thought showed her why. All through the years of separation, Fan must have looked up to her elder sister, thought of her as a lady, as respectable, as someone she might emulate. The source of Abby's wealth had come as a very rude shock to a girl fresh from the convent. Abby clasped her hands together as she sat in the cab. Fan had shrewdly guessed at Abby's long-term hopes, though; very shrewdly indeed – for a convent girl. She had seen through Abby in a way no one else had.

As for J.J., Abby's mind simply went blank. The possibility of his marriage with her sister had never occurred to her. For Abby, the idea of herself with J.J. had been like a distant mirage – something she had never been able wholly to believe in, but which might just – at some unspecified time – *might* come to pass. She would never have had the impertinence to make any overture of her own – as if *she*, with her background, would dare to presume! Their relationship, consequently, had remained studiously cool and formal, and she had never had any idea what his feelings for her might be, if he had any.

Such considerations had not hindered her sister. Fan had no such baggage to weigh her down; she was innocent, respectable, untainted.

Bedford Square stood on the seafront, white stucco, respectable terraced houses of the Regency period, four or five storeys high, with their characteristic curved fronts and canopied balconies. Katherine had been looking out for her from the balcony and was at the door as she stepped down from the cab. It was such a pleasure to Abby as they embraced, and Katherine escorted her upstairs into the drawing room, an arm round her waist.

'You're looking so much better!' was Abby's first comment. 'Your complexion, you've got your colour back and your eyes are so much brighter and clearer.'

'You saw me at a bad time when we last met,' Katherine murmured. Abby squeezed her hand, and Katherine brightened. 'But as they say – life goes on. And being at Brighton – I've only been here three weeks, but I feel so much better already. The moment I arrived I thought of you. It's wonderful to have you here. We can have good long talks like we used to do, and go for walks along the prom. Would you like to go to your room first and wash?'

'I think so. The train, you know. Try as one may, one always ends up feeling so dirty.'

Later they were sitting at the sitting room window with the brilliant afternoon light flooding the room, sipping tea.

'How is Charles?'

'They've let him out of prison at last. He'll be down at the weekend.'

'Oh – well, I'll be out of your way before then.'

Katherine smiled at this. 'You'll do no such thing. Of

course he is delicate, as you know. He has such a fierce, passionate nature, but in such a frail body, poor man. Why is that? It doesn't seem logical. It is going to take months to nurse him back to full health. That's one reason why we've taken the house.'

'You couldn't be in a better place.' She paused. 'And what's the other reason?'

Katherine smiled. 'Can't you guess?'

The light dawned. 'Really? But that's wonderful!'

As they embraced, Katherine whispered, 'Charles was so pressing. He said, you know, that after Sophie's death, it was the best thing – to hurry on and hope for another – and it was really so very easy, once he was a free man again. Very easy. It doesn't take long, Hester. Not for me . . .'

Before dinner she and Katherine walked arm in arm along the promenade, and bit by bit Abby began to unpack the story of herself and Randolph, and of Rory's escape to France. Katherine quickly grasped what an ordeal it had been for her, and as they sat at the table she said, very wisely, 'What you need my dear, is a glass of wine. Or even two.'

A bottle of chilled white wine was opened and they dined very comfortably together, the window open for the lovely summer evening, the sound of holidaymakers on the beach audible from where they sat, and when they had finished the bottle, Katherine ordered another, and as the sun was perched on the ocean's rim, they returned to the drawing room, and Abby sat in a sleepy haze, relaxed and feeling that after all not everything was lost, that she had done her duty and was, above all, very grateful to Katherine for taking such care of her.

Days merged into days; they walked, they talked, they sat on the beach. Sometimes they made an excursion up on to the Downs. At the weekend when Charles came, Abby retired to the background and was content to take walks by herself along the seafront, or take the bus to Black Rock and ramble up on to the cliffs.

She became much more cheerful, and one hot day, went into the sea and splashed in the shallows. Katherine sat on the pebbles with her parasol watching her.

Afterwards, Abby sat beside her in her bathing costume and picked up her towel. 'I never learned to swim,' she said, as she dried her hair. 'Where I come from no one ever did. But now I think I shall.'

'Bravo!'

The cold freshness of the salt sea had invigorated her, and she felt a zest, a readiness for something new. 'You know, Katherine, now that I know about Fan and J.J., it's, well, it's set me free. For the first time in my life I'm completely free.' She stopped rubbing for a moment and was thoughtful. 'I think, deep in myself, I knew he wasn't for me – or I wasn't for him, more likely.'

'You could have been. You would have made him a very good wife.'

Abby shook her head, and rubbed with renewed vigour. 'I only ever wanted to be one man's wife,' she murmured after a while, looking away. 'And that was a long, long time ago.' She sat up straight, threw down her towel, took a comb from her bag, and began the considerable task of straightening out her long hair.

Katherine watched her but said nothing.

After a moment Abby set down her comb, and staring out to sea, said dreamily, 'I wonder if I shouldn't travel.'

'Where would you go?'

'It doesn't matter,' Abby started combing again. 'Perhaps I'll emigrate. Go to America with Rory and Fergus. Perhaps I won't settle down at all; just go on travelling, seeing new places. Perhaps I'll become a famous explorer!' She burst into laughter. 'Can you see me in the jungle with a mosquito net over my hat? Or on some lofty mountain pass?' She stopped again. 'I'd love that.'

After a while, Katherine, said, softly, 'You're in a funny mood.'

'No, no I'm not. It's just that I'm free. It's very exciting.

Just wait there,' she scrambled to her feet. 'I'm going to get changed,' and she made her way to the bathing machine nearby.

That evening Katherine came up to Abby's room as she was changing for dinner. She sat on the side of the bed, as Abby stood before a long glass putting her hair up.

'You don't have to do anything, Hester,' she began gently after a long silence.

'What do you mean?' Abby was concentrating on herself in the glass.

'Don't do anything,' the other went on simply. 'Just wait.'

'What on earth do you mean?'

'Well, this morning you were all excited, talking about the future, and what you might do. I think it's too soon. Don't do anything in a rush.'

Abby did not answer for a moment, uncomfortable at what Katherine was saying.

Then unexpectedly she found tears in her eyes. 'I can do anything I want,' she said. 'It doesn't matter what I do. That's the point. There's nobody in the world who cares what I do. It wouldn't matter if I disappeared tomorrow.' And unable to help herself, not knowing what she was doing, she sat on the edge of the bed, covered her face and burst into tears. Katherine tentatively put her arm round Abby's shoulders.

'Nick went away and I'll never see him or William again. Rory went away, and I haven't heard from him, Fan's getting married.' Her words were muffled as she held her hands over her face. 'She won't want to see me now. I'm used up, finished with. I'm just nothing.'

Katherine held her shoulders, and after a little murmured, 'You have me.'

'Yes, I'm sorry, of course I do; you've been very kind.' Abby straightened herself, wiping her eyes with the back of her hand. 'I just feel very tired, I suppose. It all seems to have gone on for such a long time. And at the end of it I'm left, after all. Just left.' A nervous shudder ran through her, and she drew a long sigh. 'I'm sorry. I must wait. Thank God I have you to be so kind and patient.' She paused. 'I expect it will all work out in the end.'

'It always does,' Katherine murmured.

The next day she felt stronger, and as the days went on, she continued to take her walks and as the summer drew towards its close, and the first hint of autumn could be sensed in the air, she did begin to feel stronger, and not quite so discouraged.

Then one afternoon she and Katherine were walking in a leisurely absent-minded way, arm in arm along the seafront, when Abby suddenly stopped.

A hundred yards ahead she saw Nick. It was quite clear, and there was no mistake. He was with a woman who was wearing a broad sunhat so that Abby could not see her face. Between them was a little boy, a toddler of two or so, looking up at them as they talked over his head. After a moment's conversation, they turned to walk away, a little hand in each of theirs.

Katherine had turned to Abby. 'What is it?'

Abby was still staring after them.

'Hester, what's the matter?'

Abby was still unable to speak, but turned slowly towards Katherine, and eventually spoke, hoarse, almost choking. 'It's him.'

'Who?'

'Him. Nick.'

Katherine looked eagerly after the couple who were now lost in the crowds passing along the promenade. 'Where?'

'There.' But Abby wasn't looking. She was staring out to sea, trying to make sense of what she had just seen. Katherine turned back to her.

'Hester, are you all right?' She glanced round. 'Look, come and sit down, and tell me what you saw.'

They sat in one of the promenade shelters. Abby still had

534

not come to grips with what she had seen. 'It was him, Katherine. Definitely. And he was with a woman, and William was with them.' She paused. 'And they're here. I mean, here. You see, they were in Madeira; he went there because of his wife; and he took William with him. They went to Madeira,' she repeated stupidly, 'because of his wife.' She shook her head slightly, in disbelief. 'But that wasn't his wife. I know it wasn't his wife. It couldn't be. It was another woman.'

Katherine waited as Abby pieced her thoughts together.

'Another woman,' she repeated in a dead monotone. 'And that means his wife is dead. She must be. His wife is dead, and he has come back to England. But he hasn't come to see me.'

She was looking down at the pavement in front of them with an empty stare. Katherine waited, and then Abby started suddenly to her feet. 'He mustn't see me,' she said in an agitated tone. 'No. That wouldn't do. It would never do. Come. Let us go.'

'Go? Where?' Katherine asked as Abby took her arm, and began dragging her away along the promenade.

'Where?' Abby was agitated, speaking disjointedly. 'It would be best – Katherine, I think, it would be best, no let me see—' She stopped for a second, then hurried forward again, 'I ought to get back. It would be best if I went back to London. I think so.'

'Wait!' Katherine tried to slow her impetuous jerky pace. 'Hester, wait!'

Abby swung on her. Her face was filled with anguish. 'I couldn't bear it. Katherine, if he were to see me, I'd die, I would. I must get away. Now. I must go home and pack. If he were to see me. No!' She turned and hurried away, and Katherine followed her.

Eventually Katherine persuaded her to postpone her return until the morning at least.

'You may change your mind by then, darling,' she said soothingly, watching as Abby hurriedly thrust clothes into a

535

trunk. Abby shook her head and muttered, 'I couldn't bear it.'

But in spite of all, that evening she had cooled a little, slowed her packing and eventually sat on the edge of her bed. Katherine had retired to rest for an hour, and Abby sat alone in the quiet house. After her initial panic, a sort of curiosity began to grow in her, and eventually drew her out again on to the seafront, as if in spite of everything she had said, she did want to see him again, she did want to know perhaps if he were well, and how William was. He wouldn't mind telling her that, surely?

It was a warm evening and the beach was still crowded. She walked a little way, then this impulse too, slowed, and suddenly she felt tired and found a seat and collapsed on to it, staring out to sea. She had fallen into an empty reverie, a sort of profitless vague dreamy state, when there was a voice at her shoulder.

'Hester?'

She looked up; it was Nick. 'Don't you remember me?'

She couldn't speak.

'Why have you been hiding from me?' He came round and sat beside her on the bench. He spoke in a surprisingly light, almost casual, tone. 'I went to your house, and they said you'd gone out again,' he went on, resting his hands on his cane, but making no attempt to touch her. 'We've had to chase you all the way down here.' He shook his head. 'What a hunt we've had; I really thought I'd never find you. Never mind, I've found you now. Come along and see William – he's down on the beach with Nancy.'

He stood, but she remained seated, staring up at him. 'What do you mean?' she croaked.

He went on in that same matter-of-fact way. 'I went to St John's Wood and they told me you were here. We came down straight away. I wanted to tell you myself.'

She searched his face. 'Your wife?' she said at last hesitantly.

536

He nodded, and then sat again beside her. They still had not touched. He drew a short breath. 'Yes. It was last February. It had been such a long time coming that we were prepared for it, thank God.'

'She – she wasn't in any pain?'

He looked out to sea, speaking in a faraway tone. 'No. In the end Caroline just faded away. There was nothing we could do. Nothing anyone could do.'

'Nick, I am so sorry.'

He shook his head thoughtfully and turned back to her. 'It was so gradual, it seemed natural in the end. She just slipped out of life.'

'And now you—'

'Well, there was a lot of arranging to do, it took a lot of adjustment, of course. But eventually everything was done, and we were able to return to England.'

There was a pause.

'Then I came to find you,' he went on simply.

'And William?'

'He's down on the beach with Nancy.' He gestured.

'Nancy – oh Mrs Hardcastle. Was that her? I never recognized her, how silly of me, I was so certain she must be—' Against her will she could feel tears starting in her eyes, and struggled to hold them in. 'Yes. How silly of me –' she wiped her hand harshly across her eyes – 'I thought—' She looked at him, and he could see her tears, and suddenly she laughed, an embarrassed, awkward laugh, forced out of her by sheer relief. 'It is you, really—'

He took her hand, both her hands, 'Yes, I came to find you.'

'And you won't go away again?' she whispered.

He stood again and drew her to her feet. 'Come and see William; I want you to meet. We'll buy him an ice-cream, shall we? They do very good ice-creams here – have you tried them?'

He drew her arm through his, and they made their way down to the beach.

Historical Note

Five years later Aunt Ben died, and Willie sued Katherine for divorce the following year. It became the greatest divorce scandal in nineteenth-century England, and caused a split in the Irish party. Parnell and Katherine were married, but four months later he was dead, at forty-five, worn out by his efforts to hold the party together. He is buried in Glasnevin cemetery, Dublin. Katherine lived on another thirty years and is buried in Littlehampton cemetery.